The
Seven Bowls

The End of Mankind As We Know It...

THE TRIBULATION SERIES

The
Agenda
Book One

The
Lights of God
Book Two

The
Seven Seals
Book Three

The
Seven Trumpets
Book Four

The
Seven Bowls
Book Five

THE TRIBULATION SERIES
Book Five

The
Seven Bowls

Ralph D. Curtin

RESOURCE *Publications* · Eugene, Oregon

Resource Publications
A division of Wipf and Stock Publishers
199 W 8th Ave, Suite 3
Eugene, OR 97401

The Seven Bowls
The Tribulation Series Book Five
By Curtin, Ralph D.
Copyright©2011 by Curtin, Ralph D.
ISBN 13: 978-1-5326-8765-5
Publication date 4/6/2019
Previously published by Oaktara, 2011

The Seven Bowls is a work of fiction. References to real people, events, establishments, organizations, or locales are intended only to provide a sense of authenticity and are used fictitiously. All other characters, incidents, and dialogue are drawn from the author's imagination.

To my beloved grandchildren,
the next generations of Christians
to proclaim the coming of the Lord:

Hillary and Gregory Curtin
Raymond Joseph and Mckenzie Curtin
Alexander, Drew, and Caitlyn Elisa Bennett

Acknowledgments

This work of fiction is the product of countless of hours of research and writing, but the real credit goes to those scholars who labored for years over the Bible to arrive at the interpretations that are dramatized herein. They deserve the accolades while I only developed the characters to bring the prophecies to life.

ONE

Resplendent beams of renewed sunlight coming through the solitary lab window momentarily bounced off his monitor screen, bringing fond memories of how things were before the *terrible times,* as John L. Stern, Ph.D. in astrophysics, called them. Times like no other times. Terrible times that brought curse after curse upon the earth, its environs, and all of humanity. Curses that he believed could only be divine retribution for man's recidivous sins and his rejection of God's grace and salvation.

Before the terrible times, he thought, *a man could count on certain hours of sunlight and certain hours of nighttime—along with other natural physical and scientific laws like rain, moonlight, and seasonal changes, but that was all before the wrath of God was unleashed on the earth.* He sighed and reminded himself that it was time to return to looking outside the earth—to the distant galaxies.

Stern turned in his swivel chair from his view of the solitary window and adjusted the contrast and definition on his monitor. *Whoa! What's this?* There appeared to be an anomaly coming from WR 104, a Wolf-Rayet star located some 6,000-8,000 light years from Earth in the constellation Sagittarius, way beyond the Milky Way galaxy.

He carefully examined the data as he stroked his peppered beard, then took a deep breath and exhaled ever so slowly. In all his years as a scientist he had never seen anything like this before.

His monitor was linked to the Gamma-ray Burst Coordinates Network that displayed all incoming data from NASA's Fermi Gamma-Ray Large Area Space Telescope (GLAST). It was launched into Low-earth circular orbit at an altitude of 550 km (340 mi) from Cape Canaveral in June 2008, aboard a Delta II 7920-H rocket. The rocket carried aloft a space observatory with a Large Area Telescope (LAT) and

Gamma-ray Burst Monitor (GBM) used to study and survey astrophysical and cosmological phenomena such as active galactic nuclei, pulsars, other high-energy sources, and especially gamma-ray bursts from distant galaxies.

Stern tapped the side of the monitor, hoping it was a malfunction, then pulled out the maintenance manual from the manufacturer, General Dynamics ASCENT facility in Gilbert, Arizona, who routinely verifies the calibration and accuracy of all their equipment. This included his monitor and the orbiting space observatory.

Rats, he thought, *the calibration has just been updated.* There didn't appear to be any errors. Stern gulped down the remaining coffee in his mug, then lifted the phone. The coffee had grown cold, but he never noticed.

Marshall Space Flight Center, Huntsville, Alabama

Bernie Madras graduated from MIT with a Master's degree in quantum mechanics and quantum gravity qualifying him as an expert in astrophysics who specialized in high-energy gamma-ray bursts. He loved his job and passionately waited for the day when he would observe a burst of high energy particles coming from deep space. That day came in 2008 when he discovered the gamma-ray burst GRB 080916C in the constellation Carina, which had the greatest total energy, the fastest motions, and the highest-energy initial emissions ever seen. The explosion had the power of about 9,000 ordinary supernovae, and the gas bullets or jets emitting the initial gamma-rays reportedly moved at 99.9999 percent the speed of light. The tremendous power and speed made this blast the most extreme recorded to date.

That is, until today.

"Urgent call for you on line 01 Dr. Madras," the voice on the intercom called out.

Madras read the number off the Caller-ID and raised an eyebrow. Getting a call from Stennis raised a red flag in his mind. "Madras here," he answered with a slight degree of trepidation.

"Bernie, this is Dr. Stern over at Stennis. I need you to confirm some unusual data I just received from GLAST. You need to realign your equipment so it detects the massive burst coming from Sagittarius. My reading is off the charts and frankly I'm concerned."

"Hang on," Madras replied.

With his wireless phone in hand, he walked to the control panel to set the coordinates to realign the Large Area Telescope connected to his network for the constellation Sagittarius. Then he walked to another terminal and keyed in his password to access the encrypted data coming from the Max Planck Institute for Extraterrestrial Studies website in Garching, Germany, who would verify the data coming in from Stennis.

There was no error.

A typical gamma-ray burst released as much energy in a few seconds as the sun would in its entire lifetime. Although the typical burst lasted from milliseconds to a few seconds, this burst lasted for more than an hour, generating over 300 billion electron volts. The initial burst was then followed by a longer-lived afterglow that emitted longer wavelengths. Madras recognized the implications of the GRB from WR 104 since this binary star aligned within 16 degrees of earth. This would present serious problems for earthlings. This he was sure of. It could be on the order of mass extinction.

"We have a problem here," Madras said to Stern with heightening alarm. "I just measured the light curve, redshift, and optical afterglow of this burst using optical spectroscopy, and it looks like the core of this star is about to collapse along the axis of rotation on its way to becoming a black hole. That's what caused this massive gamma-ray burst that we're experiencing. Adding to the problem is the narrow energy beam focusing on the Earth. If the beam were more spherical, then the danger would be lessened."

NASA's Stennis Space Center, Mississippi

Stern knew his physics and knew what Madras was referring to. The influx of gamma-rays into the Earth's atmosphere would not only damage the biosphere, but the absorption of radiation in the atmosphere could cause photodissociation of nitrogen, generating nitric oxide that would act as a catalyst to destroy ozone. Without the protective ozone layer, direct UV irradiation from the burst combined with additional solar UV radiation passing through the diminished ozone layer could then have potentially significant impact on all organic life—both human and animal— not to mention the food chain. This would potentially trigger a cataclysm of Biblical proportions. Yes, he realized, the enormous distance the GRB traveled, between 6,000-8000 light years, meant that it occurred in primordial times, but as a scientist he couldn't buy into the notion that somehow God orchestrated it so mankind would experience it in these terrible times.

He would come to believe, though, that this was indeed of God.

When Stern got off the phone with Madras he quickly called the director of NASA's ELE (Extinction-Level Event) program, praying the news would not ignite a worldwide panic.

Lane Drugs, Miami

The stench coming from Biscayne Bay due to massive fish-kills filled Jonathan's nostrils as he walked briskly from the parking lot to the lobby of Lane Drugs.

"Brrr," he muttered. Adjusting to the cold weather in Florida due to the severe climatic changes would take time to get used to. He thought on the other constant reminders of the outworking of the Seal and Trumpet Judgments on humanity and shook his head in disgust. *If only man had listened to the warnings! If only mankind would turn to the Lord!* But it was not meant to be—that Jonathan came to realize as he studied God's Word each morning. Yes, the other evidences of God's displeasure toward mankind during this tribulation period were obvious as well. Astrophysical signs where the sunlight that illuminated the day was cut by one third, bringing nightfall at 3 p.m., together with the drastic dropping of the earth's temperature so that the tropical and temperate zones vanished, brought renewed fear that the end of the world was near. Moonlight and starlight suffered considerably too. With the moon turning blood red from direct comet impact and the star canopy diminishing for inexplicable reasons, mankind lived their lives in a constant state of anxiety—not knowing what disaster from the sky would befall them next.

On Earth, unceasing and powerful earthquakes dramatically altered the landscape so that mountains moved from their once-stable positions. Seawater turned red from a mysterious chemical agent that led to enormous fish kills. Freshwater supplies grew increasingly bitter and endangered from the toxic seawater infiltration and contamination by diseased fish and animals.

The animal kingdom, both wild and domestic, reacted accordingly by turning on mankind as if they were the cause of the chaos. Unprecedented outbreaks of rabies wrought havoc to animal lovers and caretakers in zoos. Man was not safe around any animal.

The insect vector of locusts and mosquitoes brought another kind of misery on the human race. The locust invasion from hell that lasted five months inflicted a terrible paralysis on its victims like that of a scorpion bite, causing millions to wish they were dead, but they could not die. Then there was the unleashing of the demonic armies. Two-hundred million fallen angels in the form of horsemen breathing fire and sulfur claimed one-third of the earth's population. These judgments only raised the indignation of man, who refused to repent of their sins against the Holy One.

The Almighty, knowing the ever-hardening heart of man, had no choice but to raise the level of punishment until His creation would yield to his sovereignty.

I must stop this constant recounting of events. I have work to do and lives to protect, Jonathan reasoned as he arrived at Lane Drugs.

"You're not going to believe this, Jonathan," his secretarial assistant, Helen, said as he walked into the lobby. "We have two hundred E-mails from people wanting some kind of drug to ease their pain from the boils."

"Boils?" Jonathan replied incredulously. "What boils?"

"Haven't you been watching TV or listening to the radio?!" Helen exclaimed. "Millions of people have developed horrible boils on their face and bodies. It happened some time during the night!"

Jonathan scratched his head in unbelief and picked up the stack of

E-mails his assistant printed out. With the E-mails in hand he walked to the TV in the lobby and looked up at the screen to see the Fox News telecast interviewing several doctors, the Director of the CDC in Atlanta, and then tens of victims suffering from the outbreak. Their faces were contorted by the eruptions on their skin, bringing many to scream in torment and others to pick at their faces with their fingernails to relieve some of the pain.

Jonathan turned in disgust when the news network focused on the yellow and green ooze that flowed from the ugly pus-filled abscesses that covered their bodies. "Ugh," he said. "This is unbelievable!"

"Some of the E-mails that came in were saying that this is another judgment from God!" Helen said searchingly, "Do *you* think it is another one?" Helen had admitted to Jonathan soon after she took the position as his assistant that, as a nominal Christian, she knew very little about the Bible and the calamities that God had ordained to come upon mankind during this tribulation period. So with each new discovery of God's direct dealing with man along the prophetic timeline, Jonathan took the time to explain each development.

"This is the start of the Bowl Judgments," he advised somberly. "I'm hesitant to say it, but we're really in for it now because God is ratcheting his divine set of judgments up to the final notch. This is only the first." He added consolingly, "But this plague only infects non-believers. So you have nothing to worry about."

Helen lowered her eyes in sorrow. "But I have an unbelieving brother in Jacksonville." She shook her head. "I'm afraid to call him about this." After another breath: "Do you think it has something to do with this crazy thing they're calling a 'gamma-ray burst'?"

"I admit, I'm out of the news loop," Jonathan confessed. "What are they saying?"

Pointing toward the TV, Helen added, "If you watch the news ticker long enough, they repeat the claims from the CDC and other sources including NASA that a gamma-ray burst from some distant star collapsing brought on this catastrophe. They are saying that the boils resemble an epidemic of anthrax. The whole thing is horrible!"

Nodding in thought, Jonathan remembered that some Bible scholars believed the Sixth plague on the Egyptians resembled an anthrax outbreak, and under modern scrutiny the plague was thought to be similar to the virulent Vollum strain of anthrax, considered highly lethal. The strain brought boil-like skin lesions that festered and eventually formed an ulcer with a black center that itched, blistered, and then oozed at the site of the infection.

Ordinarily the cutaneous anthrax boils were not painful, but not this time. These boils brought excruciating pain, causing the victim to scratch their bodies feverishly in a vain attempt to find relief. In time, the media would report that thousands inflicted with the boils ended their torment through suicide before the proper vaccine became available.

After several moments of contemplation, Jonathan turned to Helen. "There probably is a direct connection between the boils and the gamma-ray burst. It seems consistent with God's dealing with man—He doesn't need weapons of mass destruction to allow disasters to come about—He is perfectly capable of delivering these judgments on his own to fulfill his prophetic plan. As far as your brother is concerned, I'm afraid there isn't anything you can do for him if he has the mark of Kavidas, the mark of the Antichrist."

Helen sighed in despair. "He thought implanting the *MasterChip* in his body, the predecessor to Kavidas' *Masterlink*, was the right thing to do after his identity was stolen over the Internet, but now it's too late."

Jonathan added glumly, "You're right. Now it is too late. But Helen, you must focus now on God's goodness of grace and mercy that He showed you the truth and that you are saved."

Christian Fortress, Petra, Jordan

Looking up into the sky, Dalia Shamni sensed something was wrong. She didn't recognize any significant change in the atmosphere, but her instincts told her something was different. *Perhaps it is invisible*, she thought, *and these days one never knows what to expect. But I know when my spirit is troubled that spells trouble.*

"What are you looking at?" her husband, Gadi, asked quizzically.

She pointed upwards. "Something strange is going on, but I can't put my finger on it."

Discerning the times was a gift from God that Dalia possessed. It enabled her to make judgments and decisions based on the leading of God's Spirit during these dark and terrible days.

"What do you see?" Gadi asked.

"There's a force or something like it that has penetrated our world," she explained half-knowingly. "But I can't—"

"Look at Shlomo!" Gadi interrupted as he pointed to Shlomo Rubin exiting from one of the caverns in the rock city. "His face is all broken out in—" he hesitated until Shlomo walked closer, then continued—"it looks like boils all over his face!"

"Shlomo, are you all right?" Dalia asked, worried.

Shlomo held his hands to his face, exposing the boils on his hands and arms. "It...came...it came upon me so suddenly," he stuttered uncontrollably.

Gadi immediately recognized the fear in Shlomo's eyes. "You need to get some medical attention right away!"

Dalia looked at her arms and then to Gadi's face. No sign of the boils. She looked at Shlomo. "Have you come in contact with some kind of contaminate?"

"No!" Shlomo scanned his arms and then pulled up his pant leg, revealing eruptions. Then he tugged up his shirt. His body was riddled with them.

Upon hearing loud voices, Yashur Landau walked out of his housing quarters. "What's all the commotion about?"

Gadi pointed. "Shlomo has come down with some crazy—"

Yashur waved him off, then gave Shlomo a close inspection. "They're the boils from that gamma-ray burst. I heard all about them over the Internet on my iPhone. The whole planet is infected."

"But we're not—" Dalia blurted as Yashur shot her a look. She covered her mouth and went silent.

"You better take the van and go to Jerusalem and check yourself into the hospital," Yashur instructed. "There's isn't anything we can do for you here."

Shlomo nodded and dashed off toward the exit out of the fortress.

"I don't like this one bit," Yashur intoned, his breath catching in his throat. "Shlomo's outbreak is a bad sign."

"Meaning?" Gadi asked.

"From what I gathered over the Internet and in E-mailing Jonathan in Miami," Yashur began, "this plague is the start of the Bowl Judgments and only infects those who have the mark."

"But—" Dalia started and stopped.

"Yes, I know what you're thinking," Yashur replied. "We haven't seen any mark on him, right? So he may be one of those from the other side. Is that what you're saying?"

"Right," Dalia affirmed. "But then again, he always wears gloves, so..."

Yashur nodded tentatively. "It's very possible. We will have to keep him under surveillance."

Gadi crossed his arms in deliberation. "This raises many questions about what's happened last year."

Memories of Yair Kaplinsky's mysterious death flashed in Yashur's mind. When he looked into the faces of his two companions, he knew they were thinking the same thing.

K-group Leader's Home, Jerusalem

It was late evening, a time for Paul to ruminate. Regrouping was not retreating, this he knew all too well in his dealings with Kavidas, et. el. But as the K-group's team leader he made the decision to close their northern outpost at Acco to consolidate their forces. He reasoned they were spread too thin in view of the escalating persecution his people were experiencing. This thinking, together with the ongoing judgments forced him to amalgamate his people into three locations: Jerusalem, Zedekiah's cave just north of the Temple Mount in central Israel, and Petra in Jordan.

In the final days of the seven year tribulation period, he could not afford to expose his companions in the faith to any unnecessary risks. As the team leader he would rely upon the Lord for wisdom, guidance, and strength. In order to survive, he would come to realize the great need for all three in the days ahead.

"I want to have your baby!" Shira implored Paul in the privacy of their bedroom. "We've been married for almost a year. I know the inherent problems that come with having a baby these days, but there's something inside me screaming for new life!"

She pointed to the four corners of their small bedroom. "Paul, all around us is death. I can't be surrounded by continuous plagues, threats of armed aggression from Kavidas, and then ultimately, Armageddon, and not have something to hold to my breast that is beautiful and alive. I need a child who is the product of our love to hold me over until Jesus comes for us!"

"This first Bowl Judgment of the boils is only the beginning of great sorrows—more terrible than anything we've encountered before," Paul replied in an attempt to reason with his wife, "and believe me, things are going to get much worse. Do you really want to bring a newborn into this crazy world at this time?"

"Paul, Paul," Shira soothed, "you always preach to the group that 'God is in control,' so how about practicing what you preach?" She grasped his hand. "Let's just trust the Lord that He will take care of us and the baby."

Paul looked deeply into her blue eyes, the eyes of a beautiful Israeli woman who first arrested his attention at a time that seemed so long ago. She smiled at him and he felt himself weakening to her.

Within moments, things went the way of married people....

When morning came, Shira knew God had answered her prayer.

Levi sat across from Shira at the breakfast table and thought he saw a glow on her face. As a member of the 144,000, he was gifted beyond human understanding and soon recognized that in the near future he would be an "uncle" by proxy.

"Doron," Levi said, "last night you asked me about the passage in the Revelation that speaks about the warning from the three angels. I put you off until we were together. Now that we're all here at the table, I thought we could talk about it."

Doron Ya'Alon and his wife, Gilat, opened up their home in Jerusalem for the K-group soon after the Abomination of Desolation occurred. Devastated by the sacrilege committed by Kavidas where he claimed to be the messiah, they immediately sought refuge in the resistance. Days after his joining, he came to realize why he and his family refused the mark. Now as a Christian, he knew why.

"It's an interesting passage that reiterates the theme of God's wrath upon unbelievers throughout Revelation," Paul began. "It focuses on the period we're now in—the Bowl Judgments."

"While the Seal and Trumpet judgments concerned only portions of the earth, like the one-thirds, this series of judgments affects the whole world," Hershel put in. "We're talking great proportions."

"That's right," Levi added. "Then there's the judgment on Babylon, the harlot church, along with the fall of all evil powers."

Shira joined in. "These successive judgments will intensify, yet the world will refuse to repent and turn to the Lord. Mankind will curse the only One who can save them."

Doron, a heavy, jovial man, said, "And the warning that anyone who has the mark or worships the beast will be tormented with burning sulfur in the presence of God's holy angels for all eternity."

"It was close for us, Doron," Gilat said, "and if God hadn't reached down and pulled us out of our unbelief, we would have the mark today!"

"Praise the Lord for his grace," Paul said, smiling luminously. Then he shot a glance at Shira who returned the smile.

A thunderous knock sounded at the door!

"What is that?" Gilat shouted, startled.

Hershel jumped up and peered out the window. "It's Shlomo!"

"Let him in," Paul said. "He's been at the hospital." Paul had conferred with Gadi and Yashur at the fortress and shared their suspicions.

Shlomo walked in to the kitchen area. His face was covered with some kind of emollient that appeared to have lessened the size of the eruptions and his forearms were bandaged and his hands were covered with black gloves.

Gilat backed away from him but asked kindly, "Can I get you something?"

Shlomo shook his head, then looked at Paul. "When I called Yashur and Gadi, they told me to report here," he said with muffled tones. "They said you would have work for me."

Hershel and Levi exchanged looks while Doron raised an eyebrow. Shira stood up and began helping Gilat clear the table.

"That's right," Paul replied. "We are expecting the next volley of attacks from Kavidas to take place now that the Bowls are being emptied, and we will need you here."

Levi knew Paul, and he knew that Paul wanted Shlomo where he could keep an eye on him, rather than assign him to Petra, where most of the women and children were safely harbored. If suspicions grew, at arm's length he could easily deal with him.

"With this heightened security alert I am reassigning Sol Gannon from Petra to Zedekiah's cave, where they would rotate out with Asher and Simon. This will serve as a reinforcing measure now that we have only three locations to operate from. This will reduce our exposure."

It was agreed upon.

TWO

Temple Mount, Jerusalem

Stepping out of his black Mercedes, Kavidas scanned the Mount where the world came to recognize him as the messianic person. It was only twelve months earlier when he proclaimed to be the promised one, the one the Bible predicted would save Israel from its enemies; the one who would receive their worship as the Christ. The one the world would chase after. But that was then, and now new threats challenged him.

He turned and gestured toward the car. Moments later Mortimer Stein emerged to join him on the overlook. "Searching for a handle on the moment?" Stein asked.

Kavidas broke from his reflections and, with a penetrating stare, said, "We are not subject to this epidemic, but nevertheless, it is a signal that the end is near, even in sight."

Stein glanced at the sky, then nodded in assent and breathed a sigh of relief as he massaged his hands and felt his face. *No boils.* Yet he knew that the remainder of the judgments would befall him as it would the rest of the world. But that was in the future. This was now. "Is it time to make the transition?"

Kavidas knew within himself that the *transition* or unmasking was near, but it could not happen until all the components were in place. Arousing suspicions at this time would mean disaster for his plan. No, he worked long and hard to earn the trust of the Jews and in order for the final showdown to come about, three treaties and several elements of prophecy must come into alignment. "No, it is not time," he replied in a reasonably controlled voice.

"What then?" Stein asked.

To accomplish great things, we must plan as well as act, Kavidas thought, misquoting Anatole France. "We must move forward. I want you to organize a meeting with Iranian President Afrasiabi, Syrian President Hafiz Eid, and Al-Kamil, the king of Saudi Arabia. Arrange a meeting in a neutral place. Madrid will do just fine. It must be in secret, so arrange it without any leak to the media."

"Heavy ordnance," Stein quipped. "Keeping it under wraps will take some doing."

"Is anything too hard for us?" Kavidas snapped. "These are the major players in the end game, so I need them to be on board. Set it up. My meeting with them should cement the relationship and place us where I want to be."

The instructions were clear to Stein. But the niggling thoughts that reminded him of the outcome of such a meeting brought heart palpitations.

Mt. Ebal Hotel, Near Joseph's Tomb, Nablus

It was not an act of randomness that brought Kavidas to choose Joseph's Tomb as the location for Stein to meet the emissaries of the three Arab nations. No, the plan was to deliberately provoke the Arab representatives to wrath by requesting they meet at the site the Jews claimed was the actual place of Joseph's burial when the Muslims insist it was in Hebron.

Joshua 24:32 clarifies the Israeli claim where it states that Joseph's bones were laid to rest at Shechem, modern-day Nablus. Historians and archaeologists widely acknowledge the vicinity of the tomb as the important Biblical city of Shechem. There the patriarch Abraham, upon his migration to Canaan, or Biblical Israel, built an altar to God, and Jacob purchased a plot of land on which the Jews buried his son Joseph after coming up from Egypt.

The *Midrash*, the official rabbinic *Torah* exegesis, relates: There are three places regarding which the nations of the world cannot taunt the nation of Israel and say, "you have stolen them." They are: The Cave of the Patriarchs in Hebron (Burial place of Abraham, Isaac, and Jacob and their wives), The Temple Mount in Jerusalem, and Joseph's Tomb in Nablus.

Palestinian Arabs, however, claim that Joseph's Tomb is not a Jewish holy site at all, but a Muslim one. They claim an Islamic cleric who died about 250 years ago named Joseph al-Dwaik is buried there and that the tomb is actually named after him. They claim that the Biblical Joseph, who of course according to them was not a Jew at all but was a prophet for Islam, is buried at the Tomb of the Patriarchs in the ancient West Bank city of Hebron. Muslims also lay claim to the Tomb/Cave of the Patriarchs saying it is a Muslim holy site with no connection to the Jewish people. Despite these claims, it is historically documented that until Israel captured the area, Joseph's Tomb was not even considered an important Islamic site.

Yes, Kavidas would be proven right. Joseph's Tomb is a contentious place where there would never be any resolution or peace. It was a perfect setting for Stein's meeting.

Stein waited patiently in the hotel lobby, and, as expected, Al-Mamoun, the Syrian, arrived an hour late. *Another abuse by the petro-rich Arabs*, Stein thought. *Make the non-Muslims wait. That's all right; they'll get theirs someday.*

Al-Mamoun was an integral part of the planning meeting the year before at the Umayyd Mosque when the preliminary strategy for the final war against Israel began. Stein recognized at first sight that the feeble prayer warrior had put on some weight, which he camouflaged with the typical Arab garb and a peppered beard. Equally apparent on all exposed flesh was the presence of the boils.

By the time Al-Mamoun's chauffer drove out of the hotel parking lot, the Iranian and Saudi representatives arrived. Ekrima Salem from Saudi Arabia along with Nabil Salem from Iran was dressed in expensive Western clothes with dark sunglasses. Once they recognized Al-Mamoun and Stein, they threw their hands up in the air, approached them, and embraced them each with a holy kiss. "*Allah-hu-Akbar!*" they said in unison. They mutually looked each other over, then made obscene gestures as if to curse the boil plague.

They all looked at Stein sheepishly. Stein assumed Arab pride dictated they should avoid discussing it with a Jew. *Fine with me*, he reasoned.

Stein walked off toward the lobby as Al-Mamoun motioned for the rest of them to follow him as they went into the lounge. Al-Mamoun stopped short as he entered the lounge and gave a derisive snort. "What made you decide to pick this wretched place?"

Ekrima Salem and Nabil Salem agreed with Al-Mamoun's sentiments and pretended to spit on the floor. "You know the history of this place and the gall the Jews have to take possession. The Joseph Tomb monument belongs to Islam!"

"I have my reasons. You'll see, you'll see," Stein soothed as he led them to a secluded area of the lounge and gestured for them to gather at a table. "It was my way of heightening your awareness to the Israeli-Arab conflict that in turn would serve as the basis for our meeting today."

A young Muslim hostess wearing a *hijab* walked over to the table and attempted to take their drink orders when Stein shooed her away. She backed up several steps before Nabil, the younger member of the entourage, said curtly, "Don't get cheap on us, Mr. Stein!"

Stein stiffened slightly but decided to let the remark go. Even as a non-practicing Jew, his inherent dislike for Arabs had to be held in check if he was to be successful in his mission. He nodded to the hostess, who took their order for an expensive bottle of wine and walked away. "I asked you, our partners, to meet with me today," Stein began, "to build on our relationship that we established last year and to advance the agenda of displacing the infidels in Israel."

"This is good!" Al-Mamoun announced as he slammed his hand down on the table. "We will listen!" Ekrima Salem and Nabil Salem nodded in agreement. "Whatever we can do to rid the earth of those (he blurted out an expletive vehemently) is recompense for Allah's curse on them!"

Ekrima Salem glanced at Nabil Salem and said fiercely, "The sooner we do battle with them, the sooner our savior the *Mahdi* will come."

Stein's eyes flicked to Ekrima Salem's face, then away. *Now that's what I wanted to hear!* Stein thought. Our *plan is coming together*. Stein knew within himself that the Islamic world would not accept his Kavidas as the Christ. The foolish Jews, yes. The misguided Gentiles yes, but not the Islamic world. No, the majority of Muslims who knew the *Qur'an* would not be persuaded that his Kavidas could ever be the *Mahdi*, their Islamic messiah.

According to the *Qur'an*, the Muslim *Mahdi* will be an unparalleled spiritual, political, and military leader. He will establish justice and righteousness throughout the world and eradicate tyranny and oppression. He will be the *caliph* and imam of Muslims worldwide. He will lead a world revolution and set up a new world order by enforcing Shariah Law all over the earth. He will institute the new Islamic world headquarters from Jerusalem. He will cause Islam to be the only religion practiced on the earth. He will have supernatural power from Allah over the wind and the rain. He will possess and distribute enormous amounts of wealth. He will be loved by all the people on the earth.

While Stein did not agree with the *Qur'an*'s description of their messiah, he did know that his Kavidas would ultimately meet their expectations in other ways. "We have a mutual respect for each other's beliefs," Stein said, wanting to mollify them, yet determined not to reveal his whole mind. "And in time you will see that God will unite us in the common cause."

The bottle of wine, along with an assortment of hors d'oeuvres, was served.

Stein lifted his glass of wine and took a sip, then continued his conversation as the others munched and sipped along with him. "You know who I represent," he said after a moment of contemplation, "and he desires to have a meeting with your leaders to advise them of a matter of utmost importance." He set the glass down. "We wanted to follow strict protocol and speak to you as ambassadors first, yet my mission is to bring the heads of state of your three nations to the table with Mr. Kavidas."

"This sounds big," Al-Mamoun said curiously.

"It is big. It is *very* big," Stein affirmed. "In fact the meeting will change the course of history." He lifted his glass and took another sip. "I can tell you this: the Hebrew Bible speaks about the Messiah and the *Qur'an* speaks of the *Mahdi* and both books speak of the final days and the final battle." He set the glass down again. "Well, this meeting is about all of that. Is that big enough for you?"

Al-Mamoun appeared convinced. He swallowed a mouthful of nuts and dates, then said, "Speaking for President Hafiz Eid, our leader—may Allah be praised—I can say he would be delighted to meet with your

Kavidas."

Nabil Salem stroked his black beard and added with a nod, "Knowing that we Iranians must usher in our *Mahdi*, I can vouch for my President Afrasiabi that he too will meet, as you call him, *your* Kavidas." He shoveled up a handful of nuts and dates in his hand. "We will also alert our brothers the Hamas, al-Qaeda, Hezbollah, and any Al-Aqsa martyrs we can gather."

Ekrima Salem the aged Saudi agreed. "My King Al-Kamil will meet as well."

Stein stood and said with a tight smile, "We want to meet in Madrid. Advise me when you have made the arrangements." He turned and walked out of the hotel.

Nabil Salem looked down at the table and snapped, "He stuck us with the bill!"

The Messianic Wing of the Temple, Jerusalem

Israel's Prime Minister, Partlow, along with the Knesset and Temple priests, dedicated an entire wing of the Temple to Kavidas, who was deemed the messianic person. The consensus was unanimous that the messianic person was deserving of lavish quarters attached to the very sacred place where he could be worshiped. This included a security perimeter that surrounded the wing consisting of armed guards and a high-tech surveillance system. Six priests, along with ten servants, attended to his needs that included all preparations for Temple service, his worship robes, food supplies, and any luxury items he desired. Kavidas never showed any interest in women, so this was not a consideration.

A soft knock at his spacious office door shattered his moment of thought as he looked through his picture window out onto the Temple compound at the Holy Place, where a priest lit the ceremonial fires that signaled the presence of the Israel's messianic person. He reveled in the fact that this act of worship was for him. "Gregory, it's Mort," he heard through the massive mahogany door.

Kavidas walked slowly to the door to open it, then returned to his place by the window. *Silence.* Then he methodically turned toward Stein. "I've been thinking about *power* these past few moments. *Power* is everything. If we have power we can command, rule, and dictate."

"We have power," Stein asserted. "Just look at our *Masterlink* system. It is pure power! We just upgraded it so it will perform 55,000 times faster than the typical PC. It can do more than one quadrillion mathematical calculations per second. This is equivalent to having every person on the planet perform one mathematical calculation every second for 650 years! That is what this supercomputer can do in one day!" He snapped his fingers. "That is *power,* and we are controlling through that kind of power!"

"Agreed," Kavidas replied and then added with clear precision, "but I'm not talking about *that* kind of power. The kind of power I'm referring to is a gift that comes from within one's self—heightened by spiritual forces—that raises it to the ultimate level where one becomes so persuasive, so effective, so—" he gazed up momentarily as if to gain divine enlightenment— "superior. Yes, that's it. One becomes superior! The superior person is then able to exercise intellectual, moral, spiritual, and physical power far above human understanding."

"Aren't we talking about the master race?" Stein asked without a challenge. *I thought that was Hitler's....*

Kavidas waved him off. "I know what you're thinking, and Hitler did achieve this kind of control to a limited degree. Yes, he did have both spiritual and mortal help to achieve his objectives that enabled him to subjugate his people and enemies by his ideology and brute force. But the kind of power we wield will control the masses through *worship.* Hitler demanded obedience to himself, allegiance to Germany and the Reich that led to unprecedented commitment, valor, and courage by his military and people. As long as the Germans were winning, he received all of that. But what we must come to expect is that same kind of commitment, valor and courage by our followers when we begin to lose."

Stein knew what Kavidas meant. It was inevitable that they were going to lose. He knew the Bible predicted it, and that it would come to pass. But their game plan all along was to bring as many unsuspecting souls with them as possible. "So you're saying we must concentrate on bringing your followers to a higher level of worship of you that in turn will give you greater power."

"And it is not all that hard to do," Kavidas allowed. "All we have to do is to furnish their needs, give them their wants, and they will become dependent on us. Once the people are dependent on us, we will have achieved the ultimate power through control."

Stein stared blankly. "This is what I call 'Supreme Socialism.' And I note the association of the 'SSs' too. The 'SS' of your Supreme Socialism, the 'SS' of Social Security and the 'SS' or *Schützstaffel* that was Hitler's Praetorian Guard, the powerful force of almost a million men that carried out his paramilitary and police actions."

Kavidas gave a disapproving glance at the comparison. "Let's move on. What do you have for me?"

Setting the power issue aside, Stein dropped into a nearby stuffed chair. "I met with the reps of the Arabs you want to meet with," he began, giving a thumbs-up. "We're a go. They will speak to their principals, and from there we will arrange the meeting in Madrid as you requested."

"Good work! That's what I wanted!" Kavidas winked. "Now let's review where we stand with the Arabs."

After a respectful nod, Stein explained: "Regarding Israel's most sacred site, Jerusalem and the Wailing Wall, the world of Islamic apocalyptic speculation views Jerusalem as the site of the *Mahdi's* reign and the Jews as the hindrance to his appearing. Reasonably they must take control of Jerusalem. Then Jerusalem will become the seat of the new caliphate that most Islamic groups—from the Muslim Brotherhood to al-Qaeda—seek to establish. So this means they are with us, thinking that they will ultimately take control of Jerusalem."

Kavidas held his gaze. "Good. What else?"

"We need to organize a strike against the opposition." Stein pointed up. "The aid these radical fundamentalist groups are receiving from up there has brought many to question who we are. The so-called 'judgments' are expected to intensify, so I believe now is the time for us to minimize the 'competition,' so to speak."

"And your plan?"

"I am organizing something based on the intel I've received from our contact within their K-group." He ticked the points off. "First, we will eliminate one of their satellite branches. This should help to minimize them and put them on the run once again. Next we will concentrate on discrediting their helpers—those members of the 144,000 that are here in Israel. Then we will work on their fortresses."

"Discrediting the 144,000 will not be an easy task," Kavidas said, eyes narrowing. "With this other 'fellow' lurking around, that doubles, if not quadruples, the risk exposure."

Stein nodded. The presence of this "fellow," Kapporeth, represented a real threat to their plan. "I don't think we'll be able to manage this Kapporeth, so we will have to work around him." He gestured left and right. "If he's over here, then we'll act over there. He's too powerful for us to overcome."

Kavidas hesitated fractionally. He had to think on that statement. *Too powerful?* "I doubt he will be too powerful to overcome. My understanding of this character is that his mission is to turn the hearts of the people back to the Lord. That sounds like a 'preaching, soft' approach to me."

Stein vacillated. "If he's anything like his predecessor, Elijah, we have some concerns. Calling fire down from heaven to consume enemies while he was preaching sounds *hard*, not 'soft.'"

Kavidas smiled. A sphinx-like smile. "We'll see; we'll see."

Zedekiah's Cave, Near Jerusalem

Struggling through ongoing judgments for many soon became routine, like managing life during sudden climatic disasters in the weather. In the old days mankind overcame the catastrophic hurricanes, blizzards, tornados, flooding, and the like. Through preparedness and careful administration man could prevail and survive the undesirable elements, but not with God's continuous punishments that were designed to bring humanity to salvation. Global cooling due to reduced solar radiation that impacted the animal kingdom, causing wild and domestic beasts to attack humans, was only one of the many terrible God-ordained plagues to visit the world. All the judgments were an uninterrupted reminder of man's stubbornness to repent that brought the Lord to raise the level of pain until hopefully they would repent. But they would not.

With nightfall at around 3 p.m., moving out of Zedekiah's cave for Asher and Simon was an arduous task. Working with only flashlights and the headlights from their vehicle (the cave being illuminated by daylight and one generator-powered central lamp at night), hauling and loading their supplies seemed especially difficult. Yet the presence of their replacement, Sol Gannon, greatly compensated for the inconvenience.

"He's an angel of mercy," Asher said to Simon as he carried out an oversized box to the vehicle. When they turned and looked behind them, there was Sol, carrying a box under each arm.

"A ministering spirit," Simon agreed.

Sol Gannon and his wife, Ruby, were seniors in the K-group, regularly showing themselves faithful and eager to sacrifice for Christ's sake. As obedient, humble servants, they dedicated themselves to setting an example to the young married couples as well as the singles.

Counseling quickly became part of their ministry that brought them great spiritual satisfaction and fulfillment as they Biblically realigned hurting peoples' priorities.

"It must have been very hard for him to leave Ruby back at Petra," Asher remarked.

"Sure it was," Simon replied, "but thankfully Paul said it's only temporary."

After fifteen more minutes of loading, Sol pointed to the packed pickup truck and said to both Asher and Simon, "You're all set. Now be on your way." He looked over at Shaul as he emerged from the cave as the new team leader and added, "We'll hold the fort down. You guys be safe, and tell the rest of the gang to keep us in prayer."

They embraced each other.

Within minutes Asher and Simon drove out of sight. It would be the last time they would see Sol and Shaul alive.

Mohammed Jafari, an Iranian and Abdullah Mahmoud, a Saudi national, arrived on site at Zedekiah's cave slightly after 1 a.m. in the morning. As arranged, their contact met them some fifty meters from the cave entrance behind a small hillock of Acacia trees. Jafari and Mahmoud were recruited into the Wahhabi's terrorist network after masterminding the bombing of a Tel Aviv restaurant two years earlier, where twenty-five Israelis were killed. Working alone on several bombings and assassinations, Jafari and Mahmoud had experienced missions so successful that they caught the attention of Ekrima Salem, the Saudi *aged one* who met with Stein at Joseph's Tomb. The infamous duo also came highly recommended by Hamas.

Jafari, "the engineer," sat in his Toyota Tundra and unpacked the four pounds of Semtex and placed the explosives in a canvas bag. The bundle of Semtex, considered the preferred explosive by terrorists, was acquired through the al-Qaeda network. Jafari's experience had proven that the orange plastic explosive was extremely potent and would serve his purpose well when used to totally destroy this K-group fortress.

As Jafari affixed the remote detonators to each of the four bricks, Mahmoud couldn't help but break out in a sweat. "This stuff makes me jumpy," he said with a nervous titter. "My palms are all wet."

The contact nodded in agreement.

Jafari shot them both an impatient look. "So take off your gloves."

The contact looked worried as well, then removed his gloves. "Let's wait over by the cave entrance while Jafari puts the finishing touches on this," he said sheepishly to Mahmoud.

"You two go ahead," Jafari agreed. "I'll catch up with you in a few minutes." With that Mahmoud and the contact walked over to the cave entrance to wait for Jafari.

Once Jafari synchronized the remote detonators on the four charges he joined them at the cave entrance. "Open the gate," he said to the contact in muffled tones.

The contact pulled out his key and opened the lock on the wrought-iron gate in front of the wooden door that led into the cave. "Show us where the support arches are," Jafari demanded of the contact in a whisper. "We don't want to have to do this more than once."

The contact nodded, then fumbled to light off his Surefire LED flashlight. He moved stealthily along the corridor with Jafari and Mahmoud trailing behind. Within seconds he reached the first archway and motioned to Jafari to place the first charge in the crevice above the arch and force the malleable explosive and detonator in place. Then he led them secretly seven meters deeper into the cave to the arch adjacent to the sleeping quarters, then pointed to the target area. Jafari nodded once the charge was inserted.

They heard a heavy cough and froze in place!

They exchanged glances, then Jafari motioned for them to quickly head for the cave entrance where, as a last measure, he placed the two remaining charges above the doorway. "Insurance," he said with a grin.

"Let's get out of here!" the contact said in a voice fraught with tension as he nodded toward the vehicle. They had left the engine running.

"Let's get—" Jafari started.

"HOLD IT RIGHT WHERE YOU ARE!" a voice boomed from the cave entrance.

The three men stopped in their tracks and slowly turned toward the voice. In the shadows was a man holding a pump-action shotgun on them. Their eyes widened in shock. "One move and I pull the trigger," Sol said with eyes blazing.

Jafari peered searchingly at the man with the gun, then at Mahmoud and the contact. Then Jafari gazed up into the night sky as if to shoot up a prayer to Allah...and pressed the button to close the connection on the remote detonator.

A massive blast, followed by a plume of fire, bellowed from the cave simultaneously with the cave entrance exploding into thousands of large chunks of rocks and fragments.

The early morning edition of the widely circulated *Yediot Aharonot* newspaper reported that an extremist group of Christians—acting as survivalists holed up in the cave—had committed suicide.

THREE

K-group Home, Jerusalem

Y*es, it rains on the just and the unjust,* Paul thought. Tragedy befalls both the Christian and the non-Christian alike. Ideally, when tragedy strikes a spiritual man, he must fall back on God's promises and try not to reason things out. *"All things work together for good,"* he realized. *Yes Lord. And I also remember a wise sage saying, "God may conceal the purpose of his ways, but His ways are not without purpose." But Lord, why? Why take Shaul and Sol? They were your servants, and I needed them.*

Paul couldn't resolve it in his mind. He was too overwrought. He paused in his ponderings and looked over at his wife, who was watching him from across the living room in the Doron and his wife, Gilat, Ya'Alon home. She was rubbing her tummy and darting her eyes back and forth to Sol's wife, Ruby, who had come up from Petra.

Ruby was sobbing. "He was such a good man!"

Shira stroked her belly. There was death in Ruby's life as she grieved over her husband while there was emerging life in hers as she looked forward to her new baby.

"Come sit by me, Ruby," Gilat said with open arms. Shira nodded to Gilat and escorted Ruby to Gilat's side, where they both hugged her and cried with her.

"Sol and Shaul are going to be missed," Levi said to Paul and Doron with a shake of the head. "They were mighty warriors for the Lord."

"While this is terrible, it would have been much worse if Asher and Simon were there," Hershel put in.

"They can't be killed," Paul reminded him. "All the members of the 144,000 have divine protection. They all survive the Tribulation period and greet the Lord on the Mount of Olives when He returns."

Hershel just nodded in awe at the explanation.

A knock at the door!

Hershel reflexively jumped up from his chair. The fear of being discovered by Kavidas' people overwhelmed him.

Shira shot a look at Paul, who waved them off. "Don't be frightened. We should be safe here for the time being."

Both Paul and Doron walked toward the door, then glanced out. "There are two men, and I don't recognize them. But they look like friendlies." Then in one move Doron unlocked the door.

"Are you crazy!?" Hershel exclaimed once he looked out. "One of them is carrying something! They could be terror—"

Paul ignored him and opened the door.

"Mr. Douglas," the older man said as he pulled out a black leather wallet and flashed a badge, "I'm Moshe Ravitzky, the director of the intelligence-gathering division of Mossad here in Jerusalem." He turned to the younger man with him. "And this is Nachman Meschel, one of my agents."

"I remember you, Mr. Ravitzky," Doron said curiously. "You were the one who responded to the Islamic terrorists when they took control of the NPP at Yeroham two years ago."

The event at Yeroham's nuclear power plant would go down in Israel's history books as one of the scariest times since the development of the atomic bomb. It was there that Ravitzky faced his worst test to date. He had worked with the Israeli counter-terrorism task force of General Security Services, Shin Bet, against Hezbollah, Fatah, Intifada, Hamas and al-Qaeda who continuously threatened Israel's population. At Yeroham, when Islamic terrorists in an effort to bring Israel to its knees seized control of the plant at Yeroham, it was Ravitzky's mission as a seasoned veteran to bring the crisis to a peaceful conclusion. Together with his field agent Meschel, they successfully disarmed the terrorists and brought the crisis to an end.

Ravitzky nodded at Doron. "Yes, you're right. That was me." Then he shook the small sack in his hand. "And I think we have another crisis on our hands."

Paul guided Ravitzky and Meschel into the kitchen, pulled out two chairs from the table, and motioned for them to sit down. "What is this about?" he asked as he gestured for the women to leave.

Ravitzky shot a look at Meschel and handed him the sack. "We know that your group had an outpost at Zedekiah's cave," Meschel began with a nod. "That's what sent us to you. Our job is to monitor all terrorist activity here in Israel, and our network advised us there was a bomb attack on your outpost yesterday. We were directed to investigate and did a preliminary survey of the area. There were numerous body parts scattered about, along with fragments of explosive components. Our labs are testing those body parts for DNA identification and the components for the origin of the explosives. This will give us leads on the perpetrators and victims."

He opened the sack, then slowly pulled out something wrapped in a white plastic trash bag. "This was found at the site, and we thought you could help us identify it." He unwrapped the bag to show them a human hand severed above the wrist. The hand was inside a black glove. "This gets a little dicey," Meschel said with a grimace, "but we think we have something here." Then he pulled the hand out of the glove.

Doron backed up in horror. "That's disgusting!" The hand was covered in festering boils that oozed a multi-colored fluid.

Ravitzky pulled out a pocket knife and scraped a small section of the hand. "Notice the *Masterlink* ID chip that's imbedded in the hand," he said, controlling his voice.

Paul stared at the hand, moved in for closer inspection, then glanced at Levi and Doron. "I know whose hand that is," Paul said bitterly while shaking his head. "It belongs to a man by the name of Shlomo Rubin. I recognize the boils and the glove."

The realization that Shlomo Rubin would not only conspire against them but participate in the actual attack was beyond Paul's understanding. The revelation that he had the imbedded chip explained many things. One of which was the real possibility that he became the prime suspect in Yair Kaplinsky's death since he was present at the location of the so-called accident. The other thing that this explained is how Kavidas was receiving classified information about the K-group movements.

Paul motioned for Ravitzky to return the hand and glove to the sack, then Levi turned to Ravitzky and Meschel and said with a squint denoting skepticism as he gestured toward their hands, "Where are you two men in all of this?"

Ravitzky was quick to connect events and the dots. He knew exactly what Levi was asking. "You needn't worry about us," he said reassuringly. "We are with you."

"What does that mean?" Doron asked, his tone conveying concern.

"Look them over," Ravitzky said as he lifted up his hands in the air. "No mark." He turned to Meschel, who did the same thing.

Paul stared Ravitzky down. "You need to explain yourselves."

Ravitzky nodded. "I will." He cleared his throat. "I've always had a problem with the Muslims and their so-called claim on Jerusalem, so after the invasion on Israel by the Russians and the Arab-bloc nations, both Meschel and I left Mossad and went 'underground.' We had heard about the Christian view of the invasion foretold in Ezekiel so when it happened, we believed the end was near."

He turned to Meschel. "My fearless friend here may have a ferocious temperament and a rabid determination to rid Israel of the Arab presence, but he is afraid of God." Ravitzky refrained from mentioning that Meschel also had a propensity for violence when it came to Palestinian terrorists since his parents were both killed by Hamas collaborators.

"My mother," Meschel explained, "had a Christian Bible, so when millions of Christians disappeared, I was really shaken. The first thing I did was dig out her Bible and go through it."

"After he searched the Bible and realized what happened," Ravitzky said, his voice vibrating with intensity, "he brought me into it." He smiled at Meschel. "We both sought out a Christian who was in hiding, and she told us how to get saved."

"And we've been keeping out of 'harm's way' ever since," Meschel added.

"I still have some friends over at the Israeli General Security Services and the Mossad," Ravitzky noted. "So if I need to call in a few favors, I know who to contact."

Levi eyed Doron and Paul. "That may come in handy in the days ahead."

Paul looked for collaborative evidence. "By the way, who was the Christian woman who was in hiding?"

Ravitzky shot a look at Meschel, then at Paul. "Her name was Marta Shiller."

Paul hesitated fractionally, then chortled. "She's one of ours. She's with our group in Petra."

"Then we're good to go?" Meschel asked.

Paul extended his hand in friendship to both Ravitzky and Meschel. "Yes, we're good to go."

In the next two hours information was swapped feverishly. "I've come to understand," Ravitzky explained over a cup of coffee in which the women were brought into the conversation, "that Islam is connected with Kavidas in his plan to destroy Israel and take over the world."

He dunked a donut into his coffee and took a big bite. "In reflection, the International and Israeli media have been inverting truth that covers for Islamic terrorists and my investigative sources reveal that the U.S. has knowingly funded Palestinian terrorism through the UN and that the Israeli government caved into Palestinian control long ago. The relinquishing of control of Israel's third holiest site, Joseph's Tomb, to Hamas where they currently hold Muslim prayer services is an example. Our one-time PM Olmert granted amnesty to Al-Aqsa suicide terrorists and together with many U.S. groups was responsible for the rapid growth of many of Jerusalem's Arab enclaves that continue to threaten Israel's sovereignty." He dunked his donut once again and sipped his coffee.

Disdain swept over Meschel's face. "Even the name *Palestinian* gives me a cramp. Our great PM Golda Meir said that she was a Palestinian, but that she didn't like the name Palestinian because it was a name the Romans gave to Israel with the express purpose of infuriating defeated Jews. So, she argued, why would we use a spiteful name meant to humiliate us?" Meschel's face contorted in anger. "Christendom inherited the name from Rome and the British chose to call the land they mandated 'Palestine.' Local Arabs picked it up as their nation's supposed ancient name, though they couldn't even pronounce it correctly, and turned it into 'Filastin,' a fictional entity."

"Then there's Iran," Ravitzky said, his voice calm but filled with menace. "They are the big player on the field of supporting and funding Islamofascism. The Shi'ite Muslim revolutionaries of 65 million alone are determined to annihilate Israel...apart from their nuclear program which, despite all the sanctions, has developed unabated. The international community is complicit in the Arab world's plan to destroy Israel by giving legitimacy to her enemies without renouncing their lethal goals. This means that due to the U.S. and Israeli mismanagement of Iran as the breeding ground for terror, war is inevitable."

Meschel banged his fist on the table. "Why do civilized people allow terrorists to get their own way?! America has had the worst of it, and here in Israel we are following after them. Instead of these terrorist cowards being tried by military tribunals, they are tried in U.S. courts under Geneva rights. If they were tried by military tribunal that is based on the idea of providing combatants with incentives to do things that help limit the bloodiness of battle like the wearing of a uniform, carrying arms openly, not targeting civilians and so on then, we would contain terrorism. But the legal system seems to favor the terrorist, who does not recognize any of these things. They are best understood as associations of people plotting and carrying out war crimes. That means sowing fear with direct and indiscriminate attacks on marketplaces, offices, and airlines—or by engaging enemy troops without distinguishing uniforms so the surrounding civilians essentially become used as human shields. So in effect they are rejecting both the laws of war and the laws of civilized society.

"Therefore we who follow the Geneva Convention code lose because the civilian criminal justice system imposes limits on the government and gives the defendant all sorts of access to information; because we'd rather have the governments lose than unfairly convict a man. You can't take that position with an enemy who is at war with you and trying to bring your government down." He wiped a tear from his eye, and then with rabid sentiment added, "It is foolish to think that al-Qaeda, Hamas, Hezbollah or any other terror entity does not train on our system to look for our vulnerabilities. Remember what Khalid Sheikh Mohammed told his captors when he was captured in America? 'I'll see you in New York with my lawyer.' They know the weaknesses of a democratic society better than our government does."

Khalid Sheikh Mohammed, a member of Osama bin Laden's al-Qaeda organization, was the principle architect of the 9/11 attacks and the World Trade Center bombings of 1993 in New York, along with the execution-style murder of journalist Daniel Pearl. Apparently his attendance at Chowan College, a small Baptist school in Murfreesboro, North Carolina before transferring to the North Carolina Agricultural and Technical State University and completing a degree in mechanical engineering in 1986, did nothing to endear him to America. In point-of-fact, it turned him against the very land that awarded him his education when he violently protested with the U.S. foreign policy favoring Israel along with his sour view that Americans were debauched and racists.

Shira shook her head. "I remember the United Nations having the nerve to attempt to try our military leaders for war crimes! That ridiculous Goldstone Report that was instigated by Syria, Somalia, Pakistan, Malaysia and Bangladesh—all Muslim countries—accused Israel of deliberately terrorizing Arab civilians during the Gaza war, thus committing war crimes as well as crimes against humanity."

Her eyes darted back and forth as anger welled up within her. "The Report deliberately misguided the public with its unverifiable claims from avowedly nonobjective sources, some of them long-since discredited, and was a feat of cynical superficiality, without appropriate distinction between terror and defense. The Report neglected to document how Hamas uses civilian personnel for military purposes—storing weapons and snipers, or to conduct surveillance. Their top leaders hide in Shifa, Gaza's main hospital during military campaigns to avoid facing an Israeli military response who not only warn civilians of pending operations, but take great measures to avoid civilian casualties. Israel's military often overlook their rule that where there are terrorists, and especially terror leadership commandeering a facility, then it becomes a legitimate target. This step is taken to minimize civilian deaths.

"So what does the IDF get for its humanitarian policy where Israeli soldiers endanger themselves on a daily basis in order to avoid harming civilians? They get slapped with punishing rules that compromise their defenses and their future military operations are severely thwarted by threatening their officers with legal action."

Meschel stood up from the table. "Enough talk!" he said sharply. "I want to know about payback! If we don't retaliate, then we're no better off than the Jews in the Warsaw Ghetto who just let the Nazis walk them into the gas chambers!"

"Whoa," Paul said while flapping his hand up and down. "Let's not become unglued here."

"My impetuous friend is right," Ravitzky said. "We must strike them back or their attacks on us will only escalate."

"They're only going to escalate anyway," Doron added.

"Okay, okay," Paul soothed. He said to Ravitzky, "Put together a plan for us to show them their treatment of us has a cost."

"Now you're talking my language," Meschel added with a snort.

Paul glanced at Levi who sat with his arms crossed across his chest, listening. "What say you, Levi?"

Levi exhaled deeply after collecting his thoughts. "This attack on our outpost is only one of a pattern that has developed over the years, and we need to consider this from the perspective that there's a master plan in play. The relationship Kavidas has had with the Arab world is very disconcerting and becoming increasingly alarming. It seems he does nothing to offend the Muslim community while simply patronizing us Jews. While the unbelieving Jewish population has been blinded by God's Spirit and therefore welcomed this Kavidas—who purportedly is of Roman descent—as their messianic person, it raises many concerns in my mind."

"Hmm, yes," Ravitky agreed.

"The ease at which the Arabs fall in with him seems strange," Shira said in wonder.

"He does manipulate them when he wants to achieve his purpose, and then again arranges for them to be placed in compromising situations that brings bloodshed on them," Doron said. "It is a conundrum wrapped up in an enigma."

Paul sat mute for several minutes, then said, "It may be a mystery that the Lord has kept from us until now." He dropped his voice conspiratorially. "Levi, you and I will look into his history to see if there is something in his genealogy that might give us some answers to help us defeat him."

"But Paul," Shira ventured, "isn't that the Lord's job? I mean, the Lord is the only one who can stop him, right?"

"I stand corrected," Paul replied. "But we must do everything to slow him down. To thwart his progress in taking many souls with him *is* our mission."

Ravitzky stood up. "Paul, before we leave, I urge you to vacate from this location. It's too hot. If I could find you, then you know for a surety that Kavidas knows where your group is. You need to move on."

Paul scratched his head, then shot a glance at Levi, then Doron.

"Makes sense."

"There's an underground cave in the Jordan Valley that would be perfect," Meschel offered.

"Meschel's right," Ravitzky affirmed. "The cave was originally a large quarry during the Roman and Byzantine era and covers nearly one acre. If I remember correctly it is 100 meters long by 30 meters wide with 3-meter high ceilings. It's the largest manmade cave in Israel." Paul glanced at Levi and Shira, who nodded approvingly. "Where is this place?"

"I believe it's about two miles north of Jericho," Meschel added.

Paul looked at Doron and Gilat. "We will be safer there. We need to move out as soon as possible."

They all agreed.

FOUR

Miami

The drive through Miami Beach on their way to Miami was nothing like it used to be. At one time in the not-too-distant past, Brandon remembered, when he would stay with his parents in the hotels along the famous beach, the community was mostly all Jewish. As a Gentile, he witnessed Jewish merchants reveling in the fact that Miami Beach was the shopping center of the Southeast where Jewish vacationers would escape the cold northern winters to bask in the warm Florida sun. It seemed the husbands spared no expense when it came to their wives in both fashion and jewelry. Nightclubs catered to the Jewish community, bringing popular Jewish comedians and singers mostly known to the Jewish clientele. Many Jewish centers and synagogues frequented the area. But that was then.

Now the Muslim enclaves had taken over from where the Cubans and Haitians had been. Mosque towers with minarets resembling missiles dotted the landscape. Jonathan couldn't help but shed a tear as he drove through the streets and avenues that at one time had displayed the white flag with the blue Mogen David. Now the flags had been ceremoniously replaced with flags boasting of the star and crescent.

Brandon pointed to a Publix food market with the Muslim flag flapping in the wind and lamented to Jonathan, "A sign of the times."

"I hear that." Jonathan grimaced. As they passed the community centers and malls, the residential areas, it was apparent that all Jews and non-Muslims had vacated the town. It was commonly known that non-Muslims were not welcome and that if they did come into the community they did so at their own peril. Notwithstanding, it was believed these enclaves were a hotbed for Wahhabis and Islamofascist radicals. *I will never understand how the Americans tolerated these Muslims coming into their nation and taking over,* Jonathan thought.

34

Even when their terrorist comrades were arrested, they used our own judicial system in courts of law to wiggle out of justice. Our concern "not to offend the Arabs" has been America's undoing.

Other cultures had wanted to be assimilated into American society and adapted to American ways as a tribute and token of gratitude for being allowed into the United States. Historically, immigrants from Italy, Ireland, Greece, Puerto Rico, and the like would demonstrate a desire to be integrated into the surrounding nation they tried so hard to settle in. But no so with the Muslims. They kept to themselves; they wore their Islamic garb, and appeared to despise the American way of life with no interest in American history, culture, football games, or apple pie.

He remembered the former Australian Prime Minister rebuking the Muslim immigrants by reminding them that they would have to conform to the Australian lifestyle and way of life, and that the Australians were not going to tolerate the Muslims coming to their nation and attempting to change their religion, their culture, their laws and everything else in their country. If the Islamic immigrants didn't like Australia the way it was they were free to leave on the next flight back to where they came from, the prime minister said.

Soon they were at Lane Drugs.

Helen greeted them as they walked into the lobby. "Mr. Lane," she said while holding up a telephone handset in the air, "it's Paul in Israel." Brandon dashed to the reception center and grabbed the phone.

Jonathan looked on as Brandon's facial expressions contorted while listening to Paul. *Bad news; I just know it.*

"Oh, hello, George," Jonathan heard Helen announce as he turned to see George Barrett coming through the revolving door in the lobby. He nodded to Helen, then waved to both Brandon and Jonathan then proceeded to the custodian's workplace. Barrett had been hired as the custodian the year before out of necessity and out of gratitude to his grandfather, the famed archaeologist Samuel Barrett, who was a childhood friend of Brandon's father, Matthew Lane.

"Brandon," Paul said over an encrypted line, "our Zedekiah outpost here in Jerusalem was attacked yesterday and Sol and Shaul were killed."

"How dreadful," Brandon said while shaking his head.

"The perpetrators were killed in the attack," Paul explained. "No doubt it was carried out by would-be martyrs or suicide bombers. And that's not all of it. We had a visit from two men formally of the Mossad, now Believers, who brought us proof that one of ours was involved in the bombing."

"Get out!" Brandon exclaimed. "Who would do such a thing?"

"It was Shlomo Rubin, the man who worked for us," Paul said. "This of course raises the possibility of infiltrators from Kavidas' network, so you need to be careful and don't trust anybody outside of your small circle."

"I'm really grieved," Brandon said as he handed the phone to Jonathan. "Here's Jonathan, Paul. Bring him up to speed." Brandon walked to the sofa in the lobby and sat down. He hung his head in sorrow as the news was overwhelming.

Ten minutes later Jonathan joined him on the sofa.

"What did he say?" Brandon asked as a tear rolled down his cheek.

"He added that they were moving to a place in the Jordan Valley they dubbed 'Jericho,'" Jonathan replied. "And we shouldn't try to contact him until he gives us the 'all clear.' Once he determines that they weren't followed or that their cell phones aren't being tracked by GPS, he'll let us know. No matter how much information we think we know regarding these perilous times, it doesn't get easier. Losing two valuable men will hurt our cause. "We have to trust our God minute by minute because things can change in 30 seconds."

While Brandon was trying desperately to process this latest development, he spotted Helen, who was crying. "How are things with you?" he asked her while suppressing the bad news from Israel.

Helen's eyes welled with tears. "I heard from my brother in Jacksonville last night. He came down with cancer, and the doctor said it was linked to the *Masterlink* chip that he had implanted in his hand."

The human-implantable radio-frequency identification device (RFID) that was twice the size of a dime was the precursor to the universal *Masterlink* developed by Kavidas, now used worldwide. It provided identity data, along with medical information to be used by health care providers and emergency personnel. The encrypted social security number, along with the financial and religious info, was only known by *Masterlink*.

After the terrorist attacks of 2001, Homeland Security boasted that this system would protect Americans, as well as control the influx of those looking to harm innocent people. It would also expedite travel by eliminating passport use. The device was gobbled up by parents wanting to protect their children from kidnapping and predators, along with pet owners looking to keep track of their animals.

Privacy advocates protested the *MasterChip* and the improved version *Masterlink* in humans warning of potential abuse and denouncing these types of devices as "spychips," and that use by governments could lead to an increased loss of civil liberties since the microchip's dual use as a tracking device was commonly known. What was held from the public was the connection between the computer chips and cancer. When mice and rats were injected with the glass-encapsulated RFID transponders, they developed malignant, fast-growing, lethal cancers in up to 10 percent of cases at the site at which the microchip was injected or to which it had migrated.

Bible-believing Christians flat out refused to participate in the program, citing it was the system used by the Beast described in Revelation 13. The Christian community recognized early on that the 16-digit number imbedded in the microchip was too closely linked to the number of the Beast, 666.

"I'm truly sorry, Helen," Brandon told her. "Once his choice was made, there was no way back, but it's like his cancer is thrown in for free."

Jonathan joined them, gave Helen a hug, then gestured to Brandon to meet him in the office. There was work to be done.

Plantation Acres, Plantation, Florida

Pat Morrison casually arranged the folding chairs in his living room in a semicircle while his wife, Stacy, prepared the coffee and donuts. Fifteen minutes later the doorbell rang with the first arrivals for their Friday night Bible study. It was almost three years to the day that they both decided to consecrate their home to the Lord and use it as a church for other Bible-believing Christians. It was the least they could do to repay God for bringing them to salvation in Christ after the great departure, the

Rapture. Within the hour there were twenty-four people crowded into his home to hear God's Word.

Slightly after 8:30 p.m., while Pat was expounding on chapter 24 of the book of Matthew, the horror began.

Loud crashes from outside in the street!

Pat jumped up from his chair, ran to the front window, and peered toward the street. "Six men are using sledge hammers on our cars!"

Seven of the men in the group raced to the window. "Who are they?" one exclaimed.

"Wait right here!" a man named Josh announced and quickly exited the door.

Josh ran to the street as two other men from their group chased after him.

"They're all Arabs!" Josh cried out. Seconds later, one of the attackers ran to him, brandishing a knife from behind.

""Watch out, Josh!" Pat screamed from the house.

Josh turned on his heel, eyed the attacker, and then without warning went into his kick-boxing stance. Kicking the knife from the attacker, he then landed two solid punches: one on the attacker's jaw, the other on the nose. The attacker went down in a heap. The other two men were not so capable. The attackers dropped their hammers, then surrounded the two and pummeled them to the ground with their fists.

"DON'T MOVE ANOTHER INCH!" the attackers heard from behind. They froze in place.

Pat stood in a ready stance behind the Arabs, holding a Mossberg 12-gauge pump-action shotgun leveled right at their chests. "Unless you want to go to meet Allah right now," he shouted, "back off!"

They inched away from the two men on the ground mumbling something in Arabic, then reluctantly raised their hands. Pat noticed their expressions—disgust and disappointment. Disgust at the non-Muslims who intervenedm as well as disappointment they were caught.

"Call the police!" Pat shouted toward the house.

The attackers heard Pat's command and exchanged glances, then one yelled out several words in Arabic and cried out, "*Allah-hu-Akbar!*" Then they all turned and ran.

Pat fired two rounds in the air, but they kept running. He pumped another round into the chamber, then pointed at the closest one when suddenly Josh yelled out, "Pat, don't shoot!"

Pat lowered his gun, then turned in fury and hissed at the one remaining fallen attacker as he lay on the ground, "And you call yourselves 'peaceful people'! Ha! Just move one muscle and see what happens!"

Within minutes a Plantation Police patrol car pulled into the street. Seconds later both officers jumped from the car and stood in a half-crouch behind the car doors.

"Drop the gun!" one of the officers shouted. Pat waved his free hand in the air then slowly placed the shotgun on the ground away from the fallen attacker.

"What's this all about?!" Officer Flannery said roughly as he approached Pat, still holding his service weapon.

Pat pointed to the man on the ground and declared as Josh and his other two helpers walked up, "This man, along with five others, attacked our cars while we were inside having a Bible study."

"A Bible study?" Officer Flannery said, sounding amazed. "They're not outlawed yet?"

The other officer kneeled down in front of the fallen attacker, then over at the knife and looked up at his partner. "He's dead," he announced.

"Dead?" Pat said incredulously as he eyed Josh and the other two men.

The color drained from Josh's face. "But I only punched him!" As an ex-Marine and Blackwater commando, Josh was battle-trained to fight to kill when faced with an opponent carrying a weapon, be it a handgun or a knife.

"It looks like you pushed his nose bone clear up into his brain," the officer said.

Josh hung his head in sorrow as the other officer took the shotgun from Pat. "We'll need a full report," he said with a nod to his partner. His partner walked to their patrol car and radioed for an ambulance while the rest of the Bible study group gathered around to watch the rest of the tragedy unfold.

Within two months the Council on American-Islamic Relations (CAIR) filed a wrongful death suit against Josh, citing Pat Morrison and the rest of the Bible study group as accomplices. The case is presently in litigation.

Christian Fortress, Petra, Jordan

Asher tightly wrapped his blanket around himself as he walked briskly past the Treasury, Al Khazneh, a massive building hewn into the sandstone cliffs. He used his blanket to keep warm from the increasing cold that plagued the earth. With the reduction in sunlight the earth's surface temperature continued to drop, now more than 3 degrees per month. For Israel, being on the same latitude as the state of Georgia, to experience below freezing temperatures in September was unheard of.

Down from the Treasury was the Monastery, the building the K-group dedicated to large indoor meetings and sleeping quarters. Walking past the Monastery, he paused to kick the frost on the ground, then bent over to draw a cross and the words *Yeshua ha Mashi'ach* in the icy coating. "Jesus the Anointed," he whispered to himself. With only starlight lighting his path, he was able to find his way with no trouble at all. Once inside the Monastery he went directly to Simon's quarters.

"The group is assembled in the meeting room," Simon said. "They're waiting for us."

"Are you doing all right?" Asher asked, noticing his downcast demeanor.

"I'm still trying to attenuate the pain of losing our brothers at Zedekiah's cave," he replied with a shake of the head.

"Me too," Asher replied. "I think we can expect some group therapy at the meeting."

"I hope so."

Every K-group member stationed at Petra showed up at the meeting. When Asher and Simon walked in, they found Gadi and Dalia Shamni praying in a corner of the large room with Alfonse Rivera the former radical Catholic priest who migrated to Israel. Asher the son of Gadi and Dalia, one of the 144 Thousand Jewish evangelists, walked over to them and joined them in prayer. Yashur and Estelle Landau, the parents of Simon and Jonathan, along with Norman and Clara Greenbaum were praying at a table. Marta Shiller stood in the center of the room reading Scripture aloud.

Simon walked over to Marta Shiller and put his arm around her then prayed aloud with her for several minutes then motioned for her to join the others in their prayer groups. "My dear parents, brothers and sisters," he began while holding back his tears, "we are experiencing a sorrowful moment in our time here on earth as we reflect on our brothers, Sol and Shaul who are now with the Lord.

"Our brethren in Jerusalem have taken the brunt of this offense, but we all feel the pain." He nodded to Asher. "By God's predestined plan and grace brother Asher and myself are here today because the Lord intends to use us mightily in the future." He took a deep breath. "And we intend to live up to the challenge!"

"Amen!" Simon heard two group members.

Asher walked to the center of the room. "But let it be known here and now that we are entering into the final phase of God's redemption plan and this means that we should expect increased persecution from Kavidas and his gang as well as cataclysmic judgments from God. These judgments are designed to humble God's People, Israel, into receiving Jesus as their Messiah, as well as bringing judgment on the non-believing Gentiles. The remaining six judgments will also show to Kavidas, Stein, and his demonic system that God is in control of all events."

Suddenly a swirling funnel of fast-moving air over five meters high sprung up from the cave floor. Seconds later the funnel of air burst into flames—but the flames had no heat! The funnel then emitted a blinding light that drove everybody but Asher and Simon to the ground. "It's of God!" Asher yelled out. "Do not be afraid!"

Then a man dressed in a white robe with a blue sash around his waist stepped out of the swirling funnel. His white hair and beard that was long and flowing seemed to glow, causing his face to shine. "It's

Kapporeth!" Asher shouted.

"It is he who stands for mercy to bring hearts back to the Lord!" Simon hollered out.

"Yes, it is I, Kapporeth, who stands in the presence of God, awaiting His commands," Kapporeth said with eyes that bore through the heart directly to the soul. He walked to Asher and Simon and placed his hands on each of their shoulders. "You who are anointed of God to proclaim the truth must endure to the end and in your time of affliction I will come to you."

Asher and Simon's bodies trembled.

Then Kapporeth turned to the rest of the group. "The Lord of Hosts has decreed the Second Bowl Judgment to come upon the earth. Let him that knows not the Lord be afraid. Let him be very afraid."

Kapporeth slowly walked back into the swirling funnel. *Then in the blink of an eye he disappeared from sight.*

In the moments that followed Asher and Simon explained to the group that they knew their calling from God would include near-death persecutions for their faith. However the blessed assurance that God would protect them fortified them with supernatural strength.

Jordan Valley Stronghold, Jericho

Paul had sent out two trusted men to discover a safe fortress for their group. Times would get increasingly more difficult, making survival a monumental task. The fewer people who knew their whereabouts, the safer they would be. In short order the two men returned, reporting to Paul they had located a cave fortress two miles north of Jericho that would sufficiently meet their needs. Paul then divided the group up with instructions to quietly and unobtrusively leave Jerusalem and meet at the cave fortress.

When Paul and the rest of the group from Jerusalem arrived at the fortress in the Jordan Valley there were two Bedouins dressed in tribal costumes waving at them from the entrance to the cave. They were yelling something in Arabic.

"Doron," Paul said. "Go see what they want."

Doron walked to the entrance and conversed with them. Then he returned to the K-group and said, "The older one said, 'No enter! Cave bewitched with demons, wolves, and hyenas!'"

"Go tell them to clear out!" Paul boomed.

Doron approached them and spoke some warning to them in Arabic, then shooed them away. Downcast—no doubt for lack of remuneration for warding off the evil spirits—they defiantly stalked off.

Upon entering the cave fortress Paul and his group were overwhelmed to find an impressive architectonic underground structure supported by 22 giant pillars. The First-Century cave was enormous and striking, covering an area of approximately 1 acre. It measured over 100 meters long by more than 35 meters wide with 3 meter-high ceilings. Located two miles north of Jericho, it was famous for being the largest manmade cave to be discovered in Israel. Archaeologists claimed the man-made cave's primary use had been as a quarry, which functioned for about 400-500 years. Other findings definitely indicated that the place was also used for other purposes, such as a monastery, and possibly as a hiding place.

Levi walked to several of the pillars and discovered cross markings, zodiac symbols, Roman letters, and an etching that resembled the Roman Legion's pennant. Walking further into the cave, he noticed recesses in many of the pillars that appeared to have been used for oil lamps.

"Hershel, what do you make of these?" Shira asked curiously, pointing to holes in some of the pillars.

Hershel fingered the holes, then studied two of the nearby pillars. "I would say they were used to tie up the animals used to haul quarried stones out of the cave."

"Okay, let's settle in," Paul instructed after the initial survey was complete. "We need to unload all our equipment, bedding, and food stuffs while it's still light." He turned to Shira and added with a smile, "Have the women prepare the sleeping quarters and meal."

Hershel set up all the electronic equipment that included laptop computers, radios, and portable gas-powered and solar-powered generators while Doron strung some electric lights throughout the cave.

Within two hours they were all moved in and ready for dinner.

Shortly after dinner, Paul's phone rang. The call from Asher explaining Kapporeth's visit was received with mixed emotions. Part of him was excited to learn that the next Bowl Judgment was about to be unleashed while at the same time he was fearful of God's continuing wrath on unrepentant man.

There was still dew on the ground the next morning when Ravitzky and Meschel appeared before the main entrance to the fortress at Jericho. Doron met them at the entrance and waved them in. "Paul's been waiting to hear from you," Doron said expectantly.

"We had some logistical and technical problems to deal with," Ravitzky replied. "But now we're ready to move on our mission."

Doron nodded approvingly and pointed down the cave's corridor. "I'll join you as soon as I appoint a replacement to watch the entrance."

Paul and Levi welcomed them and walked with them to an antechamber, then to a rest area.

"What have you come up with?" Levi asked.

"You're really going to love this," Meschel reveled. "We've managed to acquire a UAV."

"Okay, I give up. What's a UAV?" Paul replied.

"It's an Unmanned Aerial Vehicle that will get into places we can't. It's sort of like a 'Star Wars' weapon," Ravitzky explained. "Plus it has a bullet."

"What do you mean?" Levi asked.

"I mean it carries an explosive missile," Ravitzky noted with a chuckle. He was referring to the Israeli-Made Heron that was similar to the American MQ-1C Warrior developed by General Atomics and the Lockheed P-175 Polecat. It is an Extended-Range Multi-Purpose drone that is the upgrade of the MQ-12 Predator operated by Task Force ODIN in Iraq and/or Afghanistan by American Forces. The Heron is a Medium-Altitude Long-Endurance drone powered by a Thielert Centurion 1.7 Heavy Fuel Engine capable of operating for 36 hours at altitudes up to 8,800 meters with a range of 400 kilometers. The aircraft can carry a payload of 800 pounds and can be armed with AGM-114 Hellfire missiles and GBU-55/B Viper Strike guided bombs. It's designed for targeted killings.

"So how do you plan on using it?" Doron asked as he joined in.

We're planning on sending our little bird to visit our man Kavidas and his companion Stein. That's how," he replied with a grin.

"And we're going to write on the missile the way the bombardiers wrote on their bombs during WW II: 'To so-and-so from Uncle Sam,'" Meschel snapped. "Only this will say, 'To Kavidas and Stein from the gang at Zedekiah's cave.'"

"There's only one problem with this plan," Paul observed bleakly.

"What's that?" Ravitzky inquired.

"They can't be killed. That's what," Paul said.

Ravitzky hesitated fractionally as he shot a look at Meschel. "What do you mean they can't be killed?"

"I mean both of them are under a 'special' covenant with God so that they cannot be killed by anyone other than Christ Himself," Paul explained. "And that's not going to happen until Christ comes back, which we know is going to happen really soon. So that thrill is reserved for Christ alone."

"Okay. So plan 'B' is that we get the message to him 'we're coming after you,'" Meschel added. "We blow up his building and those who are close to him. This will cut into his authority and credibility while giving us some payback."

Paul nodded. "This we can do."

FIVE

The Messianic Wing of the Temple, Jerusalem

Recurrent eschatological themes were plaguing him. Night after night he would dream—nightmares if you will—where he saw himself being cast into the lake of fire for all eternity. Unquenchable flames enveloped his body while death and annihilation eluded him. The perpetual stench of burning sulfur and other noxious gases would not yield to screams of horror or pleas for mercy. The never-ending torment would not be assuaged by repentance. It was too late.

When he awoke, he found himself in a pool of sweat. No, he was not able to share these terrifying nightmares with his soul mate for fear that he would get angry and prescribe some catharsis, such as a weekend in Cannes or Monte Carlo, while the real problem was his amygdala. *Yes,* he thought, *there is this part of my brain that processes these negative emotions, and in turn they spill over into my subconscious and rear their ugly head while I sleep. Fear seizes me, even while I sleep!*

Threatening scenes of judgment and sentencing by the One who judges continuously emerged from storage in the suppressed recesses of his mind, bringing on rapid heartbeats, increased respiration, and stress-hormone release. No, they were not confabulations. They were glimpses of the future.

The scene changed.

He stood looking out the window in Kavidas' office in the Messianic Wing of the Temple when he suddenly noticed a large predatory bird circling the building. At first it looked like a condor, but then again perhaps it was an eagle. He couldn't be sure. But it was big and threatening.

The bird seemed to pause then and hover. It stared with piercing eyes into the window where he was. He turned and squinted into the room to see his companion sitting at his desk, planning. *It's watching us!*

Just as he glanced over at the bookshelf, he heard the clock chime and took notice of the time. The bird shrieked like an osprey and flew into the window. Then there was a bright flash of light....

"Mort, are you all right?" he heard as he awoke to sanemindedness.

He stared at Kavidas who stood before him as he sat on the sofa outside his office. "I must have dozed off waiting for you," he replied, rubbing his eyes.

"Your hands are shaking." Kavidas pulled back to scan Stein's face. "What's wrong?"

"I just had a dream, that's all. Nothing," he said, passing it off.

"We're meeting with Partlow in fifteen minutes," Kavidas reminded him. "Are you up to speed?"

Stein gave him a thumbs-up as he regained his composure and walked into Kavidas' office.

Undisclosed Location, Jerusalem

Ravitzky opened up the UAV program on his laptop, then uplinked it to the dedicated satellite in low-orbit used to direct and target armed drones. The drone stood on the tarmac some 35 meters in front of him. By prior arrangement with his contact inside Israel's Mossad and General Security Services his use of the dedicated satellite was kept secret and available only for a 15-minute window to avoid detection while the mainframe computers were in redundancy.

Within minutes the target, The Messianic Wing of the Temple, appeared on his laptop. "Now that's what I'm talking about," Meschel remarked as he flicked the side of the laptop. Within seconds Ravitzky focused on the infrared heat signatures of the two men inside the wing of the building. He placed the cursor on the two heat signatures one at a time, keyed in the GPS coordinates that were uploaded to the satellite, then into the drone's software. He hit the "initiate" key.

The drone started up, taxied down the runway and, within 15 seconds, was airborne.

The Messianic Wing of the Temple, Jerusalem

Prime Minister Zola Partlow arrived early to the meeting. Kavidas immediately detected he had something on his mind. *I don't need any negativity today*, he reminded himself.

"Good to see you again." Stein extended his hand to Partlow as he walked toward one of the stuffed chairs in front of the bookshelves.

"I've been looking forward to our meeting with anticipation," Partlow began as he sat. "There are some things we should talk about."

Kavidas eyed his puppet with disdain. If there was anything he couldn't stomach, it was weakness in a man. Images of his exercising his power over Partlow during the Seal judgments flashed in his mind. *The wimp! He folded like every other mortal who caves in to pressure at the slightest provocation. Yes, I despise weakness, but it has its purpose.*

Partlow's squirming in his chair signaled his apprehension—something Kavidas would soon seize upon to his advantage. "We've called you to our meeting to discuss our future plans that involve using your political clout to help us along with our programs," Stein began. He would act as Kavidas' mouthpiece but Kavidas reminded him should the conversation become hostile, he would intervene. "We want to reiterate that God's people here in Israel have proclaimed our own Gregory Kavidas as their messianic person. But there are political activists with no religious affiliation with Judaism who could present problems in the future. These are the people we want you to round up and—" he gestured— "'coddle,' if you will, so they are on board with us."

Partlow shifted his weight in the chair, then scratched an imaginary itch on his neck. The tension in the room was rising. "Yes, I understand that part of it," Partlow agreed, "and I will do everything in my power to bring about both party and unity of faith here in Israel." He raised his index finger. "But there are some areas of concern that I need help on."

Kavidas stepped forward and said tersely, "And what might that be?"

"Well, this whole alliance with the Saudis, the Iranians, the Wahhabis, the Hezbollah, and the other Islamic radical groups has me concerned," he said as he began to stand up.

"You can stay seated!" Kavidas snapped.

Partlow's eyes darted to Kavidas, then to the floor. He visibly swallowed hard. "Sorry."

"Continue with your thoughts, Mr. Partlow," Stein said in an effort to minimize the growing tension.

"I was of the persuasion," Partlow began, "that our role here in Israel was to protect our Jewish population. But after my last briefing, I've been somewhat confused when I learned that you're making secret deals with the Arab league." He shook his head. "I've done my homework on this, and let me say that apocalyptic terrorism poses a great threat to our nation and the world. Their practitioners seek our total destruction. They want us extinguished! These terrorist adversaries are not civilized but barbaric and have grandiose ideas to take us over. So why are we 'partnering' with them?"

Kavidas and Stein exchanged glances but said nothing.

"I can tell you from history, going back to 1968 when the Palestinians hijacked four jetliners here in the Mideast, that Islamic terrorism started then. They must be stopped!" Partlow blurted out with rising rigor. "And because America failed to understand Islamic terrorism, the act of 1968 was followed on September 11, 2001 when they targeted the United States. Since then the Americans have failed to invest in resources to ensure victory. They failed to take seriously the overtly revolutionary character of Islamofascism, and I fear we are doing the same thing here in Israel.

"When I think of the weapons they used on us some five years ago when they were allied with the Russians in an attempt to annihilate us, I can't help but think on where the money came from to buy those weapons. It came from petro-dollars going back to 1973 with the staged oil shortage. Let's be honest: there was no shortage. There was only a vengeance on Israel directed on the Americans for supporting us during that war. So to get back at us for whipping the Arabs in the 1973 Yom Kippur War, they shut off the oil spigots to the West. And since then they are holding the world hostage and exacting the ransom though their OPEC outlaws."

He curled his lip. "Then there is their cowardly warfare. The Islamic terrorists use children as bombs to kill us Jews while the Hezbollah embeds in the civilian population to deter our military from retaliating as they fire openly upon our forces. How come they don't have to adhere to the Geneva Convention rules? If their leaders really believe that Allah has given them permission to fight for world domination, then why don't the leaders become suicide bombers and set the example for their cause instead of using their 'mules'? That's because they're cowards. By the way, doesn't anybody out there realize their three apocalyptic options: we surrender; we commit suicide; or they perform genocide? No wonder most of the Arab countries sided with the Nazis and *Mein Kampf* remains a best seller among the Muslims. And what's more—"

"That's enough!" Kavidas said. "You're a fool!" He turned to Stein. "Mort, I believe Prime Minister Partlow has reached that place in his career where his judgment is clouded. Maybe we ought to talk about finding another place for him in the cabinet."

Partlow stiffened, then stood and began to walk toward the door.

Stein nodded, then glanced at the clock on Kavidas' wall. He blinked, attempting to correlate the image of the clock with a fleeting thought that flashed in his mind. Kavidas' voice, along with Partlow's rhetoric and actions, caught him off balance. He couldn't think clearly.

Undisclosed Location, Jerusalem

"We're almost there!" Ravitzky winked at Meschel as he carefully directed the UAV on its course. "One more minute."

Meschel stared at the laptop as the UAV followed the GPS mapping coordinates. "May you rot in hell...."

The Messianic Wing of the Temple, Jerusalem

Kavidas raised his eyebrows. "Mort, are you still with us?"

Mort's mind suddenly locked up in terror as he stared at the clock.

He shot a look out the window and thought he saw a reflection off a metallic object traveling at high speed coming toward them.

Then the clock chimed.

Undisclosed Location, Jerusalem

Meschel smiled at Ravitzky as the drone found its target. "Boom!" he said with a chuckle.

Jordan Valley Stronghold, Jericho

Ruby sat in the corner of the main room whimpering as Shira approached her.

"You miss Sol, don't you?" Shira asked with deep concern.

"He was my soul mate." Ruby patted her eyes with her handkerchief. "We were so looking forward to seeing Jesus' return together."

"Well, you will see his return together, only Sol will be coming with Him," Shira said consolingly.

"I know, I know," Ruby lamented.

Shira put her arms around her. "I have something to tell you," she said with a smile.

Ruby blinked. "Yes?"

"Paul and I decided to name our baby after Sol," Shira explained.

"But how do you know it's a boy?" Ruby asked.

Shira rubbed her belly several times. "Because God told us."

Ruby sighed deeply. "That will be a great honor in his name. Thank you." Seconds later her tears stopped flowing.

At that instant they heard Doron and Gilat exclaim, "They did it!"

Shira hugged Ruby one more time and dashed toward Doron and Gilat as they were watching live news feeds on their laptop. "What happened?!" Shira asked.

Moments later the entire group joined in.

"Kavidas' office—the entire messianic wing—was bombed!" Doron gulped out.

"They pulled it off," Levi said matter-of-factly. "Hallelujah."

With several networks covering the bombing, views from every perspective were flashed on the laptop. The ZAKA, Israel's emergency squad of religiously trained workers, were cleaning up the bomb debris while others carried off a dead body on a stretcher. The news reporter made it clear that it was Prime Minister Partlow. Moments later Kavidas and Stein were on camera dusting themselves off while doctors hovered over them.

"Just as Paul said," Levi reminded the group as he pointed to the laptop monitor, "Kavidas and Stein cannot be killed."

"Too bad," Ruby said.

Hershel nudged Paul as they watched the newscast of the bombing and said in a whisper as he pointed to his iPhone, "Bowl Two hit. It's just now coming over the Internet."

Paul clicked on the newscast on his laptop, and the grisly scene of millions of dead fish washing ashore on the Mediterranean Sea coast all along Israel flashed on the screen. When the news cameras panned the Sea, it looked like it had turned to blood. "Probably some kind of red tide that resulted in this colossal fish kill," Doron noted. "The prophet saw red and equated it to blood."

"Oh-oh." Hershel tapped on his iPhone. "The Red Sea and Dead Sea have also turned blood-red as well."

Paul clicked on several news websites. "It looks like the only drinkable water is Lake Galilee, the Jordan River, and subterranean juvenile water." Moments later he went back to the site showing the Mediterranean Sea.

"If that is the Red Tide and it's that widespread, then it's going to be a problem," Levi said. Levi went on to explain that this phenomenon known as *algal bloom* is, in fact, a huge concentration of microorganisms that produce natural toxins and deplete dissolved oxygen in the water, bringing on vast wildlifle mortalities among marine and coastal species of fish, birds, marine mammals, and other organisms. There is a hazard to humans when the Red Tide become aerosolized and later becomes airborne. A secondary hazard is that humans can become seriously ill from eating oysters and other shellfish contaminated with Red Tide toxin. The monetary price for the closing of the fishing and shellfish industry, along with the threat to the tourist trade, was considered to be incalculable.

Paul turned to Hershel. "Contact Simon at Petra and tell him to contact his people up in the Galilee region to supply us with fresh fish for as long as this thing lasts."

"Got it." Hershel walked to a remote area to make the call.

Ruby asked Paul, "Will this affect the rest of the world?"

"Probably not," he said. "I believe that when the prophet John foresaw these prophecies that the 'whole' world was not in view. My interpretation is that it was just the 'world' of the Bible, so to speak. If the world's seas were to become contaminated, then all life would perish within ninety days. So I believe this to be contained here in the Mideast."

Most of the group spent the rest of the day organizing the food and storing drinking water while Paul went into solitude. Weighing heavily on his mind was Kavidas' vindictive nature and his certain reprisal.

Bikur Holim Hospital, Jerusalem

Doctor Eli Reich walked into the ER waiting room to a host of news reporters, held up his hand in a halting manner, and announced, "Both Gregory Kavidas and Mortimer Stein are in stable condition and expected to make a full recovery."

"What about Prime Minister Partlow?" a reporter yelled out.

"I'm afraid he didn't make it," Doctor Reich replied. "He was DOA."

There were several groans from the group of reporters, then one asked, "How is it possible that Mr. Kavidas and Stein could survive such a blast?"

Doctor Reich pointed up with one hand. "Your guess is as good as mine, but obviously God is watching over them."

Yes, that must be, the reporter thought. He had seen the damage inflicted on the messianic wing of the Temple. The damage was extensive, leading him to realize that a powerful explosive was used. *How could they possibly have made it through that horrific bombing without being killed?* He couldn't process it until he came to the conclusion that they must have divine protection. Something the people came to expect of their chosen One.

Temporary Quarters in the Temple for the Messianic Person

Kavidas clicked the remote *Off* button on the TV to dispense with the overwhelming news coverage of the attempted assassination, then walked to the window. Hordes of mobile TV stations were parked outside the Temple compound, waiting for him and Stein to make an appearance—something he'd normally welcome. But for now his anger could not be assuaged. He had to be careful not to let the public see his rage. He walked to his desk and slammed his fist down. "Do these enemies of the state really think I would let them get away with this and not retaliate?!" he said, full of outrage.

"A proportionate reprisal is in order," Stein suggested.

Kavidas turned and hissed, "Proportionate? You're kidding, right? We must respond in such a way that they will get the message loud and clear: 'Don't try this ever again'!"

"I'll plan something right away," Stein said swiftly.

"I want you to strike where they are vulnerable and where they can be hurt the most," Kavidas ordered.

"Well, they're getting help from their missionary witnesses who are under protection."

"That may be so, but we can still punish them by calling up our forces that can combat them using strategies only available to them," Kavidas argued.

Stein knew from previous actions that calling up demonic forces against God's agents and his people was a colossal failure, but then again, perhaps in these last days, the outcome would be different. "As you say." Stein carefully watched his partner for several minutes as he paced the office, obviously planning his next move. Then: "The Second Bowl has been poured out, reminding us of our timetable."

Kavidas turned to him and in a didactic tone said, "I'm aware of it, and we will leave it alone. It is not directed at us but at the Jews in an attempt to bring them to the point where they cry out for their messiah, but we know that is not going to happen."

Stein nodded. "What about a replacement for Partlow?"

Kavidas' eyes narrowed with cunning. "I thought about this. We no longer need a prime minister with me in charge. What we'll do is appoint a Temple priest to the Chief Rabbinate who will work with us—not give us any problems."

"That will work," Stein said with a chuckle.

"One more thing." Kavidas glanced at Stein while remaining utterly still, a statue. Only his eyes moved. "I believe our adversaries are sensing a need to question and probe into my heritage."

"Oh, oh."

"We need to be careful. Stay alert."

Jordan Valley Stronghold, Jericho

How do I love thee? Let me count the ways, Paul quoted to himself. *Oh, how I love thy Word. Yes, the Scriptures bring comfort and guidance.* He thought on Goethe: *"We are shaped and fashioned by what we love." Yes, my very being and thoughts are shaped by what I love—the Word of God.*

"Paul," he heard from behind, breaking him out of his reverie, "Meschel and Ravitsky are here to see you."

He turned to see Hershel waving him on. "Ask the others to join us in the big room," Paul said.

"We believe we have a time of opportunity," Meschel began once the group was assembled. "Because of our measure of success at our first strike, we want to plan another attack where we know the Arabs are vulnerable."

The group listened with increasing interest. Ravitzky walked in front of the group as if he were a military commander explaining an upcoming bombing mission. "A window has opened up for us to launch another armed drone attack—not here in Israel, but in Saudi Arabia."

Meschel held up a large photograph. "This is a satellite image of the oil fields at Ras Tanura, the largest oil facility in the Persian Gulf. It is located on a peninsula that projects into the Persian Gulf in the Eastern Province of Saudi Arabia. This will facilitate our mission by reducing the time the bird flies over land.

"This facility is operated by Aramco, the largest oil company in the world, and is surrounded by a heavily guarded security fence. This will not be a problem for us because we are launching the drone from an offshore ship since their defenses are the weakest on the Gulf side."

A hand was raised. "Yes? Doron," Meschel said.

"Why Saudi Arabia and not Iran?" Doron asked.

"At this point, Iran's defenses are impenetrable," Ravitzky explained. "Their technology comes from North Korea, who has helped them build their arsenal of intermediate-range ballistic missiles, the Sejil class, that have a range of nearly 3,600 kilometers, putting not only Israel but parts of Europe within striking distance. Then there are the Tor-M1 and S300 surface-to-air missile systems they acquired from Moscow as an added deterrent. These plus other intel tells us we could not get a drone past their defense line. But Saudi Arabia does not have this capability. Not yet anyway. So they're a better target."

"Besides all of that," Meschel explained with clenched fists and a smile, "it's time for payback. Despite the fact that the U.S. was responsible for making Saudi Arabia oil rich and that U.S. politicians support them, fifteen of the 9/11 hijackers were Saudi nationals, as well as Osama bin Laden, so that's one for the Americans. The Wahhabis and al-Qaeda that have waged war on us are financed by the Saudis and their money is funneled into our nuclear neighbors. For decades monies from Saudi banks and oil revenues have been used to finance terrorist groups here in Israel."

"What we want to do," Ravitzky added, "is to send a clear message to the Arabs that they're not getting off for what they've done to us. The

Saudi's have used their oil money to buy weapons that they use on us at Kavidas' behest and it's time they paid for it. We will paralyze their petro-rich nation while at the same time make a statement to Kavidas."

"The Muslim world will come looking for us," Ruby warned.

"They already are," Meschel noted dryly.

Lane Drugs, Miami

At first they were just anomalies that nothing normal could well explain, but after a while the mental barriers began to break down. Surreal images would form, then give way to some semblance of sane mindedness. They were images that chilled him when he would think of them and madden him when he would dream of them. These images, like all dreadful images of hell, flashed out from an accidental piecing together of separated things—in this case an old Bible story and notes from his departed aunt, the aunt who begged him to go to Sunday school.

To believe or reject God's truth was his choice; he knew that, but the rejection carried with it a price he would come to regret, for even in sleep, he found no rest, for that is when the ultimate horror that often paralyzes the memory in a merciful way came upon him.

He had heard that just as there are many mansions in heaven, there will be many rooms in hell...all have not sinned in the same manner, so all will not suffer in the same manner. Each person will suffer in the way commensurate with his sin and the character he has formed. There would be continuity of memory. There would be continuity of character. There would be continuity of punishment. There would be eternal continuity of separation from God because hell is a matter of not only of disagreeable feelings, but also of deprivation since the greatest loss of those in the damned place is that of knowing God and enjoying life with him in heaven. The damned will see what they have lost, and this will add to their torment for they will see the blessed before the judgment day and they will be grieved when they see what they have forfeited. After the judgment day, however, they will not be able to see the blessed, but they will remember what they saw before and this will continue to haunt them for all eternity.

He had heard that there are those who will be sentenced to inflict pain on one another while there are those who will live forever in solitary confinement—never, never, never, to experience anything other than loneliness.

He had read that in hell there will be knowledge of things which cause grief, but not of things which cause joy. Not only does it hold the greatest possible misery for its inhabitants, but there is never any relief from it. It is altogether vain and foolish for the unrepentant to suppose they will be able to tolerate hell by arming themselves with resolution and firmness of mind.

He had read that Aquinas maintained that the fire of hell would torture some persons more than others according to the measure of their sin because God regulates the fire in keeping with his perfect justice. The remorse of conscience would forever bring regrets on what might have been had he listened to his aunt....

"George! Are you down there?" he heard, waking him. "The meeting is going to start in thirty minutes," Helen shouted over the radio.

He rubbed his eyes, then realized he was drenched in sweat. He picked up his two-way radio. "I'm down in the basement working on the heating plant." He lied. He was taking a power nap on an old sofa put into storage by his predecessor. "I'll be right up as soon as I change my shirt," he said into the radio. He went to his locker to change his shirt and made sure he pulled his baseball cap down tight over his head. Then he walked up the stairs and onto the parking lot to the company van.

Fairchild Tropical Garden, Miami

It is not like I remember it, Brandon admitted to himself. The botanical garden had undergone a tremendous metamorphous since the Tribulation period began. When he would walk through the winding paths with his father, who would point out the colorful tropical flowers, massive trees, lakes, lily pools, vistas and overlooks, he would be in awe. But that was then. Now the 83 acres that once boasted of unparalleled beauty and conservation was a jungle of desolation. The garden had become a subordinate victim of God's wrath pointed at the very custodians of His creation, mankind.

There was no longer any scientific research or tours. The trams that ferried thousands of visitors annually were immobilized and became a nesting place for varmints and vermin. The snack bar and restaurant were vacant and the staff reduced to one man, the watchman. It was his duty to maintain surveillance over the garden and protect it from vandals. But the real enemy was the hostile environment that grew steadily perilous to both plant and human life.

"Hey, Morris!" Brandon said as he waved to the watchman from the main gate. "We need to borrow the garden for an hour. Is that okay?"

Morris knew Brandon's father well. Matthew Lane had provided a way for Morris' wife to receive chemotherapy through one of his hospital connections when his medical insurance inadvertently lapsed. An act of mercy Morris would never forget long after his wife died. "Of course, Mr. Brandon," Morris replied. "You have the whole place to yourselves."

"You're the man!" Brandon chortled, then waved in the rest of the group waiting in the company van.

The absence of birds, butterflies, and even alligators together with the dying foliage hanging from the once prolific trees rendered a somber mood among the group. But this was Brandon's way of bringing his people to remembrance as if it were a war memorial so they would never forget that God prophesied this judgment and that they must be about the Lord's business. There was little time remaining.

He directed the group to the Simons Rainforest, where towering trees supported a dense canopy of massive vines and exotic blossoms, punctuated with a meandering stream. It was the only vestige of beauty remaining in the park.

"Find a seat on the benches under the trees," he instructed his people. There were six in all: Brandon, Jonathan, Helen, George Barrett, Sydelle Swain, and Efraim Zuroff, the cyber terror expert.

"Brandon asked me to bring you all up to speed on what's happening in the resistance," Jonathan began as he stood in front of the group. "We have made what I call real progress in attacking some of the advanced areas in the Kavidas' camp. I'm talking about hitting them where it really hurts—in the heart. I just heard a report that our leadership over in Israel launched a drone attack on Kavidas' headquarters in Jerusalem—"

"Yeah! Go God!" Sydelle and Helen yelled out, breaking into Jonathan's report.

"—Go God is right," Jonathan said with a wry laugh. "But as we might expect—because of divine providence—Kavidas and Stein were unhurt. The Israeli prime minister was killed, which is unfortunate, but we believe he was only Kavidas' puppet and will somehow be replaced by a figurehead. This attack presents some problem since reprisals will certainly follow. But, as Paul believes, we must do everything to 'resist' and thwart the Antichrist's plans for people to follow him to hell. This is our mission." He motioned to Efraim. "I've asked Efraim to give us a status on the Muslim threat since that affects us all, both to us here in America and to our brethren around the world." Jonathan walked to a dry clump of grass and sat down.

"I, along with many of you," Efraim began, "have come to the place where I question, 'How did America and the rest of the world allow radical Islam to have such power and control'?" He shook his head. "Today, Shariah Law is next to our *Constitution* and holding sway in every hall of justice here in America and abroad. How did this happen?

"Well, I'll tell you. It happened little by little. Islamic indoctrination, programs, and activities were introduced into public grade schools where students were taught to say Muslim prayers, the Five Pillars of Islamic Faith, key passages from the *Qur'an*, dress up as Muslims, and build Muslim props for acting out Islamic skits. Students were told to recite aloud Muslim prayers that begin with 'In the name of Allah, Most Gracious, Most Merciful.' Memorize the Muslim profession of faith: 'Allah is the only true God and Muhammad is his messenger.' Chant 'Praise be to Allah' in response to teacher prompts. Profess as 'true' the Muslim belief that 'the Holy *Qur'an* is God's word.' Non-Muslim students were told that all religions are based on Islam and that the United States is a 'Judeo-Christian-Muslim' nation, according to the beliefs of the founding fathers. Muslims students were given 'prayer' rooms along with prayer rugs and all food considered offensive to Muslims was eliminated from the school cafeteria menus. Non-Muslim students had to remove shoes and be separated according to sex when entering the prayer area." He stopped. "And you know what the Americans did to stop this movement?" Sarcastically: "Nothing! So the

Muslims ratcheted things up!"

Jonathan stood up and walked next to Efraim. "This whole scenario is like what happened during Israel's divided kingdom period under the reign of king Hoshea described in Second Kings 17. He allowed his subjects in Israel to imitate the actions of nations around them, which had been forbidden by the Lord, to the extent where they were even sacrificing their sons and daughters in unholy fire and practicing all kinds of heathen divination and sorcery.

"The next king, Jeroboam, enticed Israel away from following the Lord and caused them to commit a great sin so the Lord sent the Assyrians to punish them. How did the Lord punish them? The Assyrians, along with other foreign peoples, settled in all the towns of Israel and systematically replaced the Israelites who lived there; the Israelites were depopulated. The Assyrians and other foreigners then made idols of their own gods and set them up in shrines and high places throughout Samaria and in turn would sacrifice their children in the fire as sacrifices to Adrammelech and Anammelech, the gods of Sepharvaim." He stopped. "Little by little they took over."

"Americans were especially targeted," Efraim continued. "The stateless Islamic enemies used our judicial system against us. The courts here in America caved into the highly paid attorneys that represented stateless terrorists where they were tried for murderous acts in civil courts instead of military tribunals and in turn made a mockery of our legal system. In point of fact, the notorious Khalid Sheikh Mohammed and his four 9/11 al-Qaeda co-conspirators had filed motions to dismiss on the basis that their constitutional right to a speedy trial had been violated and challenges to the admissibility of evidence was thrown out because it was used in a civilian court. Of course classified information necessary for military secrets was exposed in this civilian trial that seriously jeopardized America's national security. All of this happened because America did not want to do anything to offend the Muslims.

"This logic gave birth to the Islamic revolution here in America," Efraim said with a derisive snort. "When the Fort Hood massacre by Nidal Malik Hasan occurred in 2008, the radical Islamic group, As-Sabiqun, based in Washington, D.C., said that Hasan was 'victimized and the 'target of psychological warfare' defending the terrorist. This subversive group repeatedly predicted the demise of the United States and boasted of 'the Islamic State of North America no later than 2050.' This group openly declared support for terrorist organizations like Hamas and Hezbollah and even claimed it funded anti-American militants. Their leader, Imam Abdul Alim Musa, saluted the Iranian Revolution as the 'greatest epic in modern, even ancient history' and urged the students of a Muslim Students Association to have patience as the United States collapsed.

"Of course, he was given a standing ovation—right here in America—not some distant location in an Arabian province. This Musa, while making a speech to the MSA at Berkeley, explained how he funneled money to African jihadists with the intention of conquering the United States, adding that 'this religion Islam will dominate all other religions whether they be Americans, whether they be British, whether they be French, whether they be Russians, whether they be Japanese, whether all of them get together in one solid group to fight Islam—it don't make no difference—in the final analysis, Allah and Islam will rise to the forefront, will be elevated to the role of leadership in this world, whether they all like it or not.'" He stopped. Then: "And what did America do about this travesty and threat to national security? They did nothing!" Efraim shot a look at Jonathan, who seemed to be watching George intently. George looked detached, indifferent.

What Efraim, Jonathan, or Brandon did not have the presence of mind to bring out—perhaps it was because they did not want to aggravate an already explosive issue, or because they thought they already knew of it—but history did testify to the following facts that brought about the present political conflict: An Iranian-funded Hamas charter called for the destruction of Israel. This emboldened the terrorist group to perpetually wage war against the Jewish state and this fueled the Islamic hatred for Israel's sponsor, America. Saudi Arabia's homegrown Wahhabis with their global outreach of hate were responsible for promoting suicide bombers in Palestine, Chechnya, Bosnia, and then moved on to U.S. soil early in the 1960s where they infiltrated the American prison system to recruit dissidents who would perform their barbarous acts to further the Islamic ideology that included the notion that America had to be stopped since it was conspiring to seize control of Arabian oilfields. Saudi officials, recognizing the threat of Osama bin

Laden, cut deals with him to prevent him from engaging in terrorist acts in their nation due to their affiliation with American petroleum companies. As long as his ideology of killing Americans did not touch them, they would leave him alone. Accordingly, most of the bombings that took place in America were traced back to Saudi Arabia, this fact being confirmed in documents discovered by Israeli intelligence. Needless to say, this was officially denied by the Saudi kingdom.

Moving forward, the Saudis established a beachhead in Boston where local Muslims opened the Boston Cultural Center in Roxbury—a religious complex paid for largely by the Saudis and run by what federal authorities described as the overt arm of the Muslim Brotherhood, a genesis of all Sunni terrorist organizations. Flying a false flag of moderation in our Cradle of Liberty, this terrorist group was praised by all local Muslims. Meanwhile, those who criticized this arrangement were branded as bigots and dragged into court, while the press and public officials ignored the links between the leaders of the Islamic Society of Boston Cultural Center and Islamic hatred and terrorism. As it was in Britain under their 1996 Arbitration Act, Sharia Law—which contains numerous provisions that are barbaric and irreconcilable with any advanced society, including stoning married adulterers, flogging the unmarried, throwing homosexuals from roofs, amputating limbs for theft, etc.—soon made its way into American courtroom, ultimately interfacing with Kavidas' rules of engagement without anyone opposing him.

Because America was in a religious, moral, and political free fall, accentuated by America's propensity for indulgence and busyness, radical Islam found a nesting place. Their strategy during this religious morass included evicting America's God from education, law, the workplace, and school, replacing it with Islamic *Qur'an* teaching, protected under our *Constitution*. After 9/11 God "was allowed off the reservation" but quickly tucked away. The outworking of this mindset was realized when mosques and minarets replaced churches and crosses across the land, making Christian churches "tombs of God."

The divine light of Biblical revelation that God gave America was rejected so the churches became spiritually anemic. The churches brought in worldly values and pleasures to fill the void but instead of drawing men to God, paganism and pollutants that had infiltrated American culture rose to the occasion, ratcheting up the disease so that

God had to act by bringing judgment that would ultimately cure the problem. God allowed the wicked to accomplish his purpose by allowing Islam to act as his divine chastening rod.

Once the meeting was over everyone headed toward the van for the return trip; everyone but George. He remained on the bench. Jonathan took notice and dropped back. "George, are you okay?"

George was visibly shaken. *Is he ill?* Jonathan wondered. *Is it something that Efraim, Brandon, or I have said?* Something was bothering the man. Jonathan had to find out.

"Not really," George replied in a somber tone.

Jonathan looked him directly in the eyes. "Whatever it is, we want to help you."

George squirmed slightly then cast his eyes off into the distance as if to defer the pain. "Efraim's talk upset me."

"Why did his talk upset you?" Jonathan prodded. "You know that everything he said was true. We are seeing the outworking with our own eyes."

"Are you guys all right!?" Jonathan heard. He glanced toward the parking lot to see Brandon standing on the foot path with his hands in the air.

Jonathan waved to him. "We're fine. We'll be along soon," he called out.

Brandon nodded, turned, and walked off.

"Why did his talk upset you? You can tell me," Jonathan entreated.

George's hand was trembling. "I had this dream that really terrified me, and I have no one to talk to about it." Obviously he linked Efraim's subject matter with his dream.

Jonathan knew George was a loner, living by himself with few prospects for friends or companions. "Tell me," he persisted. "I want to help you with it."

There appeared to be a great debate going on in George's mind. He hesitated for several moments as he pulled his cap down snuggly on his head. Then he said, "It was a dream of hell and I saw myself there!"

Jonathan recognized fear when he saw it. It was the kind of fear that brought paralysis upon a stranded pedestrian caught on the tracks at a railroad crossing as a fast-moving train approached. "You seem really frightened," he said, wondering why such a dream would bring this reaction when Believers in the Lord were assured of heaven and that dreams of hell were not expected.

He gazed off into the distance as if to relive the dream, then grabbed hold of Jonathan's hand. "I don't want to go there!" he shouted aloud, somewhat in a panic.

"Why would you go there?" Jonathan asked soothingly. "If you belong to the Lord, you have no fear of hell." *If you belong to the Lord,* echoed in his mind.

A strange demeanor suddenly came over George. He snapped out of the anxiety attack and appeared to be governed by a tranquil spirit that brought increasing calmness. "I'm all right now," he said drawing in a deep breath. "I guess I just let the signs of the times get to me."

Jonathan nodded slowly, but his spirit was troubled. He couldn't put his finger on it, but he believed George was undergoing satanic oppression of sorts. "Are you sure you're okay?"

George bounded off the bench. "I'm fine," he said and rushed off to join the group.

Staring at George as he crossed the lawn, Jonathan couldn't help but ponder the issue of eternal security. If George truly was saved, the question of his everlasting life with Christ should have been settled at the point of his salvation. "Another conundrum wrapped up in an enigma," he said to himself. *I'll have to wait on the Lord to answer that one.*

SIX

K-group Home, Tamarac, Florida

Hosting a K-group was a new experience for Efraim Zuroff. Jonathan or Brandon frequently called upon him to decrypt a *Masterlink* coded message or to crack a complicated cyber terror communication intercepted by a K-group member, but to host a Bible study fell outside the parameters of his duties. Or so he thought, but in these perilous times there was little degree of normalcy. To avoid detection from Kavidas' forces in these times, each K-group member's home could at any moment be called upon to be the new headquarters of the resistance or the new command post or the new rallying point to mount an offensive against the regime of the new world leader.

Efraim Zuroff came to receive Christ as his messiah at the midpoint in the Tribulation. As a Conservative Jew he practiced all the rituals of the faith as well as celebrating all the High Holy Days. That is, until he came to realize the predicament Judaism was in once the Temple in Jerusalem had been rebuilt, only to have Kavidas desecrate it with the image of himself. His studies in the *Torah* and the *Tanach* explained that the false messiah would perform what Daniel the prophet called the Abomination of Desolation at the Temple. Jesus Christ confirmed the prophecy in Matthew 24. This blasphemous act drove Zuroff into the Bible and then to search out a Christian who explained the fulfillment of the prophetic word. His heart and spirit testified that he needed to get right with God in Christ and on that very day he surrendered his life to the true Messiah.

Efraim nodded to Jonathan and Brandon, who signaled for the group to hold hands. Then Efraim prayed for guidance and protection. Then it happened! Suddenly Sydelle broke from the chain, moved toward a corner of the room, and cried out, "He's dead! I know Eddie's dead! They killed him!" She began to shake from head to foot as a glaze came over her eyes. She looked like she was going into a trance. "They took him from me! My Julie has no father!" She started flouncing aimlessly while throwing her head back, then started to convulse.

A chill ran through Brandon's body as the room temperature and lighting abruptly dropped. He shot a look at Jonathan, who immediately recognized the symptoms. It was a demonic attack. "Everybody," Jonathan exclaimed, "go into prayer again!" He grabbed hold of Brandon's hand and pulled him to Sydelle's side as the others resumed their prayer, only more boldly.

"We must lay hands on her!" Jonathan instructed. "She's being oppressed by some foul spirit!" The feeling of uncontrollable power in the room was almost palpable. He nodded to Brandon; then they placed their hands on top of her head. "In the mighty name of Jesus Christ who shed his blood for us," Jonathan said fiercely, "we demand you depart from our presence!"

"You have no authority over me!" a gravelly voice resounded off the walls. The demonic tone exuded an unmistakable sense of menace, almost malevolence.

Jonathan and Brandon exchanged looks. "We don't have the authority but the blood of Jesus of Nazareth does!" they shot back.

Without warning Sydelle became inert. Seconds later her eyes widened; then she turned and focused on George. He shook his head, then his mind seized in panic. It was apparent the demon communicated with him. He broke from the prayer chain and bolted to the door.

"George!" Jonathan yelled out as adrenalin surged through his body like a jolt of high voltage, "stand fast!"

George froze in place at the command. "Efraim!" Jonathan screamed as he pointed to George. "Hold him! Don't let him go!"

Efraim vaulted over a small table to the door and latched onto George. "You're not going anywhere," he said roughly.

George began to quiver.

"Something is wrong with you, George," Brandon said as he shouted in his face. "What is it!?"

"He's been acting really weird," Efraim added in disgust.

Jonathan took a step back, then fixed his eyes on George's. A wave of suspicion swept over him as several of the events of the past few months involving George quickly came into view. This reaction with

Sydelle, together with his dream, clinched the verdict. "In the name of Jesus, George," he demanded, "tell us who you are!"

George's eyes flicked back and forth between Efraim and Jonathan. It was them he seemed to fear, but he said nothing.

Jonathan turned to Sydelle and ordered, "Sydelle, go in the other room!" She blinked several times in recognition, then scampered off.

"Let me at him!" Efraim's veins in his neck began to bulge. His face turned red as he pushed two chairs out of the way to reach George. "I'll get the truth from him!" he boomed. Within seconds Efraim had George in a chokehold. "Give it up!" he screamed in his face. "Who are you?"

George's face contorted as he gabbled something.

"Make sense!" Efraim said with twitching lips as his anger mounted exponentially.

Brandon's stomach tightened. "Now the demon's controlling him!"

Jonathan snuffled, then paused unexpectedly. "Hold it!" he said in a halting manner. Then he reached up and pulled George's cap off his head, and with his other hand brushed back his shock of hair.

"I don't believe it," Brandon said. "He has the mark and the boils!"

The three men glared at the 666 laser tattoo just above George's hairline with three unmistakable eruptions surrounding it. "He's been working for the other side all along!" Jonathan realized.

Exposed, George squirmed violently but Efraim and Brandon held him secure. Explosively with ragged gasps: "I'm working for the winning side...You and your K-group don't have a chance...Gregory Kavidas is marshaling all his forces and will crush your little resistance to powder!"

Brandon gave him a lethal glance. "Shut him up!"

Efraim nodded then clapped his hand over George's mouth and turned to Jonathan. "What are we going to do with him now that we know he's with Kavidas?"

Jonathan felt the hair rise on the back of his neck and turned to Brandon. "What's your thinking?"

"Kill him!" Efraim blurted out. "We can't take any chances with this snake! He'll squeal on us and give out our locations!"

George's eyes filled with terror as they darted between his three captors. Desperate, he motioned to talk so Efraim dropped his hand. "I'll tell you what happened to Eddie if you let me go," he choked out.

"Eddie?" Jonathan asked with piercing eyes. "What about Eddie?

You know about Eddie?"

"Eddie? My Eddie?!" Sydelle blurted out as she rounded the corner back into the room. "Where is he?"

Efraim curled his lip at George as Sydelle stood waiting. "Come clean, or we'll get word to Kavidas that you ratted him out," he said with disdain while clamping his hand on George's neck. "By this time tomorrow you'll be dead."

"He was snatched up in Extraordinary Rendition. They took him to Pakistan," George said numbly.

Sydelle snapped, "What did they do with him, you slime ball?"

Efraim dropped his hand as George said in contrition, while looking at Sydelle, "I'm sorry. I'm sorry."

Sydelle braced herself. "Sorry about what?!"

"It wasn't me"—he dropped his voice—"they killed him!" Sydelle burst into tears and ran out of the room.

"Get him out of here!" Jonathan ordered and pointed to the door.

"But we can't just let him go," Efraim said.

"God will deal with him," Jonathan replied. "Good riddance!"

Brandon opened the door as Efraim kicked him out and threw his hat out after him. A broad smirk flashed across George's face as he picked up his hat and placed it on his head while the others looked on. "Bye," he said with a mocking salute.

"I'll fix his butt!" Efraim snarled as he started after him.

Jonathan and Brandon held him back. "Let him go."

Efraim slowly closed the door as his rage subsided. Seconds later he walked over to Sydelle and comforted her until she stopped crying.

Once George reached his car he speed-dialed his stateside contact for reassignment but failed to see the oncoming garbage truck as he pulled out of his parking space. The garbage truck was fully loaded and unable to stop as George's car crossed its path.

SEVEN

Thirty-two Nautical Miles East of Saudi Arabia in The Persian Gulf

Israeli retired Navy Captain Aluf Eli Marom felt very strongly about his mission to destroy the oil fields at Ras Tanura. Recruited by Ravitzky to undertake the mission, Marom believed it was the blessing and providence of God that would enable him to bring divine retribution to the Arabs, especially the Saudis. After gathering intelligence data implicating the Saudis in the murder of his wife, he believed his conscience was clear.

Confirmation of Saudi complicity in the murder of his wife came when the United States published the commission findings on the September 11, 2001 attack on America where it was proven that 15 of the 19 terrorists were Saudi nationals. These nationals were the same perpetrators who flew commercial airliners into the World Trade Center buildings. It was the collapse of the North tower that killed his wife. It was one of her wishes that she tour the American symbol of architecture and finance during her visit to her American cousin living in Brooklyn. In Marom's mind, justice still had not been served, nor would it be until the number of American casualties had been surpassed by the number of Arabs killed in retaliation. He likened his mission to the atomic bombing of Japan's Hiroshima and Nagasaki as settlement for the attack on Pearl Harbor.

His ship, a decommissioned Israeli Navy Super Dvora MK III class patrol boat renamed *The Shadow of Haifa* after the captured clandestine immigration ships used during the 1948 Israeli War of Independence, was refitted to accommodate the latest stealth and electronic equipment known to the Israeli Defense Force. It would be determined at a later date that the boat had been purchased by a resistance group and that the use of the stealth and electronic equipment on Marom's boat was illegal. Marom would be labeled a "terrorist" by Saudi officials, but to the orthodox Jewry and K-group commanders opposed to Muslim domination and Kavidas' control, he would be labeled a hero.

Marom had carefully navigated his ship through the Red Sea into the Arabian Sea, then into the Gulf of Oman that led into the Persian Gulf. Under cover of darkness and early morning fog, his ship sat on station, waiting for the command from Ravitzky.

Undisclosed Location, Jerusalem

From their clandestine ground control station, Meschel keyed in the latitudinal and longitudinal coordinates into the Heron drone computer for the Ras Tanura oil fields while Ravitizky talked Marom through the setting up of the drone's flight parameters and arming mechanism on his Satcom phone. Ravitizky personally orchestrated the payload of 800 pounds of Semtex 10 along with four AGM-114 Hellfire missiles and two GBU-44/B Viper Strike guided bombs so as to inflict the maximum material damage.

"Set the speed at 135 knots with an altitude of 938 meters," Ravitizky ordered over the phone. "We want the bird to fly under their radar."

Marom smiled as he instructed his technician to adjust the controls of the drone. "This payback is a long time in coming," he said, his voice vibrating with feeling, "and certainly justified."

"What goes around comes around." Ravitizky chuckled. "It's time for them to learn a lesson." He nodded to Meschel. "If America retaliated in kind, it would have solved their terrorist problems, but no, they had to be 'diplomatic' with the Arabs when the only thing that stops them is force." He snarled and said to Meschel, "Let the bird fly!"

Meschel grinned, then pressed the remote switch that launched the drone off the deck of *The Shadow of Haifa.*

Najmah Residential Compound, Ras Tanura

Said Jalili stood on the veranda of the American-built condo complex at Najmah originally designed to house American expatriate oil company employees but as of late, multi-ethnic Arabs. His location afforded him a panoramic view of the refinery complex, pipeline system, and outward into the gulf to several of the off-shore oil rigs.

Originally employed to repair the pipelines between the refineries and the loading dock where the oil tankers were tied up, Said Jalili now enjoyed the position of foreman at the catalytic cracking facility where high-grade gasoline was made. With the promotion came the responsibility of overseeing security to his plant, a responsibility he believed should have fallen to qualified law enforcement who were trained in the field of security, but his superiors believed they lacked the technical expertise to avoid cyber terrorism, the new threat to the oil industry.

Suddenly Said Jalili stopped his reveling and glared into the horizon as a shape began to form before his eyes. "Allah, help!" He caught a glimpse of the sun reflecting off what looked like a metallic object flying close to the ground approaching the refinery. *An anomaly caused by the burning of the gasoline vapors at the top of the funnels?* he thought. *No, it cannot be*, he reasoned, *the object was moving too fast.*

Seconds later the refinery turned into a blazing inferno.

Jalili witnessed the flying object strike at the heart of the complex—the storage tanks. Four 750,000 gallon tanks exploded with such force that the shock wave blew the atmospheric distiller off its mounting platform. Nearly two million gallons of crude flowed into the catch basins, then ignited. The hydrotreater and hydrocracker buildings, connected to the distiller through seven pipelines burst into flames that bellowed out then lit off the coking units linked to the steam reformer. It took less than fifteen minutes to level the refinery. The only building left standing was the wastewater collection plant.

As an eyewitness and survivor of the attack, Said Jalili knew that his position with Aramco Petroleum had now been changed by fate. He would no longer be employed in the capacity of foreman but as one of the employees assigned to body retrieval and salvage.

Undisclosed Location, Jerusalem

Ravitzky and Meschel looked at the monitor, bringing the live satellite feed from what was once the Ras Tanura refinery complex. Plumes of dense black smoke ascended into the air, blocking out much of the sunlight as if it were a violent volcanic eruption. Intermittent gusts of wind blew and pushed some of the clouds of smoke into swirls that temporarily revealed the devastation. The concrete catch basins designed to contain the oil in the storage tanks in the event of a fire were unable to withstand the explosive blast of the Hellfire missiles. They yielded to the blast's concussion and fragmented in pieces then turned into projectiles that acted like mortar shells penetrating the remaining oil tanks. Mangled steel from the supporting girders, along with the aluminum pipelines, fused in the intense heat into masses of solid metal. Both crude and distilled oil was gushing freely in torrents. Most of the pipeline network was covered in crude oil and looked like logs piled up at a lumber camp. All that remained of the extensive pipeline network that crisscrossed the complex was several fractured pipes at the shoreline that used to run under the water to the offshore drilling platforms.

Ravitzky turned and gave Meschel a high-five. "We have successfully brought an end to the oil blackmail! The 'gun' to the world's head has been removed! Their production has suddenly dropped from 750,000 barrels per day to zero!"

Meschel grinned from ear to ear then said vehemently, "Now we have to work on taking out the refinery at Abadan, Iran. Then the playing field will be leveled."

Thirty minutes later several global news networks picked up the satellite feed from the Arab world's *Al-Hayat* news network of the attack on Ras Tanura. What the *Al-Hayat* network refused to show was the Jewish and American response to the attack. Thousands of elated citizens ran into the streets in various cities cheering and waving to celebrate the deed, just like the Arab world did after the attack of September 11, 2001.

EIGHT

Madrid, Spain

K avidas cunningly waited one month before calling upon the Arab leaders to convene in Madrid to discuss the demise of the Jewish nation, Israel. Allowing anger, rage, and bitterness to build would only bring better results for his partnership.

Outraged by the attack on Saudi's oil refinery at Ras Tanura, the Saudi intelligence network speedily went to work to ascertain who the perpetrators were. Using their resources imbedded in Hamas, Hezbollah and al-Qaeda, the blame fell on the Jews, to no one's surprise since they are always blamed for Arab bloodshed.

Built in 1850, the Hotel Manzanars in the center of the city where the meeting was to be held overlooked the headquarters of three of the world's largest companies: Telefonica, Repsol-YPF, and Banco Santander. An apropos setting for Kavidas and Stein, considering they were the architects of the world's massive financial network, *Masterlink*.

Kavidas equated his secret meeting with the Arab superpowers to Franklyn D. Roosevelt's request in December of 1943 to meet with Joseph Stalin and Winston Churchill at the Tehran Conference to strategize for the war against Nazi Germany and the rest of the axis powers. One of the more important products from the Tehran Conference was *Operation Overlord*, which would later be called *D-Day*. From Kavidas' perspective, the Tehran Conference decided on the dividing up of postwar Europe once the axis powers were defeated. Stalin, however, had his own secret plan to conquer choice nations once Roosevelt and Churchill did their work. Similarly, this would be his main objective: to secretly conquer nations once the Arabs did their work.

The entourage carrying the three heads of state from the Madrid airport was extremely limited and ultra secretive. There would be no pomp, fanfare, or publicity, nor any advance announcement as to the summit meeting. Saudi and Iranian security services scouted the route prior to the meeting, leaving no opportunity for anti-Arab terrorists to attack the leaders.

The first to step out of the stretch limo was Iranian President Afrasiabi, wearing a Western suit and sporting Versace sun glasses, despite the diminished sunlight. He was followed by King Al-Kamil of Saudi Arabia, who took pride in maintaining his identity as a Muslim by wearing a white gutrah held in place by a black agal. A flowing white robe covered the rest of his body, revealing only his $500 shoes. The last to appear was Syrian President Hafiz Eid who, like Afrasiabi, wore Western clothes. Finally two armed guards stepped out.

At first glance, Kavidas caught notice of what he perceived was anger in Al-Kamil's eyes as he walked up to him. *I hope he isn't holding me responsible for the hit on his oil wells*, he thought. As a gesture of recognition and humility, Kavidas bowed before Al-Kamil and said, "Your Excellency, it is my good fortune to meet with you." Then he turned to both Eid and Afrasiabi and nodded. "May Allah bring you health and prosperity." They simply blinked twice in reply. Stein walked gingerly up to them and shook hands with them. Their limp handshakes reminded Stein of their disdain for Westerners and their customs. Their intolerant facial expression conveyed the notion that they may have a problem with him being a Jew. In either case he could care less at this stage of the end game.

Al-Kamil's face looked gaunt to Kavidas. He reasoned that after last month's strike at Ras Tanura that the king didn't get much sleep. His black-rimmed glasses accentuated his bony features that appeared to be in shadow. As for Afrasiabi, his appearance struck Kavidas as odd, seeing that Iranians despise Westerners', especially Americans, who he seemed to emulate. Apparent to Kavidas was the worried expression on Afrasiabi's face. No doubt he believed his oil refinery at Abadan, along with his major nuke plants at Natanz, Bushehr, and Isfahan, was next on the renegades of Israel's hit list. Eid, short and rotund, appeared dwarfish. His countenance was of little descript.

Within thirty minutes they were all sitting at the conference table of the Royal room dedicated to diplomats and dignitaries.

"Gentlemen, I have asked you to meet with me to discuss a matter of great urgency," Kavidas began trenchantly. "You obviously—"

"Just a minute, Honorable Mr. Kavidas," Al-Kamil interrupted. "I beg your indulgence. I want to quote something to you from the *Qur'an* that should set the tone for our meeting."

Kavidas shot a look at Stein. *This is going to be just what I hoped it would be.* "Go ahead your Excellency."

Al-Kamil opened up the *Qur'an* to Surat al-Ma'idah 5:33 and read aloud: "'*The only reward of those who make war upon Allah and His messenger and strive after corruption in the land will be that they will be killed or crucified, or have their hands and feet on alternate sides cut off, or will be expelled out of the land, and in the Hereafter theirs will be an awful doom.*'" He placed the *Qur'an* on the table, then said bitterly, "The existence of Israel is an error that must be rectified. This is our opportunity to wipe out the ignominy, which has been with us since 1948. Our goal is clear—to wipe Israel off the map. We want to bring on Armageddon!"

"*Allah-hu-Akbar!*" Afrasiabi and Eid said in unison.

Kavidas made a fist under the table. *I got 'em!* "My fellow patriots, we are of the same mind." He gestured toward Stein. "My partner here met with your emissaries some time ago to set in motion what is to be the 'final solution,' and so as not to confuse this with the Nazi machine, *I mean the final solution!* I've asked to meet with you to plot the attack that will bring about the destruction of the Jewish problem that has been a thorn in the side of the Muslims for centuries.

"Although there have been other campaigns in the past that had limited success, this plan differs inasmuch as it will have complete success." He turned again to Stein and said, "Mr. Stein, please bring our partners up to date."

Stein pulled out two folders from his attaché case, then opened one. "To begin, our intelligence network has uncovered the Jews who orchestrated the attack on Ras Tanura. It is a Christian group consisting of mostly ex-Jews with several hideouts in the Jerusalem and Negev area. We know who and where they are."

Eid swore vehemently. "Then why don't you just get rid of them!"

"Ultimately we will. Ultimately we will," Stein said soothingly. "But the problem we're facing is that when we eliminate one pocket, another three pop up. They are all over Israel and the rest of the world." What he didn't add so as to invoke doubt was the Christians in these K-groups appeared to have divine protection both from the 144,000 worldwide evangelists and a host of other heavenly helpers.

"The bigger picture we must consider is that in both the *Qur'an* and the Bible there is a description of a final war." Stein turned to Al-Kamil. "It is to this final war that you mentioned we must address our attention." He nodded to Kavidas.

"Friends, and I know I can call you friends," Kavidas cleverly began, "I have come to recognize that Islam is indeed the primary vehicle that will be used to fulfill the prophecies of the *Qur'an* and the Bible about the future political and religious systems of the world. Further, I believe Islam will overtake the entire world just prior to the return of the savior, the *Mahdi!*"

All three of the heads of state and their bodyguards bolted up and shouted, *"Allah-hu-Akbar!"*

Kavidas smiled then motioned for them to sit down. Inwardly he knew that the Mahdi, Islam's equivalent of the messiah, is said to lead a world revolution that will establish a new Islamic world order throughout the entire earth and then lead his army to Israel and re-conquer it for Islam. Islam's thinking states that he will eradicate those "pigs and dogs" —the Christians and the Jews who refuse to convert to Islam—then change the law by instituting Islamic Shariah Law all over the earth. The whole concept worked well in keeping with his plan.

"My goal in asking you here today," Kavidas explained, "is for us to bind together in commonality. There are four things that do indeed bind men together. They are a common hope, common work, deliverance from a common peril, and loyalty to a common friend. All of these criteria converge in our fight against the Jews."

Afrasiabi eyed Kavidas and Stein inquiringly.

Kavidas read the look. "Question, Your Highness?"

President Afrasiabi glanced at the other two Arab leaders and nodded. "I believe I may be speaking for my fellow brothers by asking you about your loyalty to Islam." He wiggled in his chair. "After all, you are not a Muslim but a Gentile, and—" he nodded toward Stein—"your partner here is a Jew. So what are we to expect when it comes to allegiance?"

"When, in the heat of battle, can we expect you both to turn on us?" Eid ventured.

Al-Kamil would not remain silent either. "We must answer to our people. In order for us to mount a campaign of such magnitude that will require the entire resources of our military, every member of our nation will ask: *Why* should we follow you?"

Kavidas stood. "Mr. Stein, hand me the other file." Stein slid the file across the table. Kavidas picked up the file and slowly waved it back and forth while explaining, "I understand your concerns. I really do. This is why I am prepared to prove to you that there are no plans for conspiracy or deception—*we are in this together*—to achieve victory over the Jews and all infidels." He flipped open the file and handed each of them an official letter with his signatory and waited momentarily for each of them to read the brief document.

"Let Allah and Mohammed be praised!" Afrasiabi fell to the floor in humble adoration. Eid and Al-Kamil looked with astonishment at Kavidas and they too fell to the floor in worship. Obediently, their bodyguards joined them.

Only Kavidas and Stein remained standing.

NINE

Christian Fortress, Petra, Jordan

Jubilant celebrations were the plan of the day. Moments after Yashur received the call from Paul of the successful raid on Ras Tanura he told his wife, Estelle, and the entire compound broke out into festivities. Gadi and Dalia Shamni started doing the *horah* while Marta Shiller walked to the far corner of the great room and uplifted a prayer of praise for God bringing judgment on their enemies. Alfonse Rivera walked to Marta's corner and joined her in prayer as Norman and Clara Greenbaum called their son Hershel and Paul at Jericho to revel in the good news.

It was after the celebration that the conversation between Yashur and Estelle turned serious.

Estelle walked up to Yashur holding an atlas. "I don't understand why there has been so much fighting over this little piece of land. Can you explain it?"

Yashur studied the map she was looking at for several moments. It was a satellite image of Israel from space. From the vantage point of space, Israel looked very small compared to surrounding nations. He calculated that Israel stretches only 263 miles from north to south, and its width ranges from 71 miles at its widest point to only 9 miles at its narrowest point. To the northeast, Israel faces a 47-mile border with Syria; to the north, a 49-mile border with Lebanon. To the east, Israel has a 147-mile border with Jordan, and to the southwest, Israel borders Egypt. On the other side; the Mediterranean. Directly south, Israel has a small window onto the Red Sea.

"Hmm, yes," he said after a moment of contemplation, "I see what you mean. "And yes, I know why there has been so much conflict over this piece of real estate." He ticked off several reasons with his fingers: "First, we're 'locked in' by all Muslim countries, placing us at odds with them. Next, Israel is the gateway into Africa. This has always been a preferred route for invading conquerors. Then, there are the mineral deposits in the Dead Sea. There are untold amounts of potash and other minerals used for making fertilizer and gunpowder, among other valuable commodities. Then, and I believe this is the most crucial, Satan has stirred up the Gentile nations to continuous war against Israel because unto them were committed the oracles of God—the writers of the Bible, and—through Israel came the Messiah, Jesus—who brought Satan's demise on the Cross. Since his defeat, he has waged war against Israel."

Estelle mused for a minute before turning the page on the atlas. "I noticed these drawings when I was leafing through the atlas and they illustrate the condition of the land of Israel before the Jews turned it into a homeland in 1948. There is a description here by the German Kaiser Wilhelm II in 1898 when he visited Palestine that appeared in the book *The Original Sin*, by Meir Abelson. You should read it."

Yashur nodded then took the book from her hand. There were several sketches of Jerusalem and outlying regions dating back to the 1800s. Below one of the black and white images was a caption. He read it aloud: "'I was appalled at the condition of the country. The Ottomans had stripped the forests for lumber and firewood. The Palestinian Arabs had let the old Roman aqueduct fall into ruin. The ultimate ecological curse was the ubiquitous herds of black goats. For nearly 2,000 years after the dispersion of the Jews, Arabs had allowed the goats to graze unfenced across Palestine. They had eaten the grass down to its roots, and the topsoil had eroded and blown away. The Biblical land of milk and honey had become a dust bowl.'" He shook his head and handed the atlas back to his wife.

"When the Arabs had control, Israel was in ruins," Estelle added bitterly. "They had no interest in caring for our land until we Jewish people began to rebuild it into our nation—then they suddenly made claim to it."

Yashur nodded once again, rubbing her shoulders. "There's no point in getting upset over these things," he said soothingly. "Everything that has happened is to advance the greater purpose of God. Rest assured He is going to level the playing field very soon." He winked at her. "And we will see it with our own eyes."

Norman approached Yashur as Estelle walked away and held up his cell phone as he said, "I just received an encrypted text message from Paul. Ravitzky is going to give the Iranians a double whammy! He's not going to use a drone or a cruise missile this time, but he's going to attack their computer infrastructure."

Yashur stared blankly at him. "How does he plan to do that?"

"Drawing from one of his defense specialist colleagues from the Israeli Institute for Security Studies," Norman explained, "Ravitzky says the Iranians are very vulnerable to a cyber attack. So he's going to infiltrate their computer system networks and contaminate them with viruses and malicious software. Because the attacker is difficult to identify, it makes retaliation much more difficult. Only when their computers stop working do they realize they're under attack. The attack is easily concealed and extremely hard to trace."

Yashur grinned expansively and raised his fist. "Go get 'em, Ravitzky!"

Hours later, Yashur was cold. The reduced sunlight due to the shortened daylight hours continued to lower the earth's temperature. Now that it was nighttime—approaching just after 3 p.m.—he needed warmer clothing to insulate his body from the cold. Outside the cave buildings the temperature seemed warmer, but inside the dampness coming off the rock surfaces brought on shivers and shakes. It was times like this that his special reserve of aromatic tea for medicinal purposes brought relief from the bizarre weather. It also brought on sleep. After one cup, he set his head down on his pillar and thought about times past when things were different.

But his dream was not what he expected.

Standing outside and looking up, he realized the moon was still red and the sun was still partially darkened from the great astrological disturbance that occurred during the Seal and Trumpet judgments. Then light of day gave way to night and he could see the drastic reduction in starlight. It was as if many of the light sources in the star canopy had been extinguished. *How dreadful*, he thought. *How scary.*

His body began to quiver as the scene morphed into nightmarish proportions. He saw nature continuing to rebel against mankind, but now, more than ever before. The detestable ectoparasitic world would be unleashed in unparalleled proportions. He hated insects. He hated bugs. But the dream would not let him go. He had to see it. He had to warn.

Yes, he thought, *it will be pestilence. Great pestilence.* The Sixth Trumpet judgment of locusts will soon give way to an even greater scourge: ticks and ants. At first he saw the ticks. They were the American dog tick and the southern cattle tick, along with the Lone Star tick and the black-legged tick—all mutated into one species. It was a new species with resistance to insecticides. It was an unexpected kind of judgment.

Then he saw them biting and infecting. He saw the ticks lying in wait upon blades of grass and leafy trees and shrubs. Vast numbers of them. The small arachnids in the super family *Ixodoidea* living by hematophagy on the blood of mammals, birds, reptiles, and amphibians had multiplied at exponential rates. They were everywhere: infesting every patch of green left on the earth; engorging themselves on the blood of their hosts until they reached the size of marbles. Vectors, that's what they were. Disease-carrying vectors that included Lyme disease, Q fever, Colorado tick fever, Rocky Mountain spotted fever, tularemia, tick-borne relapsing fever, babesiosis, and Tick-born meningoencephalitis, as well as canine jaundice in animals.

He saw that no one felt safe when outside. Anyone who would come in contact with vegetation wore loose light-colored clothing so the ticks could be spotted quickly before they began to feed on the host. Forested regions and wooded sites that provided ticks cover were off limits. Thousands chose to shave their heads and hairy parts to avoid infestation. Domestic pets and farm animals were dying in great numbers from anemia due to a sudden influx of seed ticks that attacked in numbers up to 30,000 at a time. The worldwide death rate soared.

Then he saw the ants. They were called the Bullet Ant.

They were big, nearly 3 centimeters long and named on account of their powerful and potent sting, which is said to be as painful as being shot with a bullet. They resembled wingless wasps and their sting was described as causing waves of burning, throbbing, all-consuming pain that continues unabated for up to 24 hours. Initially indigenous to lowland rainforests from Nicaragua south to Paraguay, the Bullet Ant traveled to the United States in a larva state while mixed in with exotic butterfly pupae imported from South America.

They too were everywhere. They migrated from the woody, damp places by the bases of trees in forests to the moist places in residential communities. They sought out and burrowed into cool basements and backyard shady areas where children played. They dug into the woodwork of homes like termites to lay their eggs and continued to multiply unchecked by man. Bullet Ant colonies popped up all over grassy knolls, lawns, and areas where there was moisture. Their prey of smaller insects and nectaries quickly gave way to savagely attacking humans.

Yashur turned in his sleep, then bolted upright as the dream came to an end.

Once fully awake, he immediately called Paul to put out a warning on the K-group network that they should brace themselves for the onslaught of ticks and ants that would come upon the earth as an unscheduled judgment.

Jordan Valley Stronghold, Jericho

The problem with solitude, Paul thought, was that it brings with it the opportunity to dwell on the negatives in life. The pressure of leading the K-groups, along with Shira's pregnancy, the relentless plagues accompanying the Tribulation, not to mention the persecution and pursuit by Kavidas, was enough to discourage even the stoutest Christian. Yes, he would encourage himself with Scripture memory verses, but there were times when he needed more. *"I have been driven many times to my knees by the overwhelming conviction that I had nowhere else to go. My own wisdom and that of those about me seemed insufficient for the day,"* he remembered Abraham Lincoln saying. *Yes, Lord, that's what I need,* Paul told himself.

He dropped to his knees in the privacy of his and Shira's bedroom quarters and prayed. At first he remained silent, simply dwelling on the promises of God. Then he rehearsed in his mind all of the historical examples of how God met his needs in the past. He began to encourage himself. Then negativity began to push itself into his mind once again. "Get thee behind me Satan!" he said to himself aloud. He audibly recited more verses, then raised his hands to God like Solomon did when dedicating the Temple. More prayer! More reciting! In deep anguish of soul he stood and walked around the bedroom quarters then returned to his prayer position. He was losing it. He could feel it. *Suppress those feelings!* he commanded himself. *Don't give in to feelings!*

"Paul, Paul!" he heard.

He turned toward the voice as a corporeal shape formed behind him. "Yes?" His eyes widened in shock. He blinked several times in awe before recognizing Kapporeth. Then he stiffened. He could feel the pulse hammering in his neck.

"Paul," Kapporeth said. "I've come to encourage you!"

"Whew!" Paul said in relief as he wiped his brow. The thought of Kapporeth coming to rebuke him crossed his mind. "May the Lord be praised," he said, sounding amazed.

"We are entering into the last days," Kapporeth instructed, "so you must draw upon God's Spirit for strength."

As if he were speaking to God through Kapporeth, Paul said, "Yeah, Lord. I need a double portion of your strength to go on."

"And you shall have it," Kapporeth replied. Then he raised his arm and placed his hand on Paul's head and prayed something in an unknown tongue. The only word Paul understood was *Adonai*, which he repeated three times.

Paul could feel the infusion of God's Spirit. He felt his heart leap as his soul and will responded to the infilling of Pentecostal power from on High. His spirit revived! A wave of encouragement swept over him. *You are my chosen vessel*, he heard in his spirit. *You will endure to the end. Take heart and be strong.*

"Now be aware that difficult times are ahead," Kapporeth said, bringing Paul back to reality. "Our adversary, Satan, has directed his instrument to set in motion the plan to bring about the final conflict. He has met with his allies and laid the foundation for Armageddon."

Paul stood mesmerized as his mind absorbed the revelation.

"The time for the Third Bowl has been decreed. The Word of Truth will be rejected, and many of God's people will be martyred." He nodded at Paul. "Asher and Simon will undergo severe testing but will remain steadfast."

Paul pleaded in his spirit: *The enemy knows they have but a short while, so they will be tenacious. Lord, help!*

Kapporeth smiled. "Fear not. I will be with you."

Paul thought on Emerson. *"What a new face courage puts on everything."*

A short while later Paul read Yashur's text message to the rest of the group to warn them of the plague of ants and ticks—something they were not too worried about because of their location, but nevertheless would be on the alert. From there he asked Ravitzky to give a report on the cyber attack on the Iranian computer infrastructure and directed Doron to broadcast the developments throughout the K-group network. Then he turned to the more pressing issue: the message of Kapporeth.

"Brothers and sisters," Paul instructed the group with fervor, "I have heard from Kapporeth, who has encouraged me, and I in turn want to encourage you that we should remain faithful and steadfast in the work of the Lord. We are entering the final stage of God's dealing with mankind, and thus far He has enabled and protected us. We must remember this precedence as we go forward in time since we can expect the judgments to become more severe. This will mean that we too will undergo dangerous and perilous times."

Shira walked up to him and put her arm around his waist. He turned to her and smiled. "Was there anything else?" she asked.

"Yes, was there anything else?" Doron echoed.

Paul shot a look at Ravitzky and Meschel. "Yes. There is more." He took a deep breath. "The plan for Armageddon has been put in place. I don't know the details, but if I am able to read the times in which we live, then I believe Kavidas has met with his Arab-bloc colleagues to put together the coalition that will fulfill the prophecies in Zechariah 14 where all nations will come against Israel."

Ravitzky made a fist. "Do we know who they are?"

Paul shrugged. "I believe we can guess, but I do not know for certain. The Bible abounds with proofs that the Antichrist's empire will consist only of nations that are Islamic. Despite the numerous arguments for the emergence of a revived European Roman empire as the Antichrist's base, the specific nations that the Bible identifies as comprising his empire are today all Muslim."

Ravitzky slammed his fist down on his knee. "I will find out all the

85

details!"

Meschel nodded then joined fists with Ravitzky. "We will cut them off at the knees!"

Paul smiled at Meschel. "We won't be able to fight them, Nachman, because in this final battle, only the Lord Jesus can defeat them. But I admire your zeal." His demeanor suddenly changed.

Levi and Hershel exchanged glances. "We can read your face," Hershel said to Paul, "what else?"

Paul tried to hide his anguish. "The Third Bowl is coming soon—it is even at the door—and Asher and Simon were singled out. That must mean they are going to experience severe persecution above everybody else. As members of the 144 thousand, their testing will be greater."

There was a profound silence.

TEN

The Messianic Wing of the Temple, Jerusalem

As Kavidas walked jointly with Stein, inspecting the completed repairs to the messianic wing of the Temple and to his office from the drone attack, the thought occurred to Kavidas that being supernaturally protected from death—at least for the time being, had its distinct advantages. Yes, he realized, the time was coming when that protection covenant would be lifted, but for the present, experiencing invincibility emboldened him greatly. *I will have my way over all things!* Stein shared the euphoria and reminded him that the people of Israel recognized his superior abilities.

It was not a time for festivities or triumph, they agreed, but a time for planning. Plans needed to be in place to retain a working government and financial system both in Israel and the world at large since prophetic events were about to accelerate. This they also agreed upon.

"First things first," Kavidas said to Stein as they retired to the leather sofa in his office. "We want to help our Arab brothers to retaliate against the perpetrators of the attack on Ras Tanura and then the cyber terrorism on their computer networks, being mindful that we want to remain invisible. Use any of our resources, both natural and supernatural, and remember any reprisal must not implicate us."

Stein nodded as he made a mental note of their plans. He walked to the window. In the distance he could see continuing evidence of the Russian attack on Israel nearly seven years earlier. The Israelis were still burning the Russians weapons fashioned from synthetic materials in their electrical generating plants. Ironic, he thought. The Jews would be using weapons of destruction to power their homes. *Inventive.*

"Secondly," Kavidas continued, "we have curried favor with other nations, namely the European Union, China, and Japan, who want to join us in defeating these Christians and Jews who oppose us. I have been in secret contact with their ambassadors and it is unanimous that something has to be done to curb their aggression and their resistance to world peace. These other nations are of the same mind as both the Arabs and us to amalgamate into one strong union. But we cannot do so as long as they exist."

"The Americans?" Stein asked curiously as he walked about. "Where are they in all this?"

Kavidas snorted. "They capitulated long ago when Islam threatened them with the only weapon they have, terrorism, in the form of suicide bombers. If the Americans had stood their ground and not caved into their demands like in the case of those pirates who commandeered merchant vessels off the coast of Indonesia came to realize—that America is all bark and no bite. They are a paper tiger. That means that we can expect them to fall in line. The days where America would stand up for Israel or pirates of the sea has long past. So no, we don't have to worry about them."

Stein raised both hands into the air. "It is written that 'all nations will come against Israel,' so let's bring it on."

Surprised: "Yes, it is written. Thanks for the reminder," Kavidas said with a strange smile. "It was Karl Marx who also wrote something," he added with a note of sarcasm. "'Religion is the opiate of the masses.' So let's use the narcotic to our advantage. Religion can be a useful tool when in the hands of the right people."

"And the religion that you have started here in Israel by your mighty deeds places us in a position of power." Stein chuckled softly. "And that power has become anesthetizing."

"Amen," Kavidas said mockingly.

Stein glanced down at his iPhone and read the text message, then said, "There's a warning coming over the Internet that there is an outbreak of ticks and what they call Bullet Ants."

Kavidas shrugged. "Another unwelcome event from the other side I presume."

"Just shower more frequently and watch for crawling things," Stein replied flippantly.

Kavidas unwittingly scratched his legs several times. "Next, we need to address the issue of food control. The Christians and those Jews in those Koinonos groups need clamping down. They're bartering gold and silver coins and exchanging services so they can circumvent *Masterlink*. So I want you to put in the order to authorize the FDA in the States to distribute hybrid seeds to the food networks so we can control that part of the food chain."

Genetic engineering, recombinant DNA technology, genetic modification and manipulation and gene splicing of an organism's genes used the techniques of molecular cloning and transformation to alter the structure and characteristics of genes directly. This application allowed governments and industry to control the replication and multiplication of seeds so that corn or other food sources with contraceptive DNA cannot be reproduced without the genetic code from the supplier. A farmer would not be able to gather seeds after a harvest when he used sterile seeds. He would be required to seek authorization and then purchase them from the company that provided the seeds.

Being aware of this method of genetic engineering and potential control, many survival groups hid non-hybrid seeds in special vaults located in the Arctic Circle.

"Be sure to alert the authorities," Kavidas warned, "that any violation of this order that includes any supplies secretly hidden will be dealt with very severely."

Stein nodded again and then walked to the window once more. The view relaxed him. "We still have to deal with those Jewish missionaries. I'm wondering why they haven't been giving us problems yet," Stein whispered to himself.

"They will. But there are ways in which we can suppress them," Kavidas said.

Stein suddenly remembered Kavidas had uncanny abilities that included incredible audio and visual acuity. He grinned, reminding himself not to think aloud.

Suddenly the office door flew open!

"Sir! Mr. Kavidas!" his man servant gulped as his eyes locked on Kavidas, "the Jordan River has turned blood red!"

Kavidas and Stein simply nodded, and Kavidas said reassuringly, "Stand strong, Kedar, stand strong."

Kedar, a Palestinian in his 30s who was fully dedicated to Kavidas, exhaled but frantically paced back and forth in front of Kavidas. "What are we to do?!"

"There's nothing we can do," Kavidas said soothingly. He knew the divine oracle very well. The Third Bowl Judgment declared that rivers and subterranean reservoirs were going to turn blood red. The water would be poisonous and undrinkable. "This one is of short duration," he declared. "It will only last for forty days. Authorize a press release that I said it is only temporary and that the population of the world has enough bottled water and distillers in place to carry us over."

"Whew!" Kedar said with a sigh of relief. "Yes, I will instruct the media accordingly." He backed out of the office.

"Typical hysteria," Stein noted. "The kind we like to control."

"Right. And the good part of this—" Kavidas gestured in the air— "'Bowl Judgment' is that this one works in our favor." The three series of judgments—Seals, Trumpets, and Bowls—were all directed at bringing Israel to repentance in preparation for their true Messiah. Kavidas knew this would benefit him indirectly, while Bowl Three would serve his purpose even better.

"You're referring to the martyrdom of the Christians, right?"

Kavidas smiled luminously. "And the rejecting of their prophets!"

"Ah! Yes," Stein recalled. "Their prophecies are discredited while our interpretation is accepted. Splendid."

Jordan Valley Stronghold, Jericho

Paul sat in seclusion reading news reports on his laptop computer. It was imperative that he keep up with current events that mirrored Biblical prophecy. *Alas*, he thought, *it is heartbreaking to see humankind suffer.* Watching children roam the streets of New York and other major cities rummaging through garbage cans for food as the famine worsened; watching the effect of worldwide pestilence, drought, and never-before-seen plagues that hit both skin and eyes with boils, he believed, should bring any mortal to a saving knowledge of Christ—all because of affliction. But it was not meant to be. No, not yet.

With extraordinary events occurring in the sky above: a quadrant of the sun blackening, the moon turning red; stars somehow disappearing; and on earth: with earthquakes that shift mountain ranges and the Mediterranean Sea turning red resulting in a colossal fish kill; trees incinerated by meteor showers—he wondered why there were not massive conversions to Christ. He could not understand it in the natural man. Historically, catastrophes turn people to religion, but in the light of bible prophecy, unrepentant man would just curse God and attempt to save themselves through human invention.

Moments later he opened up a new real-time page on his laptop and immediately recognized that the Third Bowl Judgment had hit. He wept.

"You okay?" he heard from behind.

He quickly dried his eyes with his shirtsleeve and smiled as Shira walked up to him and put her arm around his shoulder. He reached around her belly. "I'll be fine," he said, forcibly focusing on her condition. "How's 'little Paul' doing?"

"You mean Sol?" Shira said with a smile. "We're naming the baby Sol, remember?"

"Of course," Paul chortled. "Just teasing." The flash report of abnormal birth rates in the world due to fears of mutations from the AIDS virus along with the pervasive thought of divine judgment brought the levels to an historical low. Something he didn't think Shira needed to hear.

"Moshe is here to see you," Shira said, giving him a gentle nudge.

Paul nodded, snapped his laptop shut, got up and walked out with his wife, hand-in-hand.

Ravitzky grinned the moment he saw Paul. "I have a surprise for you." He unclipped his two-way phone from his belt and said, "Nachman, bring him in."

Moments later Meschel walked into the fortress with a man with his hands tied behind his back. "Here's our little booty," Meschel said as he slapped the man across the face. The man sneered at Meschel but said nothing.

"This man is a Hezbollah 'mule' working out of a Shiite enclave in Lebanon," Ravitizky explained. "He was born, raised, and trained as an operative in Iran. We picked him up trying to spy on our operation." He paused and made a menacing gesture. "We Jews are staying one step ahead of the vermin these days."

Meschel grabbed the man by his hair, then pulled a large knife from his belt and held it to the man's throat. "Now it's time to tell my friend all you know," Meschel demanded.

The man grunted several times but remained mute.

"Maybe you didn't hear me!" Meschel snapped as he slid the knife across his neck. Blood dripped on to the blade. Meschel then lifted the knife before the man's eyes. "Deeper?" he asked.

Paul sucked air into his lungs and shook his head. "Be reasonable. Let's avoid any violence."

"Avoid violence?!" Ravitizky echoed. "Violence is the only thing these Arabs know and respond to. Is it not violence when these Arabs hide in elementary schools and hospitals with rocket launchers while grabbing a 10-year old boy by the collar and dragging him to deter Israeli snipers from firing at them?" He nodded to Meschel.

Meschel took the point of his knife and jabbed it into the man's ear lobe. Blood began seeping out and dripped on to the man's shirt. "Deeper?" Meschel snarled. The man stood determined to remain silent.

"Deeper!" Ravitizky said gruffly. "Tell us about Madrid."

The man winced.

Meschel detected a flutter. He had enough interrogation training to notice weakness. "See, I told you Moshe," Meschel said furiously, "something is going on!"

Ravitzky stood face-to-face with the man. "Either you tell us what you know, or I will give my ambitious friend the okay to slit your throat!"

Meschel tightened his grip on the man's head.

The man had enough common sense to know that neither Meschel nor Ravitzky were bluffing. "I only know that there was a big meeting to make plans for the future of Islam—"

Meschel slammed him across the face. "Don't take us for suckers! Our Intel told us the meeting was designed to prepare for war. We want details!"

The man's eyes flicked back and forth between Meschel and Ravitzky and then settled on Paul.

"Don't look to him for mercy!" Meschel growled. "We will give you the same courtesy you guys gave to Dan Pearl. How's that sound?" The decapitation of Danny Pearl was forever engraved upon the minds of all

Israelis as a war atrocity that few Westerners remembered.

The man weakened. "I overheard Afrasiabi's aide speaking about the meeting," he muttered.

"Speak up!" Meschel shouted, pulling on the man's hair.

The man caved. "The meeting was about the final solution," he said, voice quivering. "The heads of Arab states are aligning to bring on the Mahdi."

"The *Mahdi?*" Ravitzky replied, incredulously. "But the Mahdi is the Islamic answer to the Messiah who comes to annihilate all non-Muslims!"

The man just nodded in silence.

"This must be their idea of retaliation for your attacks on Iran," Paul said trenchantly.

"It is written. Remember?" Ravitizky replied impulsively.

"Yes, I remember," Paul said, "and I take it the Lord wants us to be in the front row when He brings down the final curtain."

"Their plan is to wipe Israel off the map," the man added in the spirit of contrition.

Ravitzky bit his lip as he thought on the man's admission. He turned to him and asked, "And for the immediate future?"

"They are planning a reprisal for the raid on Ras Tanura," he said sheepishly.

Paul pursed his lips as he thought on the man's confession. "That means they're coming after us too, no doubt," he speculated. "They must know that we're in this together."

The man stared at the wall in front of him and said nothing.

Paul scratched his head unwittingly then blinked. "Hold it," he said and added haltingly, "something is missing in this equation."

"You're right!" Ravitizky agreed. "Why would the Arabs join in with Kavidas, a Gentile and Stein, a Jew?"

"That's the big question!" Paul contemplated the matter.

"There's got to be something that we're not aware of," Meschel added curiously. With that, he tightened his grip on the man's head, then placed the knife over the man's heart. "What say you?"

The man snuffled deeply and began to whimper. "I told you everything I know!" he said apologetically.

"There's got to be a reason why they all threw in with him,"

Ravitzky ventured.

Paul's jaw tightened. "We must find out if we're to be prepared."

Ravitzky gave the man a lethal glance before he forced a smile.

The man interpreted the look. "No!" he shouted aloud. He started to quiver, and suddenly his sphincter let loose. The odor of excrement filled the room as he realized his fate.

Meschel took the cue from Ravitzky. He pulled the man toward the door as he struggled to set himself free. "We will show you justice as you have shown us," Meschel said as he regarded the Arab as a python considers a rat. Within minutes he was outside of the fortress.

Paul heard a gunshot.

This is a time for war, Paul said to himself as he thought on Ecclesiastes chapter three. *Yes, a time for war. And in wartime, it is either kill or be killed.*

Christian Fortress, Petra

At first they were only delineations but the sketchy images quickly took shape into a naked woman, and in the inner recesses of his mind he knew they were not from God. They were sensuous and provocative images that began to stir his imagination to the point where he envisioned himself laying with the woman, a voluptuous woman who lay on a large bed beckoning him to touch her. Rose petals were sprinkled on the sheets wafting an aromatic fragrance into his nostrils. *Oh, that smells so good! So inviting.*

He fled to the bedroom doorway and grasped the doorknob. He turned around and hesitated. He looked back to see her and began to lose himself in her seducing eyes. *Flee!* he heard in his spirit. The pull was overpowering. He felt his resolve weakening...

"Asher, wake up!" he heard.

Asher momentarily squirmed in his bed, then shook his head as he eyes opened. "Simon, I had this dream—" he began then stopped abruptly. He jumped out of his bed then walked to a chair and bowed his head and began praying.

"What's going on?" Simon asked as Asher broke from his power prayer moment.

"I believe a lust demon visited me last night," he said tonelessly. "The images were so vivid that I think if you hadn't awakened me that I would have fallen into sin— in my dream."

Simon thought on Asher's report as the hair on the back of his neck rose. "I don't like the sound of that. We may be under some kind of satanic attack to diminish our work ethic and testimony. We need to be vigilant."

Aggravation knotted in Simon's chest when he thought that he was probably next in line.

ELEVEN

Intracoastal Waterway, Miami

Jonathan took the final bite out of his Boston cream donut while Brandon slugged down the last of his coffee. Sitting on benches overlooking the Intracoastal and watching the yachts and sailboats go by was at one time a coveted pastime, but as of late watching the famed waterway had become a grotesque adventure. A strange adventure that brought only the curious and bizarre who dared to stare into the reddened waters to study the blood-colored fluid that brought massive fish kills. Scientists from the University of Miami and the Miami Seaquarium en masse studied the varied specimens in vain efforts to discover cause, but remained puzzled. It was this *circus of folly* as Brandon called it that brought them here. It was their way of witnessing man's incapability of ascertaining the real purpose of God's wrath.

"There's a tick on you," Jonathan said as he pointed to a red dot on Brandon's pant leg.

Brandon spit his mouthful of coffee out and quickly brushed the bloodsucker off his leg, then mashed it into the earth with his shoe.

"You know, Brandon, I've been thinking," Jonathan began, "I can cope with this aspect of Bowl Three that has come upon us," he added as he pointed to a dead fish floating in the red water in front of him. "But I have a problem with the other aspect: in today's world Bible prophecies are going to be discredited. This is going to hurt us."

"I agree. Even though the Bowl Judgments on the waters will only last 40 days and cause some to think it is simply a temporary phenomenon, the damage to Bible credibility could be long lasting." Brandon closed his eyes momentarily. "'Of all kinds of knowledge that we can ever obtain the knowledge of God and of ourselves are the most important,'" he quoted then said, "Jonathan Edwards."

"He had a good handle on God, and I think my parents named me after King David's companion and Mr. Edwards." Jonathan reflected for a minute. "But then again, this wouldn't be the first time the Bible has been criticized and discredited. From the philosophy of men to the theory of evolution to higher criticism to dismissing bible prophecy—any attempt to dismantle the truth of God's Word has always been met with the one thing that cannot be denied."

"A changed life!" Brandon said with a smile.

"You said it!" Jonathan nodded to himself in affirmation. "But for the present, we must be doubly careful of protecting the credibility of prophecy, especially when dealing with the issue of our Lord's return."

Brandon turned to hear someone walking up to the boardwalk to the bulkhead of the Intracoastal from behind him. He saw a young woman pulling a child behind her. The woman struck him as being homeless with her disheveled clothes and matted hair. The child's clothes were old and tattered. They walked to the edge of the bulkhead and stood motionless. Then the child began to pull away from the woman's grip.

"What's this?" Brandon said with heightening alarm to Jonathan. "This looks bad."

Jonathan stood up from the bench.

The woman turned and spotted him, then suddenly jumped into the water with the little girl.

Brandon and Jonathan bolted to the spot and saw the woman trying to hold the girl under the reddish water as she thrashed about.

Jonathan pulled his shirt off and flipped off his shoes. "I have God's protection, remember?" he yelled to Brandon, then jumped into the water after them.

At first Jonathan broke the grip the woman had on the little girl and pushed her up in the water so Brandon could haul her to safety. When he turned, the woman slipped from sight. "She's over there!" Brandon screamed, pointing to the middle of the Intracoastal. The slow-moving current was taking her away. Jonathan shot a prayer up to God and did the front crawl in breakneck speed to catch her.

"Leave me alone!" the woman yelled as she hit Jonathan in the face repeatedly. "I want to die!"

"Not on my watch!" Jonathan said fiercely. "Not on my watch." He glanced up into heaven and then punched the woman on the jaw. She fell limp, then he put her in a headlock and pulled her to the side.

"Bring her to the boat ramp!" Brandon shouted as he pointed to the ramp a short distance away.

With Herculean strength Jonathan swam against the current to the boat ramp. Then he lifted the woman and carried her to the boardwalk, laying her down as the little girl ran to her side.

The little girl thrust her arms around the woman. "Mommy! Mommy, don't leave me!"

The woman lay motionless for several seconds.

"Let me at her!" Brandon said, breathing in ragged gasps. He lifted the little girl away from the woman, then began the Heimlich maneuver on the mother. She coughed several times, then spit up red water. Her chest began to heave as she sucked in fresh air. "Why did you save me?" she garbled wildly.

Jonathan immediately took notice of her hands and forehead. No mark. "Because you don't deserve to die this way," he said with a tear in his eye. "God has a plan for you, and I don't believe this is part of it."

Brandon brought the little girl to her side. "Mommy, mommy," she cried aloud, then rushed to her, hugging her wringing-wet body.

The woman gazed into her daughter's eyes. "I'm so sorry, Caitlyn," she sobbed. "I'm so sorry."

"We need to get you two ladies out of here and get some dry clothes on you both," Brandon said. They helped the woman up. Brandon asked, "What is your name?"

"Lauren," she said, wiping her hair away from her eyes.

"We're going to see that you both are taken care of," Jonathan soothed as they walked them back to Brandon's office at Lane Drugs.

Lane Drugs, Miami

Helen brought hot coffee and hot chocolate to the lounge outside the ladies' restroom and placed them on the nearby table as Lauren and Caitlyn changed into dry clothes. "This is unbelievable," she said to Brandon. "I'm somewhat bewildered over this whole thing. To think she would pull her daughter into that slimy pit is too much for me to understand."

"When people are desperate and have lost hope, they will do drastic things. Things they never would have thought possible under normal circumstances," Jonathan advised. "And of course we're not living under normal circumstances, are we?"

"No, I guess not. I should feel sorry for her," she added in contrition.

"A little compassion goes a long way these days," Jonathan reminded.

Lauren and Caitlyn emerged from the ladies' room in clean clothes with their hair neatly brushed. Lauren appeared to be about thirty-five and Caitlyn about six years old. It was apparent from their frail-looking bodies that it had been a long time in-between good meals.

"Would you like some hot coffee and chocolate?" Helen asked them.

Caitlyn nodded, then looked up at her mother. "Sure," Lauren said as she began rubbing the side of her jaw.

Jonathan grimaced at the sight of the bruise on her face. "I'm sorry about slugging you," he said remorsefully, "but I had to subdue you to rescue you."

Caitlyn sipped her hot chocolate as Lauren looked around as if surveying the premises. "Where are we?"

"We're at my company," Brandon said, "Lane Drugs."

"I guess I should thank you," she said to Jonathan, slightly disoriented, "but I'm not so sure we wanted to be rescued."

"That's what I wanted to talk to you about," Jonathan said. "We noticed that neither of you have the mark—the *Masterlink* chip. Of course we know what that means, so as Christians, why would you take such a drastic measure?"

"Because Jesus lied to us!" Caitlyn blurted out.

Lauren snuffled, then started to cry. "After living on the streets and hiding from the authorities for the past six years, the only thing that has kept us alive was the hope of Jesus' soon return. But two days ago we heard this street preacher tell us that Jesus wasn't coming back like he promised—so I started to doubt my beliefs."

Jonathan exchanged glances with Brandon. "Then what happened?" Jonathan asked curiously.

"Yesterday, Caitlyn and I went to visit a pastor of a community church here in Miami," Lauren continued, "and I showed him some verses out of my Bible about Jesus' return. He told me I was wrong to take those verses literally."

"He what?!" Helen exclaimed.

"He told me that the promise of His coming was proven wrong because of the times in which we live," Lauren explained. "He said that if Jesus would allow all these disasters to kill off millions of people then He could never believe in Him. That *His* God would never allow these catastrophes and calamities to come upon the earth because he believed in a loving God. Not a god of judgment. So I started to think that maybe what he said was true."

Jonathan clenched his fist and said hotly, "No Lauren, it is not true. Jesus never lied to us but that pastor is another story. It's just like in the times of Ahab, the king of Judah. At the battle of Ramoth-gilead the Lord put a lying spirit in the mouths of his prophets."

"The father of lies is at it again," Brandon added sharply. "Heretics and apostates unite and rejoice!" he shouted sarcastically.

Jonathan, once again, realized that the construct of atheism had morphed into different forms. Now, in the newest saga in the evil development of enlightenment, Satan and his cohorts were capitalizing on the latest Bowl Judgment where Biblical prophecies and God's Word would be minimized, refuted, and then denied. Nietzsche's belief that there is no personal God had reached a new level where the modern thinking was that it is impossible to believe in God. This miscreant philosophy was being sold by gradually dismantling the promises and prophecies in the Bible. The new spirituality being a non-theistic belief opened up the door to surrendering all Biblical authority when in fact history dictated that it was impossible to rightly govern the world without God and the Bible, leaving man to his own devices and ultimate destruction.

Lauren eyed Jonathan suspiciously. "What that pastor told me wasn't true?"

"That's a big fat no!" Jonathan replied. "If what he said was true, then our lives would be most miserable and hopeless. That being the case, my friend Brandon and I would have jumped into the Intracoastal with you, saying along with your daughter, 'Jesus, you lied to us' and then 'good-bye, cruel world.'"

"In truth," Brandon added with clear precision, "you can put your complete trust in God's promises; from the promise of eternal security—where you cannot lose your salvation—to the promise of Christ's return. In fact, the evidence of His soon return can be seen by looking around. We are presently seeing the fulfillment of all the prophetic passages that predicted the Bowl Judgments we are undergoing. This proves the Bible is true. What's more, we can expect Christ to appear after the Seventh Bowl!"

"I've been a fool to believe those false reports," Lauren lamented.

"So Jesus really is coming for us, Mommy?" Caitlyn asked.

Lauren smiled. "Yes honey, Jesus really is coming for us."

Helen walked up to Lauren and patted her shoulder. "I can see you and your daughter have been through a lot but God provides. I have room in my home for you and Caitlyn. I really want you to come and live with us."

Lauren filled up with tears. "You mean it? You would invite complete strangers into your home?"

Helen assured her, "In God's house there are no strangers, and besides, you're a sister in the Lord."

Caitlyn pulled on her mother's blouse. "Can we, Mom? Please!"

Lauren glanced at Jonathan, then Brandon. "God is providing," Jonathan said with a smile.

"I can't think of a better person to stay with," Brandon agreed.

Jonathan closed the agreement with a prayer, but the specter of future lies from the other side troubled him.

Morrison Home, Plantation Acres, Plantation, Florida

Pat read the notice to appear before the plaintiff's attorney and give deposition, then shook his head and then folded it before sticking it in his bible. "It's amazing how these terrorists use our laws against us," he said to himself. *Busy yourself and don't think about it. Get things ready for the Bible study.* He arranged the chairs in his living room in his usual pattern while his wife, Kim, prepared the refreshments. *Set it aside,* he demanded of himself.

A knock at the door, then it opened. Efraim walked in carrying his Bible, a loaf of bread, and a cake. "Food for the spirit and for the flesh!" he announced.

Stacy went to his aid and lifted the offerings from his hands. "The men are waiting for you in the living room," she advised.

Efraim nodded and walked off.

Jonathan sat next to Brandon on the sofa while Pat scanned various channels on the TV with the remote control. "Praise the Lord, Efraim," Jonathan said as Efraim walked in. "Good to see you. We're trying to get more info on the latest decree that all personal weapons are to be surrendered to the Federal Government within thirty days."

"I guess the Second Amendment has been thrown out the window," Efraim said sarcastically.

"It won't be long before the Special Police Force—like the 'brown shirts'—show their ugly faces," Pat added with contempt.

"It's inevitable," Jonathan said with a derisive snort.

Stacy stuck her head into the room. "Pat, there's a car slowly circling the block. We've seen it go past our home several times."

Pat waved her off. "Probably someone is looking for a parking space."

Kim nodded and returned to the kitchen with the other ladies.

"Take a look at this," Pat said as he brought his laptop to Jonathan. "Look what's happening to gold! The prices are going through the roof!" Pat scrolled down on the Internet page of GoldPlus, the Online gold trading outlet where many of the Christians had purchased gold and silver knowing the price of the dollar and the Euro would fall. With the advent of *Masterlink,* precious metals along with the bartering system enabled the K-groups to survive.

"Praise the Lord!" Jonathan exulted. "The Lord is going to provide for His own, knowing that we need resources to last us until He returns."

"On another related issue, we may not be able to purchase seeds to continue to grow our vegetables much longer," Brandon warned. "I understand there's an unannounced Executive Order that only hybrid seeds will become available to the public so that the government can control the flow—another step toward a dictatorship."

Jonathan took a deep breath. "We only have to hold out for four more judgments; then we're home free with Jesus."

"Amen!" They said in unison.

Pat put the laptop away, then pulled the summons out of his Bible. "What do you think of this?" He handed it to Efraim.

Efraim read the highlights of the summons. "I wouldn't worry about it, Pat. We'll be out of here and in glory by the time this suit hits the courthouse docket."

"I didn't think of that," Pat said with a sigh of relief and placed it back into his Bible.

Stacy stuck her head in one more time. "Pat, I forgot to get the milk and cream for the coffee and tea."

Pat rolled his eyes. "Pat, you get things ready for the Bible study," Jonathan offered. "Brandon and I will run up to the convenience store and get the milk and cream."

"God will bless you!" Pat said with a smirk.

Moments later Jonathan and Brandon walked out the front door. "That car is still circling," Jonathan said, pointing to a BMW crawling past the parked cars lined up on the swale along the street.

Brandon carefully watched the car as it went past their field of view. There were two men in the front seat with a woman in the rear. "Seems harmless enough," he said with a shrug. *Neighbor? Community security patrol?* He didn't know. "Let's move out," he said after a moment of thought. He opened up his car door, and within seconds they were gone.

The BMW came to a stop five houses down from Pat's home. Both the passenger and the woman in the back quickly exited, each holding what resembled a canvas gym bag. In serpentine fashion they moved in and out of the parked cars until they reached Pat's home. Then, under the cover of darkness, they furtively navigated their way to the sides of the house. The man placed his bag on the west side of the house while the woman placed her bag on the east side, taking extreme caution to synchronize the timers for thirty minutes. Enough time for them to return to the BMW and disappear into the night, unnoticed.

"Pat, when Jonathan and Brandon return, we'll be ready with the refreshments," Stacy whispered in Pat's ear as he reviewed his notes for the Bible study. Then an odd expression came over her face. "You know the car that was circling our block is now parked down the street."

"Honey, don't worry about it," he replied with controlled concern. "I'm sure they are just visiting our neighbor." Stacy nodded then wandered back into the kitchen.

Several minutes later Jonathan walked into the kitchen holding a small shopping bag. "Your milk and cream," he announced.

"Where's Brandon?" Stacy asked.

"Oh, he's waiting in the car. He just received a cell phone call from Helen that the alarm at Lane Drugs went off," Jonathan explained. "So we have to leave. Give our apologies to Pat and the rest of the group." He turned and exited out the kitchen door.

Stacy shrugged. "Oh, the duties of state," she lamented. Then she walked into the living room and took her seat among the other members of the K-group.

"Jonathan and Brandon?" Pat asked as she sat down.

"They had to leave, some sort of security issue at Lane Drugs," Kim explained.

A wounded look washed over his face. "Oh." Seconds later he opened his Bible. "In the interest of current events," Pat began after a short prayer, "I've decided to review some important aspects of the Muslim threat we've been living under for the past six years or so." He turned in his Bible to Genesis 16 and read from verse 11: "'The angel of the LORD also said to her: 'You are now with child and you will have a son. You shall name him Ishmael for the LORD has heard of your misery. He will be a wild donkey of a man; his hand will be against everyone and everyone's hand against him, and he will live in his hostility toward all his brothers.'"

He closed his Bible and expounded: "I believe this text explains many things. It explains that the father of the Jews and the Muslims, Abraham, had two sons, one the son of his concubine, Hagar, who was Ishmael and then a son of promise, Isaac, who was born of Abraham's wife Sarah. The promise to Abraham and in turn to Isaac of the unconditional covenant included a promise of posterity, land, and the most important, that from Isaac's seed the Messiah would come.

"To Ishmael, no promise was made other than one of posterity. There was no promise of land or of the messiah." He patted his Bible. "This text adds that the seed of Ishmael, the Arabs, will live in hostility—

from the time of the Genesis account—for all time. That is until Messiah returns. Well, we are living today in the worst of it. For the past four decades, since the oil embargo of 1973, the Arabs have been emboldened to bring pressure on all non-Jewish nations to sever their relations, politically, militarily, and economically with Israel under the threat of future oil shortages. They have us by the throat and they know it. This is all payback for those nations that support Israel.

"But God had this in mind when he planted the world's greatest oil reserves under the desert sands of the Arab-bloc countries. His plan is to bring all nations against Israel in the very near future so that He will be able to vanquish his enemies and then set Israel up for the Kingdom period—the millennium."

A hand went up. Soon Pat realized a firestorm of sorts had been ignited. "So does that mean we have to be subservient to the Arabs until Jesus comes?" a man named Richie asked. "I mean they have infiltrated every area of American life and I'm sick of it." He pulled out a newspaper article from his Bible and went on. "In California, the 9th Circuit Court of Appeals, the same one that outlawed the Pledge of Allegiance for its reference to God, approved putting public school students through Muslim role-playing exercises. They were told to recite aloud Muslim prayers that begin with 'In the name of Allah, Most Gracious, Most Merciful.' Then they were told to memorize the Muslim profession of faith: 'Allah is the only true God and Muhammad is his messenger. They were required to chant 'Praise be to Allah' in response to teacher prompts and then profess as 'true' the Muslim belief that 'The Holy *Qur'an* is God's Word.'

"Parents of seventh-graders, who after 9-11 were taught the pro-Islamic lessons as part of California's world history curriculum, sued under the First Amendment ban of religious establishment. They argued that the government was promoting Islam. But the federal judge appointed by President Clinton told them in so many words to get over it, that the state was merely teaching kids about another culture. The parents appealed the decision in the left-wing court and lost. So they became legally in the clear to indoctrinate kids into the 'peaceful' and 'tolerant' religion of Islam while continuing to denigrate Judeo-Christian values. The fact of the matter is that only the Muslims defend their beliefs by burning down churches, killing people, and destroying embassies."

"The way I remember it," another by the name of Peter added, "is that the prophet of Islam said 'I was ordered to fight the people until they believe in Allah and his messenger.' That sounds to me like they are not going to rest until they subject everybody to Islam."

Efraim stood up. "We have not seen a single Jew blow himself up in a German restaurant. We have not seen a single Jew destroy a church. We have not seen a single Jew protest by killing people. The Muslims have turned three Buddha statues into rubble in the past year. We have not seen a single Buddhist burn down a mosque, kill a Muslim, or burn down an embassy. Only the Muslims defend their beliefs by burning down churches, killing people and destroying embassies." The group clapped as Efraim sat down.

"I am a Jewish believer on Messiah Jesus," Stacy began solemnly, "and I am appalled at the teaching of Islam that allows for rewards when female prisoners are raped."

"What?!" Peter exclaimed. "Is that possible?"

"This is true," Efraim replied to the astonished group. "It's well known to the Muslim and Iranian intelligence community that coercion by means of rape, torture, and drugs is acceptable against all opponents of the Islamic regime. When Iran's Ahmadinejad's personal spiritual guide, Ayatollah Mohammad Taqi Mesbah-Yazdi was asked about applying psychological, emotional, and physical pressure to exact confessions of political enemies he replied, 'Getting a confession from any person who is against the Velayat-e Faqih (the regime of Iran's mullahs) is permissible under any condition.'

"When he was asked about interrogating a female prisoner, the ayatollah answered, 'The necessary precaution is for the interrogator to perform a ritual washing first and say prayers while raping the prisoner. If the prisoner is a female, it is better not to have a witness present. If it is a male prisoner, then it's acceptable for someone else to watch while the rape is committed. If the judgment for the [female] prisoner is execution, then rape before execution brings the interrogator a spiritual reward equivalent to make the mandated *Haj* pilgrimage [to Mecca], but if there is no execution decreed, then the reward would be equivalent to making a pilgrimage to the holy city of Karbala.'" Efraim paused. "This is an accurate assessment of their mentality toward prisoners and to humanity in general that has its basis of belief in the *Qur'an*."

"And the Muslims terrorists of 9/11 had the nerve to object to American interrogators questioning them at the Guantanamo Bay military prison?" Pat flared.

"I guess the Attorney General agreed since he ordered them to be tried in civilian courts under the protection of our *Constitution*," Efraim said, bristling.

Stacy stood up in controlled anger. "I can't take any more of this!" She walked toward the kitchen. "Time for coffee and cake."

Inside the gym bags the battery-powered electrical timers were connected to two pounds of Pentaerythritol tetranitrate (PETN), one of the most powerful high explosives known. At 9:15 p.m. the charges were detonated. The Morrison home was completely obliterated, along with three of their neighbors' houses.

TWELVE

The Messianic Wing of the Temple, Jerusalem

Crows go in flocks and wolves in packs, but the lion and the eagle are solitaires, Kavidas reasoned within himself. *This is who we are, Mort and myself. We are solitaires within a global community of flocks and packs. But this is what leadership is. It is a solitary life.*

Secrets, yes, secrets, he thought. *We have secrets, and those secrets must remain secrets until the very end. We must protect those secrets to ensure the success of our ministry.* Having settled these issues in his mind, he gazed out his office window. His eyes rested on the Temple Mount, the very place where all the dynamics of man's history would culminate. The history of man's struggle to conquer the continents of America, Europe, Asia, Australia, and the Antarctica would pale into insignificance in comparison to the battle for this Mount. All the forces of good, be they mortal or immortal, will come to fight those who oppose those beliefs right here on this Mount. This will be the day of reckoning he feared the most.

A knock on the door.

"Come in Mort," he said.

"Some good news," Mort announced as he walked into the office. "Are we all right?" he asked curiously.

"Reflecting and planning," Kavidas replied, always disguising his innermost thoughts and worries. He turned and put on a happy face. "What's the 'good news'?"

"I just received a report that a Koinonos group in the States has been eliminated," he said trenchantly. "Our Muslim operatives over there have been very successful in knocking out a number of their cell groups." He joined Kavidas at the window. "Have you noticed those damn creatures from the pit have disappeared from the earth?"

"You're talking about the agents from the Sixth Trumpet? The 200-million?" Kavidas replied.

Stein nodded. "They have completed their mission and have returned to their dwelling place. During their stay for the past thirteen months they have aggressively infiltrated nearly all levels of pornography, homosexuality, drug addiction, and abortion-providing facilities. Their task of removing guilt and replacing it with pride was completely successful. We're sorry to see them go."

Kavidas snapped his fingers. "A triumph for our side."

"A complete triumph." Stein smiled. "This was an example of a curse turned into a blessing. What God meant for good, we turned into evil. Ha!"

I don't see the future judgments going that way, Kavidas didn't say. "Let's sit a minute," he said and waved Stein over to his sofa. "I made a pledge to our friends in Tehran that I would avenge Ras Tanura and the cyber attack. By us taking care of this we avoid a measure of retaliation that would disrupt our plans."

"You mean they were planning a nuclear attack in response?"

"They have had their finger on the trigger waiting for the slightest provocation so they could unleash a nuke on Israel for over ten years now," Kavidas explained, "but obviously—" he pointed upwards—"it wasn't in the plan. And I can see why."

"If there were a nuclear exchange between Israel and Iran, we wouldn't have much of a mission field. Right?" Stein posited, winking at him.

"Nor would the other side. So, we need them alive and responsive. Not irradiated and unable to think."

Stein's analytical mind jumped to a higher level. "I anticipated that a response would be in order to square things with Iran, so, here's the plan." For the next twenty minutes Stein reviewed the strategy of attacking both the physical and spiritual side of their enemy.

"Two more items remain," Kavidas gesticulated sharply. "We no longer have need for a Prime Minister here in Israel since any negotiations politically or religiously go through my office. But to appease the people for a religious leader apart from myself, I want you to approach the Sanhedrin group of priests and then appoint a high priest who will officiate in the priesthood who is friendly toward us."

"You mean a 'puppet,' right?"

"Call him what you like."

"Next?" Stein said after a nod.

"I want you to visit and scope out Megiddo and put together some preliminary plans for approval in preparation for the big day," Kavidas instructed.

The "big day," Stein thought to himself. *Yes, that "big day" being Armageddon.* "Sort of like a 'dress rehearsal'?"

"No," Kavidas corrected. "I mean just a planning session that I can approve. No troops. No armaments. Just on-site strategizing."

I see where he's going with this. Another overture to the Arabs to let them know he's serious about joining with them to rid the planet of the Jews. Marvelous! In addition, the Arab-bloc powers and their allies can evaluate their military advantage once they see the survey of the plan. Brilliant! Stein nodded in assent, then thoughtfully pondered the proximity of the end time prophecies. "The big hand is ticking toward midnight, isn't it? I mean we're approaching the end, aren't we?"

Kavidas sat looking at him, his expression enigmatic. "I believe so."

Lane Drugs, Miami

Jonathan read the news ticker on the bottom of the 24-hour news network as the images of the explosion of the Morrison home filled his TV screen. Both the al-Qaeda and the Wahhabis terrorist groups claimed responsibility. Two E-mails from fellow K-group members' survivors confirmed the report. It was sorrow upon sorrow.

"I guess we could praise the Lord that He redirected us and removed us from the Morrison home," Brandon said, moaning softly, "but—and it's a big 'but,' but why did it have to happen? Why didn't the Lord do something to prevent it? To lose those seventeen Believers to a terrorist bombing at a time when their work is so crucial—is something I don't understand in the providence of God."

Jonathan realized that if he knew the answer to this he would rival the wisdom of Solomon—a gift he did not possess. "The outworking of the martyrdom of the Tribulation saints is upon us, Brandon." He shook his head as tears filled his eyes. "I'm at a loss, but this too is all for the glory of God. It proves His word is being fulfilled: 'the shedding of the blood of the saints.' So in that sense we have some consolation."

"Kavidas' work, no doubt," Brandon said laconically.

"I'm sure. Satan is ramping up his persecution of the saints by using Kavidas and his gang. His real target is Israel. The Christians and the 144,000 worldwide witnesses is just an ancillary target."

"Because he can't kill off the 144,000, he will destroy everything in their midst, right?"

Jonathan nodded. "That's the way I see it, yes...especially in the areas from North American to Australia, and everywhere they have planted churches."

A knock at the door and then Helen walked in.

"Mr. Lane," she said, "a Mr. Ben-Korpel is here."

"Show him in," Brandon said.

They were expecting him. Earlier that day, immediately following the notification of the bombing, Jonathan spent two hours in prayer and would not quit until receiving an answer to his plea. He had to replace Efraim. God's Spirit directed him to Avraham Ben-Korpel.

Ben-Korpel had a commanding presence. Towering at over six-foot five-inches, this hulk of a man was former Israeli Mossad, now working for a private American security firm to protect high-profile Christians from the tentacles of the *Masterlink* system. Coming to the States after his wife and son were killed in a Hamas bombing attack in Jerusalem, Ben-Korpel had an axe to grind—no doubt.

But his vengeance was mollified when he met Messiah Jesus on the way over to America. In the providence of God he sat next to a Baptist pastor on an El Al flight returning from a Holy Land pilgrimage with many of his church members. The pastor had a love for Israel and God's people and after a brief discussion on current events discerned Ben-Korpel's pain. Before they landed in Miami, Ben-Korpel prayed with the pastor to receive Christ as his own personal Messiah and Savior. That was three years ago.

"We know you were close to Efraim," Jonathan began as he motioned for him to sit in one of Brandon's stuffed chairs. "He often mentioned you, and out of respect and honor of his name we are inviting you into our circle to work with us to continue our crusade to win your people to our Messiah as well as joining us to foil and frustrate the machinery of Kavidas and his forces."

Ben-Korpel had the reputation of having the strength of a bear, the cunning of a fox, the heart of a lion, and the dogged resolve of a wolf on the hunt. At a time when Christian persecution was at peak, this combination of animal instincts suited the needs of the K-group very well.

"Efraim was to me what Jonathan was to David," Ben-Korpel began humbly. "I had a love for him that revolved around the Jesus that we both loved. We often had prayer and Bible studies together. We witnessed to non-believers together. I came to love him as a brother in Christ. But I must put that behind me if I am to be the warrior God has called me to be. I will adamantly pursue the release of those emotional bonds we had established, but the memories of his brotherly love and fellowship in Christ are something I will cherish forever."

"That is a wonderful testimony to a fallen brother, Avraham," Brandon marveled. "And I pray that in the days ahead we may in some way soothe the pain of your loss. But for now," he said, pulling back and looking at him, "we must continue our battle against those forces that mean us harm. While we trust the Lord to protect us, we must utilize the tools he gave us."

"It was Anton Chekhov who said, 'Love, friendship, and respect do not unite people as much as a common hatred for something,'" Ben-Korpel recalled while making a fist. "So now, I look to uniting with you both in our common hatred for God's enemies—Kavidas and his Arab terror groups who continue to war against God's chosen people." He opened his wallet, removed a piece of paper, and started reading from it. "'You say it is your custom to burn widows. Very well. We also have a custom: when men burn a woman alive, we tie a rope around their necks and hang them. Build your funeral pyre; beside it, my carpenters will build a gallows. You follow your custom. And we will follow ours.' British General Sir Charles Napier on Suttee, 1842, on Hindu widow-burning.'" Ben-Korpel slowly replaced the quote inside his wallet for future reference. "You see, I'm prepared to do what it takes to see justice prevails. They want to use terror bombings to kill us, so then we will respond in kind. If it means we 'build a gallows' to rid the land of the enemy, then so be it!"

"Hatred can be a tool," Jonathan replied somberly, "but only when processed through the love that you experienced with Efraim. That's the love of Christ. We want to hate the sin, but love the sinner. Remember," he said with a smile, "we're all saved sinners who at one time were in the same place as all others—hating God. It was that hatred that nailed our Jesus to the cross."

"Yeah, I hear that," Ben-Korpel said in support.

THIRTEEN

Jordan Valley Stronghold, Jericho

Her eyes flashed open; then she felt her surroundings. She was still in bed. A glance at her wristwatch. It was 3:15 a.m. She felt her tummy. "Paul," Shira exclaimed, "the baby is coming!"

Paul jumped out of the bed, then frantically pulled his jeans over his underwear. "I'll get Gilat!"

"You need to hurry!" Shira said, "The contractions are coming quickly." She lumbered out of the bed, then walked gingerly around the room. "I don't have too much more time!"

Paul may have had the discernment of the sages, but when it came to Shira having an emergency, he behaved like a bumbling fool. He shot a look under the bed and said, "I can't find my shoes."

Shira smiled. "There're on your feet!"

Paul chuckled. "Oh."

Paul grabbed his flashlight, then bolted to Doron and Gilat's quarters. They were housed just some twenty meters from Paul and Shira in an alcove with a privacy blanket draped over their entrance. Paul stood outside their quarters and called, "Gilat! We need you! The baby is coming!"

Doron and Gilat Ya Alon were more than faithful Messianic Jews. They were a team of medical professionals who at one time worked together in a woman's clinic known to give abortions. But they had been saved by Yeshua after the great rapture of the Church. From that time on, they dedicated their profession to saving lives, not destroying them.

Seconds later Gilat emerged in her robe. "Lead the way!" she announced. Moments passed, then Doron followed with a medical bag filled with the necessary instruments to deliver a baby.

Paul paced about the room as Doron and Gilat prepared the makeshift delivery room. He got in the way. "Paul, how about you leave the worrying to us," Doron said with his arm around him. "Go visit with Hershel and Levi, and we'll call you when the baby comes."

Paul nodded. It seemed like a good idea. He glanced over to Shira, who lay on their bed with Gilat attending her. "I'll be right outside!" he said. She blinked several times in recognition as Doron escorted him to the exit.

Levi sat on the end of his bed reading a portion of his Bible. He smiled as Paul walked in. "Who could sleep with all the whooping and hollering going on next door?" he chided. Then he stood up and hugged Paul. "Let me be the first to congratulate you," he added gleefully.

"We'll know shortly if there's to be a *brith milah* (circumcision) or not," Paul replied with a grin. His eye caught a poster-size photograph of the Mount of Olives from the Temple Mount taped to Levi's wall. "I never noticed that before," he said curiously.

"I just put it up as a reminder that Yeshua will be returning shortly to that very place," he explained.

Paul focused in on the poster. "Amen to that! Even so come quickly Lord Jesus."

Levi closed his Bible. "I believe your baby will be a testimony to the Lord during these trying times. When I think on how our society views abortion, it is a joy to see a newborn child." He shook his head. "Abortion has been a plague on our world and we have been cursed because of it."

Paul couldn't get his arms around that consensus just yet. His mind was too full with what was going on next door. "Yes, I agree. It is apparently all part of God's plan."

Gilat stuck her head into Levi's room. "Paul, you're a father! Come see your new son!"

"Praise the Lord!" Paul shouted. With that he raced into the next room.

Who can describe the look on a father's face when he first sets eyes on his firstborn son? Paul rushed to Shira holding their son wrapped in a white cloth with only his face exposed. "Let me hold him."

"Careful," Shira whispered.

Paul nodded as he picked up his son and then held the child up in the air. "We name you Solomon because you will be a man of peace," Paul announced. Levi, Doron, and Gilat gazed at Shira, whose smile fit the occasion. Paul lowered him down, then opened up the cloth to look at him.

"He's perfect!" Shira said, anticipating Paul's inspection. "There's not a blemish on him!"

Paul looked up. "'Who is like unto thee among the gods? Who is like thee? Glorious in holiness, fearful in praises; doing wonders,'" he quoted.

"Sol must be proud," Shira said. "I can just imagine him looking down from glory at our son, his namesake."

"With a broad smile," Paul added.

Doron walked over to Shira with his iPhone and snapped a photograph of her and Solomon. "I'm sending this photo to Ruby at Petra," he said. "She's been waiting with bated breath."

Sol's wife, Ruby, had asked for the first photo of Solomon as a keepsake. Moments later, Doron walked up to Paul. "Ravitzsky called. He's on his way over. Fifteen minutes."

Paul nodded, then sat down next to Shira and held her hand.

Ravitzky gave Paul a 'bear' hug after looking at Solomon and said, *"Mazel Tov!* May your son be a blessing to every one!" Seconds later he pulled him aside. "We need to talk."

The two of them walked out of the room to the antechamber where Ravitzky waved Meschel over to join them. "Things are ratcheting up," Ravitzky began to explain. "The last Bowl Judgment is hitting home. Christians all over the globe are being arrested, jailed, and persecuted beyond measure." He handed Paul a report. "Here, look at this."

Paul scanned the report that showed twenty-seven locations in three continents where Christian churches and private homes were bombed. In this report alone there were over fifteen thousand deaths. "Not good," he replied with a shake of the head. "Arabs?"

"Mostly," Ravitzky answered. "Some are emerging splinter goon squads, but Islamic terrorists seem to be spearheading the movement."

"Kavidas?"

Ravitzky nodded. "He's pulling the strings. And that's not the worst of it." He handed another report to Paul. "These figures reflect another movement—apostasy. Many so-called 'Believers' who were not Believers at all have defected. They now claim that they never really believed or deny the Lordship of Christ."

"Six-hundred thousand?!" Paul replied incredulously as he flicked the report.

"And more being added every month," Ravitzky said.

It's the absence of the Restrainer, Paul thought. *That function of the Holy Spirit that retarded the expansion of evil was removed at the Rapture.* The Holy Spirit, that omnipresent, omniscient, omnipotent Person of the Holy Trinity was still present on the earth, but His restraining hand had been lifted when the Christians were removed over six years ago when the Church was removed. "Another fulfillment of prophecy," he said after a moment of contemplation. "'When the Son of Man returns, shall he find faith on the earth?'" he whispered to himself.

"One more thing," Ravitzky said after nodding to Meschel.

"Another grim report?" Paul muttered.

"More info on Kavidas." He pulled his PDA out of his pocket and booted it up. Seconds later he handed it to Paul. "I've been researching his genealogy and there's a huge gap in it. While his family tree shows both Greek and Italian ancestry there's a portion that is questionable. Here, watch this." He tapped an icon on the PDA and an encrypted file opened. "I have it locked so that if this gadget gets in the wrong hands they won't be able to open it up without the password." He keyed in the password to open the file. "Now look here," he said curiously.

A tree diagram of Gregory A. Kavidas' family appeared, showing dates and names of family members back two hundred years. "Where did you get this?" Paul asked, surprised.

"I'm former Mossad, remember? I have access to top secret information. And this is top secret, believe me!" He scrolled down several lines, then pointed the stylus to the gap. "See, here is where the big question comes in. His grandmother and mother were Italian and his father allegedly was Greek, but I think the records have been tampered with because I discovered that during the time that his mother married his father, they were living in Iran."

"Whoa!" Paul exclaimed.

"I need to research this more," Ravitzky said. "But it is really puzzling."

"I wouldn't be surprised if this Kavidas is a Muslim!" Meschel said, his voice lower, conspiratorial.

Paul and Ravitzky exchanged glances.

FOURTEEN

Fountain of Qasim Pasha, Temple Mount, Jerusalem

Qasim Pasha, the Ottoman governor of Jerusalem in 1527 during the reign of Suleiman the Magnificent, made the first public structure to be built on the Temple Mount by the Ottomans. The Supreme Muslim Council made extensive renovation in the 1920s that included a dome covered with lead panels that bestowed upon it a pointed shallower profile, later in 1998, the lead sheeting was replaced by a finely crafted stone. Muslim worshippers frequented the fountain as a source for performing ablution. Stein though it a perfect location for a strategic planning meeting with his Arab and Persian cohorts.

Sitting on the stone wall surrounding the fountain, Ramzi Yousef continued to towel himself off after his ritual bathing. He felt purified and refreshed; ready for service to his god. Allah was pleased at his obedience and dedication. Yousef, a Saudi and self-proclaimed soldier to rid the world of the Jews and American capitalists took the name of the notorious 1993 World Trade Center bombing mastermind in order to perpetuate his name. After lengthy letters to Ramzi Yousef, serving a life sentence in the United States Penitentiary Maximum Facility ("Supermax") in Fremont County, Colorado, Yousef was granted the infamous namesake with Yousef's blessing; contingent on the pledge that he would exact recompense from the non-Muslim infidels.

Sitting next to him was Moqtada al-Sadr, the Iranian electrical engineer who graduated from the Swansea Institute in Wales. Both men were recruited by Kavidas' point men stationed in both Saudi Arabia and Iran. Yousef, being an Arab, and al-Sadr being an Iranian would under normal circumstances be at war. But things were different now. Their national leaders had set aside their age-long differences in favor of conquering a common enemy, the Jews and the Americans.

Both men dressed, then walked over to the colonnade leading up to the El-Aqsa Mosque adjacent to the Temple where Stein waited patiently. He stood up and greeted them warmly.

"You've been prepped on the mission," Stein began with a nod.

Yousef raised his hand in the air and then, with his fist, thumped his chest. *"Allah-au-Akbar,"* he said with resolve. "We will serve and die if needed."

Stein admired their passion and loyalty. *Just think how different things would be if the Americans had spoken up and stood up against all the liberals trying to change our laws and get God out of every phase of life. But,* he thought, *then again Satan is the master of lies. He deceived them and distracted them with the pursuit of pleasure and the lust for materialism. The Muslim threat, on the other hand, continues to multiply.*

He pulled two sheets out of a folder and handed them to Yousef. Yousef carefully scanned the sheets that contained a photograph and a profile of certain individuals. "You need to take these two men out. They are responsible for the Saudi Ras Tanura attack and the cyber attack on Iran." Stein smiled and added with certain pathos, "Time to exact your pound of flesh."

Yousef glanced at the photos and the names under each. "Do you know these two men, Paul Douglas and Moshe Ravitzky?"

Stein nodded. "Yes, and I know they are the leaders of the resistance who have a huge following of Christians who hate Arabs."

"And do they hate you too?" Yousef ventured. "That is, you being a Jew who turned on his own people."

Stein voiced an expletive to himself, then thought, *Oh, a psych analysis.* "Yes, they hate me and all those who stand with us," he said roughly.

Yousef nodded. "Hatred is a good weapon that can unite common enemies." He gestured toward al-Sadr. "Look at us: enemies fighting a common cause."

There are many others—not of this world—who will join in the fighting, Stein didn't say.

Yousef's propensities for violence suddenly manifested itself. He winked at al-Sadr, then stiffened as he made a profane gesture. "Where can we find them?"

Stein grinned. "They're at a hideout in the Jordan Valley." He held up his PDA. "I'll download the GPS coordinates to your iPhones."

Yousef grew thoughtful. "Good."

Stein held up his index finger as his soldiers prepared to depart. "Oh, one more thing."

"What's that?" Youself said impatiently.

"Take out their comrades too," Stein added with a derisive snort.

Temple Mount, Jerusalem

Stein arrived at the high priest's quarters and realized the weather was unusually hot. The outworking of the divine judgment of Trumpet Four where one-third of the sun's radiant heat was diminished had not only brought a reversal of the popular global warming myth, but environmentalists finally admitted the event pointed to divine intervention. This was the only way they could explain the dramatic cooling that took place on the earth that defied conventional science that led to unwarranted Nobel Peace Prize rewards.

But strangely enough, Stein thought, *today seemed hotter than in the recent past.* He shrugged as he concentrated on his meeting, not giving thought to God's timetable of prophetic events.

Barry Levinson answered the door and immediately recognized Stein. He extended his hand in friendship and invited Stein into his quarters. "Your assistant phoned me and advised me you wanted to see me," Levinson said cordially.

Stein nodded as he touched the Mezuzah on the doorway then brought his fingertips to his lips and said, *"Baruch haShem."*

Levinson followed his lead, returned the blessing, and walked Stein into his living chambers. "I pray all is well," he said.

"All is well," Stein replied as he sat down on a prayer bench. "I've come to congratulate you on your service to God and to our nation," he explained with a tight smile. "What's more, I've been asked by Mr. Kavidas to extend an offer to you that we believe is in the best interest of our nation, the position of the high priest."

Levinson stared at him in shock and said humbly, "You're fooling me right? I'm just a lowly priest, and I don't feel qualified to be the high priest. I don't know if I could do the job."

Consistent with the Kavidas-Stein philosophy of ministry, Stein lied. Their real purpose in appointing Levinson was to maintain control of the Temple and the worship practices. "Of course you can do the job!" he replied with gusto. "Besides, this will afford you the opportunity of being close to the master and thus fulfilling your spiritual duties—as before—only on the highest level as the *Kohen ha-Gadol.*"

"I'm not sure of my genealogy," Levinson replied curiously. "I mean, I can't prove I'm from the priestly line of Aaron."

Stein waved off his objection. "It doesn't matter as long as Kavidas is in charge of the administration." His smile broadened. "You will be in complete control of the priesthood here in the Temple. I assure you of that," Stein lied again.

Levinson nodded and Stein took it as an assent to the offer. "I would then have to answer questions that I'm not sure I would know how," he added with a puzzled look.

"Like what, for instance?" Stein said, annoyed.

Levinson threw his hands up. "Like, do the Jews have a rightful claim to this mount we've built the Temple on? There are thousands of Arabs here who still contest our claim to ownership and as the High Priest I would be expected to answer them in a truthful, historical way. This may in turn create conflict for Kavidas."

Stein knew what he meant. The problem of the Temple Mount ownership had been a religious and political contention between Jews and Arabs for centuries. But Stein knew the real truth that the Temple Mount belonged to Israel and to no other. Scholars, both Palestinian and Israeli had declared that the Muslim denial of a Jewish connection to the Temple Mount is political and that historically Muslims did not dispute Jewish ties to the site. The problem of ownership began with the advent of Zionism that referred to political movement that supported the reestablishment of the Jewish state in the Land of Israel. Prior to that, the Jews historically revered the Temple Mount before the time of Mohammed and Islam. Jerusalem is not mentioned in the *Qur'an*, yet it is mentioned in the Hebrew Bible 669 times. Islam historically disregarded Jerusalem as being holy; Mohammed was said to loathe Jerusalem and what it stood for. Mohammed made a point of sanctifying only one place—the Kaaba in Mecca—to signify the unity of God.

As late as the 14th century, Islamic scholar Taqi-al-Din Ibn Taymiyya, whose writings influenced the Wahhabi movement in Arabia, ruled that sacred Islamic sites are to be found only in the Arabian Peninsula and that "in Jerusalem, there is not a place one calls sacred, and the same holds true for the tombs of Hebron."

A guide to the Temple Mount by the Supreme Muslim Council in Jerusalem published in 1925 listed the Mount as Jewish and as the site of Solomon's Temple. In the guide it states: "Its (the Temple) identity is beyond dispute. This, too, is the spot according to universal belief, on which 'David built there an altar unto the Lord.'"

But this truth could not be disclosed since this would settle the issue and put an end to the Israeli-Arab conflict and in turn remove the much-needed leverage Kavidas and Stein required to bring about their master plan—the destruction of God's People, the Jews.

"My answer to you," Stein paused to grab a term, "your holiness, would be to defer any questions to our Chief Counsel, master Kavidas," he replied. "This way you will not have to compromise your standards or the position of your office."

The terms seemed agreeable to Levinson as he looked forward to the exalted promotion.

Mortimer Stein's Private Residence

Stein's supernatural ability to manipulate and give orders to mortals was a natural outworking of his vast experience in the corporate world as CEO of *Redisearch*, the mega commercial and individual credit clearance and background check company where he managed the lives of thousands. Answering the call to accompany Gregory Kavidas to greatness and his subsequent supernatural ascendency to the position of the second most powerful man on the earth afforded Stein the added opportunity to draw upon those experiences only to further his nefarious career in his power to invoke the workings of the demonic world. To this art form he achieved excellence.

They are to be messengers of punishment, of that Stein insisted on. They will be from the class of evil angels that brought misfortune on the ungodly and disobedient children of Israel throughout the ages. They will be of the sort that is described in the book of Judges where "God sent an evil spirit between Abimelech and the men of Shechem..." or in the case of Saul in First Samuel 16 where "The Spirit of the Lord turned aside from being with Saul and an evil spirit from the Lord fell upon (overwhelmed, assailed, terrified) him." Yes, there will be a succession of agencies that bring disaster and horrific consequences on those who reject the promises of God. They are the vulnerable ones. But for those who claim protection from God—those who profess faith—they will also suffer. *Because in this dispensation the nature of fallen angels is dramatically worse than ever before because they know they have such little time remaining before the judgment.* It was to this end that Stein would call upon them to accomplish his work.

It was Kezef, the angel of wrath, the angel of death that he appealed. No, it was not to him alone, for Kezef had other malignant companions to which Stein invoked—those who also reveled in destruction and punishment. They were Af, Hemah, Mashit, and Haron-Peor, who commands 365,000 demons of lower rank. Stein would not depend solely on mortals to accomplish this task. No, this was a spiritual battle that required support from forces who worked outside of mortal boundaries.

The angels assured him that their mission would be carried out properly, for they too were soldiers that enjoyed inflicting pain.

FIFTEEN

The Jezreel Valley, Lower Galilee, Israel

Stein focused, then zoomed his digital camera on the West Bank cities of Jenin and Tulkarm that bordered Jezreel from the south. Then he panned to the north to view the Samarian highlands and Mount Gilboa. From there he photographed the Mount Carmel range in the west and finally the Jordan Valley to the east. *"You may not be interested in war, but war is interested in you,"* he quoted Leon Trotsky as he put his camera away.

His photography survey complete, he drove to Yohanan's roadside café at the southern tip of the valley to study the terrain and history of the valley. Moments later Yohanan's daughter brought him a cup of American coffee along with a knish, Stein's favorite.

Etymology fascinated Stein. He read in his atlas that the word *Jezreel* means "God sows" and saw an amazing clue to the end game. The sowing of both good and evil would be brought to a climatic close where goodness would emerge victorious. The phase "valley of Jezreel" was sometimes used to refer to the central part of the valley, around the city of Jezreel, while the southwestern portion was known as the "valley of Megiddo," after the ancient city of Megiddo which was located there. Over time, different civilizations have named the valley differently and as such this area has also been known as the Plain of Esdraelon. In Christian eschatology, that part of the valley is known as the place where the final battle between good and evil is to be fought. It is known as Armageddon.

He glanced at a map in the atlas then up to the valley. It was a green fertile plain, covered with fields of wheat, cotton, sunflowers and corn, as well as great grazing tracts for multitudes of sheep and cattle. In the past the valley, along with Megiddo, was an important city-state of great importance as it guarded the western branch of a narrow pass and an ancient trade route that connected the land of Egypt and Assyria. Because of its strategic location at the crossroads of several major routes, Megiddo and its environ have witnessed several major battles throughout history. The site was inhabited from approximately 7000 B.C. to 586 B.C. One of the claims to importance is the fact that since this time it has remained uninhabited, thereby preserving the ruins of its time periods pre-dating 586 B.C. without newer settlements disturbing them. As recent as 1918 at the World War I Battle of Megiddo, the British General Edmund Allenby fought and defeated the Ottoman army. The Ottoman or Islamic empire has sought to overturn that disgrace ever since. In Stein's mind, the opportunity was going to present itself very soon.

After one hour of observation, rumination, and note-taking, he returned to his vehicle and headed toward Jerusalem. *Yesterday and today have been busy days for me,* he thought, *and tomorrow promises to be just as busy as I push through our agenda.*

Jordan Valley Stronghold, Jericho

Hidden from the eyes of humankind, Kezef, Af, Hemah, Mashit, and Haron-Peor were already on station at dusk, waiting for Ramzi Yousef and Moqatada al-Sadr, their mortal counterparts to arrive at their base of operation some 70 meters from the entrance of the Christian fortress. They talked among themselves in a primordial tongue and agreed together that this would be an opportunity for them to advance in rank among the other soldiers of the nether world. As messengers of light equipped to manipulate the powers of the air, they believed they had the advantage over living souls who were bound by earthly laws. Notwithstanding, they also had an army on ready-notice to assist if warranted. They reveled in victory. They celebrated their conquest. The triumph was as good as won.

Carrying AR-15 semi-automatic assault rifles with flash suppressors, Yousef and al-Sadr arrived just before nightfall carrying 100 rounds of ammunition each. This weapon was chosen to ensure complete success in the mission. Moments after their arrival, Yousef signaled al-Sadr to move on their objective. Dressed in military fatigues and wearing body paint they stealthily approached the entrance.

Levi and Hershel suddenly bolted upright as they sat at the dining table comparing Bible notes. They exchanged glances then rotated their heads on axis. "We're under attack!" Levi shouted aloud. His divine protection mechanism kicked in.

"Everyone take cover in the deep cave!" Hershel yelled out.

In the corner of his eye Levi saw Shira grab her baby and head for the deep cave in the back of the fortress cavern. "Paul!" she screamed. "Help!"

"We'll help Shira and Sol!" Doron and Gilat cried out as they ran to shield Shira and her baby. Within seconds they were hidden in the deep cave.

"Keep them safe!" Paul shouted out as he ran to the front of the fortress to meet the threat. When he turned, Hershel, Levi, Meschel, and Ravitzky were behind him. "We're with you!" Ravitzky whispered as he pointed to the others. "We're with you!"

"Blow the door!" they heard from the outside.

Paul signaled the others to back off. "Explosives!" Immediately they turned into the stone walls and covered their ears and squeezed their eyes shut. The charge blew the large wooden doors off their hinges; then they crashed to the ground.

"Move and you're all dead!" one of the Arabs said, scanning the men while brandishing his weapon.

Paul focused on their AR-15s then on their garb. "A little overdressed for the occasion aren't we?" he said sarcastically. "I mean we're all unarmed."

"Just shut up!" the man barked and hit Paul in the gut with the butt of this weapon. Paul fell to the ground in a heap.

Ravitzky walked up to the Arab and stared him down. "You wimp! Put that weapon down and fight us like a man. Then we'll see how brave you are!"

The Arab hauled off and punched Ravizky in the jaw, sending him reeling back two meters. "Anybody else?"

Ravizky lay stunned for several minutes then began to rally.

Meschel, seeing his partner fall, clenched his fists, then jumped on the Arab. "You assassin!" he said full of outrage. With that the second Arab sidestepped, then kicked Meschel in the gut, sending him to the floor in a fetal position.

Levi turned in fury and hissed, "You would have no power over us unless it was given to you from above!"

The second Arab vaulted to Levi and raised his hand to hit him with his rifle butt when suddenly his hands froze in midair. It was some kind of divine restraint that emanated from nowhere. "What the—?" The Arab gulped.

Levi shot a look up to heaven in thanksgiving, then said with a smirk, "You dare to come against the Lord's anointed?"

Hershel darted to assist Paul. "HERSHEL! BEHIND YOU!" Ravitzky clamored as the five demons suddenly appeared out of the shadows of night. They were in the form of some alien presence that had been watching them with horrible intentness.

Formed in the infernal crucible of hopelessness, pain, torment, and horror, the alien presences shrieked and howled as the air trembled with a vibration as of invisible flapping wings. They were neither celestial nor terrestrial. They were the representatives of the ultimate horror that often paralyzes memory in a merciful way. They were fallen angels from the pit of hell. They were from the place the Bible calls Tartaros, the prison of the damned angels that left their first estate and comingled with earthly women in a vain attempt to corrupt the Messianic line to Christ.

An acute terror now rose within Ravitzky as he stood, for there, right next to him, were anomalies which nothing normal could explain. To look at them brought shivers down his spine. Biblical angels appeared in the form of men, but these creatures defied all known historical accounts. Their heads were excessively large, like what may be expected of the antediluvian giants that roamed the earth; only these denizens from beyond the grave had stubbed horns protruding from their foreheads and large bear-like noses with canine-like fangs. Their wide-open mouths seemed to hinge on some appendage on their necks, for the mouth was very large with rows of sharpened teeth behind the fangs. Their eyes were sunken orbs with dark shadows that often hid their movement. Absent were ears, only small ports next to the horns. Jutting out from behind their extended wings were claws for hands and feet resembling that of a prehistoric predatory bird.

Demonic chattering surrounded him.

Ravitzky sensed their tactics. *What was that?* He turned and listened. He thought he heard a name being called. He focused on them and could see they were strategizing as they moved toward Hershel. Suddenly they changed course. They had made a decision. They would go after Paul and Levi and leave the rest to their mortal counterparts.

The two Arabs picked up on their decision and advanced on Hershel, Ravitzky, and Meschel with their guns ready and pointed. "All three of you line up against that wall!" The first Arab demanded.

They reluctantly nodded and shot a look at Paul and Levi, whose eyes were riveted on the menace before them. Collectively the demons half-crouched in a semi-circle and slowly and determinedly targeted the two men they believed posed a serious threat as spiritual leaders. They herded Paul and Levi into a separate corner.

"Wait until I come back, and then we'll finish them off," the first Arab commanded the second as he pointed to the men at the wall. With that the first Arab began walking toward the rear cave.

Paul's eyes darted to the Arab and tracked him. He started to panic. *Oh, no! Lord help! He's going after my family!*

Moments later the Arab emerged with Shira holding Solomon in her arms with Doron and Gilat trailing behind. "Get over there with the rest of your Christian friends!" the Arab ordered. Gilat began to whimper as Doron put his arm around her shoulder. "God's going to get us out of here. Just watch," he whispered in her ear. Shira tightened her grip around Solomon as she walked to the wall with one eye on her husband.

Paul winked at Levi.

"Lord, if ever there was a time for you to help, it's now!" Levi whispered.

"No talking!" the Arab hollered, motioning for his group to face the wall.

Kezef, the angel of wrath and death, stepped forward and tapped his paw-like hand on Paul's chest. "Jesus I know and Levi I know," he mocked in a gravelly metallic voice, "but who is this Paul?"

"He is the servant of the Most High God!" Levi answered for him.

Kezef stepped in front of Levi. "I may not be able to kill you, but I can harm you!" Then he turned and motioned for his soldiers to seize Levi. Levi struggled as Af, Hemah, Mashit, and Haron-Peor held him fast. Kezef turned to the mortals at the wall and yelled out in a damnable shrill wail that reverberated off the stone walls, "Watch and see what little power your God has over us!" He stepped back in front of Paul and spit in his face. The green fluid dripped down Paul's face to the ground.

Paul clenched his teeth, then boldly yelled out, "God will not be mocked!"

Evil never surrenders its hold without a sore fight. We never pass into any spiritual inheritance through the delightful exercises of a picnic, but always through the grim contentions of the battlefield. Every faculty which wins its spiritual freedom does so at the price of blood. These demons would not be put to flight by a courteous request, Paul realized, but these demons straddle across the full breath of the way, and our victory in Christ must be registered in blood and tears. We are not born again into soft and protected nurseries, but in the open country where we suck strength from the very terror of the tempest.

"JESUS! COVER AND PROTECT US WITH YOUR BLOOD!" Paul cried out.

Kezef suddenly cringed, and his companions started gasping at the sound of Christ's blood—the sound of victory.

Without warning the earth moved! The walls began to shake and the ground floor started to vibrate. Both man and demon froze in fear. Yousef and al-Sadr shuddered uncontrollably. Kezef's soldiers stared at him, waiting for instructions. His eyes rotated, looking for cause. The earth quickly stilled. Then it happened.

A burst of refulgent light flooded the cave followed by a booming voice that commanded, "BE STILL AND KNOW THAT I AM GOD!" The overpowering presence of God to battle with the forces of darkness had arrived.

Suddenly Kapporeth appeared like an apparition inside a swirling vortex. The rotating column slowed as he stepped out and pointed his hand at Kezef, who began to cower in Kapporeth's shadow. He and his iniquitous allies knew immediately that they were outranked and defeated.

"What do you want from us, you servant of the Most High God?"

Kezef shouted.

"You evil spirits must return to your dwelling place!" Kapporeth demanded.

Kezef mechanically turned his head toward Yousef and al-Sadr. "We beg you to allow us to—" He stopped short as Kapporeth read his thoughts and nodded.

Kapporeth turned to Yousef and al-Sadr, then back to Kezef. "Permission is granted."

Yousef and al-Sadr suddenly bolted upright as the realization came upon them that they were done. The five fallen creatures from the lower world lurched forward and together leaped on top of the two would-be assassins. Seconds later their bodies began to convulse as their souls and spirits came under a new authority. They now belonged to Satan and his lieutenants.

Yousef's face contorted in rage as he mechanically turned and pointed his AR-15 on his companion. Al-Sadr instantly realized his destiny and slowly raised his weapon to face Yousef.

There was loud squealing and yowling...gunshots!

Kapporeth walked to Paul. "The Lord of Hosts has heard your cry," he said in soft tones. He turned and pointed to the crumpled, bloodied bodies of Yousef and al-Sadr on the cave floor. "And so will it be to all of God's enemies."

Then he was gone.

SIXTEEN

Jordan Valley Stronghold, Jericho

Morning brought warmer-than-usual sunshine that brightened the small patch of earth outside the fortress Paul selected for the burial site of the two Arab assassins who met with an untimely death at the hands of their demonic collaborators. It was Levi who said *Kaddish* over their graves, despite the fact that they were not Jews. It was his way of invoking a blessing from God who said, *"Love your enemies, bless them that curse you, and pray for them which despitefully use you and persecute you."* But it would not be easy to pray for those who hours before intended to kill you, your family, and all those you loved. Ravitzky and Meschel refused while the others stood around the gravesite and prayed, then tossed small rocks on top of the mound and walked away.

Once inside the fortress Ravitzky and Meschel waited several minutes then approached Paul and Levi. "We have some questions, Paul," Ravitzky said curiously.

Paul motioned for them to sit at a table and motioned for Gilat to bring them a refreshing drink. "What's on your heart?"

"You know, there's a saying in the *Talmud*, 'Whatever is hateful to you, do not to your fellow man. That is the law, the rest is commentary.' Well, I don't understand why these Arabs hate us Jews so much that they would go to these extremes to kill us." He waved his hands toward Shira and Solomon. "Innocent women, children—it makes no difference to them. How can they worship their god and still act out their terrorist activities? I just don't understand it!"

"You've been around the Arabs—the Palestinians, the Hamas, the Hezbollah, the al-Qaeda, the Wahhabis—long enough to know how they think," Paul replied. "Human life is dispensable as long as they achieve their goals that are set out in the *Qur'an*: To rid the world of the Jew and all those who support Israel. Always has been, always will be. Only this time they had help from demonkind. And I don't mind telling you that I was concerned."

Meschel nodded. "They're escalating their attacks, aren't they?"

"Their time is short, and they know it, so yes, I believe they are," Paul replied wearily.

"You know, Paul," Ravitzky said as he pulled back to look at him then scratched his cheek as he pondered his next thought. "I thought I heard one of those demons call another by the name of—" He shook his head as if to shake loose the audio fragment he heard. "It sounded like one of them said, 'Kreze' or something like that." He blinked. "No it was 'Kezef.' Yeah, that's it."

Paul looked at Levi, eyes pleading.

"Kezef is the name of a demon mentioned in the *Kabbalah*," Levi said.

Ravitzky knew the *Kabbalah* was the Jewish book of mysticism that was loosely based on the writings in the *Torah* and is not an intellectual discipline, nor does it instruct the mystic to withdraw from humanity to pursue enlightenment. No, according to the Kabbalist, they seek union with God while maintaining a full social, family and community life while interpreting the *Torah* through the eyes of folklore that said God taught the *Kabbalah* to angels, who, after the Fall, taught it to Adam in order to provide man with a way back to God. From Adam to Noah, then to Abraham and Moses, who in turn initiated 70 elders. Kings David and Solomon were initiates.

"Do you think this Kezef is really a demon that is described in the *Kabbalah*?" Meschel asked Levi.

"The name is definitely in the *Kabbalah*," Levi replied. "But I do not put any credibility in the *Kabbalah* as being a book inspired by the God of the Bible. I believe that the non-elect angels have adapted man's interpretation of the *Torah* to suit their own objectives and since they are intent on deception, they fool the unwary by pretending to be good 'fairies' and 'golem' who go around performing good deeds in 'white magic,' but in fact they are nothing more than evil spirits roaming around seeking who they may devour. The *Kabbalah* is nothing more than a compilation of those misadventures."

"Hmm," Ravitzky said, deep in thought. "I counted five of those pernicious little low-lifes. But I wonder how many of them are there?"

Levi breathed deeply. "There are many. According to one estimate there are 1 sextillion possible permutations. According to another, there are at least 100 trillion, both good and bad angels of which we know that Satan took one-third with him. Biblically speaking, stars are symbols for angels, and we know that there are billions of stars per galaxy and that there are billions of galaxies in our vast universe."

"My head is spinning," Meschel said with a chuckle.

"Let's not forget that there are good angels as well," Levi added with a smile. "Good angels are used by God to communicate His will and word to men, and on many occasions they are used to guide, just as they guided Joseph to take Mary as his wife; the women who came to Jesus' tomb were instructed and directed by an angel. Angels have ministered to physical needs such as when the angel encouraged Hagar and her son Ishmael and provided water to keep them alive. Jacob was protected from physical harm by angels as he traveled with his family to meet Esau and Daniel was protected from the lions by an angel. Not only did angels strengthen Christ Himself, but angels have encouraged and strengthened His messengers. After freeing the apostles from prison, an angel encouraged them to continue preaching. And, angels are agents in answering prayer. Twice angels were sent in response to Daniel's prayers. When he prayed for his nation's restoration, Gabriel was caused to fly swiftly to instruct him of Israel's future and final restoration. Of course there are many other examples in the Bible."

Levi seemed to have a deep understanding of the angelic realm— something Ravitzky was always interested in. "It seems that demonic activity has greatly increased during this Tribulation period. Is that true?"

"Historically," Levi explained, "demonic activity heightened before and during a time when God was going to do something special. Such as when Christ was ministering on earth, He performed many exorcisms and even battled with the head of all demons, Satan, in Matthew chapter 4 on the Mount of Temptation. Throughout the gospels you see evil spirits popping up all over the place. Now, when Satan and his henchmen know that Christ is about to return and confine them to the pit for one thousand years, they have intensified their attacks."

"This is why we have seen in the past six and one-half years more demonic activity than ever before," Paul added, "especially in the area of moral turpitude. Looking at America for instance, Toynbee noted that 'of the 22 civilizations that have appeared in history, 19 of them collapsed when they reached the moral state America is in now.' Satan is working 24/7 on America's morals to corrupt them. A noted novelist once said, 'The strongest sign of the decay of a nation is the feminization of men and the masculinization of women.' Well, my family roots are in America and my heart breaks for it. I believe our great forefathers are turning in their graves as they see what is going on there." *A great civilization is not conquered from without until it has destroyed itself within*, he didn't say when thinking of his ancestral home.

Levi looked at Paul with disdain as he finished his remarks. He suddenly felt upstaged by Paul's assessments. It wasn't right. He had to assert himself. He had to take control and prove to the K-group that he was anointed by God and that he could lead just as well as Paul. *I am from the holy priesthood*, he said within himself. *I am capable of interpreting God's will. I am capable of discerning prophecy. I am capable of perceiving when God's enemies possess a lying spirit. I possess the gift of knowledge.*

He stood up and pointed his finger at Paul and said, "Could it be possible that your leadership has brought this past attack on us?" He panned the rest of the group. "You have placed all of us in jeopardy, Paul. Your direction—even bringing us here to this cave—has brought grave consequences on us—"

"Now wait a minute!" Hershel interrupted, thumping his foot on the ground. "You can't go blaming him for what's happened! We're living in the end times and everything that's transpired is at God's hand. What's more, it's been prophesied and recorded in the Bible!"

Paul was taken aback. "Levi," he entreated, "you're not yourself. You are overtired and need to rest."

Shira handed her baby off to Gilat, then looked at Doron, Meschel, and Ravitzky. "You know what I think, Levi?" she began fiercely. "One of the evil spirits that attacked us is still lingering around here and afflicting you."

Everyone but Levi silently exchanged glances and nodded.

"Everyone hold hands!" Paul said. "This is some satanic attack on Levi! He is being oppressed by an evil force looking to usurp our chain of command and disturb our family!"

Within seconds they formed an interlocking circle around Levi. Then Paul prayed aloud for the blood of Christ to cover Levi and free him from any evil influence.

Levi shook his head several times, then yawned. "I felt overpowered," he gabbled. "What happened?"

Paul's eyes flicked to the rest of the group then back to Levi. "Things got a little dicey." His voice grew growly, like he needed to clear his throat. "We believe you were being harassed by an evil spirit."

"Your whole demeanor changed," Hershel added.

"You became very argumentative and controlling," Shira put in.

Paul waved them to silence. "Remember Kapporeth warned us that the 144 thousand would undergo severe testing." He took a deep breath. "Well, what we witnessed today with Levi is an example of that very prophecy."

"We need to be on alert," Ravitzky added. "Everybody watch your back!"

Levi yawned a second time. "I need to go and take a nap."

The Messianic Wing of the Temple, Jerusalem

His soul and spirit was unsettled as he circled his desk, wondering what his next move would be. *I need to maintain control*, he assured himself. The failure of the mission to conquer the Christian fortress in the Jordan Valley was evermost in his mind. They had taken control. He had grossly underestimated this so-called prophet Kapporeth, and it was eating at his soul.

Control is everything, and it must be maintained if victory is to be attained.

He stopped circling, then sat down at his desk. Seconds later Stein's file containing the drawings, notes and recommendations for the battle on Megiddo caught his attention. He carefully leafed through the file, and a chill ran up and down his spine. *Be strong*, he commanded himself. *Be not afraid!* The thought of his demise drawing near caught him by surprise. *There's still several more plays to be acted out*, he posited. *Vision is the art of seeing the invisible*, he reminded himself. Suddenly a vision did become clear. *That's it! I have to act upon it to regain control.* He picked up his phone and made a call.

Ten minutes later Stein walked in and took a seat in front of Kavidas.

"I looked the plans over for Armageddon and I approve of them. Good work," Kavidas said. "Now you need to contact all the major players. Give them a briefing to make sure they're on board, then move the agenda along."

Stein knew his master well enough to recognize a radical change in his demeanor. It was troublesome. "I will set that up...what's bothering you?"

"I must assert myself to maintain control of all things until the consummation," he intoned.

"I'm with you. You know that," Stein reassured.

Kavidas nodded with the reaffirmation. "I had a brief vision that the next Bowl Judgment is about to come upon the earth, and I want to capitalize on it." He pointed up and snarled, "Instead of giving Him the credit."

Stein dreaded the next Bowl Judgment and the mere mention of it frightened him. He had mentally blocked it out, but now he began to squirm in his seat. "But this Bowl involves astrophysics." He looked curiously at Kavidas. "I mean you can't do anything to change it. That is well beyond our powers—"

Kavidas gave him a dismissive wave. "I know that!" he said impatiently. "I'm not looking to change it but to predict it before the public hears it from the other side."

"Predict it?" Stein said, pulling back to look at him. He scanned his face. "It's already been predicted in Revelation 16!"

Kavidas gave off a devilish guffaw and said with a sarcastic tinge, "When did the non-believing public start reading the Bible? How do you think we have come so far along without being stopped, Mort? It's because the world at large ignores the Bible, that's how." He grinned. "No, we don't have to worry about that. All we need to do is to get the jump on it." He stood. "Get on the phone and set up a press conference right away. We don't have time to waste. The Bowl is on its way down."

Stein jumped to his feet and bolted from the office.

On the Steps of the Messianic Wing of the Temple, Jerusalem

Reporters from *Yediot Aharonot*, Israel's most widely circulated newspaper arrived first, followed by reporters from the leading Arabic-language newspaper, *Al-Hayat*. Two television news networks with their circling helicopters added drama to the unfolding scene.

Stein stood behind a stone pillar to observe the performance as Kavidas walked up to the news media assembled near the *Yediot Aharonot* mobile news vans. Three wireless microphones were thrust at him. "Your holiness," one reporter in heightened hysteria said, "why did you call this news conference? Do you have some secret information or revelation?"

The other two reporters nodded. "Can you tell us?" they asked frantically. "Are we in danger?"

Kavidas looked directly into the cameras trained on him. "Yes, I have secret information that God has revealed to me."

Stein snapped his fingers in triumph as the frenzied media swallowed Kavidas' line.

"Speak to your people!" they cried out in unison.

Kavidas nodded and then hesitated momentarily to raise the level of anticipation. "In two days our sun will go through a stage that will produce great heat, and thousands will be killed. We must be prepared! We must take precautions. No one should go outdoors without solar protection. People should be using umbrellas to block out the light. Even thought the amount of light has been greatly reduced, the light that does come to earth will be very severe."

"You mean a supernova or something like that?" one news reporter asked.

Kavidas was very skillful in how much information he disclosed since demonic forces have only limited knowledge of the future or of hidden things. Fallen angels have a source of knowledge that is found in their superior created nature and in their vast experience, as they have lived through many thousands of years observing and collecting information. Despite their great knowledge, they use all the resources of their intellects against God and His purposes incessantly.

He shook his head. "No, it will not be like a supernova that could incinerate the earth. No, it will be more like—"

"Like what happened to the sun in Portugal at Fatima in 1917?" a reporter cut in from the crowd.

Kavidas had to think on that question. It was hailed as the "Miracle of the Sun" back in 1917 when three Portuguese children—Lucia Santos and her cousins, siblings Jacinta and Francisco Marto—saw what they claimed was the virgin Mary, called the Lady of the Rosary of Fatima, in an apparition that the Catholic Church later called a miracle. The phenomenon raised worldwide attention.

Lucia described seeing a woman "brighter than the sun, shedding rays of light clearer and stronger than a crystal ball filled with the most sparkling water and pierced by the burning rays of the sun." The woman in the vision exhorted the children to do penance and to make sacrifices to save sinners. The children subsequently wore tight cords around their waists to cause pain, abstained from drinking water on hot days, and performed other works of penance. Lucia said the lady had asked them to pray the rosary every day, repeating many times that the rosary was the key to personal and world peace. In the course of her appearances, the woman confided to the children three secrets, now known as the Three Secrets of Fatima. The secrets were both visions and descriptions of Hell, along with a prophetic letter to be opened only by the Pope in 1960 of which the contents remained a secret until June of 2000. Much speculation surrounded the contents ranging from the apocalypse to a great apostasy in the church.

The Miracle of the Sun occurred when a crowd of 70,000 in number, including newspaper reporters and photographers, gathered at the Cova da Iria. The incessant rain had finally ceased and a thin layer of clouds cloaked the silver disc of the sun such that it could be looked upon without hurting the eyes. Lucia called out to the crowd to look at the sun. Sometime while Lucia was pointing toward the sun and claiming to have visions of various religious figures in the sky, it is believed that the sun appeared to change colors and to rotate like a fire wheel. For some, the sun appeared to fall from the sky before retreating; for others it zigzagged. The phenomenon is claimed to have been witnessed by most people in the crowd, as well as people many miles away.

Eye specialist Dr. Domingos Pinto Coelho, writing for the newspaper *Ordem* reported: "The sun at one moment surrounded with scarlet flame, at another aureoled in yellow and deep purple, seemed to be in an exceeding fast and whirling movement, at times appearing to be loosened from the sky and to be approaching the earth, strongly radiating heat." Although no movement or other phenomenon of the sun was registered by scientists at the time, the solar phenomenon were visible up to forty kilometers away. Despite these assertions, not all witnesses reported seeing the sun "dance." Some people only saw the radiant colors, and others including some believers, say they saw nothing at all.

Biblical scholarship challenged the claims attributing the phenomenon to the workings of the "angel of light" and the "prince and power of the air." It is alleged that Satan manufactured the vision to cause people to worship Mary as the intercessor instead of Christ who is claimed in the Bible to be the only intercessor between God and man. Having the faithful believe that salvation could be achieved by repeating prayers of the rosary was also claimed to be a satanic diversion away from the true path of salvation.

With only limited knowledge of the prophecy he said, "No. It will be different, but God has not revealed what those differences are, only that we are warned of its coming."

A woman emerged from the crowd holding a Bible in one hand and a microphone in the other. She shouted, "It says here in Revelation that 'The fourth angel poured out his bowl upon the sun and power was given unto him to scorch men with fire.'"

Stein stared at the woman with a vengeance in her attempt to steal Kavidas' attention. "So what is the big revelation since we all know it's coming?" she said in challenge.

Kavidas made a mental note of her face and would have her dealt with at another time. As for now, he grinned expansively into the cameras. "Yes, that's true that it is prophesied in the Bible, but here's what you need to understand." He paused to point to himself and added with his voice vibrating with intensity, "Only I know *when* it is going to happen!"

The crowd suddenly grew silent.

SEVENTEEN

Moriah Hotel, Eilat, Israel

R afi Nelson tied up his fishing vessel to the pier at the Eliat Marina, showered, then put on his swimming suit and walked to the beach at the Moriah Hotel. The soothing, cool waters of the Red Sea on Israel's southernmost shore is a favorite resort area for thousands of vacationers along with more than 65,000 residents who preferred to live in Eliat that is part of the Southern Negev Desert, over the busy metropolis of Jerusalem. The city is adjacent to the Egyptian village of Taba to the south, the Jordanian port city of Aqaba to the east, and within sight of Saudi Arabia to the southeast, across the gulf.

Emerging from the water was a host of snorkelers, windsurfers, water-skiers and swimmers, and Rafi Nelson, who dared to plunge in the cold water chilled by the lack of sunlight. He walked to the Sugar Shack and ordered a cold beer, then turned to survey the sensual city that caters to people who like magnificent natural beauty, lazy afternoons, spicy food, and of course, cold beer.

As a mariner of many years, Rafi realized the strategic location of Eliat. It was Israel's only access to the Indian and Pacific Oceans, and trade with Asia, East Africa, Australia and the islands including vital oil supplies from cooperative countries. Holding on to Eliat also meant a break in land continuity between Egypt and Jordan, thus offering a military benefit for Israeli defensive planning.

Off in the distance were the Eilat Mountains, a spectacular ascent of colorful stone that included the entry to Solomon's Canyon, a popular hiking area, something Ravi told himself at age 56 that he would have time for some day. But that day would never come.

In the Jordan Rift Valley some twenty-four thousand feet below the shores of the Red Sea the tectonic plates of the Afro-Arabian Rift fault line began to shift, slip, and fracture until the titanic geologic force exerted enough pressure to register abnormal registrations at the seismograph station located at Be'er Ora. The Jordan Rift Valley, otherwise known as the Afro-Arabian Rift Valley is but part of one of the longest, deepest, and widest fissures in the earth's surface. The fault lines of this rift actually extend over a distance of 4,000 miles, beginning in the Amanus Mountains of southeastern Turkey and continuing southward through western Syria, Lebanon, Israel, as far as the Red Sea. According to seismographic registrations, between 200 and 300 tremors are recorded on a daily basis in Israel.

At first Rafi Nelson noticed the waves at the beach receded dramatically. He ordered another beer to calm his nerves, but the sunbathers were alarmed when the sea water suddenly drained some twenty-nine meters from the shore line, leaving many bathers stranded on the sea bed. An intense shaking occurred as the stress built up in the rocks below, reaching the level that exceeds the strain threshold. The accumulated energy was then focused into the fault plane until the earth's mantle deformed, shearing the brittle upper crust.

The energy released by the instantaneous strain release by the earthquake sent the seaside bathers running in all directions. But Rafi, toughened by life and the elements of nature moved slowly to higher ground, while others, fearing divine retribution, raced to clear out of the area.

Then the massive rupture took place. The earth's crust suffered both a dip-slip and strike-slip—an oblique slip—that cleaved the sea bed, sending one side up twenty meters, then suddenly fell. The long line of hotels along the seacoast began to sway and collapse when a massive sucking noise took place. Millions of gallons of sea water drained into the cavity created by the slip, then undoubtedly met with subterranean volcanic heat that in turn sent a geyser hundreds of meters into the air.

Panic ensued. Rafi surveyed the scene and covertly moved away from the crowd as hundreds were trampled as they fled. When the realization that a major earthquake had occurred, Rafi hastened his departure to higher ground to watch the "big wave," his title for what geologists call a *tsunami*.

At Be'er Ora the geomorphological conditions were alarming. The intensity of the quake peaked the Mercalli scale and sent the Israeli scientists scrambling to alert the USGS that the Mideast has suffered the most severe earthquake ever recorded. They were worried, very worried.

Within an hour NASA, the USGS, and the European Space Agency conferred, arriving at the consensus that the earth's axis had shifted as a result of the subterranean upheaval that triggered the earthquake in the Mideast. Besides altering planetary speed, the shifting plates rearranged the distribution of the Earth's mass, causing it to bulge in spots it didn't bulge before and contract in others. That rearrangement shifted the Earth's inclination on its north-south axis. This major shift together with the bulge violated the law of conservation of angular momentum so the rotation of the earth did not make up for the shifting mass. Besides a wobble, the sun's rays began to strike the earth's surface at different angles—angles that would prove to be drastically harmful to mankind.

Within three hours the aftermath worsened.

With the altering of the Earth's axis, the extraordinary solar radiation on the earth began to burn the nitrogen in the upper atmosphere. This converted the nitrogen to oxides of nitrogen, which began to open holes in the ozone layer in the Earth's stratosphere. The temperature of the Earth's surface began to rise exponentially.

Christian Fortress, Petra

Asher walked out of the cavern into the night air and immediately recognized the heat coming off the surfaces of the rock formations that surrounded the fortress. After being with the group in the depths of the caves for the better part of the day, the rising temperature escaped the group's notice. It was getting terribly hot. Then, as he surveyed the fortress, he casually looked up into the night sky—clear. But something was different. He couldn't place it. Perplexed, he walked back into the cave and brought out Yashur and Norman.

"Look up," Asher said as he pointed to the sky. "What do you see?"

Three minutes passed. "The star constellations are in a different place," Yashur whispered in wonder.

"How can that be?" Norman asked. The one thing he knew about

143

astronomy was that stars don't move. The Earth revolved around the sun and accordingly, the constellations appear to move across the sky, but their position in space is constant. The entire celestial canopy moved together in concert through the universe, but the stars in their constellations remained in place. Something else had to have happened.

Yashur studied the sky for several minutes. He noticed the constellation Orion, visible from any place on the earth, was different. The three bright stars in the Belt of Orion were now oriented almost 25 degrees perpendicular to the celestial equator and the main star in the Belt, Betelgeuse, was at a different angle. "The only explanation," he said numbly, "is that the earth's axis has been altered. That must be why the temperature has risen dramatically."

Asher put it together. "It's the Fourth Bowl! That's what's happened. Only we didn't know how it would come about." He paused to recall the passage in Revelation then said, "'The fourth angel poured out his bowl on the sun, and the sun was given power to scorch people with fire. They were seared by the intense heat and they cursed the name of God....'"

Yashur moaned softly then said, "Isaiah adds that the light coming from the sun will be seven times brighter."

"Fortunately, we here at Petra have the rocks to cover us and keep us cool, but the rest of the planet is going to cook," Norman said glumly.

"You would think with everything that has happened—with all the judgments so far—that mankind would cry out to God and ask to be saved," Asher instructed, "but the rest of that verse in Revelation adds, '...but they refused to repent and glorify him.' So that means God has to turn up the heat to bring about the refining process."

Yashur threw up his hands and walked back into the cavern to advise the others of the latest event in God's calendar. Seconds later Norman and Asher followed.

Dalia Shami and Marta Shiller sat in front of the group's only real link to the outside, the K-group Internet connection on Yashur's laptop equipped with satellite reception. Within thirty minutes of the onset, nearly everyone on planet Earth knew another catastrophe had befallen man. Street scenes of New Yorkers, Californians, New Zealanders, and every other nationality walking around with umbrellas to filter out the sunlight were flashed across YouTube, Twitter, and other media vehicles.

News networks were quick to show the elderly and infirmed, who were the early casualties of the sudden heat wave and scorching, then went on to predict that, after several weeks of this intense heat from solar radiation, millions would die. Censors bleeped out the cursing, expletives, and swearing that blamed God for the judgment, but few sought out the reason why.

EIGHTEEN

Lane Drugs, Miami

Ben-Korpel sat in the research library at Lane Drugs and scrolled through the Internet photos of the ruins of the Twin Towers at the World Trade Center after the notorious 9/11/2001 terrorist attacks and shook his head in disgust. Then he reviewed the reconstructed buildings. *The newly designed buildings may be somewhat terrorist-proof,* he thought, *but they were of little consolation.* In his mind payback to the Arabs never came.

Then his thoughts drifted to Tamarac, where Efraim Zuroff, his "warrior" friend and fellow soldier, had died at the hands of Islamic fanatics. *Once is happenstance, twice is coincidence, three times is enemy action,* he thought, agreeing with Ian Fleming's James Bond character, *Goldfinger.* He could not understand why America did not recognize Islam as the enemy after their continuous onslaught on innocent civilians until it was too late. *No,* he thought on his American hero, Lincoln, *"Nothing is politically right which is morally wrong." There is no humanly justification for their hatred. Their attacks on America and their allies had to be divinely directed as retribution for their turning away from the God of Israel. It had to be,* he realized, there just wasn't any other historical or Biblical precedence he could point to other than that.

He mused for several more moments than turned in his seat until his eyes focused on the American flag standing in the corner of the room. *No regrets!* he told himself. From the day he arrived in Florida, he had no regrets about coming to America. From that time on he considered himself an American; bona fide after passing his citizenship exam and swearing his allegiance. He nodded to himself then turned back to the computer and keyed in "Theodore Roosevelt quotes." He vaguely remembered his quote but now he had to memorize it. Circumstances demanded it.

Seconds later twenty of Roosevelt's quotes appeared. He scanned the page then read the one he recalled aloud to himself: "'Any man who says he is an American, but something else also, isn't an American at all. We have room for but one flag, the American flag. We have room for but one language here, and that is the English language...and we have room for but one sole loyalty and that is a loyalty to the American people.'" He nodded several times in reflection. *If only America's leaders remembered this code, they would not be in the mess they are today.*

A knock at the doorway broke his somber reverie. "Mr. Ben-Korpel, Mr. Lane and Mr. Douglas were hoping you could meet them in the office," Helen announced.

Ben-Korpel blinked his eyes several times. "Sure, fine. I'll be right there."

Moments later as he walked through the lobby to Lane's office he noticed a woman and a little girl standing next to the receptionist center. "Mr. Ben-Korpel," Helen said, pointing to them, "this is Lauren and her daughter Caitlyn. They are living with me." She smiled. "We're going to Bayside for lunch."

Ben-Korpel took note that Lauren and her daughter were extremely well presented. Lauren had on a flowery dress and high-heels with her hair pulled up in a bun with a pair of simple earrings that accentuated her bright, sculptured face while Caitlyn wore a cute shorts outfit with her hair neatly braided in pig tails. "So nice to meet you," he said in passing. "Have a wonderful time at lunch." He made a note to sit with Helen sometime in the future to learn the story about how Lauren and Caitlyn came to live with her.

Several moments after Ben-Korpel walked into Brandon's office his spirit sensed a major change in strategy. Brandon and Jonathan were passive and subdued; something was unusual and unnerving. "Is something wrong?" Ben-Korpel asked as he surveyed the room.

Jonathan waved Ben-Korpel over to his sofa and said, "Avraham, Brandon and I have just spent an hour in prayer and we believe the time has come for us to make a radical adjustment in our approach to the enemy. "Our planet is undergoing the Fourth Bowl Judgment—and who knows where that will end—and it is because of the nearness of the Lord's return that brings us to change things. We are no longer going to physically or militarily advance on God's enemies but allow the Lord to deal with them. For the past six years we have been in combat mode and the time has come for us to assume a prayer ministry and watch God defend us."

"So you're giving up?" Ben-Korpel said in surprise as his demeanor changed to one of anger.

"Giving up? No." Brandon said. "The direction we believe the Lord wants us to go in at this late time of the game is for us to no longer use 'armed resistance' but 'prayer resistance,'" he said while flicking his eyes to Jonathan for confirmation.

"So, in other words, you're caving in," Ben-Korpel said with a tinge of sarcasm.

"Avraham," Jonathan began softly, "we have only had minor victories every time we attempted to defeat the enemies of God here in Florida, and I can tell you that I also speak for the rest of America as well. It is only when God intervenes that our enemy—be it Kavidas and his cohorts, or Islamic terrorists—that they are vanquished." He rubbed his brow. "We're growing tired. We need to 'rest in the Lord' and allow Him to destroy our enemies."

Ben-Korpel pointed to Jonathan and retorted, "And you call yourself one of the 144,000 witnesses?"

Jonathan exchanged glances with Brandon then nodded. "Yes. And my role is one of a missionary, not a soldier." He hesitated fractionally. "It's time I remembered that and acted accordingly."

Ben-Korpel shook his head then snorted in disgust. "The influence of filth and violence coming from the enemy will not be destroyed by polite talk," he said, stalking off into a corner.

Jonathan hesitated, assessed, and then responded. "This is our calling at this time of the Tribulation. But this may not be your calling, Avraham. You must do what the Lord is leading you to do, and whatever that may be, you will have our blessing."

"Will I receive your blessing if I retaliate in kind to Efraim's murder?" he replied hotly.

Jonathan shot a look at Brandon, who shrugged. Apparently the man before him had issues that stemmed from the murder of his wife by Islamic terrorists and then the murder of his friend Efraim by the same gang of thugs. He was not going to let it go. "It's not up to me to pass judgment on you, Avraham," Jonathan soothed. "I know you still have pain from the loss of your wife and friend, but remember, 'vengeance is mine, says the Lord.'"

Ben-Korpel yielded. "I know, I know," he said, his voice calm but full of menace. "I guess I must go my own way and find my peace in this crazy world that is under indictment from God." He paused, then in a reasonable, organized voice, added, "If that means I must be the instrument of justice to prevent the loss of our Christian brothers, then so be it."

Brandon and Jonathan knew this was Ben-Korpel's good-bye song as he reverted to his pre-salvation days in the Mossad. Only now he would be acting under the banner of a crusader for Jesus. Brandon walked to Ben-Korpel and put his arm around his shoulder. "This may sound trite, but remember this adage as you go forth, Avraham: that we want justice for others and mercy for ourselves."

Ben-Korpel brushed off the feeling of being unjustly accused and slightly offended. "I promise you that I will not break the law but will do everything in my power to protect those Believers God brings into my path."

Jonathan joined Brandon at Ben-Korpel's side. "Then go with the Lord today, Avraham, and let Him lead, guide, and direct your steps."

Ben-Korpel cleared his throat but said nothing as a tear appeared in his eye. The dissonance would not interfere with his love for his brothers in Christ. *"Shalom Aleichem,"* he said and hugged them both.

"Aleichem Shalom," Jonathan replied.

Ben-Korpel turned and walked out of Brandon's office and into a phase of his life he never thought possible.

The Messianic Wing of the Temple, Jerusalem

Kavidas picked up the remote control unit to his plasma TV then clicked to the Internet and entered into the search engine, *Israel, land mass.* Seconds later the screen filled with a satellite image of Israel from three-hundred plus miles up in space. The legend below the map added that

Israel's inheritance actually only encompassed no more than 10,300 square miles, or about the approximate size of Lake Erie or the state of Maryland.

He slowly enlarged the image and recognized the rugged terrain that enveloped Israel and realized that survival in Israel due to such treacherous terrain depended upon neither military prowess nor environmental ingenuity. For this nation to survive a miracle would be needed. Its future depended ultimately upon cosmic forces that lay beyond the sphere of human control. This was a fact he pushed out of his mind, knowing the consequences that would bring their ultimate survival meant his demise. He had to mitigate his fears.

He keyed in the word *Armageddon* and then smiled as the satellite image focused on the Valley of Jezreel he knew to be Megiddo or Armageddon. He propped his feet up on his desk, pushed back in his chair, and studied the topography for several moments. His heart began to beat rapidly as he thought on how the final battle would unfold. *We win at the start, then...*

A knock at the door. He immediately recognized the characteristic three-knock tap. "Come in, Mort!"

Stein walked in, beaming from ear to ear. He strode to his customary seat next to Kavidas' desk and placed a file in front of him. "Good news!"

Kavidas regarded him with a tight smile. "In view of this last judgment—" he counted them off on his fingers—"number four if I'm not mistaken—good news is welcome."

"We have the Ayatollah on board," Stein said with a gleeful nod. "Now that we have the spiritual head of Iran in the loop together with the other nations, we're ready to move on Israel."

Stein could see Kavidas' eyes dancing with anticipation.

Kavidas leaned closer and said, "The day is near, even at the door."

Stein knew that Ayatollah Mohammad Mesbah was the chief living authority on the *Mahdi,* the "Guided One," better known as the Twelfth Imam or the Hidden Imam, in line of succession from the Prophet Mohammad. He is a messianic figure who will return after an apocalypse to elevate Islam to the status of the only true religion, with the consequence that all other false religions will be vanquished. "Yes, it is very near," Stein agreed.

150

Kavidas opened the file and read off the names. "Iran, Sudan, Libya, Jordan, Morocco, Tunisia, Turkey, Saudi Arabia, and Syria."

"All Islamic nations except China and Russia," Stein said. "I didn't include them since their role is just supplying the arms to the Arab bloc states. While these states represent the bulk of the armies, I'm sure there are others that will join in the fray just as it is in Lebanon and Egypt. Historically the Arab aggressors have acted like vultures hovering over a carcass whenever Israel was attacked."

Kavidas silently rose from his chair and stepped to the oil painting of Chaim Weizmann, Israel's first president. He kept the portrait on the wall as a token for any inquiring Jewish person who might call upon him. Named "the Father of the State of Israel," Weizmann represented the consummate crusader for Israel's statehood.

In the years before the Balfour Declaration, a member of the House of Lords asked him, "Why do you Jews insist on Palestine when there are so many undeveloped countries you could settle in more conveniently?"

Weizmann replied, "That is like my asking you why you drove 20 miles to visit your mother last Sunday when there are so many old ladies living on your street."

"Humph," Kavidas muttered in contempt. "Things are very different now," he said while staring at the portrait and curling his lip. Then, with a clenched fist, he added, "Now your nation is under my leadership, and I promise you that your goal will never come to pass." From there he returned to his desk. "There's something you need to take care of, Mort," he said with a vindictive nod.

Stein recognized the look. "Who is it?"

"Remember the woman on the steps of the Messianic Wing who challenged my vision in front of the reporters? She was holding a Bible in her hand."

Stein held up his hand to halt the remainder of information. "I'll take care of her."

Kavidas grinned. "See that you do."

Four days later Hamas took credit for the bombing of a small Jerusalem restaurant known to accommodate members of the Christian K-group.

NINETEEN

Jordan Valley Stronghold, Jericho

I t was early morning and the outside temperature was already over 100 degrees Fahrenheit in the shade. Paul gave strict instructions that included 75+ sunblock lotion, eye protection, and wherever possible, to use an umbrella to reduce the sunlight falling on the body. Carrying water to avoid dehydration was imperative. In all of the central latitudes this became the uniform for humans. Instinctively animals and birds sought out water holes and shade protection, and even then, the loss due to the relentless heat took its toll. Millions of animals, both wild and domestic, were dying. Millions of birds migrated to the extreme latitudes where the climate was cooler. The evacuation left many cities without scavenger or songbirds.

But inside the cave at Jericho, the temperature was comfortable, a signature of God's hand of grace to his people.

Shira handed off Solomon to his father after breast-feeding him. "It's getting close, isn't it?"

Paul carefully manipulated Solomon so he could gently pat the baby with his right hand to burp him. Within two minutes Solomon obliged his father, then began to coo.

"You mean 'close' as in Jesus coming for us?" Paul replied.

Shira nodded and said ruefully, "Uh-huh." She rubbed her hands together—her way of showing stress. "I've been watching the reports on the Internet, and I'm wondering how long the human race will be able to withstand the judgments. I mean, the millions of non-believers with boils all over their bodies, the aftermath of the earthquake that's causing the planet to wobble and grow hotter, not to mention all the residuals from all the other plagues—the AIDS, famine, mutated insects. Then there's the moon and sun that have been divinely altered. And let's not forget the blood-red water supplies, the uncontrollable fires throughout the earth—" She began to cry. "The loss of human life is so—"

Paul held Solomon firmly and placed his other arm around Shira. "Things are bad. I know that," he consoled, "but I know in my heart that we must hold on until the Lord comes for us." He kissed her and then kissed his son. "I also know the Lord is going to protect us until He comes. He has assured me of that. So while many do not have that blessed assurance and are frightened, that confidence enables us to go forward."

Shira gazed into his eyes. "Paul," she whispered, grappling with the enormous dangers of the future, "I don't know if I can make it through the rest of the Bowl Judgments." She started to whimper. "I don't know if I can."

Paul handed Solomon back to her. "You have to make it," he said firmly. "You have to make it because of Solomon! God gave him to us, and He did not give him to us so He could destroy him. That's not who our God is."

Shira gazed at Solomon's perfect features. He seemed to return her affectionate look with a smile.

"See," Paul said, "even your son Solomon agrees. You needn't worry. God is going to take care of us."

Lord, thanks for giving me Paul for a husband. He is strong when I am weak.

Just then Doron called, "Paul, Moshe and Nachman are here to see you."

He touched Shira's cheek, then Solomon's, and headed toward the men.

"There have been some developments," Ravitzky began as he led Paul to a secluded table. Levi and Doron trailed behind.

"We've been following some leads on Kavidas and his heritage. They are disturbing," Meschel added with a snort.

"What have you got?" Paul asked curiously.

Ravitzky opened up his PDA to a document. "This is a copy of Kavidas' birth certificate that I managed to locate through some of my connections in Mossad." He enlarged a portion of the document. "Now look at his mother and father's names."

Paul peered intently at the document. "So? They look like they're both innocent enough. His father was Alexander Kavidas, and his mother was Rosella Costanza. We've always known his father was a Greek, his mother Italian."

"Yeah, right," Meschel said sarcastically.

"Now watch this." Ravitzky scrolled down to the officially recorded seal and magnified it to the max. "The seal is a phony! I checked it out with two sources since he has joint citizenship in both America and Italy. My sources were not able to locate a genuine birth certificate in Italy when I checked with the Consulate and Bureau of Records in Rome—"

"It had mysteriously disappeared!" Meschel broke in.

"The only so-called 'birth certificate' available on this guy was from the Washington D.C. Bureau of Records, and as you can see, this document has been altered," Ravitzky allowed.

"Somebody's working on the inside to cover up his true identity." Levi shook his head.

"You mean to tell me his birth certificate has never been challenged before today?" Doron asked.

"It wouldn't be the first time a high-ranking politician's birth credentials has been questioned," Ravitzky replied, "and it wouldn't be the first time that the high-ranking politician's true identity was protected by powerful people who did not want his true birthplace or genealogy revealed."

Doron nodded in assent. "Don't you remember the question as to whether or not Adolph Hitler was of Aryan or Jewish parentage?" he said glowering. "Way back before he came to power as Germany's Chancellor Hitler received a 'blackmail' letter from his nephew, William Patrick Hitler, threatening to reveal embarrassing information about Hitler's family tree so Nazi Party lawyer Hans Frank investigated and claimed to have uncovered letters revealing that Hitler's father, Alois Hitler, was the illegitimate child of Alois' mother, Maria Schicklgruber, who was employed as a housekeeper for a Jewish family and that the family's 19-year old son, Leopold Frankenberger, fathered Alois."

"So Hitler was really a Jew?!" Levi asked incredulously.

Ravitzky shrugged. "Hitler made sure any records that could connect him to Judaism were either permanently expunged or destroyed so it could never be proven."

"So what about Kavidas?" Paul asked. "Are you saying that he has done something similar?"

Levi raised an eyebrow. "They're both from the same mold."

"The collage is slowly coming together," Ravitzky reflected. "Paul, don't you remember when we interrogated the 'mule.' and he 'fessed up about the big meeting with the Arabs and Kavidas' 'go-to' man? The question as to why he, a Gentile, and his 'go-to' man, Stein, a Jew, would secretly turn to the Arabs for support may soon be answered."

Meschel sat silently grinding his teeth while cracking his knuckles. "I have a hunch—and I pray my explanation is wrong—but it will make clear many things."

"Let's throw it out there!" Doron suggested. "Maybe your hunch is what we've all been thinking."

"Here! Here!" Ravitzky said in agreement.

"Okay, here goes," Meschel said with a shake of his head. "I bet you my pension that Kavidas is really Persian, not Arab —in point-of-fact, an Iranian in disguise, and that he's really the Antichrist. That means the Antichrist is a Muslim."

A wave of silence came over them. Then...

"The evidence has been building, hasn't it?" Paul said, eyes narrowing on Ravitzky and his PDA.

"What about bringing in some help?" Doron shrugged. "You know, an expert to examine his genealogy who will confirm our conclusions."

"You mean someone learned in comparative linguistics, or semiotics?" Paul said, pulling back to look at him.

"What about an etymologist?" Levi asked.

"We need to be sure." Paul asked Ravitzky and Meschel, "Can you find someone who knows languages—an etymologist, who is not afraid to dig into Kavidas' past?"

"Kavidas has a phenomenal 'snooping' system in place, so it won't be easy to find someone who is qualified and will keep his or her mouth shut," Ravitzky replied.

Paul scanned the faces of the men in front of him who he trusted his life to. "Well? Your thinking?"

They all nodded simultaneously. "The evidence so far is compelling," Levi said solemnly.

"We need to go for it," Hershel said, summarizing their consensus.

TWENTY

Miami

It was early morning on I-95, and the discussion with Jonathan and Brandon was still very fresh in Ben-Korpel's mind. The debate as to whether or not Christians should retaliate to violence and persecution in like manner was troubling him. One part of him applied the principles Joshua and David used when fighting God's enemies, the Canaanites and the Philistines. *Did not David kill Goliath to defend God's honor and rid Israel of the terrorist threat from the Philistines?* This argument included not only defending God's honor but also one of self-defense. When Nehemiah was rebuilding God's Temple in Jerusalem after the Babylonian captivity he advised the laborers to put a shovel in one hand and a sword in the other to defend themselves. The other part of him wanted to apply Christ's principle of "turning the other cheek."

"The Lord will fight for you; you need only to be still. Today the Lord will deliver you into my hand; and I will kill you and take your head from you, you champion of the Philistines, and I will give your body to the fowls of the air." The words of the Bible haunted his conscience. *What do I do? Should I stand and fight for the Lord to defend His honor and His people like Joshua and David, or should I simply submit to aggression and let God take care of it?*

He dwelled on Masada, where over 900 Jewish zealots committed suicide rather than be captives to the Roman government. He remembered the Holocaust, where over six-million Jews were exterminated while the rest of the world stood by and let it happen. Then he remembered the more recent Israeli mentality: The "Samson" option. Israel will not allow them to be exterminated without inflicting collateral damage on their enemies. This warfare mentality has prevented the nation of Israel from being annihilated.

Should I consider myself a warrior or a martyr? He didn't know. He

156

would have to let the Lord help him with the decision.

He needed a cup of coffee and one of these sweet-sticky buns. A blast of caffeine and sugar in the morning always helped him think more clearly.

He drove his car into the Bayside Mall and walked to the Bayside Coffee Shop. He immediately recognized several K-group members from the Miami chapter, along with many patrons with yarmulkes from the nearby Jewish center. The coffee shop, owned by a K-group member, attracted Jewish folk with its kosher menu of lox and bagels. K-group members reveled in the shop since they were able to share the good news of Jesus with whoever would listen.

"Morning, Avraham," Jim, the owner said as Ben-Korpel walked in the door. "The usual?"

Jim had a thing for faces. At one time he could remember a patron's face but not always the name that went with it. A quirk he soon overcame that became his trademark when he took photos of his frequent customers then labeled them and made a collage on the wall next to the cash register. When *Masterlink* took over, he simply ran a private tab for all of his K-group members. At the end of the month they settled their private accounts with gold coins. The non-K-group patrons paid by *Masterlink*.

"Yeah, the usual," Ben-Korpel said. Jim nodded then proceeded to prepare a gourmet coffee with a glazed cinnamon bun—Ben-Korpel's favorite.

Jim brought his order then studied Ben-Korpel's face. "You look distracted. Are you okay?" he probed.

"Heavy schedule the past few days," Ben-Korpel said with a cryptic smile.

"This should fix you up." Jim smiled expansively.

"Jim, look!" he heard from the front of the shop. Jim turned reflexively to see his counterman pointing to a strange-looking man standing in the doorway. The small-framed man wore an overcoat and a baseball hat with one hand in his coat pocket. At first glance he looked like a homeless panhandler about to ask for a handout. But his eyes gave him away. His eyes were that of a predator.

"This looks bad! Very bad," Jim muttered.

Ben-Korpel immediately assessed the situation. "Move slowly to one side," he whispered.

Jim flashed his eyes in agreement, then inched to one side while keeping the rest of his body inert.

The man grinned in triumph as he pulled a push-button trigger out of his pocket and slowly opened his overcoat as the patrons began to recognize the horror. They saw multiple sticks of what looked like dynamite wired to a device that was flashing green with another wire connected to the push-button trigger.

Ben-Korpel coughed several times to muffle the sound as he slowly, yet methodically pulled his Smith &Wesson M&P 9-mm weapon from its holster and held it under the table. He briskly drew the slide fully rearward to chamber a round from the magazine, then waited.

"*Allah-hu—Akbar!*" the man shouted. "All those who do not follow Islam will die!"

Ben-Korpel's Mossad training and his keen animal instincts sensed the tension of the moment and recognized that he had to control the scene. It was the terrorist's life or the lives of those in the coffee shop. He acted accordingly.

A flash came from under Ben-Korpel's table. The man blinked as the 9mm round found its mark in his forehead. His body jerked backward from the force of the bullet just as another round struck him in the neck. He never had a chance to press the button. He dropped in a heap on the sidewalk.

From that moment on Ben-Korpel knew what his calling was to be: a warrior.

Central Avenue, Miami

Central Avenue boasted of fine apparel shops that catered to the elite of Miami. Despite the calamities besetting the world, there were those who found relief from the perils and associate anxiety when spending money. It was the American way. Brandon thought it an excellent location to spread the Word of God.

He walked up to a passerby, handed her a gospel tract, and said,

"Jesus is the Good News."

The woman glanced at the tract, then gave him a dirty look before throwing the tract on the ground and walking on. Brandon smiled, picked up the discarded tract, and approached another passerby on the busy street where shoppers frequented.

"'Jesus is the way, the truth and the life,'" he heard as he turned to see Jonathan standing on the corner with his Bible in hand. "'No man comes to the father but by him.'"

A disgruntled man walked up to Jonathan. "Take that Bible and stick it—" The man used an expletive as Jonathan smiled in return.

"The Lord is coming soon! We all need to repent!" Jonathan called out. "He will never turn away from those who come to him!"

Brandon glanced into an appliance store window and caught a glimpse of a news broadcast. He stopped short. "Jonathan, come here quickly! Avraham is on TV!"

Jonathan bolted to Brandon's side as he looked into the window at the TV and read the news ticker below the live feed coming from the network covering the shooting at the coffee shop. They exchanged glances as reporters interviewed the shop's patrons and then the owner with several brief shots of the terrorist now covered by an FBI body blanket. "This is unbelievable!" Jonathan said. His tone conveyed disbelief.

Brandon continued to read the news ticker. "They branded him a hero." Then he paused and read that the al-Queda terrorist network took credit for the failed attempt, saying the next time there will be no such failure. "They'll put a *fatwa* on Avraham. He'll be a target from now on."

"It looks like Avraham is already prepared to meet the threat," Jonathan said.

Moments later Jonathan walked back to the street corner. A special feeling came over him. He recognized the leading of the Spirit believing his ministry had now been changed. He would take on the challenge of street witnessing with gusto. With power! *Yes, Lord, I want to be used in any way you want, even if it means shouting out your message from the street corners.*

Turn around, he heard from within himself.

Jonathan did a 180 and saw a young man reading one of the tracts

Brandon handed out. *Go to him*, the internal voice directed. *Speak to him*. Jonathan recognized the voice. "Yes, Lord," he whispered.

"Can you explain this?" the young man asked as he flicked the tract. "It says that Jesus is coming again very soon and that a person must get right with God before He does." He looked into Jonathan's eyes, pleading. "What does that mean?"

Jonathan shot a look up to heaven. *Help Lord!* "First of all, what is your name?" The man's eyes bored into Jonathan's. The man was searching, Jonathan just knew it.

"Yasser Sabri," the man replied.

Jonathan knew enough about languages and nationalities to make a calculated guess. "You're Palestinian?"

Sabri nodded. "I've been in America for ten years," he said in relatively good English.

Jonathan shook his hand. "Let's talk," he said and walked him out of the foot traffic to a nook between two stores.

Sabri looked inquisitively at Jonathan. "Can you explain what's happening all around us? I mean the world is falling apart and it seems like all the religious leaders, politicians, and intellectuals don't seem to have any answers." He scratched his head. "Then there's this Kavidas over in Israel who seems to be leading the show." He shook his head. "I'm very confused."

Jonathan realized this was a divine appointment. "All of what you said is true. But what you might not understand is that these events are all in the providence of God. God spoke through the pages of the Bible and predicted well in advance what we are seeing today."

"This 'business' with the homosexuals," he began in a whisper, "is this also in the Bible? I mean things are really very much out of hand with all the laws to protect them. Then there's the AIDS and the millions of people that have died from the plagues—" he stopped short, as if to gather his thoughts, then: "I'm wondering if God is dead."

"God is very much alive," Jonathan reassured Sabri. Then he whistled at Brandon and motioned to him that he was about to invite Sabri into a donut shop. Moments later they were both sitting down at a table. *Lord, it's moments like this that remind me of my calling*, he thought. "Since you asked me, Yasser," he began, "I would like to appeal to both your spirit and conscience."

"I'm listening," Sabri said curiously.

"First, let's order our coffee and donut." Jonathan chuckled then turned serious. "Think about this," he began. "Our society has deviated so far from sound moral principles that they have ended up paying a high price that has recoiled back on us, forcing mankind to re-evaluate the path they have chosen. Unfortunately, it is too late. Venereal diseases and AIDS is the price paid for sexual license. Violence and poverty is the price we paid for the breakdown of the family. In the past societies have been driven back to their senses by the sheer cost of misconduct. But now something is new. The state—our government—no longer sees itself as a moral institution, but as a secular one that took on the role of the alleviator of bad consequences. The state is called upon to remove the inconvenience and costs of misconduct. God and the Bible—even the influence of the corporate church has been rendered impotent. So the reaction to diseases and illegitimacy is not sexual responsibility and abstinence but handing out condoms. And the antidote to drug addiction is clean needles.

"While we think we are solving problems we have actually subsidized them. And by lowering the cost of misconduct, the government has perpetuated it. The corrosive impact on society has continued unabated for decades, and like most solutions that deal with symptoms rather than causes, things only got worse."

Sabri appeared to contemplate the summary of society's condition. "Things look rather grim," Sabri noted dryly.

Jonathan's eyes lit up. "That's when God shows up, Yasser. He shows up when we come to the place where we see that life is very grim without a relationship with him. This is supposed to drive us to him since he is the way, the truth, and the life."

Sabri blinked several times as the coffee and donuts were served. "When I was a boy, I had a Jewish friend who would always say 'oppose bad things when they are small.' But it seems we are well beyond that now. Right?"

This man is a deep thinker, Jonathan thought. *Besides that, he seems ready to act on God's leading.* He prayed he would reach his soul for Jesus. "'We are way beyond that now,'" he repeated. "When the moral compass of this nation pointed in the wrong direction, the Church sat back and let the spiritual, moral, and ethical standards continue to slide down the slippery slope until the stench was so great in God's nostrils that he said, 'It's time to draw the final curtain.' The timetable has been set and we are in the final stage." He said warmly, "Jesus will be back before the end of the year. What is God calling you to do, Sabri?"

Sabri's hand was trembling and sweaty as he prayed to receive Christ as his Savior, but when they finished praying, his hand was calm, steady, and dry.

TWENTY-ONE

The Messianic Wing of the Temple, Jerusalem

The first thing Stein saw as he walked up to the Messianic wing of the Temple were six uniformed men with red berets standing guard. Their posture, insignias, and sidearms typed them as military. As he approached they bolted upright, stood at attention, and then gave him a military salute. "You're with whom?" he asked the one who wore several combat decorations and looked like a leader.

"Sayeret Matkal, Mr. Stein," the man answered in Hebrew.

Stein nodded and continued into Kavidas' office. He was perplexed.

Stein recognized Kavidas' mood immediately: he was somber and reflective; uncharacteristically. "Problem?" Stein asked.

Kavidas' eyes flicked to Stein's face, then away. He looked worried. "Undoubtedly you've noticed that I've invoked my executive privilege to bring in the *Sayeret Matkal* to protect us." He sucked in a deep breath. "Our timetable is rapidly moving along and we are going to need their help to insure there are no interruptions or sudden roadblocks."

Stein blinked. *This sounds serious.* He knew the *Sayeret Matkal* was Israel's finest elite Special Forces unit of the IDF. Specializing in counter-terrorism, deep reconnaissance, intelligence gathering, and hostage rescue, bringing them in was a signal that things have been ratcheted up considerably. "It's your identity, isn't it?" He sensed the other side brought in etymologists who knew Biblical and ancient texts.

Kavidas bit his lower lip, then slowly, almost mechanically, nodded. "Our enemies are working hard to decipher my name. It won't be long before they crack the etymons. Although we have ongoing powers we can call upon in the event of an unexpected attack once my identity is revealed—" he made a sweeping motion—"I thought it best to cover all our bases and bring in armed guards."

"I know the date is fixed and beyond our control, but what does this mean as far as Armageddon is concerned?" Stein asked almost sheepishly.

"You need not be concerned about that, Mort," he replied with renewed gusto, obviously setting his fears aside. "While you're right about the date and time being fixed, we can be sure we are prepared to give the greatest fight since time immemorial. This means you must make sure all the players are in place with all their hardware."

Stein mulled Kavidas' edification over momentarily. Seconds later an overwhelming wave of anxiety swept over him. *"I need not be concerned"? With my eternal future at stake, I shouldn't be concerned? I know the end game, and we lose! If you showed signs of cracking as we near the end—and you're the one who is worshipped—where does that leave me?* An image flashed in his mind. He saw himself in a distant place, a fiery place where the flames were never quenched, and a place where he would never be consumed despite the everlasting torment....

"Mort!" he heard, snapping him out of his daze. "You're drifting again!"

"Sorry," he half-apologized. "Just daydreaming."

"Mort, you need to stay focused."

"Right," he replied penitently. But the troubling thoughts lingered. He had to willfully suppress them, or he couldn't function. "I'll make the necessary calls to the other players to check their readiness."

"That's more like it," Kavidas said with a wry grin. One that Stein hadn't seen before that only aggravated his restless spirit. He made for the door when: "One more thing, Mort," Kavidas said, "the next Bowl Judgment is on its way. This one, like the others, is going to bring great consternation. Be ready."

Stein slipped his shaking hand into his pant pocket to hide his apprehension. "Right."

Jordan Valley Stronghold, Jericho

Spending time alone with you keeps me going, Paul thought as he looked up into the sky outside the fortress. *I need that private time with you, Lord, because every life that would be strong must have its Holy of*

Holies into which only God enters. Of this he was sure. The final curtain of the world's drama was soon to be drawn and this demanded spiritual vigilance in order to maintain mental acuity.

"Encrypted call for you on the satellite phone," Doron interrupted as he walked up with the phone. "It's Jonathan in Miami." Paul smiled then walked off near a grassy knoll with the phone.

"Hello, brother Jonathan," Paul said with a long, theatrical smile. "Give me some good news from the States."

"We've turned the corner over here," Jonathan began. "We have entered into a new phase of our life in the Tribulation. We have 'laid down our guns and picked up our Bibles.'"

"What do you mean?"

"We've come to the conclusion that we've been hindering the Lord from doing His work here by remaining in 'combat' mode," Jonathan explained. "So now we are going to wait and see what the Lord will do."

"A 'hands-off' approach, right?" Paul replied.

"Only from the perspective of 'returning fire,'" Jonathan said. "If one of us is threatened with bodily harm, we should defend ourselves. But, we have to believe that the Lord is going to protect us from Kavidas and his gang now that we are entering into the final quarter."

Paul did an internal assessment then quoted a verse that had become very familiar in the K-groups. "'The Lord will fight for you, you need only to be still,' right?"

"Amen," Jonathan replied.

"How are you managing with the heat from the last Bowl?"

"It's abominably hot," Jonathan replied. "And if that weren't bad enough, the electric companies have mandated restrictions so air conditioners can only be used at night. During the day—the hottest times—we're told to 'tough it out.' Normally people would go to the ocean or to lakes to cool off, but most of the water in those places is contaminated.

"With all the judgments thus far man has reacted against God by becoming very angry and striking out at their fellows. This unbearable heat has just 'raised the temperature' of the crimes. There are senseless murders and beatings every day here in Florida. Home invasions, robberies, smash and dashes...and on and on it goes. Secret police who apparently came out of nowhere—not National Guard or Regular

Army—are acting like we're under Marshall Law. They're keeping what little peace can be gathered." A pause, then: "Few people know what's coming next on God's schedule. That might cool the air down a bit...but not their temperaments, that's for sure."

"Yes, and from what I read, it's on the way." Paul groaned.

"Time to go," Jonathan said. "Be sure to give my brother Simon a big hug for me." He clicked off.

Paul walked slowly toward Doron and handed him the phone then said, "Ask the group to assemble so I can talk to them." He had made a command decision after Jonathan's call.

"You got it!" Doron said and walked off.

The grassy knoll featured two pomegranate trees that allowed shade to fall on the group amidst the heated air. There were no complaints while they sat in the daylight.

"We all know that the darkness Bowl is coming," Paul began as the group fanned themselves. "So I thought we would come outside and enjoy the sunshine while we have it."

"How long will the darkness last?" Gilat asked.

Paul raised both hands in the air. "Unknown. Maybe days; maybe months."

"Local or worldwide?" Doron followed up.

"Unknown," Paul repeated. He heard several sighs emerge from the group. They were getting tired of the Tribulation. He had to say something. "'Be not weary in well doing for in good season you will reap if you faint not,'" he quoted. "I wanted to encourage you to keep your faith and spirits high as we come into the final stretch, my friends. We may not know the details on how the Lord is going to do things, but we do have his light, promises, and road map in our Bibles so we are not completely in 'the dark.'"

"Paul, we have company," Levi said, pointing off behind his field of view.

Paul turned and saw Ravitzky and Meschel approaching with a strange woman. "Greetings in the name of the Lord, Yeshua," Ravtizky announced while walking toward the group. He nodded to acknowledge the others then walked to Paul. "This is Roni Shukrun, our own linguist and polyglot."

166

Paul extended his hand. "Welcome, Roni."

Roni was a beautiful Sabra in her early forties who must have turned the heads of many Israeli men.

"Roni and her husband worked for the Mossad at one time," Ravitzky explained to Paul quietly, "until her husband was killed by an IED planted by Hamas in Nazareth where he was working on an arms smuggling case. Right after that she went 'into the wind,' but we tracked her down. Now she's been working with us."

Paul motioned for Shira to join them and then introduced Roni to her. They seemed to hit it off well as they walked together back to the group. "I need to address the group with a change in tactics," Paul said to Ravitzky.

"Oh?" Ravitzky replied as he swallowed hard. "A little late in the game to change, isn't it?"

"We've gone before the Lord," Paul intoned, "and we have his assurance that we must stand down and watch Him work."

Ravitzky stood looking at Paul, his expression enigmatic. "Does that mean we're going to just lie down and let them crush us?"

"You can't mean that!" Meschel joined in as they exchanged glances.

Paul waved him to silence then moved to stand in front of the whole group. "I called this meeting here in the glorious sunlight to share with you why I believe we must change our approach to the adversaries we face daily." He paused and held up his satellite phone momentarily then continued. "I spoke with Jonathan in Miami, and my heart was pierced after he told me that they are no longer going to face off with Kavidas' gang and the Islamic terrorists who have thrown in with him. No, they are now relying totally on the Lord for protection."

He raised his voice an octave. "They are no longer equipping themselves with weapons but are relying on the Lord to defend them. You might say they have adopted a 'martyr' mentality—meaning they are willing to die for what they believe—if need be. However, let me add that they believe if they 'stand down,' the Lord will show up. Their thinking is that spiritual forces cannot work while earthly forces are active."

Ravitzky's hand shot up in the air. "If we are threatened and our life is in danger, do we just stand there and allow them to behead us?" He smirked and crossed his arms across his chest to wait for the answer.

Paul knew that question was coming. He nodded and pulled out his pocket Bible. "For a time we have neglected some of the more salient principles Christ gave us pertaining to survival during this period, but it is time for us to dig them out of our Bibles and apply them."

He turned to Matthew 10 and read, "'But when they arrest you, do not worry about what to say or how to say it. At that time you will be given what to say, for it will not be you speaking, but the Spirit of your Father speaking through you...when you are persecuted in one place, flee to another. I tell you the truth, you will not finish going through the cities of Israel before the Son of Man comes.'"

He turned to Luke 21. "'They will deliver you to synagogues and prisons, and you will be brought before kings and governors, and all on account of my name. But make up your mind not to worry beforehand how you will defend yourselves. For I will give you words and wisdom that none of your adversaries will be able to resist or contradict...but not a hair of your head will perish. By standing firm you will gain life.'" He said with vigor, "And here is the part I love the best: 'When these things begin to take place, stand up and lift up your heads, because your redemption is drawing near!'"

When he lifted his eyes off the pages of Scripture, the group was standing with their heads bowed in prayer. Paul had his answer. There was no need for a vote.

Hershel and Doron approached him. Hershel gave him a thumbs-up and said, "We will prepare to relocate and wait on the Lord."

"I will take it upon myself to inform the group at Petra," Doron said with renewed gusto.

"That's the spirit!" Paul replied with a smile as he recognized his words penetrated their hearts. All but two.

Ravitzky and Meschel approached Paul. Their expressions spoke volumes. "Your little 'pep talk' had its effect on those who the Lord has called to be 'martyrs'," Ravitzky said, glowering. "But let me remind you that those who oppose the battle sit at leisure at the expense of those committed and willing to serve to defeat the enemy—be it Kavidas or terrorism." He pointed to Meschel and added, "We are not among those 'martyrs' you spoke of. We have been called to resist aggression against the Jews, as well as resist those who seek to destroy our faith."

Paul put his hand on Ravitzky's shoulder. "Brother, we are not going to be 'at leisure' but very active in witnessing and proclaiming the Gospel of salvation. Justification and vindication will come when Christ returns." He breathed deeply to garner strength. "But as for you, you must act as the Lord directs you. If your calling is to guard the Holy of Holies by force, then so be it."

Meschel blinked several times. "Can we have your blessing as we go forward with our purpose and calling, Paul?"

Paul called Levi and Ruby over to form a prayer circle, then called God's anointing down on the two newly cast warriors.

Moments later Paul turned to Ravitzky and Meschel. "Bring Roni into the fortress so we can talk."

Ravitzky quickly realized that Paul shared his mission to uncover the true identity of Kavidas and that the mission would include Roni Shukrun. "Right away," he said.

He walked two meters toward Roni and Shira, then froze in place and looked up into the sky. A massive black hand came out of the heavens.

"Oh, God!" he exclaimed as the horror of the next judgment unfolded before his eyes.

A great darkness swept over the land as the hand touched the earth. A heavy darkness that could be felt.

TWENTY-TWO

The Mosque of Al-Aqsa, Temple Mount

Solidarity was the theme behind Kavidas' meeting at the Al-Aqsa Mosque located at the southern part of the Temple Mount. The mosque stands almost on the site of Solomon's palace and was used in ancient times as the headquarters of the knights of the Templar's, a fitting place Kavidas thought to gather the leaders of the Muslim population for a rally. It was his way of avenging the atrocities of the Crusades.

But the cloak of darkness was disturbing to him. He had to overcome the divine judgment to bring glory to his cause; a plan was needed that ran counter to Stein's suggestion of bringing in generators and floodlights to illuminate the site, adding that automobile headlights could be used to light the area in the middle of the day. No, he rejected that plan to further his own glorification.

Despite Kavidas' assurances, the anxiety of the judgments wouldn't leave Stein. He hated darkness, of which this new Bowl Judgment brought out renewed fears. The adjustment in his life cycle due to the reduction in the sunlight was difficult, but he managed. But this eerie darkness—a total darkness over the land of Israel—raised new questions. He questioned himself. He questioned his messiah. He questioned the providence and the Scriptures that foretold of his future. He questioned everything. *What am I doing and where am I going?* The darkness really troubled him seemingly much more than it troubled his messiah.

The weakness was noticeable, especially to Kavidas.

Kavidas stood on the step of the mosque and waved the large group of designated imams over to him, then pointed to the bank of votive candles Stein had brought in that provided a slight rendering of light for

170

the occasion.

"You see these lights?!" he boomed defiantly. "Well these represent the side that brought this darkness upon us." Then he pointed to himself and then made a sweeping motion in the air. "But I represent the light of the world and whoever walks with me will never walk in darkness!" With that he dropped to his knees and began praying.

The Islamic scholars exchanged glances, then looked at Stein standing next to Kavidas. "What do we do?!" an aged imam shouted out.

Stein looked skyward then held out his upturned hands as Kavidas continued in his prayer posture. "Just be still and see the salvation of the lord," he said in mock solemnity.

Seconds later a brilliant white light burst forth from the Al-Aqsa mosque that radiated out in all directions and lit up the entire Temple Mount. The dazzling rays stunned the imams, who stood awestruck, waiting for some word from their leader. But they would have to hold their breath and wait.

The light intensified exponentially until the imams could no longer tolerate it. Many shielded their eyes from the blinding beams with their hands, while others fell to the ground in fear and trembling, covering their heads with their prayer shawls. "Save us!" they began to chant. "Save us!"

Kavidas slowly stood up and raised his hands while the imams looked at him and fell silent in anticipation of his words. "God is light, and in him is no darkness at all." The crowd stood up and mumbled amongst themselves. "I know that you believe in God," he added, his voice vibrating with intensity. "So believe also in me." He paused momentarily, then cried out, "Allah is to be praised!" Suddenly the light emanating from the mosque mysteriously began to dissipate. The imams looked on in wonder then shouted, *"Allah-hu-Akbar! Allah-hu-Akbar!"*

Stein waved them to silence then turned to Kavidas. "Listen to the anointed one!" Stein yelled out.

A hush came over the crowd.

"I have special powers from on high," Kavidas said reverently. "This command I have received from heaven. And these powers were given to me as a sign to authenticate my calling to unite us in one common purpose and that is to proclaim goodness over evil and God over Satan! You adhere to this creed and God has raised me up to bring in his kingdom through Islam. Now I am going to prove to you who I really am."

Two elderly imams exchanged quizzical looks, then stepped out of the group. "But we were told you are the Jewish messiah. Does not your wondrous works confirm this?"

"What do you have to do with Islam?" a voice from the group asked.

Kavidas motioned for them to calm down. "I have already met with Islamic heads of State and have vowed to join with them in their battle for victory over the Jews and other infidels," he asserted. "Plans are in place to see that victory to fruition and our meeting today is an extension of that plan. Does not the sacred *Qur'an* predict that in the end Islam will conquer all? Therefore I must have your support!"

One of the elderly imams stepped forward. "Your Excellency," he began as he momentarily turned toward the rest of the group. "I, along with the others am confused. Why would you, a Gentile with a Greek and Italian heritage who has been called to be the Jewish messiah now offer to join with us in our battle against the very people you represent to God?"

"Because I am not Greek or Italian," he said dogmatically. "I am Iranian."

A great hush came over the site as the darkness returned.

TWENTY-THREE

Christian Fortress, Petra

Despite the melancholia brought on by the darkness, the regathering of the two K-groups was to be a celebration. Paul and Yashur agreed that wine be served at dinner as another reminder of the need to rejoice in the Lord when adversity comes. The wine would make the heart of man merry.

Marta and Gilat led the women in festive dance music while the men headed off to an antechamber to discuss weightier matters.

"What is your thinking on this darkness?" Hershel asked his father as the other men found their comfort station in the cave.

Norman shot a look at Paul then back to his son. "I believe it's only temporary. Biblically speaking, I think it will only last 40 days—God's number for testing."

"We know that it is only local—here in Israel—because Jonathan in Miami tells me things are normal over there," Paul added.

"This judgment of darkness reminds me of the account of our Lord on the cross at Calvary," Levi explained. "It wasn't an eclipse or a sandstorm as some liberal critics claimed but a heaven-sent darkness." A tear formed in his eye. "It was as though all creation was sympathizing with the Creator as he blacked out the scene when the sin of man was poured into His Son's body. He was made sin for us who knew no sin."

"Like the darkness in Egypt before Passover," Asher said.

"Yeah, like in Passover, when the darkness preceded the putting of the blood of the lamb over the doorposts of the Israelites' homes. It was like unregenerate man living in darkness before the Lamb of God—our Passover—is applied to the doorposts of our hearts," Doron explained. "Afterward the light appears."

"Paul, come quick!" Shira shouted. Paul bolted out the cave to the meeting place as the other men rushed behind him.

An awesome scene awaited them as they came to a sudden halt. Kapporeth stood at the end of a golden staircase that extended from the cave floor, beyond the field of view, all the way up into space and on into the heavenly sphere. When looking at the staircase there were angelic beings ascending and descending on it. They were traveling from earth to the very abode of God.

"It's Jacob's Ladder!" Marta shouted out. The rest of the group stood in silence as the marvel of God unfolded.

Kapporeth walked to the group, then lifted up his hand to the Most High who dwells in the Third Heaven. "The Lord has heard your prayer of dependence upon Him and has sent me to instruct you."

Many began to bow down in reverence and worship when Kapporeth lowered his hands and cried out, "Stand up! I am a fellow servant! Bow down only to the God of the universe and his Anointed!"

Estelle and Dalia began to shake when Kapporeth walked to them and put his hands on their shoulders. "Fear not!" he hollered in a booming voice. Immediately their shaking ceased. "The God in whom I serve has decreed this judgment of darkness to be a sign that the end is near, it is even at the door!" He made a sweeping motion and shouted out, "Mankind will refuse to repent of their sin! Mankind will gnaw at their tongues in torment, for this thick darkness will bring gloom! Mankind has not seen neither shall be any more after it a darkness of this kind that will bring great trembling! Mankind will continue to blaspheme the Name of the Most High because there is no remedy!"

Time stood still until Kapporeth walked to Paul and silently touched his forehead with his thumb then walked to Levi and did the same. From there he walked to Asher, Simon and Hershel repeating the anointing. "You men will proclaim the gospel of Jesus Christ in Jerusalem and the Lord will do a mighty work," he said to the five men, then turned to the rest of the group. "Your calling is here. You will receive shelter from the storm as long as you obey the word of the Lord: do not depart from this place alone." All the other men and women silently nodded.

Kapporeth held up his hand to the group as if to pronounce a blessing and then walked up the staircase to go back to where he came from. His image grew smaller and smaller as they watched until the golden staircase faded from view.

"This vision confirms our mission," Paul announced as the room returned to normal. He nodded to the other four men. "We should leave as soon as we're able."

He went to Shira, who was crying. "I'm afraid for you," she lamented. She handed Solomon to him. "You have a son now. You must not take any chances."

He placed Solomon over his shoulder and patted him. "I don't believe the Lord sent Kapporeth from heaven to come and anoint us then turn around and see that we're killed," he asserted calmly.

Shira sighed. "I must believe the Lord will keep you in safeguard." She began to sob. "If anything happens to you—"

He placed his fingers on her lips to stop her from speaking her fear. "Shush!" He held her and Solomon tightly, then closed his eyes and prayed, "'The LORD God is a sun and shield; the LORD will give grace and glory. No good thing will he withhold from them that walk uprightly. O LORD of hosts, blessed is the man who trusts in you.'"

"We will watch over her and your son," Doron, Gadi, and Yashur said collectively. Norman and Alfonse Rivera smiled in agreement.

"Time to go, Paul," he heard from behind. He turned to see Levi, Asher, Simon, and Hershel assembled.

"You need to go," Shira said as she dried her eyes with her free hand.

Rapid footsteps from behind...

"Paul! Moshe and Nachman just arrived with that woman Roni Shukrun!" Yashur thundered as he bolted into the room. "He said he has urgent news about Kavidas!"

Paul stared at Shira while processing the bulletin. His heart raced as he rushed with Levi, Asher, and Simon to Ravitzky's side. His mind conjured up all kinds of possibilities that constituted the urgency, but he was not prepared for what came next.

"We cracked the code surrounding the *mysterious* Kavidas!" Ravitzky announced. Standing next to him by the table piled with papers were Meschel and Roni Shukrun, who had a large book in her hand.

"What have you come up with?" Levi asked.

"Kavidas is Iranian!" Ravitzky blurted out. "And his real name is not Gregory A. Kavidas that we have been led to believe all these years. His real name is *Reza Pahlava!*"

"My gut was telling me this guy's a Muslim all along!" Meschel said, full of outrage.

"This is confirmed?" Paul asked, looking at Shukrun.

Shukrun nodded then opened the book she was carrying and invited Paul to sit down at the table. "This is the *Gematria*, and I have carefully examined all the possibilities of this Kavidas. I am convinced his real name is Reza Pahlava. When we convert this name into Farsi Iranian, the numerical equivalence is 666!"

Paul knew about Jewish books. He knew about the *Torah*, the *Tanach*, the *Talmud*, and the *Kabbalah*. But he knew little about the *Gematria*. "Explain it to me, Roni."

Shukrun nodded. "The *Gematria* is a system of assigning numerical value to a word or phrase, in the belief that words or phrases with identical numerical value bear some relation to each other, or bear some relation to the number itself as it may apply to a person's age, the calendar year, or his name. The word *gematria* is generally held to derive from Greek *geometria* or geometry."

"Do you see the link to his alleged Greek heritage?" Meschel asked Paul curiously.

Paul nodded. The link being Kavidas' claim to both Italian and Greek parentage all being a cover-up to his true identity.

"Now watch this," Shukrun said as she began writing on a pad while referring to the *Gematria*. Within one minute she wrote out:

R=108
E=30
Z=156
A=6

P=96
A=6
H=48
L=72
A=6
V=132
A=6
666

Paul studied the letters and the numbers. "This explains everything," he said at last. "Now we know why he's been pandering to the Muslim population while pretending to be on the side of the Jewish people."

"Could this be incorrect?" Hershel asked.

"No. I've been a professor of etymology at Bar-Ilan University for the past 20 years. I know my work. There is no error," Shukrun asserted.

"To think that the nation of Israel would go after a Muslim Antichrist is just unbelievable!" Yashur said from behind. They turned to see him in the archway, listening to the entire conversation.

"That's because they are predisposed to believe a lie," Levi said. "Satan is the father of lies and this has to be his best lie yet—duping the nation with a false messiah who is, in fact, a Muslim while rejecting the true Messiah, Jesus Christ."

Yes, Paul thought, *Satan is the liar that convinced Islam that their religion is the only true religion and one of peace.* Satan even convinced Islam that when the Mahdi came that he would bring together with love people from all faiths and holding all kinds of ideas, will enable them to see one another's good sides by strengthening their feelings of friendship and brotherhood, and will ensure they treat one another with understanding. They were taught that when the Mahdi appeared, love would rule the world and people would abandon all feelings of hatred and anger. So much that, the writings in the *Qur'an* described how even the fish in the sea and the birds in the air will be content with the environment of beauty and love of which the Mahdi will be instrumental, and that love for the Mahdi will descend on everyone's hearts. The sincere love people feel for the Mahdi will be instrumental in them trusting each other with love, affection, and compassion.

Yeah, right, he thought. When he reflected on Kavidas, now Pahlava the imposter, he recognized that this prophetic utterance never happened. Not only did Pahlava bring division in the world between Jews, Christians and Muslims—a far cry from the promised peace, but this false messiah is indeed the Islamic Antichrist that will take millions with him into eternal damnation.

"So *what* is their belief about our Jesus?" Yashur asked.

Shukrun closed the *Gematria* and turned to Yashur. "Muslims reject the idea Jesus was or is the Son of God. According to Islam, Jesus is not as the Bible articulates, God in the flesh. Second, in Islamic belief, Jesus never died on the cross for the sins of mankind. The *Qur'an* specifically denies that Jesus was ever crucified or that He ever experienced death. Muslims believe that after Allah miraculously delivered Jesus from death, He ascended into heaven alive in a fashion to the Biblical narrative regarding Elijah. To Muslims, Jesus was merely another prophet in the long line of prophets that Allah has sent to mankind. When Jesus comes back, they believe He comes back as a radical Muslim.

"This Muslim interpretation of Jesus," Shukrun continued, "is for Jesus to kill a figure known as the *Dajjal*, or the Muslim version of the Antichrist. Jesus will kill not only the *Dajjal* but also all of the *Dajjal's* followers, most of whom will be Jews. They make Jesus out to be a vigilante or an avenger. Also, they claim Jesus will also marry, have children and eventually die.

"The *Dajjal* will claim to be divine and will claim to be Jesus Christ, the Jewish Messiah, according to the *Qur'an*. He will defend Israel against the Mahdi and the prophet Jesus, and he will deceive many people into leaving Islam. If the Islamic prophecies are indeed intertwined with the unfolding of Biblical prophecy, then we can see that part of Satan's strategy is that, when the real Jesus returns, there will already be a worldwide religious leader claiming to be Jesus, namely the False Prophet. If this were the case, then Muslims worldwide would accuse the real Jesus of being the *Dajjal*, the Muslim Antichrist. According to Islamic apocalyptic traditions, Muslims expect two Jesuses to come: the real and the false one.

"This Muslim Jesus is a contorted version of the Biblical Jesus who espouses the cause of the Mahdi. Instead of saving those followers of His whom the Father has placed under His oversight, the Muslim Jesus instead slaughters those who remain faithful to the words of Jesus as found in the Bible."

"Now that's sick!" Hershel said. "How do they explain that Jesus— born a Jew to the house of David—suddenly becomes a Muslim? Is there some conversion that occurs in heaven that we don't know about?"

Paul turned and hissed. "Hardly!"

"So his entire operation is one of deception, right?" Hershel asked. "He deceived the Jews, the Gentiles, and now the Arabs, right?"

Asher nodded. "Now you're getting it."

"This slaughter you mentioned, Roni, what's that about?" Yashur asked, definitely upset.

"For the past twenty years Islam has been fulfilling Jesus' words where he predicted future persecution against Christians and explained that those who committed this persecution would think they were performing a service to God. Both Islam and Christianity—Catholic and Protestant—have been guilty of this very thing of murdering those perceived as heretics from the only true religion. Whether it is Jihad, the Crusades, The Inquisition—they all fit the requirements of murder for and in the name of God. It is impossible to imagine any belief system or philosophy on the earth that could carry out such a thing if it were not a well-organized and established world religion. The system that carries this out in the final days will be a religious system that believes it is the earthly custodian of some form of global divine government." She pointed to her papers on the table. "Only the religion of Islam has fulfilled these requirements."

Hershel raised a finger. "I see it as—" He stopped to collect his thoughts then added, "It's almost like the Lord has been using Islam to punish humanity since they rejected Him and turned to their own devices for salvation. Then He brought in the end game where the Islamic Antichrist would fulfill the desires of man, who would accept him as the true messiah."

"Now you're getting it," Levi confirmed once more. "And Kav—" he stopped himself. "And Pahlava is the main man!"

"I've heard enough!" Meschel said sharply. "We need to take care of this Pahlava right now before he kills any more innocent people!"

"It's no longer our way," Paul argued. "We have to leave him to the Lord."

Meschel shot a look at Ravitzky. They both nodded. "Well then, maybe the Lord has commissioned others to take care of him," Meschel snarled back.

"It's not God's way," Paul persisted.

"Did not David tell his men 'gird you on every man his sword...'?!" Ravitzky snapped.

Seconds later both Ravitzky and Meschel bolted out of the fortress heading toward Jerusalem.

TWENTY-FOUR

Miami

Moments of nostalgia seized his heart as he sat in his car in front of the Galleria Mall watching the corporate owner's workmen board up the windows of the countless shops and stores that once captivated the well-to-do of Miami. *Oh, how the mighty have fallen*, Jonathan thought. The mighty businesses and enterprises of man have all come to nothing in the wake of the Great Tribulation. When he turned his head he saw several faded posters on the walls advertising high-end fashion pocketbooks, wristwatches, and shoes—things that no longer were of interest to those in the Great Tribulation. No, the time had come when mankind was fighting for their survival against the judgments of God. Video games, DVDs, and other vehicles of entertainment have been replaced with textbooks and manuals that were once relegated to sunken ship survivors on deserted islands. So-called "victory gardens" and homemade water distillers had replaced lawnmowers and golf clubs in man's effort to stem the tide of starvation and thirst. Items of relaxation were no longer important as man sought to stay alive.

A tap-tap-tap on his window.

Jonathan slowly turned his head to see an unshaven man in a disheveled, stained suit holding a plastic shopping bag. He lowered his window. "Say mister," the man said, "can you help me out with some food or some *Masterlink* credits?"

Jonathan's heart sunk as he looked at the man. "I don't have any *Masterlink* credits because I don't believe in them. But I have some granola bars in my glove box that you're welcome to."

The man nodded. "I would appreciate it," he replied in a hoarse whisper.

Jonathan reached over and grabbed two granola bars out of his glove box, then asked the man, "What's your name?" He was hoping for a divine opportunity in which to share the Lord with him.

The man peered at him suspiciously then grinned. "You look like a nice man," he said as he stuffed the bars in his bag, "So I'll trust you. My name is Michael Weinstein."

"Would you like to come inside? Or maybe I could drive you someplace?" Jonathan asked. It was apparent the man was homeless, but Jonathan believed there was something else the man needed beside some food.

The man looked around in wonder, then said, unsolicited, "I used to be a loan officer in Bank Gibraltar here in Miami, but as you can see, I'm no longer employed."

"Please come inside for a few moments," Jonathan urged, "and then I'll drive you to get something more than just those granola bars to eat."

Michael glanced sheepishly around again. "You're sure it's okay?"

"Yes, it's okay."

Jonathan quickly recognized as they drove off that it was probably a long time since Michael had a shower and no doubt even longer since he had a decent meal. "Tell me your story, Michael. How did things come to this?"

Michael nibbled on one of the granola bars, then said with a sigh, "It seems like decades ago, but it was just over six years when that *Masterlink* system started. At first everyone in the banking system believed a cashless society would ease our workload while increasing our revenue, but that didn't happen. What the banking officials didn't realize was that banking laws were modified so that the banks were converted into credit clearing houses while all the revenue was funneled into the *Masterlink* system. At first the banks received a small percentage, but when the system went global, the percentage reduced so that your mainline banks were unable to operate. I was terminated—and that was after twenty-two years of service.

"I took a second mortgage on our home to tide us over until I could get another job, but that never happened. Within a year we lost our home then went to live with my sister-in-law, but that became too much of a hassle because she interfered too much in my family's life, so we moved out and eventually wound up on the streets. In time my family went their separate ways." He turned and stared out the window. "Now it's just me."

"Never saw them again?" Jonathan asked.

"My wife picked up with another man—I guess it became 'every man for himself' after a while, and my two sons wandered off someplace." He took a deep breath and repeated his refrain. "Now it's just me."

"Well, Michael, today things are going to be different," Jonathan said with a smile. "Has anybody ever shared Jesus with you?"

"You can let me out here, Mac," he said, becoming defensive. He started pulling on the door handle. "At one time I prayed to God to help me and my family—" he pointed to his soiled clothes—"and this is what I got in return."

Lord, I need help, Jonathan prayed. *Help me to reach this man.* "Just relax and hear me out. Whatever disappointment you have with God, I want you to know that He loves you and has a plan for your life. God's ways are so far above our ways. Sometimes our Lord allows situations in our life to develop in order for us to see out great need for Him. Man has always applauded his own achievements, leaving God out until a crisis. His word tells us that He will have no other gods before Him. He is not a crisis God. He is God, and there is no other. You just need to trust in Him and ask for forgiveness of your sins. Once you do that and the Lord becomes your Savior, you have a new relationship with God. Your sins are forgiven and you are a new creature; old things are passed away and all things become new. He will provide all you needs according to his riches in Christ Jesus. "Having done that, you begin to see things from God's perspective. He opens your eyes so you begin to realize His sovereignty and that all things that happen in your life are for a reason and His purpose."

Michael stared blankly out the car window. "So what would be the purpose in my losing my job and family?"

"In the providence of God, if that hadn't happened," Jonathan explained as he dropped his voice, "you may never have run into me and you may never have heard about God's plan for your life."

He wiggled in his seat. "Okay, I'll bite. What's this plan?"

"The plan is for you to surrender your life to Christ, short and simple," Jonathan replied. "Admit that you're unable to manage your life so that it pleases God, that sin has separated you from Him, and that you need Him in your life, first to manage your sin, next to manage your future." He reached over and patted Michael's shoulder. "That's it."

"There's got to be more than that," he argued.

"No, there isn't." Jonathan tapped the steering wheel twice. "That's why most people miss the whole plan of salvation because they make it too complicated." He could tell from Michael's expression that he connected with him. He was thinking. He was processing the data. He was getting it.

"It's the only thing that makes any sense in this crazy world," he said after several moments of contemplation. Then he turned and asked, "Is everything that's going on in this crazy world in God's plan as well?"

"Everything," Jonathan replied with certainty. "In fact, the Almighty has orchestrated *everything* we are experiencing and will experience until Jesus comes back very soon."

Horns honked.

Jonathan suddenly realized the traffic light he stopped for was now green. "Time flies when you're having fun, right?" he quipped. He stepped on the gas pedal and they continued on.

"This whole business with *Masterlink* and these catastrophes—are they all from God?" Michael whispered in wonder.

"All of it," Jonathan replied with a smile. "God's purpose is to bring mankind to salvation, first through His love and if that fails, through the pain of judgment."

Michael nodded several times. "Do you think His plan is working?"

Jonathan shot him a look—straight in his eyes. "I'll answer that after you answer this question: Do you want to pray to receive Christ?"

Michael bit his lip as he pondered the question then said, "Yes."

Jonathan pulled the car to the nearest curb to pray with Michael. "See, to answer your questions, yes, I believe it *is* working."

They prayed together.

"I feel washed and cleansed inside." Michael sighed blissfully.

"Jesus' blood has that purifying power," Jonathan said as he pulled back into traffic. "Now that you belong to Christ, you will see how he will use you mightily as a Jewish believer."

"I look forward to that!"

Jonathan's cell phone vibrated and chimed at the same time. He glanced at the caller-ID. It was Paul in Jordan. "I have to take this," he said and pulled over to the side of the road once again.

"No 'hands-free' phone system?" Michael pointed to the overhead microphone.

"My phone is encrypted and we don't want it on the Net or any other surveillance system," he said. "No *Bluetooth* for me."

Michael blinked and shrugged.

Jonathan's expression piqued Michael's curiosity as he listened on his cell phone for the first two minutes. He heard bits and pieces while trying not to eavesdrop, but in the confines of the vehicle privacy was difficult.

Then suddenly he heard: "Kavidas is really a Muslim? Somehow that doesn't come as a shock. He's been playing both sides, now that we're nearing the end of days he's drawing the Arabs in for Armageddon." Then with a nod Jonathan added, "His real name is Reza Pahlava? No doubt it adds up to 666, right?" A pause then: "Yeah, that's what I figured." Jonathan looked askance at Michael. "The master of *Masterlink* is really an Arab," he said.

Michael just shook his head ever so slowly in unbelief.

Moments later Jonathan ended the call as they pulled into the parking lot of Lane Drugs.

Michael sat rigidly in the passenger seat. "Why doesn't God do something about this Kavidas or Pahlava, or whatever his cursed name is?"

"He will very soon," Jonathan replied. "But for now, the Holy Spirit as the Restrainer of evil is allowing him to manifest his full propensity to create chaos and mayhem to punish mankind for their rejection of Christ, as well as bringing Israel to their knees until they cry out the messianic greeting, 'Blessed is he that comes in the name of the Lord.'

"A Christian theologian by the name of John Calvin once said, 'There remains in a regenerate man a smoldering cinder of evil, from which desires continually leap forth to allure and spur him to commit sin.' If that is what we can expect from Christians who have been regenerated, how much more evil can we expect from the unregenerate man during these times when the Restrainer has been ordered to withhold his influence."

"So non-Christians can do whatever they want now, right? Full bore? Full vent?"

Jonathan nodded in assent. "Look around you. What do you see? Do you see the confusion and lack of purpose in society? The lack of spiritual integrity? The moral turpitude? The moral relativism? The emotional and physical dependency on drugs, porno and alcohol? Society has finally been unleashed to do whatever it wants as you say, and look at the mess it has made of things."

Tears welled up in Michael's eyes as he shook his head. "God help us," he lamented.

Jonathan smiled. "He will. That's his promise." He pulled the handle to open the door and said, "Let's go!"

Michael was surprised to meet Brandon in his T-shirt. The heat generated from Bowl Four was more than the air conditioners at Lane Drugs could manage. Nearly all his employees wore sweat bands on their foreheads to curb the perpetual perspiration. The constant slugging down of bottled water quickly became an acceptable sight throughout the company.

Brandon handed Jonathan a bottle of water and said as he looked at Michael, "Who's your friend?"

Jonathan picked up the cue. "This is my newfound 'friend' Michael. He is now a new babe in Christ."

Brandon shook hands with Michael while his eyes assessed his condition. He walked him over to a chair and said, "Have a seat."

Michael gave Brandon a strange look as he pointed to his soiled clothes. "It's all right, Michael," Brandon said. "We have long since dropped protocol." Michael slowly sat down then Brandon asked, "How long have you been on the streets?

Michael shot a look at Jonathan. "I guess—" he fumbled for words— "two years three months."

"Well, today is your last day at being homeless because you're coming home with me to a nice bed and a good meal," Brandon said with a smile.

"You mean you trust me enough to take me into your home?" Michael replied incredulously as he sat in the chair, his shoulders hunched.

"With Jesus coming back very soon, we don't have time to fool around," Brandon said, pointing to Jonathan. "If you're good enough to ride in his car, you're good enough to sleep in one of my beds."

Michael shook his head in disbelief at his newfound friends and fortune. "Is it okay to use the rest room to wash up a bit?" he asked humbly.

"Of course," Brandon said and motioned in the direction of the rest room as Michael rose from the chair and walked out.

"Did you receive a phone call from Paul?" Jonathan asked the second the door closed.

"Unbelievable," Brandon replied with a nod. "This Kavidas thing explains many things in my mind. The direction our world has taken with Islam becoming the dominant religion—sure it makes perfect sense."

"He explained the darkness over there?"

"Yeah, he told me about that as well," Brandon replied as he walked over to a book case cabinet and opened the door. Taped to the door was a chart of some sort. Brandon took out his pen from his shirt pocket and said as he wrote on the chart, "Now we're at Bowl Five, the darkness in Israel."

"And Bowl Six is not far behind," Jonathan added as he raised an eyebrow.

"Come quickly Lord Jesus," Brandon replied as he walked to Jonathan and handed him a copy of the *Southern Sentinel* newspaper. "Look at the article on page two where three members of a radical Islamic group jumped a Christian woman as she came out of her church here in Miami. It so happens that a 'Lone Ranger' came to her rescue and took all three out with a 9-millimeter." He handed the paper to Jonathan and added, "Any idea who this 'Lone Ranger' might be?"

Jonathan's lips pursed in a soundless whistle as he opened the paper and started reading. "Are you thinking it's Avraham?"

"Who else? I mean his signature is all over the slaying," Brandon suggested. "Don't you remember what he said at our last meeting? It has to be him; no question about it." He shook his head. "He's become a renegade of sorts as he defends the helpless Christians against Muslims—sort of like a 'caped crusader."

Jonathan snapped the page on the paper. "Or maybe he's an angel

186

looking out for the innocent. I guess justice must be served if the courts will not protect God's people," he said with a sigh. "But this doesn't seem like God's way." *I wonder how many more notches Ben-Korpel will cut into his belt before Jesus returns,* he didn't say.

"The K-groups here in America are hailing this crusader as a hero," Brandon explained. "There's a part of the human psyche that wants justice now, like you mentioned, and also later when they go before the Lord at the GWT. For the most part, the K-groups are waiting on the Lord to return and have gone passive, but there's an internal element who is cheering for this guy who is acting like a David against the Islamic Goliath."

Jonathan had to think on that statement. *With all that the Believers during the Tribulation have had to endure: The judgments from God and the human response that resulted in man eating their domestic animals for food, seeing their children die from mutated diseases, watching vegetation being consumed by pestilence and wild beasts, enduring massive earthquakes, observing frightening astrophysical disturbances in the heavens, adjusting to the reduction in daylight and then add the unbearable heat and drought—is it any wonder that humankind triumphed a hero like this Lone Ranger?* No, even as one of God's chosen evangelists, he couldn't argue with them.

"Am I interrupting something?" they heard from behind. Brandon turned to see Michael in the doorway

"No, Michael," Brandon said, "we were just finishing up." He nodded at Michael. "You and I need to go. It's time you saw your new home."

Michael's eyes lit up.

TWENTY-FIVE

Temple Mount, Jerusalem

Ravitzky's message to his Mossad contact inside the *Yediot Aharonot,* Israel's widely circulated newspaper, paid off. By the time Paul and the others reached the Temple Mount, several thousand curious Jews were assembled. The newspaper article promised that the true identity of the messianic person would be revealed to the shock and horror of every patriotic Jew in Israel suffering from the judgments of God. The news item incensed Pahlava and Stein.

Office of the Messianic Person

"Call the *Al-Hayat* TV station and have them send a crew to the Mount so that by the time we get over there, we'll have plenty of Arab coverage to offset all the Jews," Pahlava ordered.

Stein nodded in agreement then hesitated fractionally as he looked out the window to the Mount where the waiting Jews were carrying portable lights to illuminate the darkness. Moving shadows mixed with half-lit faces together with the specter of the unknown reminded him of his future. The eerie sight unnerved him. "Is this going to be like Elijah and the priests of Baal on Mount Carmel?" he asked with an edge of skepticism.

"Maybe so," Pahlava replied. "They will have their people, and we will have ours."

"Yeah, but who wins?" he muttered under his breath. More waves of troublesome doubt were washing onto the shores of his mind. "These

Christians now know who you are, and they are going to make it public. It's going to be like a bursting bomb! This bomb is going to be more explosive than when you declared you were the messianic person." He shook his head. "What are your plans to compensate?"

Weakness! I despise weakness! Must I be questioned by my subordinate? Are my decisions to be challenged? No! This is going to be my finest hour! "Mort, lately you have been giving me the impression that you are succumbing to doubting."

He pointed his finger in Morton's face, raised his voice two octaves, and flared, "This is not the time to doubt!" He stared at Mort momentarily, then offered a cryptic smile: "You know who wins! We don't win! You know that! It was ordained before the creation of the universe. Do I need to remind you of that? But we will take millions with us. And that's where our victory will be."

Mort stiffened. The reminder that his destiny was irrevocably engraved in the annals of time and predicted in Scripture had escaped him. He was being controlled by forces outside the bounds of his authority, unable to alter the path he had been chosen to walk on. "I'll call the TV station right now and put that in motion."

Pahlava raised a finger, knowing the rebuke served its purpose. "One more thing, Mort. Contact all your liaisons and inform them that the time has come for them to begin to assemble their armies. The march to the Valley of Megiddo will begin soon."

Stein knew exactly what that meant: the end of the world as he knew it.

Robinson's Arch Platform, Temple Mount

They unobtrusively meandered through the crowds until they reached the platform above the reconstructed Robinson Arch. It was here, Paul decided, they would preach truth. It was an elevated platform that overlooked the Temple pavilion, where thousands were gathered in the dark. It would be the perfect location to make one of the most important announcements Israel ever heard from God.

"Where are Ravitzky and Meschel?" Hershel asked once they were on station. He peered into the poorly lit crowd, but there was no sign of them.

Paul shrugged. "They'll show up, of that I'm certain."

"They're not the only ones to show up," Hershel announced. "Look over there." He pointed to two media mobile trucks at the base of the pavilion steps. "It looks like this is going to be a really big show."

"And let's add two more *actors* to the show," Levi said sarcastically. "The main stars." With that he nodded toward the priest's quarters, where Pahlava and Stein were standing, apparently waiting for the right moment to make their appearance.

Paul motioned for the group to form a huddle. "Let's have a short prayer before show time." He gestured to Levi, then they all linked hands as he prayed for God's protection.

Two minutes later Paul walked to the edge of the platform and cried out, "You men of Israel! Hear what I have to say and be warned! This man you have held up to be your messianic person, this Gregory A. Kavidas, is an imposter! He is the Antichrist who will bring ruination to your nation and your souls!" He stepped back as Levi stepped forward.

"My fellow Israelites!" Levi shouted. "I am your brother who believes in the Law of Moses and the Prophets and am here to say that my companion, Paul, is speaking truth! This man who you are following—who you have revered as your messiah—is a fraud! His real name is Reza Pahlava, and he is an Iranian with fake credentials and a forged birth certificate!"

The crowd quickly moved from curiosity to anger.

"How could he perform the miracles he's shown us over the years?!" a voice from the crowd yelled.

"Because he's empowered by Satan—the angel of light—the prince and power of the air," Levi replied hotly. "He is the master of illusion and delusion—plotting to take as many unsuspecting victims with him to hell!"

Hershel saw movement coming from the priest's quarters. He watched the area closely. "Paul, the *stars* are here. It looks like they're waiting on something."

Paul's eyes darted back and forth, then spotted them. "Asher, take Simon with you through the crowd and work your way over to Pahlava and Stein and wait for my signal. We are not going to let them perform any parlor magic today."

Asher and Simon sneaked off the platform into the crowd, then stood behind a support column, waiting.

"Why should we believe you?!" another voice clamored.

Paul stepped next to Levi. "Don't believe me, friends! Believe God! What you are hearing is truth that is spelled out in your Bible—the *Tanach*. These things that we have witnessed for the past six-plus years were written thousands of years in advance in Daniel, Ezekiel, Joel, and Zechariah. They predicted the rise of the Antichrist, and this Kavidas person is him! Stein is his false prophet. What's more—"

"Paul, they're on the move!" Hershel yelled, pointing to Pahlava and Stein as they walked stealthily and menacingly toward the platform.

Paul knew Asher and Simon were protected by divine decree from the Antichrist's powers. "Asher, seize them!" he cried out. "Bring them to me!"

Asher and Simon lunged forward as Pahlava and Stein moved through the crowd and grabbed them from behind. Stein turned to see who restrained him and raised his fist to punch him when his arm suddenly froze in place. It was paralyzed. "Take you hands off us!" he shouted.

Pahlava cunningly assessed the present threat from both Paul's group and the crowd. He realized he was temporarily powerless against God's anointed evangelists. Under his breath, he uttered a string of curses. "Remain silent," he said to Stein.

"PAUL, LOOK!" Levi broke in as he pointed to Ravitzky and Meschel forcing a man through the crowd.

Second's later Ravitzky and Meschel arrived at the platform with a man cuffed with a cable tie. Ravitzky turned to Paul and said, "This is one of Pahlava's imams, who will confirm Pahlava's identity for us!"

"Hold him aside for now," Paul instructed, then motioned to Asher and Simon to bring Pahlava and Stein to him. Once on the platform next to him, Paul cried out, "Men of Israel, hear me! I bring these two fakers before you today for you to pass judgment on them so they can be tried before God and your priests."

He pulled several papers from his pocket for reference, then said aloud, "This Gregory A. Kavidas was born in Iran, and his real name, as we said before, is Reza Pahlava, and the numerical equivalency of this name in the *Gematria* is 666! That's right," he repeated, "666, the number of the Antichrist! We have this on the highest authority. Documents provided to us have been verified by Roni Shukrun, who is a trusted linguist and etymologist at Bar-Ilan University. We can believe her implicitly!" He pointed to Pahlava. "The long arm of God is reaching out to throttle this evil that is standing before you. He is the monument of man's inhumanity to man. He is Satan incarnate!"

Pahlava and Stein said nothing. They remained silent.

"They're acting like Christ before Pilate!" Levi whispered to Paul, "They're playing on the sympathy of the crowd."

Paul nodded. He knew their game. "Bring that man over here," he said to Ravitzky.

Ravitzky beamed from ear to ear as he marched the imam to Paul. "Now you're talking." Stein blinked when he recognized the imam and nudged Pahlava, who ignored him but made sure he stared into the news cameras.

"My friends," Paul shouted out, "we have an eyewitness who will verify everything I've told you." He gestured to Ravitzky, who pushed the imam to the front for the crowd to see plainly.

Ravitzky held the imam by the neck as Meschel held him by the arm and said aloud, "Now you tell these people who you are and what you told us about this man before you, this phony Pahlava!"

The imam said nothing. Meschel waited momentarily, then reached behind the imam and twisted the cable tie to inflict pain on the man. The man grimaced but remained silent.

"Speak up!" Paul demanded. When he looked at Pahlava, he detected contempt.

The imam stared into space and stood mute.

Paul nodded to Ravitzky, who in turn nodded to Meschel.

Meschel then whispered into the imam's ear. "If you don't tell us what we want to hear, I will personally kill your wife and children in front of you, and then I will see that your house is bulldozed and burned!" He tightened the cable tie one more time to restrict the blood circulation as tears formed in the imam's eyes. "You know enough about my reputation to know that I don't make idle threats!"

The imam weakened. He turned and pointed to Pahlava and then to the crowd. "I was with this man at the Mosque of Al-Aqsa when he stated he was an Iranian to all the Islamic scholars who were with me!" The man began to shudder as fear grabbed his heart as if some kind of supernatural reprisal would befall him.

The crowd was horrified and held its breath in anticipation. Suddenly a strange parenthesis in time occurred—there was a peculiar silence that swept over them.

Pahlava turned to Stein and whispered, "Hold on, my friend."

Stein looked at him curiously. *Hold on? What do you mean?*

Levi studied Pahlava's eyes and began to see what he saw. He saw the scene and recognized it! *Does Pahlava have precognition? Does he have future sight?* He didn't know for sure, but parapsychological or extrasensory perception was not out of the realm of possibility for demonic forces.

The ground started to shake under their feet! Massive rumblings from the bowels of the earth thundered!

Levi shot a look at Pahlava. He was smirking.

Paul turned to Levi in surprise. "The Sixth Bowl already?!"

Levi nodded as his spirit confirmed the next judgment. "This time it's going to be a big one!"

Pahlava and Stein quickly assessed the unfolding drama. This was their chance.

Suddenly like the opening of giant jaws, a gaping fissure in the floor of the Temple, appeared! It came from far beneath the earth's surface. The Afro-Arabian plate had shifted again, but this time the subterranean plate exerted such titanic force on the adjoining plates that they began to shift and uplift as well. Unparalleled geologic history was about to begin.

The Arabian plate collided with the Eurasian plate landmass, whose boundary was contiguous with the Indian plate. The three tectonic plate cataclysms would bring gigantic gashes, fractures, and upheavals in the earth's crust throughout the Mideast and into Africa.

Panic ensued. Men were running everywhere to escape the horror at the Temple Mount.

"Paul, look, the crevasse swallowed up hundreds of men!" Hershel cried out as he pointed to the bottomless opening. Men were toppling into the pit like cascading dominos.

Meschel peeked over the edge of the chasm and turned to Ravitzky and winked. Then with one quick move Meschel pushed the imam into the crevasse. The imam screamed curses as he fell headlong into the crevasse. "Good riddance!" Meschel said in triumph.

"Watch out!" Paul heard from behind. He turned to see Simon pointing to portions of the Temple crumbling under the stress of the shaking. Stanchions and columns were toppling around them as the structure struggled to remain intact.

"Clear off the Mount!" Paul ordered his men, then turned to Asher and Hershel. "Take Pahlava and Stein out into the open, away from the building."

Events were happening at rapid speed. Paul needed time to think. *No time!* He watched Asher and Hershel march Pahlava and Stein off the Mount as they sidestepped the debris that had fallen from the quake. There would be more tremors and shaking, of that Paul was certain. This was going to be the *big one* as Levi predicted. "Move them along quickly!" he shouted.

"The next one is on its way!" Levi yelled above the catastrophe. When he looked around, Ravitzky and Meschel they were carefully shadowing Asher and Hershel.

The flow of men running out of the Temple and off the Mount heard Levi exclaim the warning. Fear gave way to panic that gave way to terror. The terror gave way to confusion. Asher and Hershel held onto Pahlava and Stein, but the gushing of men jammed against them, their fears heightening exponentially. The frightened crowd of men shoved and grabbed anybody they could and swept them along to exit the Mount—it was madness. It was pandemonium.

It was the perfect time for Pahlava and Stein to make their move. Pahlava suddenly stopped short, punched Hershel in the left side of his chest, then yelled out, "He's having a heart attack!"

The crowd ignored the plea and veered around them as Hershel clutched his chest and dropped to the ground. Asher fell to the ground after him, then opened Hershel's shirt before crying out, "Paul, help!"

"Now!" Pahlava said to Stein. They immediately inserted themselves into the maddening crowds as they poured out of the Temple and within minutes were out of sight. Ravitzky and Meschel immediately reverted to their training and split up to follow them.

Asher instinctively massaged Hershel's chest in an effort to assist him, then dragged him to one side to keep him from being trampled on as the building emptied.

Then the next tremulous jolt hit.

Paul, Levi, and Simon arrived at Asher's side and quickly laid hands on Hershel. "Lord, heal this man!" Paul pleaded to the heavens amidst the crashing noise of the quaking.

Hershel bolted upright and blinked several times in astonishment. "I don't believe it. I feel fine!"

Paul realized that Hershel had just experienced a demonic assault and that nothing was wrong with his heart. Pahlava was unable to attack Asher, so Hershel, being the weak link, fell prey. "We need to clear out of here right now!" Paul commanded.

They all ran.

History would record that the Mercalli-Sieberg scale maxed and that this earthquake that involved the intense converging of three major plates was the most severe Earth had ever suffered. It would be the last earthquake of all time.

There was a rapid separation of three underlying geological plates that produced primary fault lines as well as secondary fractures resulting in the splitting, rifting, and chiseling of the earth's crust. This reconfigured mountains, valleys, and lakes. Multiple epicenters brought major resculpturing of the landscape throughout the earthquake zones, especially along the Euphrates River that transects the Southeastern quadrant of Turkey, where the Ataturk and Karkamis Dams are located.

TWENTY-SIX

Christian Fortress, Petra

Paul carefully navigated through the USGS website to study the geodetic monitoring maps and earthquake charts that highlighted the recent geologic upheaval in Turkey and other outlying regions in the Mideast. The posting reflected the truth that this quake was historic and devastating.

"You seem mesmerized by that site. You okay?" Shira asked as she peeked over his shoulder while thumping little Sol on her hip.

Several panes of various viewpoints of the earthquake from the USGS perspective brought major concern to Paul. "This was no ordinary quake, love," he said with his notebook open and his pen poised over the page. "This was the quake to end all quakes. Look at this..." He clicked on the satellite imaging of the Euphrates River at the Karkamis and Ataturk Dams. "See this?" He pointed to the river.

"The river no longer flows after the dams," she replied. "Why?"

"Because God said in Revelation 16:12 that he would cause the Euphrates to dry up so that the forces that would come against Israel could travel over it," he instructed solemnly. "So He used this agent of destruction to make it happen. The dams collapsed from the quakes, shutting off the headwaters."

"The quake being the Sixth Bowl Judgment," she affirmed.

"Yes, this is the outworking of it," Paul replied as a news ticker streamed on the bottom of the website.

"Dear Lord!" Shira exclaimed as she read the report moving across the screen. "You mean over three million people were killed in this earthquake?"

Paul nodded as he finished his notetaking. "I'm afraid so. There are casualties in many countries such as here, in Israel, but Turkey, Syria, and Iraq are those sustaining the most deaths; all the countries where the

Euphrates River flows."

Other images of the cataclysmic destruction cascaded across his laptop screen. Panic-stricken men in prayer shawls running from the Temple Mount as the walls collapsed gave way to graphic videos of nature's mountains and plains, as well as man's testimonial to self—his cities and tall buildings—being reshaped by the Hand of God. Mankind was once again realizing that their fate and memorials are not in their hands but in the One who holds the sovereign right to the Earth.

Shira shed many tears as she watched the news reports, then turned aside and walked out with little Sol to find comfort in her other Christian sisters in Christ. Once alone, Paul navigated to the military website that showed in real satellite time the amassing of troops on the banks of the dried-up Euphrates in response to Pahlava's order.

"Looks like God's plan is coming together," he heard Levi say as he walked up, glancing at Paul's laptop.

Paul took a deep breath. "Apparently we're in the final act that culminates in the curtain coming down in what is called Armageddon."

"What is the latest from this military channel satellite feed?"

Paul flicked the side of the laptop. "It tells of the alliance of powers that are coming against God's people here in Israel. The 'kings of the north, south, east and west,' as the Bible puts it, have now been identified. They are the remnant of the Russian war machine, together with Iran, Syria, Lebanon, and the coalition of Arab-bloc nations in Africa, the kings of the east that is China and others of the Orient, and we can expect the 'kings of the west' that includes the European nations to come against Israel as well."

"You mean like the forming up of the nations in the axis verses the allied powers in World War II?" Levi said.

"Yes, only this invasion against Israel will be met by the Lord Jesus who will vanquish his enemies and save his People, and then bring in the Millennium," Paul advised tonelessly.

"Ah, yes! The Millennium." Levi revelled in the thought of it. "To be with our Savior-King for one-thousand years in Israel is the ultimate this side of heaven."

Paul agreed and added, "It will be interesting to see the unseen hands of the evil spirits that will convince all these 'kings'—these enemy nations—to come up against Israel. If they only knew the Bible, they would know that these evil spirits that direct them are leading them to their deaths."

"Orchestrated before the world began," Levi summarized.

"Paul," they heard, "I need to get some air. Is it all right to go out and walk around?"

Paul turned to see Alfonse Rivera, the ex-priest, now a long-term resident of Petra looking very anxious. "Yes, Alfonse, it is fine—only remember—Kapporeth instructed us that we are not to leave the compound alone."

Alfonse nodded in assent and walked out of the room.

"Levi, assign someone to go with him," Paul said as Alfonse left the area. "He doesn't look too well."

Levi left the room, then asked Doron to accompany Alfonse on his walk.

So here we are, Lord, Paul thought, once left to his private ruminations. *We have arrived at the end of a long, hard road. You have brought us through the Seal, Trumpet, and now—finishing up the Bowl Judgments—a long, hard road. So I ask that you continue to watch over us and keep us safe from the evil one. Keep us from this Pahlava and Stein, who seek to destroy your good name and your people.* He closed his eyes as his thoughts morphed into prayers. Then he added aloud, "Assign your angels to watch over Shira and Solomon, should something happen to me."

"Paul, come quick!" he heard. He turned to see Levi, flushed in the face, panting. "Alphonse has been killed!"

They ran out of the fortress building into the open to join with the others who were lowering Alphonse's body off one of the crumbling rock embankments that forms the lower layers of the rock sentinels that surround the city. Once on level ground Paul cried out, "What happened?"

Doron, gasping for breath, shouted above the melee, "He got away from me and climbed up the wall. Then I heard him scream and saw his body flying through the air—landing on top of the rock pile!" He turned and pointed to Yashur and Norman. "They helped me get him down."

Paul looked down at Alphonse's crumbled body and shook his head. "I warned him not to leave."

"He told me he was going 'stir crazy' being locked up in the compound all these months," Doron lamented. "I guess he couldn't take it anymore."

Paul looked at the women back at the compound with their hands over their mouths in grief. "Kapporeth warned us that evil forces are lurking outside of our protected zone and that we should not venture out alone. There is God's protection in obedience." He nodded to Yashur. "Put together a burying detail so we can give our brother a decent funeral." He kept his head lowered all the way back to the living quarter's compound.

TWENTY-SEVEN

Ash Sheikh Ri'han Street, Muslim Quarter, Jerusalem

The house on Ash Sheikh Ri'han Street doubled as a showplace for wealthy Palestinians as well as the central headquarters for the Hamas movement led by a man referred to only as Tema. Tema served as a munitions specialist under Yasser Arafat in his youth, then graduated into leadership by instructing others in the art form of martyring for the cause of Palestinian emancipation by ridding the land of the Jews in Israel. His philosophy of ministry was very successful: utilizing the asset of Muslim youth as suicide bombers to further the cause of Islam.

His house was a perfect place for Pahlava and Stein to find refuge until the storm blew over.

Stein sat in Tema's recreation room watching a TV program where Temple engineers assessed the damage to the Temple and the adjoining pavilions and patios. The broadcast reminded him of the old Discovery stations on cable TV that interviewed the experts as well as taking camera crews well underground to film the damage to the foundation and earthquake-stabilizing rocks of ancient buildings. From there he scanned the stations showing footage of the earthquake devastation. He would dwell on those reports since they fascinated him.

"Mort," he heard as Pahlava walked into the room, "tune into the live satellite feed on the troop movements. I need to know if we're on schedule."

Stein navigated on the military cable channel that gave real-time footage of the crossing of the Euphrates River by Chinese coalition forces. Then he moved to the Worldwide Telescope satellite channel that gave close-up real-time access to the Arab-bloc troop build-up on the Syrian-Lebanese borders. "We're right where we need to be," he said with a nod.

"Yes, we are," Pahlava replied with a gleam in his eye.

Rapid-gunfire erupted!

"What the—?!" Pahlava shouted.

Mort dashed to the nearest window. "It's that crazy Jew Ravitzky and his partner! They just shot two of Tema's bodyguards!" Frantically: "They're coming after us!"

Pahlava made a rapid assessment of the crisis.

The door burst open!

"Master," Tema shouted to Pahlava as he gulped in mouthfuls of air, "gunmen are coming! They killed my men!"

Seconds later Ravitzky stood in the doorway. Tema turned to him as Ravitzky stared him down, then pointed his weapon of choice, a 9-mm Browning BDA9 double-action pistol, at his head and pulled the trigger. Ravitzky asked no questions.

Tema dropped to the floor with a thud as Meschel appeared in the doorway, carrying an Israeli Uzi with smoke spiralling out of its barrel. "Next?" he said with a sardonic grin.

"Up against the wall!" Ravitzky ordered. "Being an ex-director of Mossad gives me clearances and resources to seek out Israel's enemies. You can't hide from me." He motioned with his gun. "I want to see you two beg for your lives before we end them and put this madness you created to rest once and for all."

Stein shot a look at Pahlava as fear gripped his heart. He sluggishly moved to the far wall as ordered along with Pahlava. Once against the wall, Pahlava glared at Ravitzky with malevolent eyes and retorted, "You don't really think you are in control here, do you?"

"SHUT UP!" Meschel called out as he exuded an unmistakable sense of menace. He raised the Uzi and pointed it at Pahlava.

Stein felt his hackles rise as his hands began to shake. *This is the end; I just know it.*

"You know nothing!" Pahlava screamed in Stein's face. "This is not the end! We are protected, you should know that!"

"SILENCE!" Meschel said and fired several rounds into the wall next to Stein.

Stein's physiognomy gave him up. He was crazed with fear and doubt. "I don't want to die!" he screamed.

Pahlava raised his brow in challenge. "You have no power over us!"

"That's what you think!" Meschel said and slammed the butt of his Uzi into Pahlava's stomach. Pahlava doubled over and fell to the floor.

Pahlava groveled on the floor for only a moment before a supernatural strength came over him. It was time for him to exert his powers that he had been granted from below. He slowly rose to his feet as his eyes blazed with rage.

Meschel saw the rage and took a step back, then pulled the clip back on his Uzi to reload it.

"You have no power over me," Pahlava repeated with repellent savagery.

"Kill them!" Ravitzky ordered.

Just as Meschel started to pull the trigger, an unseen hand pushed Ravitzky into the path of the bullets. Ravitzky took four rounds in the chest, propelling him against the wall where Pahlava and Stein stood, knocking them to the floor like bowling pins. Ravitzky groaned only once, then was motionless.

Then in a split second Meschel placed the Uzi on his right Temple and pulled the trigger. One single shot was heard; then he teetered on his feet before dropping to the floor in a heap.

Pahlava gave out with a loud maniacal laugh that echoed throughout the room. It was a cry of victory.

Turning to Stein, Pahlava saw that he had soiled himself. "You are becoming an embarrassment to me, Mort," he said with a shake of the head. "Go clean yourself up."

Pahlava was troubled. Not over the attack as he surveyed the bodies of the would-be assassins and his supporter, Tema, as they lay on the floor. No, he was troubled over Stein. His character was weakening and his fears strengthening. With the end being so near, he wondered if Stein had the backbone, resolves, and faith to see the plan through to completion. *I cannot dwell on this now!* No, he would have to leave it alone; it was too late in the game to make changes.

TWENTY-EIGHT

Parkside Drive, Miami

Brandon stood looking out his kitchen window at the bizarre behavior of the fire ants building their mound in a patch of ground that received bright sunlight. He studied the ferocious little bugs that notoriously infested southern Florida for several minutes and concluded that the mound had risen at least four inches overnight. He remembered being bitten by those insects and how Floridians dreaded the voracious creatures. This unusual growth was a telling commentary on the abuse of nature. Nature was rebelling against man's wanton disregard for the environment over the past seven years in comparison to their utter fascination to protect it prior to the Tribulation. Now man had more important things to worry about: surviving the wrath of God.

He turned away from the window as Michael entered the kitchen. "Coffee, Brandon?"

Brandon nodded and pointed to the electric percolator. "Yes, I'll have a cup with you but only if we have coffee and—"

"I'm a 'coffee-and' person myself," Michael chortled.

Brandon pulled a loaf of banana nut bread out of the refrigerator, sliced off three slabs, then put them on a paper plate and placed it on the table. "Good stuff," he remarked with a wink.

As they sat down at the table, Michael said, "We're in the final throes, aren't we?"

"Yes, we are." Brandon took a sip of his coffee. "But we have a unique opportunity, Michael, because it has been said, 'the problem in getting great things from God is being able to hold on for the last half hour.' If that be true, we *will* receive great things from God since we are in the 'last half hour,' so to speak."

Michael went to the cupboard to get a jar of peanut butter.

Returning to his seat, he spread a wholesome portion of it on his slice of banana nut bread, then bit off a chunk to enjoy with his coffee.

The doorbell rang. Within seconds Jonathan appeared in the doorway. His face was ashen. "Paul called and advised me that two of our comrades in Israel, Moshe Ravitzky and Nachman Meschel, have been killed by Kavidas—Pahlava, that is!"

Michael dropped the remaining piece of banana nut bread on his plate. "Oh no!"

Brandon shook his head. "Our people are being systematically eliminated," he said with deep pathos. "It's times like this that you want an Avraham Ben-Korpel around to even the score. It's times like this that I can't fault Ben-Korpel for his vigilante methods to rid the land of those killing off our compatriots."

In his mind Jonathan agreed with Brandon. *There needs to be some justice now. I know things will heat up again later when Jesus comes back and makes things right. The bad guys are having it all their way—or so it seems.*

But it was not the way of the Lord. It was not the way of the Spirit, but the way of the world. No, they had to leave the outcome with the Lord, despite their frustration. It was now a matter of faith: that God would bring about His justice so there would be no regrets. But, he rationalized, Brandon and Michael had to come to that place by themselves. God would have to meet their personal need to settle that matter with Him as the world marched rapidly toward Armageddon.

"Come look at this," Jonathan said as he sat down at the table and then popped open his laptop computer. "The armies of Pahlava are moving along." He navigated to the military satellite site showing troop movements toward Israel through Syria, Iran, Lebanon, and Egypt. Live news pop-ups on the screen featured high-ranking heads of state claiming that strategic air space had been cleared to allow Syrian and Egyptian fighter jets to move on Israel to shadow the ground troops.

Michael looked over at Jonathan's laptop and backed his chair away two feet from the table. "I have to admit that I'm new to all of this. What is going on?"

"It's the beginning of the end," Jonathan explained. He motioned for Brandon to give him a piece of paper, then said as he scribbled some notes, "'The battle of that great day of God Almighty' as the Revelation puts it is about to happen. The confluence of the nations of the earth is in a place called Armageddon that is located west of the Jordan River in north central Israel, some 10 miles south of Nazareth and 15 miles inland from the Mediterranean seacoast. It is an extended plain on which many of Israel's battles had been fought. There Deborah and Barak defeated the Canaanites. There Gideon triumphed over the Midianites. There Saul was slain in the battle with the Philistines. There Ahaziah was slain by Jehu, and there Josiah was slain in the invasion by the Egyptians. It is also known as Megiddo in the Plain of Esdraelon, which has been a chosen place for encampment in every contest carried on in Palestine from the days of Nebuchadnezzar, king of Babylon. There God deals in judgment with the nations because of their persecution of Israel, their sinfulness, and because of their godlessness.

"The Book of Revelation also says that the blood will flow to the bits of the horse bridles for 1,600 furlongs, and it has been pointed out that 1,600 furlongs covers the entire length of Palestine. But Jerusalem will no doubt be the center of the interest during the battle of Armageddon, for God's Word says: 'I will gather all nations against Jerusalem to battle.'"

Michael looked puzzled. "Every nation on the planet is going to come to Palestine to fight?"

"No," Jonathan said. "It's a figure of speech that the Bible uses. It's called a hyperbole. It's like when the Pharisees said in John 12:19 about Christ, 'The whole world has gone after him.' Obviously the 'whole world' had not gone after him. Likewise, the prophet Zechariah did not mean 'all nations,' but he meant that the great battle of select nations would represent all the kingdoms and nations of the earth."

Brandon moved alongside. "Pahlava is being used by God as the agent that brings His plan to fruition. He is a mere pawn in this colossal chess game where the enemies of God and His people, Israel, will be crushed. Then the Lord will deal with Pahlava and Stein."

Jonathan clicked on several websites and news clips. "When I examine the Bible, I come to the conclusion that the Lord is going to use man's propensity for evil against himself."

"Meaning?" Michael said.

"Well, the way I see it is that many of the Arab-bloc nations, especially Syria, Iran, Lebanon, and Egyp,t are coming against Israel to conquer it for Allah as their prophet Mohammad predicted. Their hatred for the Jews will fully vent during this war. They will be initially supported by the remnant of the Russian armies left over from the invasion that took place seven years ago. Then there are the kings of the east, or Asia, represented by China and Japan, who come to aid the Arab nations in their conquest but then turn on them since they want the oil reserves under Arab sand for themselves. They have been in cahoots with the Arabs to ensure the flow of oil to fuel their mechanized world does not diminish. They seize the opportunity during this campaign to turn on the Arabs so they can keep the oil for themselves without having to go through any Arab brokerage. The other Gentile nations—America and Europe—are considered part of the kings of the west, but they sit on the sidelines and let the others do all the dirty work and the fighting. But in God's eyes they are complicit."

"You mean like the so-called 'neutral' countries during World War II?" Michael asked.

"Yes, they don't do any of the fighting, but reap all the benefits of the victory," Jonathan replied. "Yet, in their heart of hearts they chose their sides and are accountable for it."

"Yes, I remember seeing the documentaries of the citizens of Germany and Poland at Auschwitz and Treblinka being ordered by Allied commanders to properly bury the Holocaust victims they reportedly said they knew nothing about. Their turning a 'blind eye' did not cut it with the liberating American and Russian forces."

"Sad but true," Brandon added with a nod.

"The coalition of powers coming to Israel is nothing more than the armies of the Antichrist, the Beast," Jonathan continued. "And they all unwittingly are following God's plan of marching to their deaths at Armageddon because when Jesus arrives on the battlefield, these armies turn and attack Him as he arrives on his white horse from the heavens."

Michael clapped his hands in triumph. "That is going to be some scene!"

"Tell him about the part where the heavens are shaken when Christ returns," Brandon suggested.

"I'd rather read it direct," Jonathan replied as he reached over to get his Bible on the cupboard. "Listen to Jesus' own words in Matthew 24: 'Immediately after the Tribulation of those days shall the sun be darkened, and the moon shall not give its light, and the stars shall fall from heaven, and the powers of the heavens shall be shaken. And then shall appear the sign of the Son of man in heaven; and then shall all the tribes of the earth mourn, and they shall see the Son of man coming in the clouds of heaven with power and great glory. And he shall send his angels with a great sound of a trumpet, and they shall gather together his elect from the four winds, from one end of heave to the other.'" He closed the Bible and smiled. "Exciting stuff, isn't it?!"

"Exciting?" Michael asked in wonder. "For us, yes, but for those outside of God's forgiveness—those who do not have Christ as their Savior—-it is very frightening."

Both Jonathan and Brandon nodded.

Moments later Brandon read the news ticker inching across the bottom of the laptop screen and said aloud, "God is cooking up something over in Yellowstone National Park."

"'Noxious gas leaking from subterranean portals kills off bison in national park,'" Jonathan read. He navigated to the Yellowstone National Park website that showed both images of the dead animals, along with trees and shrubs throughout the massive park being cooked from underground heat sources. Spiraling yellow gas plumes were easily distinguished from the age-old geysers in the images. "This doesn't look good," he remarked suspiciously. "This has the makings of a big one."

Michael blinked.

TWENTY-NINE

Christian Fortress, Petra

The gathering to listen to Asher and Simon's account of the marshalling of forces at Megiddo reminded Paul of the meeting that occurred when the twelve spies reported to Moses after surveying Canaan in readiness to enter the Promise Land. But instead of observing the terrain, they were directed to observe troop movements. Instead of observing whether the people were strong or weak, few or many; they were to report on the Israeli defenses; whether they were ready or not. Instead of bringing back a sample of the fruit of Megiddo, whether or not it flowed with milk and honey, they were ordered to observe the weaponry being transported into the valley.

Paul sat at the stone table and listened to both men as if they were giving briefings before a bombing mission over hostile territory. Asher used a stone wall and a stick of chalk to outline the configuration he observed while Simon provided some of the technical support that brought Paul to form a conclusion: this was indeed the staging and marshalling of forces for Armageddon. "What is your opinion of the Israeli forces?" he asked after several minutes of contemplation.

"To use the Biblical vernacular the spies used when reporting to Moses," Simon began, "the Israelites are like 'grasshoppers' compared to the 'giant' Arabs. The Israelis have sophisticated protection, like the Iron Dome short-range missile defense system, but the Syrians are bringing in the Russian-made MiG-29 fighter jets and advanced anti-tank armored vehicles."

"Millions of armed personnel are pouring in from every side," Asher added.

"What about the Israeli air force?" Doron asked.

"They are on alert status and are doing aerial reconnaissance 24/7, but it's almost as if they're waiting for some allied support before they take action," Asher surmised.

"You mean like waiting for America to come alongside them?" Yashur asked.

Simon shrugged. "Maybe."

"If they knew the U.S. isn't going to support them like they have in the past, they probably would've taken action by now," Norman argued.

"I agree with your assessment, Norman," Paul said. "Asher, give me your best estimate on when you think the shooting will start."

Asher nodded. "I believe the Arab forces are waiting for the 'kings of the east,' the Chinese coalition, to form up with them. And in the interim I believe they are amassing in huge numbers to intimidate the Israelites like the Philistines and their champion Goliath did when fighting against Saul in the valley of Elah."

"Hmm, yes. That sounds like a plausible scenario," Paul agreed.

"It sounds to me like the final drama on the world stage is being acted out," Levi added positively, "and that the Lord is going to return and do some amazing things to bring glory to God."

Hershel walked up to Paul and handed him a slip of paper. Paul read it aloud: "'Pahlava has turned against the Israeli forces and is now siding with the Arab alliance.'" He asked Hershel, "Where did you get this?"

"I just pulled it off my iPhone and wrote it down so you could read it just as it was announced," Hershel replied.

Paul nodded. "This is it, then. Things are moving into place with the Antichrist turning against the people who once worshipped him. If only they had listened to God's Word, they could have avoided this."

"Let God be true and every man a liar," Levi retorted. "God will not be mocked when it comes to his Word. All the miseries and evils men suffer from vice, crime, ambition, injustice, oppression, slavery, and war, proceed from their despairing or neglecting the precepts in the Bible."

Paul gazed at Levi in admiration at his voicing an oracle from God.

Yellowstone Caldera, Wyoming

The extremely high level of sulfuric acid in the atmosphere coming from the newly developed fissures surrounding the Upper Geyser Basin had become very alarming. New fumaroles showed enhanced activity, and increasing water temperatures indicated an imminent eruption. In many of the older geysers the water had become so hot they were transformed into purely steaming features, bringing greater concern to volcanologists. Then there were the dead animals that dotted the national park. Hundreds of bison, deer, and black bear had inhaled toxic geothermal gases, killing them off in minutes. Park officials were forced to close the national monument to the public to allow geologists and volcanologists to survey and assess the degree of danger while they buried the carcasses.

Thirty-four-year-old Stanley Royce, with a Ph.D. in Volcanology and Geothermal Exploration, now working for the U.S. Geological Survey, had researched the 1980 Mount St. Helens and the 1991 Mount Pinatubo eruptions. Although these eruptions came in with a Volcanic Explosivity Index of VEI-5 and VEI-6 respectively, he feared those cataclysmic events would pale into insignificance if Yellowstone blew. The present violent seismic activity, along with the history of Yellowstone being a "megacaldera," troubled him. All the elements needed for this super volcano to explode were falling into place since he'd arrived ten days ago. For this reason, he'd venture no closer than the visitors' center while making his scientific observations and calculations.

Considered to be a "mantle hot spot" below the crust of the earth, the Yellowstone caldera is the largest volcanic system in North America. It was termed a "super volcano" because the caldera was formed by an exceptionally large explosive eruption in prehistoric times, which released 240 cubic miles of ash, rock, and pyroclastic materials. That eruption was 1,000 times larger than the 1980 eruption of Mount St. Helens. It produced a crater nearly two thirds of a mile deep and 52 by 28 miles in area. That disaster blanketed much of central North America with volcanic debris that fell many hundreds of miles away. The amount of ash and gases released into the atmosphere undoubtedly caused significant impacts to world weather patterns and led to the extinction of many species in the world; including millions of humankind.

Of utmost importance was the pronounced uplifting of the structural dome surrounding the caldera along with the severe rise in temperature near the uplifts. The ground had risen at a rate of 2.4 inches or 3.8 to 6.1 cm. per day since he began his surveying. The uplifting together with the accompanying earthquake activity was enough evidence to warrant immediate evacuation of the potential blast zone. In Royce's mind, together with the accumulated evidence, when this super volcano blew, it would eclipse every volcanic eruption in recorded history because of the potential volcanic winter. The death toll of the Mount Tambora eruption in Indonesia in 1815 of 92,000 would be easily eclipsed.

He remembered the ashy plume that hovered over Iceland in 2010 for months when the *Eyjafjallajokull* volcano blew. The Icelandic volcano kept much of Europe land-bound while it spewed out its grit and forced European air travel and trade to come to a screeching halt. Air space across a swath from Britain to Ukraine and New Zealand to San Francisco was closed and foiled the plans of millions of passengers. And this was, in his mind, a small volcanic eruption. The thought of this super volcano blowing plumes of grit into the atmosphere, together with the wind driving the toxic ash around the globe, brought chills down his spine. Then there was the fluoride-laden toxic ash that brings long-term bone damage to man and beast. Add to this the poisonous gas and pyroclastic surges and flows that will kill off both animal and human life for an interminable period, and you have the makings of a global catastrophe of Biblical proportions. He was frightened.

He heard frequent and insistent rumblings—many of the subterranean ones resembled thunder, and on the surface, they sounded like deep bellowings. His fear heightened. At that instant there was a portentous crash, as if mountains were tumbling in ruins. He looked into the distance and saw huge stones hurled aloft, rising as high as the very clouds; then came a great quantity of fire and endless smoke, so that the whole atmosphere was obscured and the sun was entirely hidden, as if eclipsed. Day turned into night and light into darkness. "The whole universe is being resolved into chaos and fire!" he cried out.

The huge cone suddenly ejected an inconceivable quantity of ash and dust that mushroomed into the air! Then pumice and rocks burned and shattered by internal fires rained down upon him. Massive tremors!

A THUNDEROUS BLAST!

Seven minutes later the 800° C. pyroclastic surge traveling at 1050 kilometers an hour reached Royce and completely enveloped him. All that remained was a charred cinder.

THIRTY

Parkside Drive, Miami

Brandon watched the live news feed of the horrific explosion of the super volcano at Yellowstone on his iPad. "This is the end, isn't it, Jonathan?"

Jonathan nodded slowly. "It sure appears that way. This must be the beginning of the Seventh Bowl."

Brandon added the narrative as he watched the feed. "The super volcano triggered a series of massive earthquakes that in turn brought down huge hailstones that have killed over eight-thousand people here in America already."

"The Revelation Sixteen passage describes all of that," Jonathan said.

"...unbelievable lightning strikes and..." Brandon stared at the iPad. "There's a man in Wyoming pointing to a huge chunk of ice that fell from the sky onto his car—crushing the roof, and the news ticker says it weighed 75 pounds! They're like wrecking balls from God!"

"The prophecy says that hailstones during the Seventh Bowl will weigh a 'talent,' and that's about 75 pounds," Jonathan explained. "It is likened unto an 'exceedingly great plague.'"

"Here it comes!" Brandon gaped at the iPad. "Look at that ash cloud mushrooming! It looks like an atomic bomb was detonated!" The continuing volcanic eruptions were spewing forth massive amounts of black soot-like clouds that ascended high into the atmosphere, blacking out the sunlight. Then the upper-atmospheric wind currents seem to be blowing the cinders in all directions. The video feeds were fading in-and-out as the sunlight shifted into darkness.

"I wouldn't have guessed it," Jonathan said, "but this explains the passage in Matthew 24 that describes the earthly scene before Jesus returns where the sun, moon, and stars are darkened."

"Meaning?"

"What's happening here is called a 'volcanic winter,'" Jonathan said in somber tones. "Once this ash gets sucked into the jetstream, it will spread around the Earth in a matter of hours."

"I never heard of a 'volcanic winter,'" Brandon replied.

Jonathan shook his head. "Without doubt it's a verdict from God. I remember reading about the Lake Toba, Indonesian eruption that plunged the Earth into a volcanic winter, eradicating an estimated 60% of the human population, not to mention the devastating effect across the globe that killed off huge amounts of plants and wildlife. Then add that the eruption was responsible for the formation of sulfuric acid in the atmosphere that corrodes and blinds much like what is happening here."

"Doomsday," Brandon muttered in anguish.

"No, Judgment day," Jonathan corrected.

When Michael walked into the kitchen and saw their faces he immediately knew something terrible had happened.

THIRTY-ONE

Christian Fortress, Petra

Shira stroked Solomon's legs as she breast-fed him, thanking the Lord for the precious gift of motherhood. When the thought of America's abortion rights came to mind, she could never understand how a mother could terminate life within her womb and still live with herself.

"How's our boy doing?" Paul asked as he entered their bedroom. It was really only a carved-out cave with a makeshift door, but to them, it was a special sanctuary.

Shira smiled, detached Solomon, and burped him. "He's doing well, especially with a full tummy."

Paul meandered around the room. "The end is near," he said laconically.

"Are you worried?" Shira scanned his face. "We knew it was coming."

After a few moments of reflection, Paul said, "Now that it's upon us, I'm getting a little nervous." He finally sat down next to her.

Shira patted his knee. "My husband," she said lovingly, "God has used you mightily these last seven years to lead the K-groups and God's other messengers against the forces of Satan, Kavidas, and Stein, but now, as the Lord begins to bring the curtain down, he is preparing to bring in the final act Himself. Very soon we will be free to just sit on the sidelines and watch Jesus do battle and bring in His kingdom."

Being in perpetual motion while leading a band of soldiers in a crusade against the Antichrist and at the same time proclaiming the Gospel was a mission that few could manage—Paul knew that. He also knew that if it were not for the empowerment of God's Spirit, he would have failed miserably.

Nevertheless he tried to shake off the unnerving feeling, even if it were only for a short period, that he felt like a retiring Billy Graham who suddenly lost his edge. But then again he realized it was God's will. "Thanks." He sighed with relief. "I needed that reminder."

When Paul walked out of their bedroom, Hershel and Norman were reading E-mail on a laptop.

"Paul," Hershel announced, "we just received an E-mail from Jonathan and Brandon in Florida that Ben-Korpel has 'laid down his guns' and joined the ranks of those waiting for the Lord to bring justice on our enemies."

Just as Paul was about to smile in triumph, Norman added: "He also writes that Islamic terrorism has reached an all-time high and that Shariah Law has taken control of the U.S. Congress. Mankind in America must be so frightened from the judgments that they are openly performing lewd and lascivious acts in the streets without any shame. The only ones left in the closet are the Christians."

"Come quickly, Lord Jesus," Paul replied with a shake of his head.

Asher broke into the group, shouting, "We're being attacked!"

The scene of an approaching assault force outside the fortress at Petra was a familiar one. Only this time the armaments were different. An armoured column of three personnel carriers along with two Soltam Rascal Light 155mm SP Howitzer self-propelled artillery vehicles drove up to the Siq entrance of the fortress and slowly took up strategic locations as three teams disgorged from the personnel carriers carrying B-300 Light Support Weapon (shoulder-fired rocket launchers). The three teams began to patrol the area to scout out vulnerable targets.

"Pahlava's men are all Hamas using Israeli weaponry," Yashur whispered to Gadi from their observation perch atop the east escarpment that overlooked the valley floor being used as a staging area. He quickly recognized the attackers and the Israeli military hardware from his former days in the IDF.

"They're going to finish us off before the Lord comes back!" Gadi said, full of outrage.

Yashur called Paul on his two-way phone. "Paul," he whispered frantically, "they have brought in the 'big stuff' with at least fifty foot soldiers."

"How close?" Paul replied as a muscle jerked in his left cheek.

"Five minutes."

Paul turned to Doron. "Gather the women and children into the deepest cave." Doron saluted, then ran out of sight. Paul spun. "Levi, Asher, and Simon, you three stand in front of the cave entrance to form a prayer barrier. The rest of us will go to the Siq to fend them off as long as possible."

Norman hissed, "With what? Harsh language?" He reached down and picked up three small stones off the ground and said mockingly, "Slingshot, David?" He shook his head in despair. "We're finished!"

Paul took the three stones from Norman's hand and quoted Elisha: "'Fear not, for they who are with us are more than they who are with them.'" He prayed, "Lord, open Norman's eyes that he may see."

Norman blinked several times, then looked to the top of the rock walls that enclosed the fortress. "I see the mountains full of angels on horses and chariots of fire! Praise God!" Seconds later he motioned for Yashur, Gadi, and Hershel to follow him to the underground chambers along the Siq that were the most defensible. They ran ahead, leaving Paul alone in the middle of the compound.

The Siq (Arabic, *al-Siq,* translated *the shaft*—a dim, narrow gorge that in many places was no more than three meters wide) wound its way approximately one mile and ended at Petra's most elaborate ruin, the Treasury. Known to few, however, were the underground chambers along the Siq used by the ancient Nabatean guards to defend the main entrance to the fortress. It was here that Yashur, Gadi, and Hershel set up their ambush. It would not be an ambush fortified with weapons, but one of faith, trust, and prayer—believing deliverance would come from God alone.

Paul glanced toward the front of the cave at Levi, Asher, and Simon standing sentry and thought of his people and his family. He prayed aloud: "Lord, we are looking to you to protect our women and my son. You have been our redeemer, our defense, and our high tower. Now, in these desperate hours, we call upon you to show yourself strong and humiliate our enemies." He turned toward the Siq entranceway and then to the mountain ridges. "Lord, use your angels to humble the enemy so you may be exalted!"

Then he ran toward the Siq to be with Norman and the others.

One team of attackers split into three squads, then strategically entered the Siq passageway in a zigzag pattern on their way to the fortress. "This looks bad," Yashur whispered to Paul inside the chamber.

Gadi nudged him and nodded in an upward direction toward the angels. "Our protective umbrella."

"Against rocket launchers?" Yashur said discordantly.

"Is anything too hard for the Lord?" Paul answered.

"We're being attacked!" Paul heard Asher cry out over his two-way phone. "They used climbing equipment to scale the rock wall."

Flashes of fear struck Paul. His family was in grave danger. "Lord, help," he muttered as his mind began to seize in panic.

"What do we do!?" Hershel asked.

"We wait on the Lord," Paul replied, regaining confidence.

"PAUL!" Asher called frantically through the phone, "THEY'RE ADVANCING ON US!"

Paul covered his ears to mute the flow of information and fell to his knees. "Lord, it's the eleventh hour!...No, Lord, it's 11:59!"

"Look, Paul!" Norman yelled out. "The angels are coming!"

Paul looked up to the ridges to see the angels swooping down with swords in their hands, loping off the heads of the intruders. Within seconds the bodies of the three squads of men lay on the Siq floor with their severed heads just inches away.

"Ha! Ha! Now that's what I call a surgical strike!" Norman announced in triumph.

The frenetic moment passed in a heartbeat. Then Paul ran out of the Siq toward the cave. "Shira! Solomon!"

Once he cleared the Siq, he stopped short and gazed toward the cave entrance to see Levi and the others standing gallantly over the dead bodies of their assailants. The would-be murderous Hamas attackers were strewn on the ground, each divided in two. Holding his golden sword in his hand up toward the heavens was Kapporeth.

Kapporeth's voice boomed: "THE LORD REIGNS! All honors for making this victory possible go to Yeshua ha Mashiach!"

Gadi ran to Paul's side, gulping in air. "All the men outside the compound are dead, and their equipment is in flames!"

Paul viewed the field of dead. "The Lord has pounded into impotence those who have lifted up their arms against us. Blessed be the name of the Lord."

THIRTY-TWO

Tel Megiddo Prison, Overlooking the Valley of Jezreel

I

t's fitting, Pahlava thought, *that we should observe the final conflict from the site of the remains of the Megiddo Prison, where archaeologists uncovered the oldest remains of a church in the Holy Land. Oh, what irony! The beginning and end of the Christian era here in Israel to take place right here!* He stared at the excavated floor that revealed a large mosaic with a Greek inscription stating that the church is consecrated to 'the God Jesus Christ.' He nudged Stein standing next to him and snorted, "Ha! We'll see if this Jesus Christ is really *God!*"

Stein scanned the horizon, looking beyond the Valley to Mount Tabor in the distance, then back to the famed Valley to see the huge troop build-up taking place. From there he turned to see the Megiddo Stables atop the Tel Megiddo and then back to the Valley. Many battles were fought here, he realized. Battles dating back to the fifteenth-century B.C. between the armies of the Egyptian pharaoh Thutmose III and a large Canaanite coalition led by the rulers of Megiddo and Kadesh up to the Battle of Megiddo in World War I between Allied troops under General Edmund Allenby and the defending Ottoman army. But they were nothing compared to what lie ahead.

"The existence of Israel is an error that must be rectified," Pahlava said with utter disdain. "This is the great opportunity to wipe the ignominy off the map once and for all."

"Incalculable odds against them." Stein scratched his head. "Divine intervention?"

"Never!"

"It is written."

"Don't start believing the Book now!"

Stein nodded silently.

The mood in the Valley is right for war, Pahlava thought. The predominantly Muslim states simply could not conceive of the idea that the Jews, destined to humiliation in their *Koran,* could actually possess a sovereign state in the middle of the so-called "World of Islam." *This battle will suit our purpose.*

The defeat of nearly seven years ago, whereby the Russian-sponsored Arab-bloc nations invaded Israel, was about to be reversed. The world of Islam would no longer have to tolerate the disgrace. Now, with Israel outnumbered by Arab and Iranian forces 3-to-1 on its borders and with superior air power to protect the tanks and other heavy armor, together with ground forces, victory for Islam was certain. Or so it was believed.

"Syrian paratroopers coming in," Stein announced, pointing his field glasses at the northern end of the Valley.

Pahlava tapped him on the shoulder and pointed south. Stein swiveled and focused his field glasses on the incoming aircraft. It looked like the IDF unleashed many of its fighter jets. There were three squadrons of F-16Is, Lavis, and Kfirs bearing down on the Syrian and Iranian artillery being moved in. Seconds later one squadron split off and fired their rockets into a line of heavily fortified Syrian bunkers, trenches, and gun emplacements. Then they strafed the paratroopers both on the ground and in the air.

"Let the action begin," Stein said stoically.

Historically, Israel relied on its fast-moving offensive armor and its preemptive striking ability to avenge the murderous record of terrorism waged upon it by the Arab states, but this was not the case in Armageddon. The massive Arab, Iranian, and Asian forces, with their 20-to-1 edge over Israel's infantry forces and their 5-to-1 advantage in tanks, would not be easily overcome.

"With this immense assault force, the enemy has achieved a strategic and tactical advantage already. "They are fighting for Allah, for Islam, and for their supremacy." Pahlava smirked.

"What about the Samson option?" Stein asked as the sound of the artillery bombardment filled the air. "If things go according to *your* plan, they have threatened to annihilate their enemies with nukes, even if it means their total destruction in the process."

Pahlava shook his head. "It will never come to that." In his mind, he knew why but left Stein to his own ruminations.

The rattling of sabers had passed. Threats had given way to the evidence of the enemy's determination to destroy Israel: the sky above the Valley of Megiddo was filled with war planes. Iranian IRIAF Azarakhsh and Shafaq fighter aircraft eclipsed the volume of IAF warplanes. Their Russian sponsors furnished them with Mi-171Sh transport helicopters that continued to ferry in Iranian troops to the staging area while their MIG-29A/UB and Su-30MKM fighter jets guarded the Russian-supplied Su-24 fighter bombers in transit to Jerusalem. Additional IRIAF air support included Chinese-manufactured F-7M, FT-7, and J-10 fighter jets. Clearly, the Persian Islamic Republic of Iran had planned this showdown with the cooperation of their Muslim neighbors very carefully and with the full intention of seeing that Israel would never recover. Israel was doomed to defeat.

Jet engines roared overhead! Two IRIAF fighters flew just above the heads of Pahlava and Stein and engaged two IAF fighters in a dogfight. "Whew, that was close!" Stein gulped.

Two missiles from one IRIAF jet were fired and streaked toward their Israeli jet target but exploded on a mountaintop after narrowly missing the elusive IAF fighters.

Then it happened!

"What's *that!?*" Stein pointed into the sky.

Pahlava stiffened. "It's him!" Pahlava screamed with rage into Stein's face. "It's—"

"Who? What are you talking about?!"

"IT'S THAT JESUS!" Pahlava exploded. "THIS IS HIS WORK!"

Several kilometers from the Valley, enormous dark, ominous clouds had suddenly rolled in and filled the horizon. Building in strength, the clouds at first resembled a front of tornados. But as they approached, their character continued to change.

"It's a dust storm," Stein shouted. "It extends from the ground up to the cloud cover!"

Pahlava flared. "It's not a dust storm, you fool! It's the volcanic winter!"

"The what—?"

"The volcanic ash storm from the eruption in the States!" Pahlava growled.

The wind flowing over the Valley whipped the volcanic ash into millions of swirling eddies that were quickly swept up by warm-air convection currents coming off the valley floor into the atmosphere, producing a blinding ash blizzard that blackened out the sun, obscuring its light and lowering the Earth's temperature.

"I can't see any further than four meters!" Stein shouted.

Booming crashes!

Two Iranian fighter jets collided midair and fell, killing hundreds of foot soldiers as they marched. Other crashes signalled the end of the air battles as jet engines fouled from the corrosive sulfuric acid-laden ash.

Blanketing!

Stein stared at his arms in horror. Two millimeters of ash were all over his body. Pahlava too was covered with ash from head to toe as the storm raged around them.

Burning!

"We have to get out of here!" Stein said as panic ensued. "My body is on fire from the acid!"

"We can't leave yet!" Pahlava shouted.

Stein shot him a look. Pahlava's body was trembling. "Are you all right?!"

Pahlava's jaw tightened as the ash continued to fall all around them and on them. He quickly brushed himself off. "We can't leave yet!" he repeated frantically.

"What are we waiting—?" Stein gulped in silence as he abruptly realized what his messiah was waiting for: the destruction of Israel!

The attacking armies regrouped amidst the cataclysmic storm, using infra-red equipment and satellite coordinates. To them, it had become night-time warfare. They were not going to be defeated this close to victory. Their air forces were paralyzed, but their ground forces were equipped for all-weather operations that included poisonous and corrosive gas.

Thousands of shots were fired, echoing off the valley walls. In his mind's eye, Pahlava could see the Israeli forces being decimated by his armies of mercenaries. "Ha!" he cried out. "The hour of disaster has come, Jesus, and you are nowhere to be found!"

Stein shuddered and thought, *Don't say that!*

THIRTY-THREE

Tel Megiddo Prison, Overlooking the Valley of Jezreel

"Yⁱou fowls that fly in the air, come and gather yourselves together unto the supper of the great God that we may eat the flesh of kings, and the flesh of captains, and the flesh of mighty men, and the flesh of horses and of them that sit on them, and the flesh of all men, both free and enslaved, both small and great!"

"Did you hear that?!" Stein turned his head toward the sky. His knees knocked together. "The roar of battle may be clamorous and the air may be filled with volcanic ash, but I heard that loud and clear!" He was increasingly edgy as he witnessed the unfolding of God's timetable.

Pahlava gave a deep sigh of anticipation. "It's the angel of Revelation 19 announcing the end."

"The end?" Stein shook his head. In his mind the words *the end* were kept from him. In his heart he knew it had to come to this, but he was under the same delusion that beset all those who deny Christ and the promise of his return. The god of this world blinds them to the truth that the end is near and that God's Word will indeed be fulfilled. "What are we to do?" he choked out.

"We wait for deliverance from the one we placed our trust in," Pahlava said as he kneaded his temples.

Stein's eyes bored into Pahlava's as his anxiety heightened.

The Valley Floor

IDF'S Brigadier General Davi Almog clutched the Mogen David that hung on a gold chain around his neck. After brushing the volcanic ash off

222

his goggles and reached into his pants, he pulled out his pocket Bible and turned to chapter 14 in the Book of Zechariah. He read the first four verses aloud to his Chief of Staff standing next to him, then said, "We will see the fulfillment of this prophecy before the day is out, for destruction is the benediction paid by those who war against God."

The ground shook violently beneath them! Lightning strikes electrified the battleground!

Almog's Chief of Staff trembled. "Earthquake?"

Almog scanned the horizon to see hundreds of his men being swallowed up in the earth. Its giant jaws opened and closed as the screams of mortals ascended in the blackened air. Hundreds defaulted to zigzag patterns to elude the targeting lightning bolts as they stuck the earth.

"Yes, it's God's judgment on—" He turned to see his Chief of Staff's body twitching on the ground from a bullet to his head.

Almog raised his head to the heavens and cried out with the lament, "Armies are made by nations and battles are won by men! But this is one battle that can only be won by the Lord!" He fell to the ground and prayed over his fallen comrade.

Tel Megiddo Prison, Overlooking the Valley of Jezreel

Pahlava clapped his hands in triumph as the armies of Israel continued to fall to the Muslim conquerors. "Ha!" he exclaimed in a moment of revelry, "the earthquake is consuming both the Jews and the Arabs!" His goal of taking as many souls into hell with him was being realized before his very eyes. His gaze raked the area and then focused on an intense skirmish in the southern quadrant in the valley. Then he pointed and shouted, "Look, Stein, *our* forces are throwing the bodies into the pit!"

Stein peered in the southern direction and only saw mortals in intense combat with heavy casualties. "*Our forces?*" he blurted out.

"Look hard!" Pahlavah said in fury. "Look hard!"

Stein once again stared in the southern direction. At first he saw nothing unusual. But when he focused his thoughts on belief, he saw thousands of dark shadowy figures kicking, hauling, and throwing the dead soldiers' bodies into the newly opened crevasses in the valley floor. He realized the forces were the fallen spirits of angels who were ordered to claim the dead and remand them to the pit.

The Valley Floor

Almog stood next to the body of his fellow warrior and pulled out the commemorative sword he was awarded after the Yom Kippur War in 1973. "You Arabs have no part in Israel! We are a nation for peace, but you are for war!" he called, brandishing his sword. He pulled out his radio from his jacket and then keyed it before yelling to his command center, "Commit *Operation Samson!*" He raised his voice an octave. "I repeat, Commit *Operation Samson!*"

It is finished! There will be no more Israel, this I know. We are finished as a people. We are finished as a nation. Oh, Lord, where are you? Oh, Lord, where is your Messiah?

Tel Megiddo Prison, Overlooking the Valley of Jezreel

Stein continued to survey the battle through his field glasses, then stopped abruptly. "Reza!" he shouted. "Many of the Arabs are turning against each other!"

It was madness. Utter chaos. The armies, blinded by the ash, were flung into a state of confusion. The Iranians were shooting the Syrians, and the Saudis turned on the Egyptians. Moments later, most of the forces were fighting each other.

"I never expected this," Pahlava mumbled to Stein. He turned his nose up in the air and made a fist at the Sovereign Lord. "This is your doing, isn't it!?"

One hour later he added, "There's a decisive turn here. The Chinese and Japanese appear to be winning."

"If they can beat the Arabs here, the Asians will go on to seize all the Arab oil assets," Stein speculated.

Pahlava didn't have time for speculation. "Damn them all!"

"THRUST IN THE SHARP SICKLE ON THE EARTH AND GATHER THE CLUSTERS OF THE VINE OF THE EARTH, FOR HER GRAPES ARE FULLY RIPE, AND CAST THEM INTO THE GREAT WINEPRESS OF THE WRATH OF GOD!"

"Did you hear that?" Stein said with a quiver.

"I heard it. And so did the rest of the earth."

"It's an angel of God, isn't it?" Stein asked frantically. When he looked down, he realized he had wet himself.

Suddenly the volcanic ash began to dissipate as an easterly wind pushed through the valley. Moments later the air cleared. What appeared to be hundreds of thousands of dead bodies were strewn across the valley. In other areas heaps of soldiers were piled up by some unseen force but hundreds of thousands remained to fight.

Giant hailstones came barrelling down from the sky and pummelled the armies and the land!

"God dammit!" Pahlava screamed. Seconds later, as if his blasphemous expletive were turned on him, the fighting men stopped in their tracks and cried out in curses against God, then returned to their folly.

The Valley Floor

"They're cursing the only one who can save us!" Almog shouted. He keyed his radio once again. "Commence *Operation Samson!* There is nothing left for us! We are all doomed!"

Seconds later he raised his eyes to see millions of large birds flying into the valley. Within minutes two of them landed on his fallen friend. They were turkey vultures sent from above to fulfill the curse.

"General Almog," he heard on his radio. It was his commanding officer. "There are strange phenomena occurring on the Mount of Olives, and we cannot initiate *Operation Samson* until we investigate it. There are underground disturbances taking place along with bizarre cloud formations swirling. We're not sure, but we think it could be enemy action or some divine oracle about to unfold."

Almog stared at his radio. "What—?"

"FEAR GOD, AND GIVE GLORY TO HIM, FOR THE HOUR OF HIS JUDGMENT IS COME; AND WORSHIP HIM THAT MADE HEAVEN, AND EARTH, AND THE SEA, AND THE FOUNTAINS OF WATERS," the angel cried out to the world.

When Almog heard the plaintive cry, he peered up into the clouds, realizing the time of his nation's redemption was about to begin.

Tel Megiddo Prison, Overlooking the Valley of Jezreel

With the curtain of ash lifting and the hailstorm subsiding, Pahlava smiled as the fighter jets returned to the sky to wage war. There would be more bloodshed—this he was sure of.

Once the air cleared, the Arabs realized who the real enemy was and, with the Chinese and Japanese marching alongside them, resumed their attack on Israel. The IRIAF Shafaq fighter jets and the Syrian air force greatly outnumbered the Israel Air Force F-16I warplanes. Within 30 minutes of the commencement of the exchange of air-to-air missiles, Israel lost all air superiority. All 85 remaining Israeli fighter jets were destroyed.

The Valley Floor

"All hope is gone. We are finished," Almog said with complete resignation. He started to whimper as he waved to his remaining subordinates on the ground in what he believed was a gesture of surrender. When he gazed at the panoramic view of the valley, his heart sunk in despair. Never before in the history of Israel's military was there a picture of defeat and destruction. *God has abandoned us!*

Tel Megiddo Prison, Overlooking the Valley of Jezreel

"We got 'em," Pahlava said, clenching his teeth. "Israel is finished!"

Stein stared at him in helpless frustration. "But what about that Jesus?"

"Forget about him! We got 'em." Pahlava recoiled with every word like a whiplash.

The skin on the back of Stein's neck began to crawl; then he was flooded with terror. "But—"

Pahlava waved a hand to stop the flow of doubts. "Enough!"

Stein went mute, but when he felt his chest, he realized he was suffering from heart palpitations. His mind raced ahead to the end game. *All this time I thought things would really be different from what was in the Book. I was wrong.* He glared at Pahlava in disgust. *You lied to me....*

THIRTY-FOUR

Golden Gate, Temple Mount

The ground outside the ancient Golden Gate located on the eastern wall of the Temple Mount began to vibrate. Within seconds the vibration increased exponentially to an earthen seizure. The earth shook violently until the stone gate leading to the Temple Mount, which was sealed by the Ottoman Sultan Suleiman I in A.D. 1541 to prevent the Messiah's entry, gave way to the enormous pressure being exerted.

Moments later the Muslim cemetery in front of the gate, placed there in the belief that the true Messiah would not be able to pass through, suddenly tumbled into a crevasse that opened in the earth to swallow every vestige of Arab presence on the eastern side of the Mount.

Jewish Cemetery, Kidron Valley

The subterranean tremors extended directly across the Temple Mount, through the Kidron Valley, and in to the Jewish Cemetery, where the prophets Haggai, Zechariah, and Malachi were buried, along with thousands of other Jews. When the violent shaking stopped, many of the tombstones took on a strange glow, as if they were being singled out from the rest. The stone gates and doors of many of the crypts and mausoleums suddenly opened in anticipation of something spectacular about to happen.

God was not only preparing a path for his Anointed One, but was preparing the graves to be opened.

And so it was throughout the entire earth....

THIRTY-FIVE

Tel Megiddo Prison, Overlooking the Valley of Jezreel

Terror was in the air. Pahlava may have denied it, but Stein could feel it. He was terribly frightened. The armed forces brought to the Valley were hardened soldiers with many years of military experience, but he knew in his heart they would be no match for the armies of God.

All the signs were in place. All the Scriptures leading up to this point were past. He knew it was only a matter of minutes before God would intervene.

THIRTY-SIX

Above the Valley of Jezreel

"THE TIME HAS COME TO BRING AN END TO DESOLATION AND DESTRUCTION!" an angel cried out from the heavens. It was God's signal to get man's attention.

All enemy action ceased. Every warrior on the battlefield stood frozen in time as they looked toward the sky to identify the bellowing voice.

"ALAS, FOR THE DAY OF THE LORD IS AT HAND! DESTRUCTION FROM THE ALMIGHTY SHALL COME!" the angel added.

Hundreds of the Arabs, Chinese, and Japanese fell to the ground out of sheer fear. Thousands of others raised their fists to the sky in defiance.

Then it happened...,

A strange quiet came over the valley, extending to the uttermost parts of the earth. It was like the interlude of a dramatic play, or the pause before the crescendo of a great symphony movement...but eerie and foreboding.

Every eye looked up to the heavens.

THIRTY-SEVEN

The Return of Jesus Christ

An incalculable number of angels suddenly appeared above the horizon, each with a golden trumpet in hand in preparation to announce the coming of the King. It would be forever unknown to mankind how it was possible for the entire earth to see this at the same time in simulcast, but God was about to make sure His Son was visible to the world. His first appearance was in relative obscurity, but His second would be worldwide.

Voices from heaven shouted: "HALLELUJAH! SALVATION, AND GLORY, AND HONOR, AND POWER, UNTO THE LORD, OUR GOD, FOR TRUE AND RIGHTEOUS ARE HIS JUDGMENTS! FOR THE LORD GOD OMNIPOTENT REIGNS!"

The echoing gallop of a horse followed. The sound intensified until the figure of a horse appeared in the distance. He appeared to ride out of a multitude of white clouds that were symbolic of his glory.

On the earth, every eye remained riveted on the heavens above. The hearts of humanity raced as the anticipation of the unfolding events brought both fear and hope. Fear to the enemies of God; hope to those who longed for his appearing.

Millions of trumpets blasted! The earth shook!

"I AM THE RESURRECTION AND THE LIFE," the earth heard. "I SAY, ARISE!"

The world's Believers rose from the dead at Christ's command! Graves of God's saints throughout the earth released their inhabitants! Millions upon millions of graves throughout the earth burst forth as those who trusted Christ as their Savior fulfilled the promise to rise again from sleep.

"LOOK UP!" was all that was heard throughout the earth as the world pointed to the Son of Man, who appeared riding down an invisible ramp on his magnificent white charger. As he drew closer, man began to tremble when they saw his battle dress and long shining sword at his side. In one hand he held a sickle and in the other a gold book that was called the Lamb's Book.

Flames! Flames! Flames!

Flames of fire shot out of His eyes as a token of his fierce righteous anger.

"I AM HE WHO IS FAITHFUL AND TRUE!" he cried out so the world could hear. "I HAVE COME IN RIGHTEOUSNESS TO JUDGE AND MAKE WAR!"

The armies on the ground at Megiddo looked at each other, then brandished their weapons and ran toward the coming Christ. Millions of soldiers raced toward He who sat on His white horse as He descended through the sky.

Refulgent light radiated out from the angelic host as their vesture reflected Christ's glory. Then they ceremoniously stepped aside and raised their hands toward the heavens from which they came and cried out with a thunderous voice, "BEHOLD THE BRIDE OF CHRIST!"

There were millions of them dressed in white linen. Grandeur and splendor accompanied them as brilliant, dazzling white light radiated from their beings. Oh, the glorious appearance of the Bride!

Together with the raised saints they heralded the coming King.

"LOOK UPON HIM WHOM YOU HAVE PIERCED!" the host cried out.

All those on the earth stopped up their ears. Man could not bear to face the truth of God as He appeared. Man's hearts either burst with sorrow and repented or filled with indignation and rebelled.

Now, the Lord Jesus would separate the wheat from the chaff.

He drew near!

He stood hovering above the earth for an interminable period. Time stood still so that His presentation would be forever engraved on the minds of men. It is He, Jesus Christ, that the world mocked and ridiculed, who would have the final word. It is He, Jesus Christ, who came as the suffering servant, the Lamb, who now held the world captive as the King of Kings and Lord of Lords.

He drew nearer!

On His head He wore a gold crown, and His vesture was red from the blood of His saints. As He neared, the earth held its breath, and then the angelic host together with His Bride shouted out: "BEHOLD, THE WORD OF GOD!"

He was upon them!

Tel Megiddo Prison, Overlooking the Valley of Jezreel

"OH, NO!" Stein squealed. "HE WILL COME FOR US!"

Pahlavah spun, glared at him, and hollered in his face, "SILENCE!"

The Valley Floor

"This can't be!" Almog said numbly to those around him as he pointed to the rider on the white horse. "That's Jesus!"

"I AM THE LORD AND VENGEANCE IS MINE!" the Lord Jesus shouted for all to hear. Then, swiftly and purposefully, He trained His eyes on the enemies of Israel. Swooping down on His white charger with sword in hand, He began to slaughter all those who came to war against His people. Seconds later His angelic host followed Him.

Eye has not seen, nor ear ever heard, neither has it entered into the hearts of man, the great massacre that followed. The prophesied day of reckoning had finally come to all those who had gathered together to make war with the Christ and against His army.

Almog shook in his boots as the reign of terror from above escalated. He gazed off into the distance to see Jesus on His white charger swinging His sword on the neck of the intruders. His heart leaped within him, and then he fell to the ground. His stomach retched. He breathed in ragged gasps and squeezed his eyes shut. "Lord!" he cried out. "Save me!"

He opened his eyes and saw hundreds—maybe even thousands...he wasn't sure—of his fellow Israelites falling on the ground in repentance as well. "Blessed is he that comes in the name of the Lord!" he yelled out.

The killing was well organized. The Almighty on His white horse ordered His legions of angels to systematically attack the enemy individually. He could have sent fireballs from heaven to burn up the enemy who refused to repent, but He did not. He could have opened the earth to swallow up those who defied the Living God, but He did not. He could have sent wild beasts to trample down His enemy who denied His second coming, but He did not. He could have smote every last man with a dreaded disease because they mocked His Name, but He did not. No, the Lord God chose to assign an angel to every last man so that men would meet the holiness of God face to face. As the angels were about to plunge their sword into each man, the angel asked, "Are you for the Lord of Hosts, or are you for the Antichrist?" The answer they gave determined their fate.

In celestial time, the duration of the battle would be brief, but to those mortals on earth, the time seemed infinite and intolerable. Time seemed to stand still as the slaughter went on. There would be no victories for men, nor would there be any war heroes to receive medals. No, all glory and honor will go to Messiah Jesus, the Lord of Hosts.

Mounds of human carcasses filled the valley. If their blood were let, it would have reached the bridle of a horse, for the slain of the Lord was very great, and the fowls of the air were filled with their flesh.

THIRTY-EIGHT

Tel Megiddo Prison, Overlooking the Valley of Jezreel

A great and supernatural lull came over the Valley. It was another interminable pause, a dynamic separation between events as it were. The end and yet beginning of another episode in the divine schedule. It was time for the evil ones to pay.

Stein carefully scanned the Valley and attempted to measure the carnage. It was too great to calculate. All the enemies of God were dead. More than a million bodies lay on the surface of the earth in layers. Some layers were ten meters high, while others were only five.

He looked up to the sky and estimated that 200,000 birds of prey, those that lived on carrion, were circling and hovering over the mounds, deciding on the best place to feast on the flesh of men.

He turned and his eye caught a vast gathering of men in the eastern quadrant of the Valley. He focused the field glasses and gulped. "They're all Jews! They're on their knees praising God and His Holy One!" He handed the glasses to Pahlava.

Pahlava waved him off. "I know who they are," he said as his face contorted with rage. "They are the Jews who suddenly realized this Jesus is the Messiah and cried out with the messianic greeting, that's who they are!" They were the remnant who acknowledged Jesus as Lord and were preserved from the executioner's sword.

The resonant sound of horses galloping toward them!

Stein's mind seized up in panic as the Rider on the white horse approached in the air with two other angels on horseback. "He's coming for us!"

Pahlava stood fixated on the approaching Messiah, whose eyes blazed with anger and holiness. He clenched his teeth, but said nothing.

Realization crashed in on Stein. He threw the field glasses at Pahlava and roared, "YOU LIED! YOU LIED!"

Stein stood paralyzed with fear as the Returning Messiah rode through the air with two of His officers, then abruptly came to a halt above them. Stein gazed into the face of the One he'd denied, and for once in his life realized his unworthiness. He realized his sinfulness. He realized his evil nature. He realized his destiny, but it was too late. His doom had been sealed before the foundation of the world had been laid.

The Messiah then gazed at Pahlava, who immediately turned away. He was unable to look Jesus the Messiah in His face, for His face was one of righteousness and judgment.

Jesus summarily judged them. "TAKE THEM!"

The angelic officers dismounted, walked to them, and bound them with scarlet ropes. The angels then presented them to Jesus, who bellowed out, "YOU WHO HAVE DECEIVED THEM THAT HAD RECEIVED YOUR MARK OF THE BEAST AND WORSHIPPED YOUR IMAGE ARE SENTENCED TO SPEND ETERNITY IN THE LAKE OF FIRE IN THE OUTERMOST PART OF MY UNIVERSE!"

Both Pahlava and Stein stood speechless before their accuser.

The Lake of Fire

At first there was what appeared to be a vast hole in the sky that extended up to the star canopy and beyond, and then it looked like a corridor opened to reach up into the outer limits of our galaxy.

Jesus held up His sword and, behold, a gigantic, swirling mass of fire slowly descended through the corridor and stood suspended above the earth. The flames shot out a great distance and gaseous vapors ascended up through the corridor, giving the appearance of a bubbling caldron of napalm that would scald, burn, and scorch the flesh. The insidious fires destined to burn forever and ever beckoned Pahlava and Stein. These same fires also beckon all those who are presently in hell that will ultimately be cast into the lake of fire.

Jesus nodded to His two angelic officers who held Pahlava and Stein firmly in their grip. They bowed in reverence to He who brings judgment, then lifted Pahlava and Stein from the earth and transported them above the lake of fire so every soul on the planet could see them receive their just punishment. A repulsive sulphurous smell permeated the air while a greenish-yellow nonmetallic substance splashed out for kilometers as they were dropped from a great height into the lake of fire...their divine punishment meted out.

The Abyss

Jesus nodded to His two officers, who in turn returned to heaven on their beautiful steeds. Then He raised His sword toward heaven and shouted, "GABRIEL AND MICHAEL, COME FORTH!"

Moments later the majestic archangels appeared before Him. Michael held a gold key, and Gabriel held a golden chain. They bowed to Christ's glory and holiness, then stood erect, awaiting His command.

"HE IS ROAMING THE EARTH SEEKING WHOM HE MAY DEVOUR. BRING HIM HERE!" the Almighty Christ demanded.

The archangels both bowed the second time, then flew away.

His location when he was apprehended would never be disclosed, but historical precedence dictated that Satan would be found where the highest level of debauchery, hedonism, materialism, and depravity was present. Reason dictated that his field of play would be in the society that encouraged such behavior. He was given temporary authority over all the earth to reign, tempt, and deceive, subject to God's omnipotence.

Three trumpet blasts announced the return of the archangels!

As God's sentries flew through the air toward the Holy One on His white horse, their prisoner whom they held bound in chains squirmed and yowled, howled, and wailed as his judgment drew near. But God's sentries held him fast. With Michael on one side and Gabriel on the other, Satan was unable to escape. As their superior, Satan held power over the angels, but at Christ's command, he was powerless.

He was beautiful to look at as he stood before the Lord Jesus. The Tempter or Lucifer displayed his natural side, which appealed to man, then transformed into his supernatural side, which appealed to other fallen angels who were also deceived. Both sides were condemned before the Lord.

Jesus held up His sword, the symbol of His Word, and shouted out, "BECAUSE YOUR HEART WAS LIFTED UP AND YOU SAID, 'I AM A GOD' AND I SIT IN THE SEAT OF GOD, THOUGH YOU ARE BUT A CREATED BEING, AND NOT GOD, THOUGH YOU SET YOUR HEART AS THE HEART OF GOD. WITH YOUR WISDOM AND UNDERSTANDING YOU HAVE GOTTEN RICHES AND HAVE GOTTEN GOLD AND SILVER INTO YOUR TREASURIES, BUT I WILL BRING YOU DOWN TO THE PIT!

"YOU WERE IN EDEN, THE GARDEN OF GOD; EVERY PRECIOUS STONE WAS THERE FOR YOU, AND YOU WERE PERFECT IN ALL YOUR WAYS UNTIL INIQUITY WAS FOUND IN YOU AND YOU WERE FILLED WITH VIOLENCE AND YOU SINNED. THEREFORE I DID CAST YOU OUT OF HEAVEN, AND I WILL DESTROY YOU, O COVERING CHERUB. YOUR HEART WAS LIFTED UP BECAUSE OF YOUR BEAUTY, BUT YOU CORRUPTED THE WISDOM YOU WERE GRANTED BY REASON OF YOUR BRIGHTNESS. YOU HAVE DEFILED MY SANCTUARIES BY THE MULTITUDE OF YOUR INIQUITIES; THEREFORE WILL I BRING YOU BEFORE ALL MANKIND SO ALL THAT KNOW YOU AMONG THE PEOPLE SHALL BE APPALLED AND NEVER SHALL YOU BE ANY MORE." When He finished speaking the charge, He once again nodded to Michael and Gabriel.

Michael released Satan into Gabriel's custody, then flew to the earth in the middle of the Valley. Once he landed on the earth, he struck the ground with his gold key three times.

Then it happened! The earth beneath his feet cleaved and opened wide to reveal a massive crevasse that appeared to go down to subterranean caverns and abodes in the middle of the earth.

Screams and shrieks of torment from the denizens of the pit echoed off the walls of the crevasse. The horrific sounds seemed to reverberate around the planet, as if the Lord were allowing all to hear the terrible cries of those who denied Him.

"SPEAK YOUR DEFENSE!" Gabriel shouted at Satan.

"I will ascend into heaven and exalt my throne above the stars of

God," Satan began limply. "I will sit also upon the mount of the congregation; I will ascend above the heights of the clouds, I will be like the Most High." His shoulders rose and fell as his sentence was about to be decreed.

"HOW YOU HAVE FALLEN FROM HEAVEN, O LUCIFER, SON OF THE MORNING!" Gabriel announced. "HOW YOU HAVE BEEN CUT DOWN TO THE GROUND, YOU WHO DID WEAKEN THE NATIONS. YET YOU SHALL BE BROUGHT DOWN TO HELL, TO THE SIDES OF THE PIT. THEY THAT SEE YOU SHALL NARROWLY LOOK ON YOU AND CONSIDER YOU SAYING, 'IS THIS THE ONE WHO MADE THE EARTH TO TREMBLE, WHO DID MAKE KINGDOMS, WHO MADE THE WORLD LIKE A WILDERNESS, AND DESTROYED ITS CITIES AND CAST INTO HELL HIS PRISONERS?'"

"CAST HIM IN TO THE BOTTOMLESS PIT AND SHUT HIM UP AND SET A SEAL UPON HIM, THAT HE SHOULD DECEIVE THE NATIONS NO MORE UNTIL THE THOUSAND YEARS SHOULD BE FULFILLED, AND AFTER THAT HE WILL BE RELEASED FOR A LITTLE SEASON," the Almighty Christ pronounced.

Michael stood on the precipice of the pit. Pulling his sword out from the scabbard beneath his wings, he held it in the air and shouted, "WHEN THE THOUSAND YEARS ARE ENDED, YOU WILL BE RELEASED FROM THIS PRISON AND SHALL GO OUT TO DECEIVE THE NATIONS, WHICH ARE IN THE FOUR CORNERS OF THE EARTH, TO GATHER THEM TOGETHER TO BATTLE. UNTIL THEN, YOU AND THOSE WHO FOLLOWED YOU ARE REMANDED TO BLACKNESS UNTIL THE GREAT WHITE THRONE IS CONVENED." With that he flew up into the air to join Gabriel; then together they released Satan, who plummeted headlong into the pit.

Moments later the earth in the Valley convulsed!

Never before in the history of man did the earth spew forth like vomit the dead that were torn and picked over by the birds of prey. Gouged and ripped, the bodies of the millions who came against God's people were tossed and thrown in the air. Then the ground opened its jaws wide to allow God's angels to shovel the dead into the pit along with Satan.

Another great calm came over the earth.

THIRTY-NINE

The Mount of Olives

Finally, Jerusalem, the city of peace, was free from the threat of war. There would be no more fighting over the ownership rights to the Temple Mount. There would be no more terrorist incursions into the land rightfully given to Israel. The Creator of Heaven and Earth had from ancient times decreed the rightful owner. Now there would only be a millennium of celebrations with their long-awaited King.

Three hundred feet above the Kidron Valley on the Mount of Olives a small remnant who survived the terrible Tribulation in Jerusalem stood waiting His return, praising their Lord with unspeakable joy.

Then, without warning, the rest of the earth's Believers began arriving.

By divine transport, similar to that which carried Philip from Gaza to Azotus after sharing Christ with the Ethiopian eunuch, they started arriving, beginning in Jerusalem and extending to the uttermost regions of the earth. Millions came forth.

Suddenly a staircase from the earth to the heavens appeared!

It was a pure, clear, gold flight of stairs that hung suspended in the air, reaching from high above the earth—even to the heavens—to the top of the Mount of Olives. Then a parade appeared. An incalculable amount of redeemed Believers dressed in white robes marched thousands abreast from their station in glory down the stairs to the Mount.

A frightening flash shot across the earth to announce their arrival!

"BEHOLD THE BRIDE OF CHRIST!" angels boomed. The Bride who died in Christ continued to descend the staircase for an interminable period as the Kidron Valley filled, extending into the glorious city of Jerusalem.

Paul found himself walking up the slope of the Kidron Valley toward the summit of the Mount of Olives with his family and the entire

Petra clan following behind him. Sol Gannon and Yair Kaplinsky, his worthy companions who died in the Tribulation, were among them.

As they neared the summit, the sky quickly filled with Believers summoned from the four corners of the earth. From every continent they came. Millions of survivors who hid from the terror of the Antichrist and refused to take the mark of his *Masterlink* system were ushered in by angelic escort. The innumerable angelic host had received their orders to accompany every single Believer to the Mount and await the Return of the King.

"Glory is to God," Paul said as Jonathan arrived and touched down on the summit. Along with Jonathan there was Brandon and his father, Matthew, Eddie and Sydelle, Efraim Zuroff, and Abraham Ben-Korpel.

"Paul, look!" Jonathan pointed to the far side of the Kidron Valley. "There's Levi and Simon, joining up with the other 144,000!"

"Oh, that man would praise the Lord for His goodness and His wonderful works to the children of men!" Paul shouted out.

Strangers and fellow companions and laborers alike met on the summit. All men of all color and creed who believed on Jesus were being harvested. Time? Time was no longer of importance. How long did it take for the full regathering? No man knew. But with great anticipation, those already on the Mount waited for the glorious moment when He whose rightful place on the throne would appear.

"Paul, look to the heavens!" Jonathan shouted as he grappled with the enormity of things. "There's David, and Solomon and —" he stopped to catch his breath—"yes, and it looks like Moses and Elijah!"

Paul's eyes widened in shock. "All the Old Testament patriarchs and Believers are coming down to join us!"

Shira clutched Solomon ever so tightly and ran to Sol to show him his namesake. "I will forever crucify the word *why*, now that I see that trusting in Him was the right thing to do."

A voice from heaven!

"THIS SAME JESUS, WHO WAS TAKEN UP FROM YOU INTO HEAVEN FROM THIS PLACE, SHALL SO COME TO YOU NOW IN LIKE MANNER AS YOU HAVE SEEN HIM GO INTO HEAVEN."

"HERE HE COMES!" the great multitude shouted aloud. Millions of voices sang the "Hallelujah Chorus" as the angelic host blew their trumpets in unison to announce the coming King.

His magnificent white steed galloped through the air to the Mount and came to an abrupt halt just above it. Then He who rode on him slowly and royally dismounted. As His feet touched the Mount, a great hush came over the earth as the Scriptures in Zechariah were fulfilled to the last detail. Then every being on earth fell to their knees in worship and cried out, "HAIL TO THE KING OF GLORY!"

"ENTER NOW INTO THE JOY OF THE LORD!" He said with outstretched arms.

King Jesus then led his Bride and all the others down from the Mount of Olives and through the Kidron Valley, up to the Golden Gate. As he walked through the Gate He touched the archway with his fingers as if to kiss a mezuzah fastened to the doorway. But it was to signal the transformation.

The procession stopped! Then the entire angelic host appeared, filling the sky up beyond one's view!

"THE CREATOR OF HEAVEN AND EARTH SHALL REIGN FOR THE NEXT ONE-THOUSAND YEARS!" they shouted.

Working outside the boundaries of the earthly time and space dimension, the angelic host began their labors. There were no sounds of tools or machinery, only the songs the angels sang to their Lord as they reconstructed the city to God's specifications written in Ezekiel.

Their work would only take a short while. It would be a glorious city where Christ will rule as King of kings and Lord of lords; where a new Temple will allow His priests to perform sacrifices to commemorate the final sacrifice of the Lamb on the Cross at Calvary; where David will be His co-regent and the Glory of the Lord will fill the Temple because the LORD is there.

THE BEGINNING OF THE MILLENNIUM...

Bibliography

This novel is a fabrication of the author's interpretation of Bible prophecy. It is completely fictitious, but the support research is real. The following reference works may assist the avid reader of prophetic fiction and eschatology to learn more about the events that may soon come upon the earth.

BOOKS

Aarons, Mark and John Loftus. *Unholy Trinity: The Vatican, The Nazis and the Swiss Banks.* New York: St. Martin's Press, 1998.

Anderson, Sir Robert. *The Coming Prince: The Marvelous Prophecy of Daniel's Seventy Weeks Concerning the Antichrist.* Grand Rapids, MI: Kregel Publications, 1975.

Ankerberg, John; Jimmy DeYoung. *Israel Under Fire.* Eugene, OR: Harvest House Publishers, 2009.

Archer, Gleason L. *The Rapture: Pre-, Mid-, or Post-Tribulation.* Grand Rapids, MI: Zondervan Publishing House, 1984.

Backhouse, Robert. *The Kregel Pictorial Guide to The Temple.* Grand Rapids, MI: Kregel Publications, 1996.

Baer, Robert. *Sleeping With the Devil.* New York: Crown Publishers, 2003.

Biblical Archaeology Society. *The Origins of Things.* Washington, DC, 2002.

Brickner, David. *Future Hope: A Jewish Christian's Look at the End of the World.* San Francisco: Purple Pomegranate Productions, 1999.

Bullinger, E.W. *Number in Scripture.* Grand Rapids, MI: Kregel Publications, 1996.

Chapman, Colin. *Whose Promised Land?* Grand Rapids, MI: Baker Books, 2002.

Cohen, Gary. *Understanding Revelation.* Chattanooga, TN: AMG Publishers, 1987.

Colson, Charles. *The Faith.* Grand Rapids, MI: Zondervan Publishing, 2008.

Cooper, David L. *An Exposition of the Book of Revelation.* Los Angeles: Biblical Research Society, 1972.

Corsi, Jerome R. *Black Gold Stronghold. The Myth of Scarcity and the Politics of Oil.* WND Books, 431 Harding Industrial Dr., Nashville, TN, 2005.

Ibid. *Why Israel Can't Wait. The Coming War Between Israel and Iran.* Threshold Editions, 1230 Avenue of the Americas, New York, NY, 10020, 2009.

Crichton, Michael. *State of Fear,* New York: Avon Books, 2004.

Dalin, David G. and John F. Rothmann. *Icon of Evil.* New York: Random House, 2008.

Darwish, Nonie. *Cruel and Usual Punishment.* Nashville, TN: Thomas Nelson Publishers, 2008.

Dickason, C. Fred. *Angels, Elect & Evil.* Chicago: Moody Press, 1995.

Edersheim, Alfred. *The Life and Times of Jesus the Messiah.* McLean, VA: MacDonald Publishing Co., circa 1979.

Evans, Michael D. *Beyond Iraq, The Next Move.* Lakeland, FL: Whitestone Books, 2003.

Folger, Janet. *The Criminalization of Christianity.* Sisters, OR: Multnomah Publishers, 2005.

Friends of Israel Gospel Ministry. *Eye on the Middle East.* Bellmawr, NJ: The Friends of Israel Gospel Ministry Publication, 2001.

Fruchtenbaum, Arnold. *The Nationality of the Antichrist.* New Jersey: American Board of Mission to the Jews, Inc., circa 1978.

Gabriel, Brigitte. *They Must Be Stopped: Why we must defeat radical Islam and how we can do it.* New York: St. Martin's Griffin, 2009.

Gold, Dore. *Hatred's Kingdom*. Washington, DC: Regnery Publishing, 2003.

Grant, George. *The Blood of the Moon: The Roots of the Middle East Crisis*. Brentwood, TN: Wolgemuth & Hyatt Publishers, 1991.

Guiley, Rosemary Ellen, *Encyclopedia of Angels*. New York: Checkmark Books, 2004.

Hagee, John. *Jerusalem Countdown*. Lake Mary, FL: Front Line Publishers, 2006.

Hamada, Louis Bahjat. *Understanding the Arab World*. Nashville, TN: Thomas Nelson Publishers, 1990.

Hays, Daniel J. and J. Scott Duvall. *Dictionary of Biblical Prophecy and End Times*. Grand Rapids, MI: Zondervan Publishing, 2007.

Hislop, Alexander. *The Two Babylons or the Papal Worship*. Neptune, NJ: Loizeaux Brothers, 1959.

Ice, Thomas, Randall Price. *Ready To Rebuild*. Eugene, OR: Harvest House Publishers, 1992.

Ironside, Harry A. *Revelation*. Neptune, New Jersey: Loizeaux Brothers, 1976.

Kennedy, D. James. *The Real Meaning of the Zodiac*. Ft. Lauderdale, FL: TCRM Publishing, 1997.

Kent, Phil. *The Dark Side of Liberalism*. Augusta, GA: Harbor House Publishers, 2003.

Kinnaman, David. *Unchristian. What A New Generation Really Thinks About Christianity*. Grand Rapids, MI: Baker Books, 2009.

Klein, Aaron. *The Late Great State of Israel*. Los Angeles, CA: WND Books, 2009

Koch, Kurt. *Occult Bondage and Deliverance*. Grand Rapids, MI: Kregel Publications, 1976.

LaHaye, Tim. *No Fear of the Storm*. Sisters, OR: Multnomah Press, 1992.

LaHaye, Tim, Thomas Ice. *Charting The End Times*. Eugene, OR: Harvest House Publishers, 2001.

Lindsey, Hal. *Apocalypse Code*. Palos Verdes, CA: Western Front Ltd., 1997.

McCall, Tom and Zola Levitt. *Raptured*. Irvine, CA: Harvest House Publishers, 1975.

Ibid. *Satan in the Sanctuary: Israel's Controversy: The Temple, Fantasy or Tomorrow's Reality?* Chicago: Moody Press, 1973.

Missler, Chuck. *Prophecy 20/20*. Nashville, TN: Nelson Books, 2006.

Mohler, R. Albert, Jr. *Atheism Remix*. Wheaton, Illinois: Crossway Books, 2008.

Ibid. *Desire and Deceit. The Real Cost of the New Sexual Tolerance*. Colorado Springs, CO: Multnomah Press, 2008.

Netanyahu, Benjamin. *Fighting Terrorism*. New York: Farrar, Straus and Giroux, 2001.

Parris, Edmond. *The Secret History of the Jesuits*. Ontario, CA: Chick Publications, 1975.

Patterson, Lt. Col. Robert. *Dereliction of Duty*. Washington, DC: Regnery Publishing, 2003.

Pentecost, J. Dwight. *Things To Come*. Grand Rapids, MI: Zondervan Publishing House, 1975.

Posner, Gerald. *Why America Slept, The Failure To Prevent 9/11*. New York: Random House, 2003.

Price, Randall. *Fast Facts On The Middle East Conflict*. Eugene, OR: Harvest House Publishers, 2003.

Ibid, *Jerusalem In Prophecy*. Eugene, OR: Harvest House Publishers, 1998.

Ibid. *Unholy War*. Eugene, OR: Harvest House Publishers, 2001.

Richardson, Joel. *The Islamic Anti-Christ. The Shocking Truth about the Real Nature of the Beast.* Los Angeles, CA: WND Books, 2009

Ritmeyer, Leen and Kathleen. *Secrets of Jerusalem's Temple Mount.* Washington, DC: Biblical Archaeology Society, 1998.

Rydelnik, Michael. *Understanding the Arab-Israeli Conflict.* Chicago: Moody Publishers, 2004.

Scofield, C. I. *Will the Church Pass Through the Great Tribulation?* Grand Rapids, MI: Baker Book House, 1967.

Sears, Alan and Craig Osten. *The ACLU Vs. America.* Nashville, TN: Broadman and Holman Publishers, 2005.

Seif, Jeffrey L. *The Iranian Menace in Jewish History and Prophecy.* Dallas, TX: Zola Levitt Ministries, 2006.

Shanks, Hershel. *Jerusalem's Temple Mount.* New York, NY: The Continuum International Publishing Group, 2007.

Shoebat, Walid. *Why I Left Jihad.* Top Executive Media, 2005.

Shorrosh, Anis A. *Islam Revealed.* Nashville, TN: Thomas Nelson Publishers, 1988.

Simmons, Matthew R. *Twilight in the Desert.* Hoboken, NJ: John Wiley & Sons, Inc., 2005.

Spencer, Robert. *The Politically Incorrect Guide to Islam.* Washington, DC: Regnery Publishing, Inc., 2005.

Ibid. *Stealth Jihad.* Washington, DC: Regnery Publishing, Inc., 2008.

Steadman, Ray C. *Waiting for the Second Coming.* Grand Rapids, MI: Discovery House Publishing, 2007.

Walls, Jerry L. *Hell, The Logic of Damnation.* Notre Dame, London: University of Notre Dame press, 1992.

Walvoord, John F. *Daniel: The Key to Prophetic Revelation.* Chicago: Moody Press, 1989.

Ibid. *The Revelation of Jesus Christ.* Chicago: Moody Press, 1966.

Ibid. *The Prophecy Knowledge Handbook.* Wheaton, Illinois: Victor Books, 1990.

White, John Wesley. *WW III: Signs of the Impending Battle of Armageddon.* Grand Rapids, MI: Zondervan Publishing House, 1977.

Wohlstetter, John C. *The Long War Ahead and the Short War Upon Us.* Seattle, WA: Discovery Institute Press, 2008.

Woodrow, Ralph. *Babylon Mystery Religion.* Self-Published, 1966.

PERIODICALS

Biblical Archaeology Society. *The Origin of Things.* Washington, DC: 2002.

Discerning the Times Digest. *The Global Environment Agenda to World Government and Religion.* www.discerningtoday.org, 2001.

Spiritual Counterfeits Project, Inc., Box 4308, Berkeley, CA 94704.

You won't want to miss...

THE TRIBULATION SERIES
Book One

The

Agenda

Ralph D. Curtin

**An AIDS vaccine is being developed in contemporary America,
but the cost is higher than anyone can imagine....**

When pharmaceutical magnate Gregory Kavidas announces that he has
discovered an AIDS vaccine, people laud him as a wonderful
humanitarian. But could he and his partner, entrepreneur financier
Mortimer Stein, have something else in mind?

David Douglas, a Christian college professor, is wary. He's convinced
that Kavidas—an energetic, charismatic man of Greek descent—is the
Antichrist of Bible prophecy. He believes the joining of forces between
Kavidas' Rainbow Pharmaceuticals and Stein's *Redisearch* is the first
move toward world dominance through a unified medical and monetary
system. But will Douglas be able to expose Kavidas and Stein before they
dupe the world?

Book Two

The
Lights of God

Ralph D. Curtin

**How much would you pay
to know the mind of God?**

In 31 B.C., the Temple high priest, Amariah, flees to the ancient Essene fortification at Qumram, on the shore of the Dead Sea, to avoid Roman persecution. Hidden in his saddle bags is the Urim and Thummim, the revelatory device used to ask and receive answers from God, which hasn't been seen since the Babylonian captivity in 586 B.C. When Amariah is murdered, the Urim and Thummim are buried with his body in a cave-vault, later sealed by an earthquake that strikes Judea in 32 B.C. There they remain until the present day, when they are discovered by Ishmael, a treasure-hunting young Arab Bedouin, then are passed to Rehavam Krasnoff, an unscrupulous chief investigator for the Israeli Antiquities Authority.

When two masterminds in Athens, Gregory Kavidas and Mortimer Stein (who've developed the global financial network *Masterlink*—the precursor to a cashless world economy) become alerted of the stones' discovery, they set out to seize the stones for themselves...before their evil agenda is exposed.

Book Three

The
Seven Seals

Ralph D. Curtin

**A sinister plot advances.
But who will believe the shocking truth?**

When the Arab-bloc nations begin to encroach on the land of Israel, Israel's Prime Minister Zeman makes a deal with Gregory Kavidas, head of the European Union (formerly the European Economic Commonwealth) to ensure Israel's defense. But is all as it seems? Is the heralded Kavidas really the savior of Israel—or the prophesied Antichrist, out to destroy God's people and their land?

As PLO/Hamas sympathizers seize a nuclear power plant in Israel, Russia is set to invade. On the Mount of Olives, two strangers appear out of nowhere, with a special message for the *Koinonos* resistance group. But can such a small contingent make a difference against the supernatural, evil forces marshalling their efforts in a campaign of death?

Book Four

The
Seven Trumpets

Ralph D. Curtin

**Earth is in its final days…and God is displaying His wrath
Against everything unholy.**

Meteor showers blanket the earth. Volcanoes erupt. Famine is rampant. One third of all trees and grass on the planet are consumed. Plagues and demonic forces are unleashed. The world is in chaos.

K-groups—the Christian resistance, *Koinonos*—join forces in Jerusalem, America, and Rome to war against the infamous duo, Gregory Kavidas and Mortimer Stein, the masterminds behind the evil plot to take countless souls with them in the Lake of Fire for all eternity.

About the Author

DR. RALPH D. CURTIN is a family man, pastor, and counselor in a large Christian denomination and a college professor at Trinity College, where he teaches Biblical Studies. When he's not preaching or teaching, he's either writing a book or riding his big Harley.

Other interests include a passion for nature photography, of which he has had many of his images published by a stock agent in national magazines. Photographing his grandchildren and making DVDs for the family gives him great pleasure as well.

"Through many years of Bible research and being a bit of a news junkie," says Dr. Curtin, "I arrived at the place where I earnestly desired to transform Bible prophecy into reality so that it would be believable. Many people don't read the Bible, but will read Biblical fiction. This is my way of educating the public in a non-preaching manner, while giving them a taste of my interpretation of what we may expect in the future. I don't like fluff, so my writing is designed to intrigue the reader, give them facts that interest them, as well as raise their level of understanding on a particular subject. Readers are fascinated with science fiction, so prophetic fiction—which has a great degree of the supernatural—will only excite the reader who craves suspense, yet knows that our Good God will win in the end."

You may write Dr. Curtin at: **drrcurtin@bellsouth.net**